We Interrupt This Program

Other Books by Randee Dawn

Tune In Tomorrow
The Only Song Worth Singing
Leave No Trace

We Interrupt This Program

BY RANDEE DAWN

We Interrupt this Program
First published 2026 by Solaris Nova
an imprint of Rebellion Publishing Ltd,
Riverside House, Osney Mead,
Oxford, OX2 0ES, UK

www.solarisbooks.com

ISBN: 978-1-83786-775-2

This book is a work of fiction. Names, characters, places and incidents are products of the author's imagination or are used fictitiously.

A CIP catalogue record for this book is available from the British Library.

Printed by Ingram Spark

To my funny, sweet, open-hearted and
adorable husband Maury,who's probably thinking
about time she dedicated one of these to me
right now – and who helps me live
a better story every day.

Prologue

Provoke the Muse

"ZEUS' SHORT HAIRS," Calliope muttered to Janus. "I'm bored."

Instantly, the stack of paperwork in the goddess' 'To Do' box shot up an inch.

"You look too busy to be bored," said Janus, lowering their pair of stylish sunglasses.

"That's not how this works," said Calliope, who was the Muse of epic poetry, among other things.

Janus drummed their fingers on their thigh. The two-faced god of gates, change, and other shifting spaces had dropped into the office of Muse Central on the 925th floor of the Seelie Court Network building on a godlike whim, and with a mundane expectation: to take Callie out to lunch. Unfortunately, Callie had kept them waiting for an exceedingly long time, and they were starting to get hangry. "I don't know how any of this works," they said. "It's been a minute since I visited."

"Indeed," the goddess noted archly. "About a century or two. You've been conspicuously absent since you 'recommended' that We pair up with the Seelie Court Network honchos on their TROPE Town experiments."

Janus shifted uneasily in their cloud chair, which floated in front of Callie's desk. "I've been around. Ever heard of a little fae-run streaming show called *Tune in*

Tomorrow?" Janus had spent the last several decades in the self-created position of 'writer's assistant' at that reality series, where they'd spent their days alternating between reading and stirring shit up.

Immortals had time to do that sort of thing.

"No. You see, *I've* been working." Callie kept her eyes glued to the computer screen. The Muse's lustrous curls strained at a bejeweled hair clip. Dark wisps escaped, making her look frayed. And were those *bags* under her eyes?

"You can't ignore lunch!" Janus sat up straight. "I hear the commissary has a new ambrosia recipe: grapes, Mandarin oranges and a fluffy human concoction that combines being both cool and whipping. We must indulge."

"Go, then. Report back," Callie sighed, lifting a sheaf of paperwork as thick as her head. The inbox inched up with more paper. "It never stops, the requests for inspiration from Showrunners. Humans were challenging enough; Seelie requests are worse. I forget what day it is."

It was, in fact, Thursday 15th of November, 11:57 Greenwich Mean Time, midway into the 21st Century—but immortals like the Muses and Janus only cared about the component parts of time as a hobby. Callie's wall calendar was merely decorative. It featured a different half-clad legendary poet offering a sultry gaze to the camera each month. It had last been updated in April 1916.

(Yeats. It had been left on W. B. Yeats.)

Janus glanced around the bright, high-ceilinged room to get the full 360-degree view of Muse Central. Like the entirety of SCN's alabaster and marble edifice, the wing devoted to Muses was cozy and sterile simultaneously, shaped by curved, stark walls and a floor-to-ceiling set of window panels. An azure sky filled every glass pane. Ringed around the room gleamed nine crystal desks, each with its own hovering cloud chair, though only four were currently occupied.

Callie hit 'send' on her latest inspirational request. The computer rang out: ting! She winced, then stared at Janus. "Will you *please* remove those glasses? I can barely see your face and you don't even need them."

"But they look so glam." Janus pushed the sunglasses up on their head. The pair came from a basket that had been set atop a plinth at the far end of the Muse Central corridor. The sign hovering over the plinth read:

SCN Employees Required to Wear
Ray-Banning Glasses from This Point On

"They're for Seelie," said Callie, glaring at her computer as if daring it to ting! again. "Inspiration isn't just something We Muses *do*. It's something We *are*. Fellow gods are immune. Humans used to be more receptive. But with Seelie, it appears We passively affect them at a distance. They are quite helpless"

"I love it!" Janus clapped their hands together. "Seelie are *delightful* to mess around with."

The Muse glowered. "Do not interrupt Me."

Janus held up their hands in exaggerated submission. No need to provoke the Muse. Not before lunch, anyway.

Callie continued: "We consciously inspire individuals and groups. But even when We *aren't* doing that, it's impossible to turn off the effect entirely. Unseelie are less receptive to Our charms, but Seelie positively get their wires crossed. Fuses blow. Catatonia is possible. A human visitor once explained that it was like holding a magnet close to a computerized device. Seelie brains overload with too much presence."

Janus nodded, twirling their sunglasses. "So, these ban your inspirational rays."

"They diminish them." She gestured at the room. "Hence Our private wing here at SCN HQ, to avoid disorienting the executives."

Janus tucked the sunglasses in a pocket. "Understood. So, about lunch—"

Ting! Callie's computer chimed again.

More sighing. "So boring," she said. "Being bored was new once, and now it's also boring."

"You sure that's the word you want?" Janus wondered. "How about 'overwhelmed,' 'underappreciated,' or 'melismatic'?"

"*I'm* melismatic!" piped up Euterpe, Muse of song, music, and lyrics, from her nearby desk. She was taking a break after conducting a score in the air.

"Of course you are, darling." Janus gestured around the room. "By the way, where is everybody? You're barely half-full in here."

"Some of Our sisters are less dedicated to the idea of a 'job' than We are," noted Thalia, Muse of comedy, as she wrapped up inspiring a new challenge video involving sliced mangoes and nostrils. She pressed a button on her keyboard that would make it go viral on Arachne's Veil Wide Web in an hour. "We're the responsible ones."

"Imagine Me, responsible," Callie told Janus. "I will never understand how you convinced Me to spend some of the best years of Our immortality doing *this*."

Janus pressed their fingers on their chest, scandalized by the attitude. It had seemed like such a good idea at the time. For hundreds of moon cycles, SCN had created entertainment series for mythical creatures, by mythical creatures, starring humans. At first, this had been a fae lark not unlike the creation of pop music, or fairy cakes. But Seelie survival depended on being believed in. Without belief—without being seen, noticed, and acknowledged—Seelie began to fade into irrelevance, which was essentially death for their immortal kind. But it turned out that creating endless entertainments to be endlessly watched by an endless array of mythical creatures—who couldn't get enough of human shenanigans—filled up those belief coffers beautifully.

Then, approximately a hundred years ago, the Seelie announced a grand experiment: Topographically Restricted Outer Perimeter Environment (TROPE) Towns, which would be small thematic villages on this side of the Veil, stocked with humans (almost all volunteers) who would live there full time, and star in SCN-produced movies. Janus, who had expertise in working alongside human actors on SCN TV series, was invited to advise. Loving being both a problem creator *and* a problem solver, Janus found the idea of human terrariums run by Seelie irresistible.

Give them a safe village to live in, free housing and a guaranteed job, Janus had suggested to the SCN executives. *Humans will be happy to surrender their privacy and independence for the perception of safety.*

And they had. True, a hundred years in, TROPE Towns were still in the 'working out the kinks' stage, but the official SCN Guide could be amended as needed by SCN executives. For example, deciding what to do with human younglings in TROPE Towns was an ongoing debate. But the first big hurdle had been in selecting Seelie who would run the towns and direct the films created in each TROPE Town. They were known as Showrunner/Mayor/Directors, or SMDs. The hitch was that while Seelie were great organizers, leaders, and movie directors, they had no idea how to create compelling stories. Keeping the flow of scripts constant required the skills of human writers, and a source of regular inspiration.

Enter the Muses. Seeing an opening for the sisters, Janus put their names forward, deciding it would keep the ladies useful and entertained, not bored.

Backfiring had occurred.

"I was only trying to share the love!" they cried. "I've had such a delightful time with nutty human actors. It was so *edifying* to help out those adorable brownie assistants at *Tune in Tomorrow*. And you ladies were restless. Humans no longer worship you properly. They're all captivated by their odd little screens now and call what they put on them 'content creation.' You nine were positively pining away, and pine is not a good look on you. Oak, maybe, but not pine. And now with—"

"AI!" shouted Erato, Muse of love poetry, clicking 'send' on a list of fan fiction inspirational concepts. "Horrors. Creative *machinery*? Inspiration from ones and zeroes fed the good stuff, then regurgitated like bird pap?" She shook her head in disgust. "Humans."

Ting!

Calliope's left eye twitched. "I know your heart was in the right place, Janus. When this enterprise started, there were barely four T-Towns. Any idea how many there are now?"

"Five?"

"Seventy-eight!" Callie shouted. She pruned off an additional inch of requests from the stack, stared at it with glowing dark eyes, and then crumpled them in her fists. Her regal brow was coated in a thin film of sweat. "The mythical audience is *insatiable* for human to-ings and fro-ings. It is an Atlas-sized burden and honestly things—"

Ting!

"Are out of—"

Ting!

"Control!" Yanking the crystal computer from its stand, Callie hurled it over her shoulder. The device crashed through a windowpane and disappeared into the empty sky. Wind swirled into the newly created aperture, sending the discarded papers into the air.

"Aw, Callie, that's the third time this week!" Euterpe's voice was full of minor notes.

Whirling from the shattered window, Calliope was a vision of frustration, flushed and full of thunder. On the human side of the Veil, at least three poet hearts imploded. The wind whipped at her curls, and she was magnificent in her office attire—half-toga, half-pantsuit, both white—her shoulders heaving.

"I'm losing hair!" she cried over the rush of wind. "I've got hives on My knees! I haven't opened a book in years! Guess when I last went swimming? Finished a crossword puzzle? Baked spanakopita?"

"You could quit," mused Janus.

Callie leaned across the desk and nearly clunked foreheads with the god. "And prove to these ridiculous Seelie that I'm not up to the task? Never!"

"Well, at least you won't have to think about that computer for a while—" Janus stopped. A new device was sprouting from the crystal base on Callie's desk. It was the size of a hand for ten seconds and then stretched until it was as broad as Janus' shoulders. Then it turned on and went ting!

Behind Callie, helper brownies scurried from the walls, silently sweeping up the glass shards. The wind died down as a second battery of the small, wizened assistants emerged in overalls and caps, painting on a brand-new window that turned translucent in minutes. A few waved at Janus, who smiled back. The god had a soft spot for brownies, who wanted nothing more than to be useful.

Thalia, Eutie and Erato were staring at their sister with admiration. "I know where You're coming from, dear sister," said Thalia. "I inspire 5,289 viral vids on ArachneWeb each day. And I 'like' them. And I leave snarky comments. And I start flame wars! It is relentless!"

"I've just sent out inspirations for the next sixty volumes of fanfic crossovers," said Erato. "I'm considering inspiring authors to kill everyone off. My nightmares are full of these characters."

"Ladies." Janus held out their hands for calm. "This is not boredom. You are all 'burned out.'"

Callie looked offended. "I have never been on fire. I am not made of ash."

"Metaphor, my dears." Janus's tone was soothing, but a strange tickle in their mind was goading them to make this situation more dramatic. *Maybe I'm not entirely immune from inspiration*, they thought. *It seems Musery loves company.* "It means you are so engaged you can't disengage. You are like a candle with no more wick."

Ting!

Callie clenched her fists.

"Foxtacular," Janus called to a window repair brownie with a swirl of hair piled so high it doubled the size of his head. "Please adjust Calliope's computer settings—unless you plan to return in an hour to paint a fresh window."

The brownie (and his hair) bowed to the deities and darted to the computer. A few button presses and there were no more tings. "All set, your worships," he said, and trotted back to the drying window to collect his supplies.

Callie's trembles abated.

"You goddesses deserve as much as humans," cried Janus, now getting into the swing of their new idea. "More!" They'd never been a trickster, but they had watched Loki and Anansi's joint GOD Talk on ArachneWeb a few times. Encouraging drama was an excellent way to brew trouble, which led to the stirring of shit. "This brings me to a human concept you will find tremendously appealing." They paused, enjoying the attention of so much beauty. "When did you all last… hang out?"

"As in, trees? On ropes?" Callie folded her arms.

"Metaphor, sweet sister." Talia turned to Janus. "I mean, it has been a tick."

A knock came at the open office door. Clio, Muse of memory, wandered in from the hallway. "I put it at nearly five hundred years," she said. "Recall when that intense Italian painter convinced Us to pose?"

"Tintoretto!" Euterpe chirped. "Good old Tin-Tin."

"I heard there was a ruckus," said Clio. "Was there a ruckus?"

"There was. Got it out of My system." Callie gripped her desk.

"You seem a bit drained, dear." Clio tsked. "Good thing I was in the building for a meeting. They had Me holed up in that conference room where the T-Town map is and we went on for *ages*. Those nutty Seelie want to start a new T-Town for re-enactments of human history—featuring humans given too much wine. Naturally, I had to take that meeting. But now I see it was fated for Me to join you. Loop Me in."

"Janus is godsplaining to Us that We're not bored, just burned up." Callie brushed hair from her face.

"Out," corrected Janus. "Burned *out*. You've overdone it, and you need a break. Humans have this problem. Ever wonder what they do in these circumstances?"

"Should We care what humans do in any circumstances?" Clio wondered.

"They go on vacation. Take a holiday." Eutie's minor notes turned to major chords. She shimmered.

Janus nodded.

Callie relaxed. Then she brightened. Her curls rearranged themselves. Her smooth, bronzed tones returned. "Vacation, hmm? Swimming. Horseback riding. Crossword puzzles. Sleeping in. Manicures. *Badminton!*"

"Karaoke!" cried Eutie. "A hot tub!"

Janus was so excited they'd gone up on tiptoe. What a grand way to shake up the status quo! The Seelie could survive without their inspiration machine for a short while. They'd have to. And maybe, Janus began to wonder, maybe *they* themselves could come up with a few stories of their own. With the ladies stepping away for a bit, they could have the whole of Muse Central to themselves. Another new thing had been discovered!

The god leaned forward, tapping their fingers together. "I know of worlds you've never visited," they said. "Olympus is so last millennium, and Athens is overrun with tourists. No, I have a better idea. A place where you can just be yourselves."

"And no one else is there?" Clio raised an eyebrow. "We can be alone?"

Janus' grin was pure Loki. "Well, of course there are others there. But you just… move them aside. You're *goddesses*."

"I want Our Own house," said Talia. "With a pool."

Eutie squealed a sonata. "I like the ocean!"

Callie tilted her head. "I require a badminton net out back."

Clio squeezed her sister's hand, and the others gravitated to Janus as if they were the only one in the room who knew how to truly live.

Yes, thought Janus. They would go to the TROPE Town map room. They would zoom in on villages until they found one with a pool, an ocean, and a badminton net. And that was where they would send the nine Muses. Who cared if they got in someone else's way? They would leave and stay away as long as they cared to. They were goddesses, after all.

"Ladies," said Janus, eyes twinkling. "Let's get you a gal-cation!"

Chapter 1

A Garden of Unseelie Delights

Two Years Later

As a rule, it was unusual for Unseelie fae to adhere to rules. But there was one directive every fae understood about Smash gatherings:

No Smashing Before Sundown.

Who made up the rule? No one knew. Why did it matter? Maybe it didn't. Had anyone violated the rule and lived? How would they know? The Smash Rule was one of the few directives Unseelie paid attention to. Adherence to chaos was generally their way of existence, but adherence to seemingly random rules was *also* a type of chaos. It was best not to think too hard about it, as brain matter was known to stiffen if Unseelie creatures tried puzzling things out for too long.

The fae called Finch knew he was Unseelie. He could insist on being so for hours. ('Finch' was not his True Name; pronounced correctly his True Name caused patches of hair to turn purple and spontaneously braid themselves.) He had proudly committed himself to being a full, destructive member of the Unseelie community, whose pantheon included other ne'er-do-wells like boggarts, ogres, fachan, kelpies and gnomes. All of them did their best to stir things up, preferring to exist in a 78.3 percent chaos-to-rationality ratio. During wild celebrations, though, they could tolerate up to 92.4 percent spikes of unvarnished anarchy.

And a rule here and there was necessary to avoid one hundred percent pure anarchy.

No one knew what might explode if that occurred.

Currently, Finch was standing outside a rickety wooden cottage in the Kingdom's remote Northwest-Downsouth valley, and he had high hopes for tonight's Smash. Namely that it might reach 92.6 percent chaos, plus a side of utter nonsense. Numbers that high would boost his prestige level in SCN's Unseelie Deconstruction Internship Program (UDIP)—and, he hoped, impress his jaded mentors Laurel and Hardy enough to assign him to field work.

But gaining their confidence was not easy, Finch had learned.

You're such a floofy lightweight, Laurel had sneered last week when he'd approached them in the SCN commissary with a Big Idea. *Barely a mark on you. What kind of Unseelie is unblemished?*

I am Hideously Deformed, okay? Finch had said in a low, trembly voice. *You want me to show you again?*

One key factor in determining Unseelie from Seelie was a lack of personal bodily perfection; Seelie were so radiantly lovely they could give lesser creatures sunburn. But the dark secret no one liked to talk about was that despite SCN's commitment to absolutes, no fae was truly full Seelie or entirely Unseelie. It was just that at some point in their immortal lives, creatures had to pick a side. Long ago, Finch had embraced Unseeliedom, and once committed to a path, Finch never wavered. Besides, destructors like Laurel and Hardy were the essence of *cool*. Creators were dull, weakling *nerds*.

Ugh, keep your shoes on, Hardy had snapped back, then waited. *Spit it out, what's so important you had to interrupt our lunch? The cafeteria has ambrosia today.*

I've found an unexploited, unprotected location for the next Smash, Finch had said.

That had gotten their attention.

Now, Finch stared out into the grand backyard of the otherwise unimpressive house and plucked a blueberry the size of his thumbnail from a flourishing bush. The expansive acreage, ringed in hedgerows of yew, spread before him like someone had vomited up a rainbow. Fruit tree branches drooped with the weight of unfallen bounty; berry bushes were arrayed like stuffed clouds on the ground, speckled with bright explosions of color. Medicinal herbs and flowers alike sprouted enthusiastically. Rows of squash, carrot, tomato, eggplant, and eight types of lettuce overran their rows. In the distance lay a lush meadow which during the day came alive with bees, butterflies, and hummingbirds. It was all so *admirable*. Beautiful, even.

Finch felt nauseated looking at it. *It's not beautiful*, he told himself again. *It's horrible. Wretched. Itching to be mown.* He pressed the blueberry between his thumb and forefinger and savored the juice dripping into the earth. *That is what Unseelie do.* Finch often had to remind himself to enjoy Unseelie things. It was all part of the internship learning process—and he was, after all, entirely committed.

"Quite an evening." Agatha, Witch of Backyard Sheds and Third Tuesdays, sidled up alongside Finch.

Finch started. He'd almost forgotten she was still here. "Hey, Ags," he said. "Sun's going down."

They stared at the faraway Mountainous Mountains in silence as the first rays touched the faraway peaks.

"That's my sign to be off," she said, pressing a small golden key into Finch's hand. "Appreciate the house-sit. As we discussed, I'll be at CovenCon for three nights, and Queen Meow is coming with me—"

Hearing her name, Agatha's ebony-furred familiar leaped onto the witch's shoulders and hissed at Finch.

Finch raised his middle finger at the cat. Then he pocketed the key and saluted Agatha. "I got this. No problem." But his throat tightened and sweat collected in his armpits.

"Might think of weeding your own patch," she said absently, digging around in her satchel. "Starting to look overgrown. You were so attentive at first—"

"Shh," he said. "Keep it down." Finch was deeply embarrassed by his terrible proclivities; namely, the garden patch he'd planted in a spot Agatha had donated.

"I'll take the plot back if you've lost interest, kiddo. I could use more rue and mandrake."

"Mmph." Finch was noncommittal. After tonight, it wouldn't matter.

Agatha was the closest thing Finch had to a friend in this part of the Veil. Their love for SCN programming had bonded them—particularly TROPE Town movie series—and they spent long evenings watching it at Broadcast Lake, where it streamed nightly. During breaks in the films, Agatha gossiped with Finch about her neighbors: who was pranking who, what the ogre down the block was doing with his newest dungeon captive, and spellcast recipes she had picked up in the latest issue of *Who Witch* magazine. In return, Finch shared whatever gossip he had come across in the SCN headquarters, though it wasn't much—UDIP interns were among the lowest of ranks in the building, and little came his way.

I find you entertaining, Agatha had told him. *And you're just the right kind of mess I like to hang out with.*

Still, even with Agatha, Finch kept his guard up. He was afraid of anyone knowing too much about him and his level of proper Unseelieness. He was fine if she knew the colors of his hair (gray with streaks of red), and that his green eyes shifted to gold under stress. It was all right that she knew he had problems portaling around, and was overfond of shortbread. But even Agatha had never seen his Hideous Deformity.

Yet she always seemed to know his secrets anyway. Maybe it was a witchy thing. One night he'd asked Agatha how her garden grew, and she'd gone on for the next hour explaining every row and patch and plant. Then she'd waved at a small rectangle that had been cleared but wasn't growing anything yet. *It's yours*, she'd said. *You should have a place to be yourself, whoever that is.*

Finch had begun making regular visits to his garden patch, staring at the soil for a long time before adding seeds: nightshade, foxglove, castor bean. Agatha had drawn the line at poison ivy. To his astonishment, they'd grown. Then they'd grown more. Some afternoons he'd sit alongside the plants and set his hand on the soil. He imagined he could hear the patch calling to him: *Water me. Pick me. Need more worms!*

He'd been astonished by how much he enjoyed seeing the insignificant seeds turn into full-on plants. His chest had swelled with pride, though his stomach roiled in disgust.

Stupid Unseelie spectrum, Finch often thought. *Why can't I just be abnormal?*

Agatha never questioned his interests. As a witch, she had intimate knowledge that there were shades of gray in the world—nothing all yin, nothing all yang. But Finch could not afford such in-between thinking. He would have to be more Unseelie than any other Unseelie to prove himself to Laurel and Hardy and to get ahead at SCN. Agatha's garden was about to prove the perfect vehicle to do so—and it was time to get rid of the evidence that he had weird *growing* interests.

This year's Smash would take care of *that*. The Smash was a bi-annual celebration of the most wonderful time of year to be Unseelie, held when humans and fae alike reveled in the dark, the in-between, the *end* of things. Across the Kingdom at this time of year Unseelie partied hard, tearing, rendering, uprooting, and destroying whatever they came across. But finding an unprotected location was difficult; Seelie were on to the practice and often set out wards to keep out troublemakers.

Not Agatha.

"Well, I think you've tended a fine patch for your first effort." She pulled a tube of black lipstick from her satchel and applied it. "Next year, you'll grow better."

A soft bustling in a far hedgerow caught Finch's attention. If he squinted, he could see a group of early Smash arrivals hanging out in the yew—a motley, roiling gang of invitees and crashers alike. Smash crashers were *de rigueur*, since mayhem-loving Unseelie weren't much on patience, etiquette, or engraved invitations. If they couldn't hold back until sundown, though, Finch's plans would be ruined. But he felt their dagger stares poking at him to get this party started.

Finch's fingers twitched. "Yeah, sure I will. Thanks. Hey, are you going to be late? Better to take to the skies before dark."

Agatha snapped her fingers, and her hazel broomstick darted over. Taking a sidesaddle seat, the witch hovered a few feet off the ground for a moment. Queen Meow leapt into her lap. "Look at me, Finch," she said.

He had a hard time dragging his eyes to meet hers.

"There's nothing wrong with what you do, or what you are," she said. "Embrace all of it. You'll be a much happier fae." And without waiting for a reply, she shot into the sky and flew into the oncoming night.

"I don't want to be a happy, sappy fae," Finch called after her. "I'm Unseelie!"

The garden was silent for a brief pause.

Then a face appeared in the leaves of an apple tree—a human-like creature with a spray of blue freckles across its nose and two long ears that suggested both donkey and rabbit. "Whatcha waitin' for, weirdo?"

"Fitzwilliam," Finch told the púka. "You know the rules. Nothing till sundown."

Somersaulting from a branch, the púka landed on his feet, pockets and arms bulging with apple bounty. "Kinda sus' how you always point out *rules*," Fitzwilliam spat. "All of us dragged ourselves way out here 'cause we heard there'd be classic Unseelie craic. An *untouched* Smash spot—that's a find, so it is."

Finch instinctively wanted to reason with the púka, but that would be an error. Púkas didn't respect logic, and they'd think less of an Unseelie who tried using it on them. "S-sure," Finch stammered. "Rules are for suckers. But a single rule, well—"

The púka unhinged his jaw and released an ear-splitting siren of a wail. Finch clapped his hands over his ears in time, but every fruit the púka had touched had already turned brown and rotten. They smacked to the ground like soft, wet turds. The jaw hinged back into place. "Oops." He grinned. "Guess I started early." Then he froze, staring over Finch's shoulder. The grin fell like a rotten apple. "Oops," he repeated, this time in a more chastened voice.

Finch turned. Behind him stood two Unseelie in white overalls. Their bronzed skin glowed, and even at this distance their ice-blue eyes gave Finch itchy palms. They looked nearly identical, except that one was hefty with platinum hair and the taller one sported shocking blue hair. But they were equally glaring in Finch's direction.

The sweat under his arms increased.

"Stand aside, DIPster," said Laurel, the taller, more slender one.

Hardy barreled past Finch. They grabbed Fitzwilliam's collar and lifted the púka in the air. "You will *respect* the Smash Rule!"

"He hasn't, though," said Laurel. "What we gonna do?"

They both looked at Finch.

Give him another chance was on the tip of Finch's tongue and he bit down hard on it to keep the words inside. His mentors were riding to his rescue, and he was beside himself. Laurel and Hardy were legends at SCN, top-of-the-line Unseelie Deconstructors who appeared as Nos. 34 and 35 on the official SCN Trading Card Set. As a youngling fae, Finch had hung up posters of them in his bedchamber. Little was known about them, which only enhanced their enigma. They might be related to one another. Might be mated. Might be just friends. But they were never seen singly. And he'd been assigned to them at SCN by random selection.

Finch would not let them down. "Uh, uh—revoke his invite!"

"Pah," snorted Laurel. "There are no invites, DIPster."

Finch searched for something better. "Bury him in the compost heap! Headfirst!"

Hardy gave him an odd look. "Too much work. Here's what you do." With a flick of their wrist, the Unseelie flung the púka toward the darkening mountains in the distance.

Fitzwilliam's final shout of "I regret nothing!" faded as he flew away.

The Unseelie mentors turned to Finch. "When you've only got one rule, you better enforce it," Laurel told him. They gazed around the backyard, evaluating. "Smaller than I imagined."

Hardy nodded. "But plenty of trees. Trees are good. They take time to pick apart."

Laurel narrowed their gaze at Finch. "Curious that you chose this spot. Thought I'd heard you were tight with the third-tier witch owner."

"Nah." Finch waved his hand to one side. "She's stupid. I was cultivating her. Like a plant."

Hardy raised an eyebrow. "Cultivating?"

"For the Smash, of course." Finch didn't worry about what might happen when Agatha came back. Probably nothing. Probably she had all the spells needed to resurrect her place—that was what made it such a perfect Smash spot. But also, Finch insisted to himself that he didn't really care what she thought.

It sort of worked.

Laurel laced their fingers together and inverted them, making the knuckles crack. "Finchola, tell me. What *are* you doing in UDIP, other than taking up space a more natural Unseelie could use?"

Finch's mouth dropped. "I'm doing my best— I mean my worst—"

Hardy clapped Finch on the back. "They're just messin' with you. I mean, yeah, you're still our lightweight, but we'll get that hammered out of you in time. What my partner means is you showed initiative finding us this sweet Smash spot. Point in your favor. But what are you gonna do for your next trick? What's the goal here for Finchola the Floofy Unseelie?"

This was the most either of his mentors had ever spoken to him, and Finch's brain was breaking a little bit. *Embrace all of it*, Agatha's parting words came to him. The words popped out before he could filter them. "I wanna tear shit down," he said. "Just like you! Gimme a TV series—a human hamlet—a sacred grove… even a TROPE Town!"

There it was. The unvarnished truth. Only the most elite UDIP success stories achieved Laurel and Hardy's levels of access and expertise, but Finch had big goals. TV series got canceled all the time and needed tearing down; TROPE Towns were less likely to fail but occasionally needed re-evaluation when not enough eyeballs were tuning in anymore. Finch wanted to be the kind of deconstructor they gave the most difficult jobs to, the Unseelie they wrote legends about. And it was all going to start with an impressive Smash—

Why were they laughing?

Finch's mentors were bent over in hysterics, pointing at each other, pointing at him, red-faced and almost weeping with amusement. "As if!" Laurel gasped.

"It'd take ten immortal lifetimes!" cried Hardy.

"Nothin' like blind ambition!" Laurel held their sides. "Emphasis on the *blind*."

For a moment, Finch's face burned with shame. His green eyes turned golden. His mentors weren't taking him seriously. But then he took a step back and glanced at the garden, and back at the nearly identical pair in their starched white overalls. An odd calm came over him.

They don't get it, he thought. *Old and tired, those two. Past it. They have no idea what I'm capable of.*

Turning, Finch plucked a second oversized blueberry. Holding it up to the sun, which was about to disappear behind the mountains, he closed one eye and blotted out the light. *I made an eclipse*, he thought, a brief godlike power curling his toes. With a pinch, he crushed the berry between his fingers and this time let the juice run down his arm.

I'll show them, Finch thought, mind racing. *I have resources.* Interns didn't have a lot of spare time outside of classes, but they were given free range of the SCN corridors—and Finch had spent hours in the library, reading through the ever-growing official SCN Guide. He'd pulled down appendices and manuals on deconstruction. He'd memorized meeting procedural rules, the hiring process, even the commissary recipes. Until now it had all felt just like accumulating facts. He hadn't felt a need to put those rules and that knowledge into play.

Turned out all he needed was a feeling of righteous ambition.

Time to carpe the destruction, he thought. *They're gonna have* me *on their walls someday.*

At last, the sun and the light disappeared from the sky.

Whirling, Finch raised his arms toward the garden. He wanted to launch mayhem, to give a speech of importance. It was all on the tip of his tongue. But the moment the sun winked out, invitees and crashers alike surged into the garden like mudslides down a mountain. Someone shoved Finch aside. Laurel and Hardy wiped their eyes and dove into the crush. Finch leaped to grab an apple tree branch and dangled from one hand while gesturing widely with his other arm.

He shouted, "Welcome to the Smash! I'm your host—"

"Nobody's listening, Finchola!" Hardy called over their shoulder. "Nobody needs you!"

I'm gonna change all that, thought Finch.

Then he released the branch and dropped into approximately 91.3 percent chaos.

Chapter 2

Smashing Decision

FINCH DUCKED AROUND the side of Agatha's cottage, disappearing into the shadow of the overhang. Mere feet away, havoc reigned, participants illuminated by a moon so full he wondered if they might try pulling it down to smash it into wedges of cheese.

He was coated in layers of fruit and dirt and smelled like a three-week-old parfait. Peering around the house, Finch spotted boggarts blasting bananas. Kelpies kicking kale. Gnomes grabbing grapes. The cool evening air echoed with shouts of delight, mayhem, and occasional outrage when someone pelted someone else with vegetable matter. At some point Fitzwilliam had wandered back into the Smash, using a hollowed-out tree branch as a pea shooter with berries as ammunition of choice.

Finch had gone at it with gusto for three hours but leaving the melee he was happy for a shortbread break in relative solitude. Unseelie could get drunk if they liked on uisce beatha, but homemade shortbread was a secret weapon on his type. Few Unseelie would admit to making it themselves—they'd just steal it from an unwitting baker—but Finch always had a tray cooling somewhere. It gave him a heady, confident feeling. It made his ears tingle. Once he'd had a few bites, he'd be ready to rejoin the fracas.

One thing nibbling on shortbread was doing for him now was to quiet the voices of the garden he'd heard in his head all evening. *Why? Why? Why?* the produce mewled at him—or he imagined it did—in pathetic, reedy voices. But with every bite, he felt more himself. Shortbread just did that for Finch, muting the weird itchiness he woke up with every day that made him want to see what he could make sprout in the dirt. That made him whisper and coo at things beneath the soil. Roots responded to him, worms wriggled at his vibrations, and seeds sprouted at his song. Soil practically sighed when he murmured to it.

Utter nonsense. Not good Unseelie behavior at all.

Shoving a third rectangle of shortbread into his mouth, he spied Laurel and Hardy parting from the main scrum. A loose game of rugby had broken out between two even looser teams, who were using squash to hurl into the 'goal' of a spindly pear tree. With a casual wave over their shoulders, the deconstructors hopped onto the reasonably chaos-free front steps of Agatha's cottage. Their formerly pure white overalls and T-shirts were now covered in pulp and seeds.

Finch began scrambling to his feet, prepared to share the shortbread. He'd claim he stole it from Agatha; they'd never know he prepared it yesterday—then paused while Hardy lit a clove cigarette and drew down deep.

"You know, not horrible," said Laurel. "The moon, a destroyed watermelon patch, and thou."

Hardy blew out smoke rings. "Not that we're gonna tell ol' Floofster that."

"He calls himself Finch." Laurel plucked drying pumpkin seeds from their overalls and licked their fingers.

"He can call himself whatever he likes. He's a floofy lightweight and I sometimes wonder why he's even a UDIP intern."

Finch slid deeper into the shadows of the overhang.

"Same," said Laurel, taking a puff on the cigarette. "Notice how he's not out there with everybody else right now?"

Crumbs rained down Finch's chin. The shortbread in his mouth tasted like stone and he couldn't swallow. Why did what they said matter? Hadn't he just psyched himself up to decide that he was going to surpass those two old-school yo-yos?

"Still," Laurel said after a pause, "you gotta admit it's beautifully wretched to go after a *friend's* garden. That witch put a lot of love and care into that patch, and she didn't do it overnight. A modicum of respect for Finch on that one."

Hardy laughed. "I doubt we'll be wondering about his UDIP cred once she gets back. She might be third-tier, but I bet he'll be slinking around as a newt this time next week."

Finch hung his head. How had he failed so badly at being awful? Except to Agatha, who was surely going to be *very put out* once she returned. Being a newt was nothing. If she reported his gardening to the Seelie Court, he could be cited for trying to fake an Unseelie nature. Fae found out to be faking were frequently sent just one place: to live on the other side of the Veil, in exile. Among *humans*.

Finch shuddered. He wouldn't let that happen. Not again. He was still scarred from his earliest youngling days as a changeling among a human family. They'd been so strange, even stranger than the humans who appeared in SCN programs.

The Unseelie cleaners were still talking.

"So, what's your verdict? If he turns up at HQ next week and he's not a newt, do we make space for him at the Emergency All-Hands meeting in the map room?"

The map room! That was Finch's favorite place to have

lunch when he was at SCN HQ. When no meeting was scheduled, he could hide out under the table and dig into his most pungent meal—sardines stuffed with red kimchi, with a side of durian. If no one kicked him out after he finished eating, he would linger over the dynamic TROPE Town layout that covered the conference room table, watching from above as treetops waved in the thick forests that separated the towns, sometimes following a lone car winding its way down the narrow highway from one to the other. If he leaned close enough, he swore he could hear the tiniest voices down below. Not that he could affect anything in the T-Town.

Hardy flicked the cigarette butt into the ongoing havoc. "Nah. Above his pay grade, and he doesn't even get paid yet. Probably never will. What do you think that whole meeting's about, anyway?"

Laurel leaned closer to Hardy, and Finch could barely make out what they were saying next. "T-Towns… map room… missing… something… something."

Finch leaned closer, wedging himself behind a bush. Leaves adhered to the drying fruit pulp on his outfit and the residual clove smoke made him want to cough.

"Somebody was posting on Arachne's Web that—" A noise obscured Laurel's next few words. "And there's no new stories—" A gnome rolled like a bowling ball across the yard, quacking. "So they're doing reconnaissance—"

Finch leaned even closer, and abruptly several things happened at once. A cantaloupe soared out of the still-raging party, smacking and exploding against the cottage. Seeds and orange pulp rained down. Hardy took out a new clove cigarette and lit up, sending smoke directly into the bush. The burning scent tickled Finch's throat, and he coughed, spraying remnant shortbread everywhere. Then he fell forward out of the bushes, landing at the feet of the Unseelie.

They stared down at him and said nothing.

Hardy rolled their eyes and flicked the cigarette into a pile of dry plants. The plants caught alight.

A watermelon hunk plummeted from the sky and landed on top of the nascent inferno, dousing the flames in juice.

Finch stared up at his mentors. "Gah," he gasped, embarrassed into incoherence.

This time, Laurel and Hardy didn't laugh. Instead, they stepped over Finch as though he wasn't even there. "Ready to act like a hockey stick?" Laurel asked, clapping Hardy on the shoulder.

"And get the puck out of here?" Hardy nodded. "You know it. There's a rave the ogres are throwing at the—"

The pair portaled away mid-sentence.

Finch closed his eyes and sighed, wishing he could vanish himself. But then a shadow fell over him and he blinked once. Twice. Three times. Despite his prone position, he could feel the blood draining from his face.

"Evening, Finch," said Agatha. "Something you forgot to tell me?"

THE SMASH OVER, Finch grabbed some of the last bits of Agatha's former garden and hurled them into the bonfire. Watching as flames licked the ravaged pieces of plant matter and turned the leaves into curled black fists meant he didn't have to look the witch in the face. He kept expecting to look up and see her waving a wand or flailing her hands at him to cast a newt-like spell, unsure what the Witch of Backyard Sheds and Third Tuesdays could really do with her powers.

But she wasn't doing any magic. She just sat in her Adirondack chair, alternating between gazing up at the bright moon and twinkling night sky and watching him with dark eyes and an unreadable expression.

As he stared into the flames, Finch couldn't stop running Laurel and Hardy's words over in his mind. Maybe they were right. He *was* a lightweight. He *was* a weirdo aspirant destructor Unseelie who didn't fit the mold. But he was learning. He'd learned so hard he'd let his only friend's garden turn into the site of a four-hour Smash, leaving it looking like an army *and* a herd of centaurs *and* an earthquake had all recently visited. If Laurel and Hardy had called it a triumph, he would be soaring as high as an errant cantaloupe launched into the air. Instead, he felt like *he'd* been smashed up against a cottage.

I will have to try harder, he decided. *They're going to respect me.*

With the last armload of garden delivered to the fire, Finch turned. "Anything else?"

Agatha didn't answer.

The witch hadn't actually asked him to clean things up. After revealing that she'd left Queen Meow's catnip behind by accident, she'd quickly put an end to the yard-invading Smash by magicking up a giant backyard shed that sucked every reveler inside, folded in on itself and vanished. Then without a word, she'd made herself a cup of tea indoors, lay a plate of chocolate-covered biscuits on a plate, and took a seat in her favorite chair. It was the one she usually brought to Broadcast Lake where they had enjoyed so many hours of SCN programming.

Seeing the chair reminded Finch of those nights. For years, he'd avoided SCN entertainments, wrapped up in his own problems and going to five-times-per-week therapy for changeling trauma issues. But once he connected with Agatha, they'd begun spending time each night at Broadcast Lake, watching the short, weird lives of humans unspool in TROPE Town movies. That had been therapeutic, too. Humans had come a long way since Finch's changeling days. They now traveled on wheels. They were more concerned with taking baths. They smoked meat in outdoor metal devices. They clipped their toenails and threw away the remnants, as if they had no idea witches paid top dollar for human body discards. Finch began to understand the horrid beasts a little better.

But then Agatha had burst his bubble. *TROPE Towns aren't real, exactly*, she'd said. *They're real enough for humans to live in them, but it's like putting fish in a tank in your home.* T-Towns were contained spaces on the fae side of the Veil where they organized humans who fell into their orbits. Nearly all were happy volunteers. Nice ones went to places like Swee'ton, a T-Town where life was full of bakeries and holidays and never ran out of sugar. Dastardly ones might end up in Second Chance, a town where everyone had a dark secret. Agatha had a soft spot for Los Esposos, aka Flashback Spouse, village.

I once dated a Seelie Showrunner for a heartbeat, and what I understand is they let humans run around in these bubble towns and come up with stories based on their lives and film their doings, Agatha had explained. *Take the one you like so much—Seaview Haven—for example. You don't imagine that little seaside village is ground zero for hundreds of crimes, do you? That one gray-haired woman—*

Winnie Arrowmaker, Finch had added.

Right, her and her frenemy sheriff—you really think they solve everything in two hours? It's all a scripted story. It's not really *happening in the movie, even if it did once happen in real life.*

That had been a mind-blowing evening for Finch. One reason he liked the Seaview Haven mysteries so much was that he could side with the wrongdoers whose crimes

Winnie ultimately solved. But he hadn't thought of Winnie or Seaview Haven since they'd stopped making original movies a couple years ago. Who wanted to watch a rerun of a whodunnit? You already knew who'd dunnit.

Finch had entertained the idea of portaling himself into Seaview Haven and complaining to the Showrunner/Mayor/Director: *How dare you leave us hanging? Make something new! Or maybe it's time the cleaners come in to close up your town!*

Agatha told him that wasn't how it was done. *You don't complain to the town's Seelie Mayor*, she said. *When a show stops drawing enough eyeballs, or the humans stop doing interesting things and Seelie get bored, SCN orders that the town gets dismantled. That's where your heroes come in.*

Now, Finch knew that Unseelie dismantled things that didn't work. Spells, relationships, even the occasional forest. He hadn't realized they could be in charge of dismantling an entire *town*—and the concept blew his mind. The next day, he'd signed up for SCN's Unseelie Deconstructor Internship Program. Over the ensuing months, he'd learned that a failing town would be taken apart piece by piece. Some of it was thrown into a bottomless pit, some was burned, and some was magicked away into storage for later use. The good parts were often sent out to other T-Towns, but most humans were portaled back onto their side of the Veil to fend for themselves. In time, their memories faded, and they were never able to talk or write about their T-Town experiences.

It's a delicate process, I was told, Agatha said. *Once a show goes bad, there's no saving it—you just have to cancel it. There's a whole cancel culture to it all.*

Finch felt he'd found his métier as an aspiring Unseelie deconstructor. But he struggled, every day. And after tonight's Smash, he wondered if Laurel and Hardy would even allow him to graduate the program.

While the bonfire continued to consume the former garden, Agatha continued to consume her biscuits, staring at Finch. It was as if she expected something more than cleanup from him. Queen Meow curled around Agatha's legs and hopped onto her lap. She gave a half-hearted hiss to Finch.

"You know who I am." Finch folded his arms and tapped his foot. "Who trusts Unseelie with the key to their home? Who gives Unseelie a garden patch to grow poisons? Who..." He trailed off.

Agatha removed a biscuit from her cooling tea and took a bite. She dabbed the crumbs from her mouth and swallowed. "The thing is," she said at last, "I didn't give my key to Unseelie."

"Of course you did! I've told you everything, I've been very clear that—"

"I gave it to my friend," she said.

Another blood-draining-from-his-head sensation came over Finch. He threw up his hands and stormed around the former garden. "Well, la-di-da. You showed me. Maybe I should thank you because you proved I can be one hundred percent committed to the Unseelie way—"

"Finch, you're blustering."

He stopped and held his arms out wide. "Fine. Then do what you have to do. Make me a newt, or whatever. I'll take your punishment."

"No," she said.

"No?"

"No."

He wasn't blustering anymore, but now Finch was flustered. "Then... everything's okay? You can just go ahead and magic the garden back—"

"No, I can't," she said. "That's not how gardens

work. Not real ones. And I'm not going to change you into another creature or make your hair fall out or your tongue cease to function, though Wicca knows that last one would be a blessing. I'm going to do something else. Because you're right, Finch—this is partly my fault. I knew who you *said* you were. Who you were working so hard to be. And I kept thinking to myself, *He'll figure it out. He's misdirected.* I was once confused about who I was, too. Now I know better. So, what I'm going to do with you, Finch, is—"

He leaned forward, afraid but expectant.

"Nothing."

Finch blinked. "Nothing?"

"Correct. You will figure out your own punishment, in time. Maybe then we'll talk again."

Finch sagged dramatically, tilting his head back. "Oh, come on. Just make me a newt for an hour and we can go watch the lake again."

"That's not going to happen."

"You're making this very hard."

"It's not supposed to be easy."

Irritation bloomed in his head. "Fine. Keep your high ground. I'm going to go."

"I think you should."

"I'll come back in a couple days, when you're more like a normal witch."

She shook her head. "First, I've never been a normal witch. Second, you're not permitted back." She held out her hand. "The key, please."

Reluctantly, he pulled it from his pocket. The gold still shone brightly as he placed it in her palm. "You'll change your mind. I'm going to be the greatest dismantler SCN ever had. I'm going to that Emergency All-Hands meeting Laurel and Hardy said got called and—"

"I don't care, Finch."

"—I'm going to wreck something, but good. And you'll see—"

"Goodbye, Finch." Agatha fluttered her fingers.

"But I—"

And he was portaled away without another word.

Chapter 3

A Trash Bag of Infinite Capacity

Malvous V. Hill had done well. The brownie paused at one end of the east-southwest-north corridor of Floor 1037 of SCN HQ, gazing with satisfaction at the extremely long hallway behind him. It had taken eleven days to make the alabaster walls sparkle and the gold-threaded marble floors shine like mirrors. He'd spent long hours dusting, feeding, and complimenting the Will O' the Wisps that clustered in the ceiling, illuminating the space.

As a brownie, Malvous was on the high end of the Seelie class spectrum. But he did not construct. He helped. Also, he knew he was unusual by Brownie standards. Unlike his brethren, Malvous was neither short-statured nor graceful. His fingers were calloused and awkward, and instead of a squared-off head and oversized eyes, he had squared-off eyes and an oversized head. Brownies—who these days preferred being called 'Bros'—could come in any shade, but Malvous had turned a pale green hue thanks to his vegetarianism.

Malvous appreciated the value of work. He took pride in his one accomplishment, which was also his job: to keep the hallway of Floor 1037 at SCN HQ pristine. It was a job with no beginning and no end; by the time he finished, the hall needed re-cleaning. He'd gone through this soothing repetition so often that he could daydream his favorite streaming series' plotlines all day while still turning out an exceptionally clean surface. And while daystreaming—as Malvous thought of it—he sometimes envisioned himself in those stories, too.

Tonight, when Malvous squeezed himself within the walls of SCN HQ to join his brownie companions, folded awkwardly into whatever drinking establishment they'd chosen for the evening to swap stories in, he would have this great accomplishment to share. If he was fortunate, one particular brownie—Foxtacular Frayo Featherweight, he of the bold chestnut eyes and gravity-defying pompadour—might be there. If he was insanely favored, there might even be some hand-holding.

In relationships, as in his cleaning duties, Malvous was focused and methodical.

Sighing at those future delights, Malvous heaved the packed silk trash bag from his cleaning cart's holder and set it gently to one side. Silk bags were only one of the wonders he could fashion. Virtually unbreakable, they could expand to hold far more than their flimsy structure would suggest. And while they weren't sentient, they were imbued with the desire to contain. They eagerly made room for whatever was given to them to hold. Malvous himself could fit into one, not that he'd tried it or anything. Packed with Seelie and visitor detritus, the bag would enter the garbage chute and transform into butterflies, dreams, and 72% dark chocolate drops that dispersed around the world below. Until then, it was a messy combination of tissues, food scraps and something unspeakably slimy and green that smelled of dragon vomit. Probably *was* dragon vomit.

Reaching into the cleaning cart, Malvous withdrew a silver flask. Glancing around—he was alone in the hallway—he took a slug of the uisce beatha within, the burn of the alcohol a comfort and joy. He permitted himself one jolt of the whiskey at the end of every completed hallway, after which the flask would be tucked safely back on his cart among the bottomless spritzers of cleaning solutions, self-replicating tissue boxes and newly woven trash bags. Today, however—perhaps distracted by the idea of Foxtacular's small (compared to Malvous) delicate hands—he slipped the flask into a pocket of his olive linen jumpsuit and reached for a new silk trash bag.

With a practiced snap of the wrist, the bag billowed before him like an opaque balloon. Through the fabric, he swore he saw a flash of light, a whisk of movement. Had a Will shorted out?

The light flashed again and a large *something* burst from it, limbs flailing as if it had just discovered gravity. The Something tumbled through the air and landed with a giant *whoomph* on top of the full trash bag, which Malvous had not yet tied shut. Tissues and half-eaten snacks and dragon-associated effluvia splashed on the walls, the floor, and Malvous' ankles.

The pristine hallway was no longer pristine.

Malvous wailed.

The Something scrabbled like a crab from its soft trashy landing and rolled to the marble floor, gasping. It was filthy even without the added layer of trash, wearing boots covered in clots of dirt and dressed in torn jeans and a ripped T-shirt that said *Wyvern World Tour '93* in looping, sparkling letters. The ends of the bag quivered, looking to contain things, and one crept close to the Something's left foot.

"Well," the Something said, catching its breath. "Not as bad an entry as usual." It turned its head, which was covered in straggly gray hair threaded through with crimson streaks. "Do you have any idea how hard it is to portal into this building? Every day I do it wrong in a whole new way. I keep landing in recycle bins, on the roof—and once I ended up in this squishy, fruity salad in the cafeteria. The cooks did *not* like that one bit." The Something kicked itself to a standing position. "This is the 1037th floor, right? Map room just down thataway?"

Malvous shook a fist at the Something. "Look what you did to my hallway!"

The Seelie elf, or the Unseelie boggart, or whatever the Something was, glanced up and down the hallway. "Meh. I've done worse." He turned to stare at Malvous' chest and craned his neck back. "Great googly eyes, you're a tall drink of water."

"This took me a week to clean!" Malvous gestured at the filth around him.

The creature took a second glance. "Well, you're clearly not done yet." His eyes were green with gold flecks in them. "Seelie don't put up with slackers. You've got to do better if you want to get ahead." The creature set a thumb on his own chest. "Think big. Do whatever it takes. That's what I'm here about."

Malvous glared at him. Not a Seelie elf after all. "You could at least apologize!"

"Unseelie don't apologize." Somehow, despite their height difference, the Something looked down his nose at Malvous. "Even if they want to. Not even to stupid old cranky witches."

Malvous didn't know what any of that meant. "Who *are* you?"

The Something rose up on tiptoe. "Some call me an ollphéist beag."

"A Little Monster." Malvous fought the urge to cringe. "They should call you Dirty Boots! Just look at your feet!"

"Can't be helped. Dirt happens in a new garden—I mean, when you walk around in the woods." Distracted, the Unseelie Something continued to scour the hallway, muttering to itself. "You'd think I'd've memorized this by now, but this place would disorient a compass." He glanced at Malvous and gestured. "That way. Map room, right?"

"Down there—" Malvous' words stuck in his throat as he pointed, only realizing now what was about to happen. "Wait—"

But the Unseelie Something wasn't waiting any longer. Whipping around, he galloped down the corridor, leaving in his wake sticky, muddy, fragrant boot prints. And attached to one heel, trailing after him like a silky shadow, was the still mostly full trash bag.

Malvous wailed again. Everything was *ruined*, and just as he'd completed a round! He would have to start all over again. He would miss drinks with his friends. He would not beguile Foxtacular with his accomplishment. It was untenable—and his union could do nothing about it. The brownie's green-tinted face reddened. Something in his head went *pop*.

No! he thought and dashed after the interloper. Malvous wasn't particularly fast, but his long strides closed the distance between himself and the fae in moments. Equal parts uisce beatha and fury raced through his veins. Pursuer and pursued zapped past frosted crystal doors down the extended hallway of Floor 1037, footsteps pounding on the marble. "Halt! Cease! Desist!" Malvous cried, but nothing would slow the Unseelie Something down.

Desperate, Malvous let out a cry and hurled himself forward, trying to tackle the creature. He missed by several inches and pancaked on the ground—yet he still moved. Something had wrapped itself around him and was drawing him inward. As was its nature. A soft silken shroud slurped itself over his body, containing Malvous with ease. He was engulfed in his own trash bag, which simultaneously continued to curl its drawstrings around the fleeing Unseelie's boot.

This is ridonculous, Malvous decided, struggling to break free. But the bag wouldn't give. In fact, if a bag could rejoice, this one would be doing it; not only had it contained one square-eyed brownie with an oversized head, but it was also doing its best to swallow up a fleeing, mysterious, filthy Unseelie Little Monster, a fae unfazed by dragging a not-insubstantial brownie behind him. Bits of dirt kicked into the brownie's face, taken in eagerly by the overambitious bag.

Malvous couldn't do a faun-cocky thing about it. He squirmed, he wailed, he pushed back, and it changed nothing. In fact, the bag tightened around him.

And then—the ride ended. Fully swallowed, Malvous could only move an inch here and there, and was able to peer out of a small aperture at the top with one eye. That one-eyed gaze discovered a frosted conference door before them. The Unseelie Little Monster yanked it open and heaved himself inside, tumbling to the floor.

And Malvous V. Hill heaved along with him.

Chapter 4

Failure Is Not a Seelie Option

For the entirety of its existence, the Seelie Court Network had been run by, well, Seelie. Also, run well by Seelie. As the correct creatures to undertake such a fiddly, complex task, far-end spectrum Seelie were perfect beings, namely perfectly symmetrical, perfectly unblemished, and perfectly toned. They smelled of nice scents like freshly laundered linen and toasted sugar. The air they breathed out was cleaner than what they took in. They positively glowed with heightened magic, like an electric blanket or radioactive glassware. Their sweat was purer than a mountain stream, their outgassing toots the finest of melodies.

With Seelie in charge, SCN had always been orderly, efficient, and entertaining. They had many ideas (bright and brilliant), concepts (high and low), pitches (elevator and curve), loglines and synopses for potential series and films. Most importantly, they knew how to delegate. They hired other creatures to do the drudge work of actually *writing* the projects, and left cleanup on the rare failures to a troupe of Unseelie in the Cleaning and Waste Management crew.

As a system, it had flaws—none of which Seelie would admit to, including the Executive-Vice-Vice-Vice-Vice-Vice President in Care of TROPE Town

Allocation and Programming (EVVVVVPCTTAP for short; nomenclature was a tricky, ego-driven business). The EVVVVVPCTTAP was a Seelie Queen descendant known as ꝁ— (a word that sounded like 'the,' if the speaker's tongue was stuck to the roof of their mouth), and as such was a model of Seelie greatness. She trusted her instincts. Was tough, but fair. Open to fancies, yet traditional in her choices. Drank as much as eighty-two cups of strong tea every sun cycle. The surface of her forest-green hair was bedazzled with living butterflies and ladybugs. She wore a different crisp, tailored outfit every day that predicted the next fashion trend. She was a vision of faedom.

For centuries, ꝁ— had worked at SCN and run her various offices like a ship's captain, sailing through calm oceans with barely a ripple. Officially, she was the inventor of TROPE Towns, a concept she claimed came to her in a dream but really was just an outbranching of her need to organize, pigeonhole, and reduce. Mythic audiences had become so picky in what they wanted to see of human stories that it was easier to just group the mortals together and make films of them doing the same things over and over again. Mortals had such short life spans they never noticed the repetition. Or so went the theory. But long-lived Seelie saw centuries pass in a blur. A hundred years of TROPE Town existence was barely a beginning. There were still lessons to be learned. Fortunately, Seelie *could* learn. They could evolve.

ꝁ— was certain that her key to success lay in knowing both her strengths and weaknesses. She loathed two things: meetings and Thursdays. By this, her 419th year at SCN, she'd managed to keep meetings down to two every year, when she caught up with SMDs of TROPE Towns and series alike. They had to operate on a timescale that dealt with humans, and so she bore the oppression and boredom of endless meetings stoically. This method had produced results: TROPE Towns had gone from four experimental villages to nearly eighty, and she liked leaving them to function like well-magicked machines.

But all machines, even magic ones, were subject to hiccups.

Approximately two years ago, something had begun gumming up the works. Memos began arriving, fluttering like birdless wings into both of ȝ—'s assistants' offices. Each memo featured a similar complaint: T-Town stories were drying up. Humans were still living their wildly entertaining mundane lives, but for some reason, SMDs were running on fumes. The mythics hired to write new scripts were claiming they'd been 'blocked' somehow, and were writing sequels, prequels, spin-offs, and reboots in lieu of new original scripts. It was a bad, recursive look.

And from what ȝ— could determine, Unseelie folk had nothing to do with it.

Early on, she'd ordered her Right Side Assistant to check in with Muse Central to determine what was going on. Seelie didn't like the idea of relying on immortals outside the faeverse for anything, but it had been a goddess-send to have the Muses on board, inspiring from afar.

"They're out to lunch," Right Side Assistant had reported back.

"You verified this?"

"I called." This made sense; no Seelie with any brains *visited* Muse Central. Even with the inspirational ray-banning Ray-Ban glasses, a short trip could invoke a week-long migraine. "Whoever answered the phone told me they were ladies who lunched."

Six months later, when things hadn't improved ȝ— told Right Side Assistant, "Call again."

This time, the Muses were out on a coffee break,

according to the voice on the phone.

"Have a coffee machine installed in their office," said ɮ—, who loathed the sludgy stuff but was willing to make concessions for goddesses.

More time passed, and ratings revealed that shows were dropping eyeballs left and right. T-Towns had run out of prequel, sequel, spin-off, and reboot material and had resorted to reruns. Reruns were not capturing mythic attention. In fact, formerly obsessed audiences were starting to rediscover the joys of the great outdoors, or face-to-face conversations.

ɮ— placed the call herself this time.

"Muse Central," a voice answered.

"This is EVVVVVPCTTAP ɮ—," ɮ— said in her most officious tone. "Put a Muse on the line."

"Not possible."

"Don't tell me they're at lunch or having a coffee break," ɮ— barked. "Lunch and coffee breaks do not take twelve months to complete."

"Okay," said the voice. "I won't tell you that."

A long silence ensued.

"Anything else?" the voice asked.

"Who is this?" ɮ— demanded.

"Janus," said the voice on the other line. "What's the issue?"

A god answering phones for Muses? ɮ— shook her head. "I must converse with a Muse. Any Muse. Our TROPE Towns are suffering without their inspiration, and things have to get back on track."

"And you're trying to blame the *Muses*?" Janus's voice was somehow both authoritarian and playful. "Let me take a note here about how you think they're failing—"

"No— no," ɮ— backtracked. It was a direction she could never recall having gone in before. But then again, she'd never had to solve a mystery. This was not her bailiwick; she was an EVVVVVPCTTAP, not Sherlock Holmes. "Of course not. Perhaps I misspoke. If you could alert me as to where—"

"Look, lady—"

"I am EVVVVVPCTTAP ȝ—!"

"That's a mouthful of rocks. The ladies are gonna do what they want to do and you're just gonna have to suffer along until they get back to doing what they were doing before, when they were doing whatever it was you were having them do. Gods and goddesses are *not* responsible for running your goofy little network."

"No, that is my responsibility—"

"Exactly. So, go be responsible. Go… I don't know, go check out your Twerpy Towns. Maybe there's a hairball in the pipeline."

If Janus hadn't been a god, ȝ— would have magicked them into an ice cube and plopped it into the ocean. But no one wanted a war between immortals. They went on *forever*. She had to placate them, something that didn't come naturally to her. "That… sounds like a clever plan," she allowed. "I will entertain it."

"Great. It's a plan. So, stop calling here. I'm busy putting together my memoirs, and you're breaking into my procrastination time."

The call had disconnected.

ȝ— had stared at her phone receiver for a long time.

This raised the level of mystery to a new level: Why was *Janus*, of all gods, hanging out in Muse Central? *Writing*, of all things? And hanging up on ȝ—, of all Seelie?

The logical thing would be to march over to Muse Central and demand answers. But here, ȝ— hesitated. Her delegatory nature rose up and insisted that there must be another explanation. They should clear out all other possibilities before turning to the most logical one. Wasn't that how one solved a mystery?

Frantic, ꝫ— was running out of ideas, and Janus' suggestion was as good as any. Without audiences, the great dream factory of SCN was in peril. Fae worlds existed when they were believed in—by humans, by mythics, by gods and goddesses. Without audiences watching their shows, there was no SCN; without SCN they would be stuffed back into the days of living underground, waiting to be worshiped and feared again. It was untenable. It was impossible. Not on her watch.

But as two years ticked on of slowly failing TROPE Towns, ꝫ— feared she was *this close* to being the first EVVVVVPCTTAP to fail, a nightmare on its own. Failure would lead to firing. Firing meant she would be evaluated in front of the Seelie Court and possibly Exiled.

Something had to be done.

And so, in desperation, ꝫ— called an Emergency All-Hands Meeting.

For Thursday.

Chapter 5

Some Enchanted Meeting

FINCH BLINKED UP from the floor of the map room at the luminous, distractingly beautiful faces of dozens of Seelie executives and Showrunner/Mayor/Directors. Wide bright eyes of every color of the rainbow (and a few outside of it) nestled among skin tones of equally great variety, all without a blemish or scar among them. For a moment he flashed back to being a newborn changeling, observed by startled humans.

He coughed once. "Tah-dah?"

Seconds before opening the door, Finch had been certain he'd heard chatter on the other side of it. He'd hoped they were still in the preliminary phases of the All-Hands meeting—he'd had the location and date from Laurel and Hardy, but not the time—and that he wouldn't be barging in on anything important. Now, among the hovering faces, slender legs, wheeled transport devices (largely for selkies and other finfolk) and body-contouring cloud chairs around him, there was nothing but silence.

Finch had thought he was prepared. He'd spent the last several days since his Smashing Success of a party by first ignoring the disastrous elements of it then plotting how he could best join the All-Hands Meeting that Laurel and Hardy were excluding him from. He spent an extended time in the map room, studying the TROPE Towns and paying special attention to a strange mark over one in particular. Then he spent more hours in the SCN library, looking for a special loophole in the Guide. In time, the plot thickened, coagulated, and was finally ready to be put into action.

Finch's plan had been this:

1. Portal in to SCN at daybreak, hours before his official hours began
2. Dodge 'Stabbin'' Stanley, the pink unicorn who worked as the overnight security guard
3. Hide out in the map room in an optimum location
4. Reveal himself
5. Deploy loophole
6. Stake claim
7. Await applause

But his sleep had been poor, and even a late-night walk in the woods to his new, hidden garden plot hadn't helped. Eventually he'd fallen into bed still wearing his hiking boots and gardening gloves, woke up way past sunrise, and had to portal in a hurry. Portaling had never been a real strength of Finch's. He was going to have to improvise, but improvisation was not a huge strength of Finch's either.

Sometimes he wondered what his actual strength was.

"What's that stench?" a bell-like voice said from the head of the map room's table—the Seelie in charge. Finch perked up. If the forest-green-haired fae at the end of the table was EVVVVVPCTTAP ɮ—, he was in the right place.

He nearly asked *what smell*, but then several sensations struck Finch at once. First, his leg was entangled in strong vines. Possibly kelp. Second, he was shedding forest soil all over a gold-threaded marble floor so shiny he could make out his clay-smeared face in it. Third, something smelled like an overripe durian—which made his stomach growl.

"Get me out of here!" a distinctly un-bell-like voice mumbled from the large silk bag on the floor, a bag whose drawstrings Finch discovered were entangled around his hiking boot. A squarish eye peered from the center of the bag. The bag shifted. Another eye popped into view. A hand lashed out and grabbed Finch's boot.

"Yikes!" Finch jerked upright, slamming his head into the underside of the map room table, which took up the majority of the room. "Nuts!" The boot pulled away from his foot into the hand, exposing his blue woolen sock with its worn heel. Backing up, Finch blundered into a cloud chair. It left a wet spot on his trousers and skittered across the room, still carrying its occupant. Finally, he rose to standing height and hopped on one booted foot.

Executives on all sides scrambled backward.

"That's not mine!" he pointed at the wriggling bag, whose boot-thieving resident continued to protest in a muffled voice. "Never saw it before."

Everyone was still staring. Finch counted forty-eight individual fae of various executive and Showrunner levels, plus a full complement of Unseelie—including Laurel and Hardy. Finch's mentors stood to one side, lips curled against their teeth in barely suppressed annoyance.

An elfin fae tapped Finch's shoulder, and when he turned, blew a palmful of dust into his face. Finch sneezed. Instantly, the durian stink dialed down to a slightly-off mayonnaise scent. The dirt clods on the floor disappeared. He felt as if he'd been scrubbed with gravel.

"Who *are* you?" ɮ— demanded once Finch stopped coughing.

He stood ramrod straight. "Unseelie Finch of the UDIP!"

Laurel coughed into their fist. "One of our *lesser* interns, your EVVVVVPCTTAP-ness. I'll discard him—"

ʒ— held up her hand. "Stand down, Unseelie. I said All-Hands and I meant All-Hands. Even *those* hands." She lifted her chin at Finch, who quickly stripped off his gardening gloves and tossed them to the side. She lifted an oversized cup of tea for a sip, returning it to exactly where it had been before—over the stain Finch had noticed during his reconnaissance. "Now. As I was explaining, SCN is facing a crisis of existential proportions—"

Executives closed in again, crowding against the expansive mahogany map table. Finch was jostled aside by elbows, knees, and flippers alike, but he elbowed back and pressed forward. Within the knot of fantastical beings, he glimpsed ʒ—'s gesture at the table's opposite end. One assistant at ʒ—'s side pressed a button, while a second assistant on her other side whispered at the Will O' the Wisps surrounding the table. The grand TROPE Town map lit up, hummed, and came alive. An intricate, eagle's-eye view of a densely forested countryside dotted with small, cleared areas came into sharper focus. With a brief tap or pinching movement of ʒ—'s fingers, the map zoomed in to reveal humans, buildings and other specific elements shifting around in real time.

That was the angle Finch had never witnessed. During his visits to the map room, he'd only ever been able to see TROPE Towns from an extremely high vantage point. The ability to examine fine details caught his throat and he—like a few other newer hires—gasped.

During Finch's hours poring through SCN's several-thousand-page rules and regulations Guide in the library, he'd gone down multiple rabbit (and a few fox) holes. He'd learned how a Seelie was assigned a TROPE Town, and what requirements had to be met before Unseelie were invited in to take charge. But the rules and subrules and exceptions and commentary were so detailed and arcane he had to wonder when was the last time any fae had bothered to read this stuff?

Finch might have been the first one in centuries.

After the Guide, Finch then spent hours poring over the table itself. He hadn't had the spellcasting ability to make it possible to zoom around, but he'd had plenty of patience to watch it shift dynamically in time. That was when he'd noticed a pale ochre ring atop the far end of the table. It was at the location where ɮ— was standing. Where she always stood. Where she always rested her mug of tea. And in doing so, she'd made a practice of covering up a not-insignificant square acreage of the T-Town world.

Now, as ɮ— maneuvered around the map, Finch made a soft squealing noise and raised his fists to his mouth in excitement.

The elbowing from the others in the room was getting annoying, though. Finch was squished so tightly that he could muster no effective defense. And he was down a boot. Sweat emerged under his armpits again. At last, he realized he had two choices: stand on someone's shoulders or take refuge.

He ducked under the giant map table.

"As you are aware from the series of reports that were forwarded to you, many of our TTs are down significantly in ROI and eyeball attention has plummeted among all key demos," ɮ— was saying, her chiming tones muffled beneath the thick mahogany. Far from fluent in the dialect of Seelie CorporateSpeak, Finch tuned her out and waited for his moment.

"Psst," said the bag next to Finch's knee.

He ignored it.

"As you will note from the initial eighty-nine pages of introduction in your reports, my plan had been to parse

EECs and JOIs that have led to the precipitous fall in fresh content these last moon cycles, and initiate discussion as to whether reruns are sustainable," the executive continued. "However, if you flip to page one hundred and twelve, you will see my thinking has evolved in this matter. There are three lists of town categories before you: Treading Water, Drowning, and Flatlining. The latter category will be our first focus today, and we will work our way up the chain from there until we happen upon a solution. All SMDs were invited here today—hence the lack of cloud chairs for all—and anyone whose town is resident in the latter two categories will leave here today with an appropriate Unseelie Evaluator to return with them to their Towns for… well, Evaluation."

Finch perked up. He expected Laurel and Hardy were doing the same; there were only a few Unseelie who could be assigned this kind of job, and it was one of the more exciting roles a worker could land. Everyone knew a town getting Evaluated was just a precursor for total and complete future cancellation.

"Hey," said the bag.

Finch kicked it.

"Ow," snapped the bag.

Taking a risk, Finch peeked briefly over the tabletop. A high-level Unseelie banshee knocked on the table and signed, "You mean whether the town goes to the Chopping Block." (It was best for Banshees not to speak in a crowd, being that they could unleash their Death Wail at any moment. Mistakes had been made.)

"Indeed, Cancellation is an option," said ɮ—. "But as this issue is ongoing and global, we will not be hasty. The goal is to understand what has gone wrong, and for that we need trained, experienced Unseelie who will not be charmed by the T-Town experience. I expect evaluations within fourteen sun cycles before any decisions are made."

Finch clapped his hands together in delight.

No, he was neither trained nor experienced.

But that wasn't going to stop him from making this work.

THE INSIDE OF an unbreakable silk trash bag packed with garbage was not a happy place. Malvous, twisted into a position where he could wriggle but not escape, with seemingly sentient drawstrings that battered his face each time he tried to push his way out, was cranky and claustrophobic. As a large brownie, he was accustomed to folding his way between crawlspaces in the SCN walls to reach various brownie-colonized locations. But this was different. The only exit here wasn't letting him out.

And he was *hot*.

The idiot Little Monster who had announced himself as Finch, who'd ruined the east-southwest-north corridor of Floor 1037, then dragged him into a room of executive fae, was being as Unseelie as he could be. When his captor failed to acknowledge the obvious large sack filled with brownie inches from where he'd ducked under the table, Malvous tried to get his attention. When that was rewarded with a kick, Malvous did something unheard of for a brownie.

He hurled the loose boot. It smacked into Finch's head.

"Faun-cocky!" the fae hissed. "What'd you do *that* for?"

"*Let me out of here.*" Malvous pitched his voice low, respectfully fearful of a room of Very Important Executives and Showrunners, but also desperate to cease being folded up while perspiring like a troll in a Zumba class.

"Hold your horses," said Finch.

"I have no horses."

"I'm busy."

"You are not."

"Well, I'm busy listening." Finch cocked his ear, then turned back. "This is an Emergency All-Hands TROPE Town meeting, and I have plans." He beamed. "It's going to be glorious."

Malvous doubted that anyone who showed up as a stinkpot, late to a meeting, wearing one boot and who was now hiding under the world map, had a shot at glory. "My patience wears thin," he said.

The LM thrust a hand into the bag. "Call me Finch. You?"

"Malvous V. Hill." The words had the texture of sandpaper. "Also, Sweaty and Oppressed. When my union hears about this—"

"Do you have any idea how important this meeting is?"

"Can I stop you from telling me?"

Finch grinned. He launched into the wonders of SCN programming, and how exciting it was that entire T-Towns were going under.

Unimpressed, Malvous interrupted, "This is not news to me. I work here, too. And I occasionally watch select shows in a puddle at home."

But he was downplaying things. Some SCN series Malvous had been watching his whole life, and he'd paid such close attention that the humans in them were like personal friends. He hoped that Foxtacular might share a fraction of that passion and frequently dreamed of their fingers touching over a bucket of roasted caterpillars shared during a screening of the *La Grande Ménagère* series.

"You get it!" said Finch. "Human lives are *so* interesting! They deal with overdrafts, fender benders, love triangles, cosmetic surgery, leaky pipes—"

"Fondue sets!" Malvous interrupted. "Mortgages!"

"Shopping for linoleum tiles!" Finch nodded. "And you've heard of Bridezillas, right?"

"Naturally." Everyone knew about the monsters clad in white with painted claws, chewing up their loyal friends and barking impossible demands. Malvous rather liked sharing his streaming obsession with someone else for once, even if that someone had led him to be confined in a trash-filled bag. "I dream of meeting one of those humans someday," he continued. "They live such incredible lives."

Finch's face changed. Became hungry. No—happy but also filled with a bit of meanness. "Shows what you know."

Malvous blinked.

"Turns out, they're all *scripted*." Finch pointed at the underside of the table. "That's why they're in such a tizzy, since for some reason nobody's writing new stories anymore."

The brownie's stomach sank. "I don't believe you."

"'Course you do." Finch grinned.

Malvous remembered: *Unseelie*. What a jerk. The brownie's eyes burned, and he felt like crying—until he realized there was an onion peel attached to his cheek. "Some fae might have kept that to themselves."

Finch's smile grew even wider. "Thank you! I'm still in the training process to be properly Unseelie."

Malvous sulked.

"Unseelie like me are going to be *so in charge* now that all these T-Towns are crashing and burning. Some are going to need canceling. That's where Unseelie come in—we swoop in and clean stuff up. We're Un-everything."

Finch's eye twitched. He glanced off to the side, and the delight disappeared from his face.

Malvous squinted—then *understood*. It was like having a bandage ripped from his vision and being blinded by the sun. The fae was almost *too* pleased with himself. A little too eager to underscore his Unseelieness. Malvous had encountered a few Unseelie in his time, and real ones didn't make a fuss about it. They just went around fiddling with things that worked perfectly well. Then Malvous remembered a few other things about this particular Little Monster. The dirt on his boots, for one thing. The fact that he smelled like lavender—or had, before the trash situation. Something wasn't adding up here.

"All I can see is that you're unconscionable," said Malvous. "Everything else is up for debate. Are you even really Unseelie?"

Finch's face hardened. He tugged on the drawstrings and the small, cinched opening in front of Malvous' face sealed off. The brownie protested, but his arguments were muffled by silk. "Help! Help!" he cried. "Save a worthy brownie, won't you?"

A greenish eye with gold streaks appeared in the tiny remaining opening. "Keep your trap closed. Soon as I take care of business, I'll take you back to your stupid cleaning cart. We never have to talk again. Deal?"

Malvous was bewildered. He didn't care whether Finch treated him right, but clearly he'd hit on a sore spot. "What kind of business?"

The eye widened, then disappeared.

Chapter 6

Rules of the Game

The strange interruption of the Emergency All-Hands meeting by that klutzy Unseelie intern and his bag full of odiferous brownie aside, ɮ— felt things had gone precisely as planned. She'd paired off every trained Unseelie on staff with appropriate Showrunner/Mayor/Directors in the suffering T-Towns with the assignment to evaluate and report back. Unseelie were now murmuring with delight all around the map room, rubbing their hands in anticipation of investigating failing TROPE Towns, and every SMD was anxiously knotting *their* hands, worried about whether their T-Towns would survive the investigations.

All in all, a success. The Seelie executive lifted her tea—this would be cup forty-nine of the day—and finished off the liquid inside before setting it back down again in its usual place.

Hmph, she thought. *Seems to be leaving a mark on the map. Perhaps I should use a coaster. Or get a more attentive brownie cleaner.*

"If there is no other business..." ɮ— scanned the room. Slumbering Seelie executives awoke as everyone else started toward the doors.

"Actually— ow!" Something thumped against the underside of the table. The map shook. The interloper from before—what had his name been? Fluff? Frowzy?—emerged from the back of the room and pushed aside a few Seelie. He rubbed his head. "Ahem. Point of Order."

ꝁ— froze. An intern? In training? Was calling a Point of Order? She shot a look at Laurel and Hardy, whose jaws hung open. "Yes, intern Fluff?"

The Unseelie leaped on the table. On the *map*. He only wore one boot. Dangling Will O' the Wisps lighting the room scattered. "I'm Finch, m'EVVVVVPCTTAP"—though he didn't say 'Finch,' he said his True Name, the sort of thing a fae would only do in a room of fellow fae, where no one would be altered by the side-effects of such a pronouncement—"of the Far Valley. And I am Unseelie!"

The strangely formal re-introduction angered ꝁ—, but she wasn't sure why. "As you noted earlier." ꝁ— hadn't touched her copy of the Guide in centuries but recalled vaguely that a "Point of Order" required immediate attention. Even if it was a half-baked Unseelie intern making the call. "Proceed."

Finch, who now had the attention of every awake individual in the room, gazed around. He met as many eyes as he could before turning back to ꝁ—. "I hereby claim an unrepresented TROPE Town for my own!"

The only sound in the room was a silky rustling from beneath the table and a soft squeal.

The EVVVVVPCTTAP tapped a fingernail on her empty mug of tea. "There are no unrepresented TROPE Towns." Her tone was enough to raise blisters on human skin, had any humans been around. "We have been meticulous. And you are getting yuck on the T-Town map!"

"I'm afraid you are mistaken!" Finch's brio was almost too big for the room.

"We are never mistaken." Blistering became frozen in a heartbeat. "We are Seelie."

This was followed by faint applause.

Finch traversed the length of the table and towered over her. "What about the TROPE Town that lives directly under your *tea*?"

Fae buzzing filled the room. Right Side Assistant asked ꜩ— if she would like a refill. Without waiting for an answer, the assistant lifted the cup and began to decant more liquid, revealing a circular ringed stain that perfectly circumscribed a small patch of trees, buildings, houses, and piers set on the ocean, at the very edge of the Veil's T-Town universe.

"Seaview Haven," Right Side Assistant noted, oblivious to the tension in the room. "'The Coziest Mystery Land of Them All.'"

ꜩ— shot a glare at Right Side Assistant, who transformed into a puff of smoke and vanished along with the tea kettle. Then the executive turned to the tea circle. "Naturally, I knew that was there." But it was a lame excuse even to her own ears. Seaview Haven *was* on the Flatlining list. But she had already gone through every Showrunner and every Unseelie. How could they have missed it?

"Of course, m'EVVVVVPCTTAP," said Finch. "So, can you point out the Showrunner/Mayor/Director to me?"

Flustered, ꜩ— sputtered. She wanted to order him to get down from her T-Town map. She wanted to vanish him in a puff of smoke. But while that was easily done with assistants, those with valid Points of Order had special dispensation. "Seaview Haven Mayor—" she paused as Left Side Assistant whispered the Showrunner's True Name in her ear. She repeated it for him to make himself known.

Silence.

She called more loudly.

Continued silence. ꝁ— felt a distant chill. This was covered in the Guide, she was certain. A need to wait until it came back to her seemed prudent, but over the last three hours ꝁ— had lost her patience. She called a third time for Seaview Haven's SMD to step forward.

The Showrunners looked around.

The executives looked up and down.

Laurel and Hardy looked quite pale.

But nothing happened.

"Three times!" Finch gestured at the ceiling, holding three fingers aloft. "Three times and a town is deemed *abandoned*. Page 732 of the SCN Guide, Paragraph 18, sub-paragraph 8, lines 10 through 15. *During meetings called in times of emergency of an All-Hands or All-Feet nature, Showrunner/Mayor/Directors who fail to appear when summoned thrice are considered in dereliction, and their towns shall be handed over to the one who makes this fact a Point of Order.*" He took a deep breath. "Them's the rules! I stake my claim!"

ꝁ—'s Left Side Assistant produced a Guide from the air, flipped to the correct page, and whispered that he was accurate. But, as Left Side noted, the rule had never been invoked before.

Laurel whispered something to Hardy that ꝁ— could not make out.

"I see," said the EVVVVVPCTTAP after a long pause.

The room erupted. Seelie who had been asleep jolted awake and were informed by those who'd been alert the whole time. Showrunners waved their hands at one another. Laurel and Hardy attempted to get the attention of the EVVVVVPCTTAP, but she had broken into a floral-scented sweat. She grabbed Finch's shirt and yanked him down to his knees.

He met her gaze. He smelled like vinegar and worms. But he did not waver—though his eye twitched, just a bit.

"*Silence*!" ɮ— roared without averting her gaze. The room hushed. "You are an *intern*. You have not even completed the UDIP."

"And he's awfully fond of rules!" cried Laurel.

"Which is not very Unseelie of him!" shouted Hardy.

They had a point, but not a useful one. "Which T-Towns have you worked in before?"

Finch pretended to enumerate them on his fingers, then paused. "None."

"I must speak!" Laurel burst out. "This half-formed Unseelie is unprepared! Is unwarranted! Is untrained!"

"I do put on a Smashing good Smash, though." Finch replied, not breaking his stare with ɮ—. "Quite well attended, really. I believe even my mentors were present."

"We were not!" Laurel was practically apoplectic. "We never would!"

"Enough." ɮ— waved them aside. Laurel tried clawing at Finch but finally collapsed against the table and was helped back to the wall by Hardy.

"Well?" asked Finch. "When do I start? I'd love to see what an Unseelie Showrunner/Mayor/Director can do to shake things up."

"You will *never* be a Showrunner. Or a Mayor. Or a Director," said ɮ—, whose head was roaring.

"I beg to differ," said Finch, sitting down on the map. Several in the room gasped; he was, in essence, mooning several TROPE Towns.

Seelie loved rules. Seelie hated having rules used against them. But there was an in between, liminal space here. Some might call it a loophole. Because unlike in other failing TROPE towns, Seaview Haven hadn't produced bad programming, just *no* programming. This was an essential difference. "Then I have no choice. To follow the rules in our own Guide, I must cede oversight of the town." She held up a hand to prevent further argument.

Finch made a triumphant jabbing motion with his elbow.

"However."

Finch's hand fell limp.

"Ceding the town to an untried intern whose very mentors are questioning his abilities is *not* what this Emergency All-Hands meeting was about. We are here to *evaluate* the T-Towns to see if they are in trouble. It seems clear that Seaview Haven is, indeed, not just Failing but possibly has already failed as a T-Town." She took a deep breath. There would be questions later, and she had to walk a fine line here. "And so, before any ceding of anything can be done, Seaview Haven requires a Very Special Evaluation. As all of my qualified Unseelie are now assigned elsewhere and seeing as how you know the Guide a little too well, Finch of the Far Valley, I will assign *you* to do the Seaview Haven Very Special Evaluation."

Finch opened his mouth, raised his finger as if to argue, then lowered it. "And if I determine that it's a great big old Failure? That we gotta rip it apart and demolish it and sell the parts for scrap?"

"Then we will revisit that at a later date."

"That's when I'm going to stake my claim again."

"No Unseelie has run a TROPE Town," said ƀ—. "And no true Unseelie should *want* to run one. So, what is it, Finch of the Far Valley? Will you be satisfied with the role of Evaluator for the time being—a role we *only* assign to Unseelie? Or do you aspire to run a town as a Seelie? Because if it is the latter, I believe our next step is to set a Seelie Court hearing in which you *could* be charged with Fakery."

Finch blanched.

"Which is it, Finch?"

"I accept," he said, only slightly deflated.

"Which part?"

"I'll evaluate Seaview Haven. Should be pretty easy, what with a missing SMD."

"Approved." ɮ— didn't like bargaining with an intern, but his point was valid. She *had* overlooked Seaview Haven until this moment.

Finch made to leap in the air.

"With *conditions*."

Finch remained half-bent over. "Conditions?"

"There is no way on this side of the Veil that you can be permitted to go alone. You might break something that isn't already broken. So I will send you with an assistant—and I choose that poor brownie you have hiding in that trash bag under this table. Brownies are sensible and cautious, and clearly you are not. So, you will work together, and I will listen to both of your evaluations."

Finch groaned. But that was drowned out by an even louder moan from beneath the mahogany table. "Mistress EVVVVVPCTTAP," came the sad voice of the brownie. "My hallway is not *clean*."

ɮ— eased around the table, with various Seelie parting in front of her. She lifted the bag into the air, upending it until it coughed out more trash, some dragon slime, and one bent over brownie covered in all sorts of effluvia. "Here," she said, offering a silken handkerchief.

He held it as though it were made of precious jewels.

"Malvous V. Hill, I have witnessed your industriousness on Floor 1037 for many moon cycles," said ɮ—. "But this is a matter that supersedes your devotion to that location. Will you heed the call to duty? Will you ensure that this… *intern*"—she gestured at Finch, who stood on the table with his fists on his hips—"does what he has been tasked to do, and nothing more?"

Malvous stared at the floor and nodded.

"Then all is agreed," said ɮ—.

"But you see—" Finch tried to interrupt.

The executive shushed him with a look. Then she spelled out the rest of her conditions.

Chapter 7

A Town Called ~~Seaview Haven~~ Nowheresville

SIGGY SOMMERSDAY SPUN her wheels, going nowhere fast. Head bent, her thin, fourteen-year-old legs churned on the pedals as she poured everything she had into propelling her bicycle forward down the empty two-lane road—and moved not an inch forward. Sweat coursed down her dust-covered face, leaving glistening, clean, brown streams. Her thick raven hair was a wild profusion of twists coming undone.

Behind her lay Nowheresville. Ahead of her lay the impossible.

There's a way to science this out, she insisted to herself. *There's always a way to science things out.*

"Sig! Quit it!" A boy a few months older than Siggy rolled up behind her on his modified wheelchair and halted. While she continued pedaling, he tapped on her shoulder. A section of sun-bleached, shaggy hair tumbled into his face and obscured curious, hazel eyes. He finger-combed it aside without a thought and Siggy nearly fell off the bike.

"Lock your wheels, Martin," Siggy said through gritted teeth. "I'ma getting through this today."

She pedaled harder, keeping her head down. *I am an unstoppable object, and this is an irresistible force*, she thought. *If this is a shield, I'm a giant, sharp arrow. On a bicycle. Who needs a drink.*

That first part had come from one of Miz Winnie's lessons: unstoppable objects meeting irresistible forces. Siggy often had Miz Winnie's voice running through her thoughts. Sometimes the voice repeated lessons from a school nobody bothered with anymore; sometimes she got snippets of bedtime stories about Siggy's mom, Eve. Who used to be the town sheriff. Who Siggy hadn't seen in over a year.

Who nobody had seen in over a year.

Martin inched forward, bumping up against the invisible barrier that crossed the street and disappeared into the forest that ringed Seaview Haven, a barrier that had encircled the whole stupid town. Maybe even the whole stupid ocean, too. Exactly when it sprung up wasn't known, but as of a year ago people could still drive in and out of Seaview Haven whenever they wanted. And that was a year *after* other things started going kerflooey.

"Experiment's over." Martin tapped his watch. "You're gonna wear through the rubber on those tires and you know we can't replace 'em. Besides, have you *looked* past your own shoes recently?"

He pointed, mashing his forefinger against the unseen barrier.

Siggy stopped pedaling, bringing her feet to the ground, panting. Then her breath stuck in her throat as she gazed down the road. "Wait. What *is* that?"

The two teenagers stared through the barrier to the other side. Just down the road the pavement had split, leaving a several-yards-wide gulf between the two halves. Bits of asphalt had crumbled like cake into the crevasse, which extended horizontally across the pavement and into the thick woods beyond. Pine trees slid together, their pointed tops supporting one another. Beyond the crumbling, the road continued extending south.

"That wasn't there when we got here today," said Martin. "And we're out here every day, practically."

"Sure as shootin' wasn't," said Siggy. "But you know what's weird?"

"Other than the *road* breaking up out of nowhere?"

"Yeah. How come we didn't *hear* it happen?"

Martin didn't have a snappy answer for that one.

Now, as they watched, a small piece of asphalt on the Seaview Haven side—that was, the *Nowheresville* side—broke off soundlessly and fell into the gap. Siggy pulled out her notebook and wrote down what they'd seen, like any good scientist. Other pages in the notebook detailed the efforts they'd been making since it got warm enough to use the bikes again: they'd tramped (or in Martin's case, rolled on his modded chair) through the woods, looking for a break in the barrier; sent kites into the sky to see if they would soar *over* the barrier (they'd hit something unseen and crumpled, then sank to the ground); and recently abandoned digging by the beach to try and reach under the barrier. An eight-foot hole they'd created flooded with seawater and Siggy realized no matter how much they scienced, they'd never empty the ocean.

Still, Siggy was one of those people who believed there was a good, solid answer to everything. Thanks to science, everything was—with time and diligence—knowable. And why shouldn't she think this way? She'd grown up in Seaview Haven, and science always worked like the books and her teachers said. Birds laid eggs. If you threw something in the air, it came back down again. If you got sick, Doc Mallard had a disgusting, warm, brown liquid called Medicine to drink, and you got better. Because science.

If there was an opposite to science, Siggy didn't want to know what it was. But this barrier, that chasm, and all of the other awful things that had been going on in Seaview Haven since she'd turned twelve felt like that opposite.

"I didn't think things could get worse," she said in a small voice.

"Things can always get worse!" Martin rolled back, popped up on his motorized chair and started doing wheelies. He'd never been able to use his legs properly, but his arms were full of muscles. "Who knew? The great Sigfrieda Sommersday might not *know something*! Total failure!"

"Shut up, Martin Timmlerwicz," said Siggy. "Or I'll pound you, chair or no chair."

"Have to catch me first!" he shouted and raced off down the road. He paused, then called back, "C'mon, Sig! We can fail again tomorrow!"

"Ugh! Not. A. Failure." No scientific experiment was a failure. You just learned new info. Siggy noted the date, time, and weather conditions in her notebook, which was nearly full. She'd have to scare up more scrap to add to the book. Paper, like most things in Nowheresville, was in short supply. Yeah, Ms Wordsworth at the card store had been mashing up used pages into pulp and pressing them into fresh paper, but that was *expensive*. Siggy would have to trade, like, half of Miz Winnie's vegetable patch to get a single sheet.

Giving one last hard push on the pedals out of sheer cussedness, Siggy released them to spin on their own, holding her legs out wide. The bike held its physics-defying position—wheels whirring, dust kicking up, but not moving forward. The barrier across the road had rendered it a stationary bike.

That was Not Science.

It was darned close to magic.

"*Football*," she muttered.

Now, magic and football didn't have a lot to do with one another. But for some reason, if Siggy ever thought the word *magic*, it came out of her mouth as *football*. She could think the word *fairy*, like in *fairy* tales, but if she spoke the word, it came out as *referee*. There were a bunch of other words that came out a lot different than they looked when you wrote them down. That was another bit of Not Science she'd never understood about Seaview Haven.

One bizarre mystery at a time. Seaview Haven—now best understood as *Nowheresville* among the few remaining residents—had always been full of mysteries, and it was hard to tackle more than one at a time. Miz Winnie was usually the one to solve them all—but so far on this one, nada. Still, Siggy had faith in her.

Martin was rolling his way back. He had a hard time being left alone for too long, which Siggy alternately found annoying and endearing. She wiped her sweaty face with the bottom of her shirt and tightened the band holding her thick twists into a ponytail.

"You done being fruitless today?" Martin asked.

"We got results," she said, tucking the journal away. "Miz Winnie's gonna want to know. 'Specially about that gap in the road."

"Bet she already knows. There's, like, nothing she doesn't know."

Siggy didn't disagree. In the before times—as in, before Seaview Haven was Nowheresville—if there was a mystery Sheriff Eve Sommersday couldn't figure out, Miz Winnie Arrowmaker was the one to call for answers. Or to at least locate a good clue. Miz Winnie and Eve worked together to solve all kinds of crimes around town, after which Miz Winnie—with some help from her friend Mayor Neal—wrote books about those mysteries. Then Mayor Neal transformed into Director Neal, and he made movies about the books. Everyone in town had a role in those movies—or, rather, *nearly* everybody.

"Maybe we should try the woods again," said Martin, staring into the greenery. "We'll get a machete—"

"Where you gonna get a machete?" Siggy shook her head.

"Or a chainsaw! My dads have one in their barn. Or a can of gas and matches—"

"Martin, you want to *burn down* the whole town?"

"It's better than doing nothing." For the first time, she noticed his eyes were wet. His lip trembled. "Somebody has to do something."

Siggy's chest tightened, and she swallowed hard. Crying wouldn't help anything, and if Martin started she might never stop. She thought about giving him a big hug, but kept her arms folded. That was dumb, too. They didn't have that kind of friendship, even if they'd known each other since basically Day One. But now she was thinking about her mom again. And her dad. And how they'd tried to science things out a year ago and also failed.

Now she really did want to start crying. *Not very scientific, dummy,* she thought. "I miss my mom," she said, and let one lone tear drip down her cheek, the way the sweat had just a few moments earlier. "And my dad."

"At least they got out," said Martin.

"But without me!" Siggy shouted.

Martin touched her shoulder again and she calmed a few degrees. Everybody knew the story of how the Sheriff and her husband had vanished, leaving their daughter behind. Siggy's father Hal had lost his job at the village newspaper when he started writing stories about weird things that were happening in Seaview Haven. Stories about the missing Mayor Neal, or the faltering supply delivery to the village grocery. Hal was told he was *riling up folks* by the paper's publisher and was told to quit it.

So he quit the job instead. Then one day, Siggy's parents announced they were driving to the nearby town of La Ciudad Grande to look for work for him, just a normal excursion to explore options.

That was the official story. Unofficially, Eve had told her daughter the drive was about more than just a job hunt. *Something funny's happening in Seaview Haven*, she'd said. *Winnie and I are worried about Mayor Neal and the sporadic deliveries. People are filing reports saying their property is vanishing overnight, but not stuff that usually gets stolen. Like front yard trees. Or backyard fences. Or driveways. Or basements. I need to see if this is happening in other places. I'm going to do some science. But we have to pretend things are normal. I don't want everybody here panicking. Scared people get crazy.*

It was supposed to have been an overnight, maybe a weekend trip. Eve and Hal Sommersday had left Siggy in care of Eve's best friend Winnifred. That wasn't unusual; Miz Winnie had looked after Siggy on and off her whole life. But then the overnight turned into several overnights, and months, and now years.

"So where are they?" Martin asked. "You don't think they fell into another big gap in the road, do you?"

Siggy's eyebrows shot up. "I didn't until you just said that!" She punched his shoulder.

"Ouch," said Martin. "That's disability abuse!"

"You're the least disabled person I know," said Siggy. "And the most annoying."

Martin sulked, pounding on the invisible barrier. His fist bounced off the nothing. "I don't think science is going to help us here, Sig. We've tried everything."

Siggy wouldn't believe it, but she was too tired to argue with him. "C'mon," she said. "We've got the Counting. And we should stop at Miz Winnie's house first."

"She'll have lemonade," said Martin, perking up. "And if we're lucky—"

An enormous crackle sounded in the clear blue sky, like the biggest lightning bolt Siggy had ever heard. A narrow gap rent the air above the forest like someone gouging open an envelope. The space where there was no sky was deep, dark blue and full of swirly things.

Martin grabbed Siggy's hand. His touch was ice. Goosebumps ran up and down Siggy's arms, despite the heat of the day.

Shouts faded in through the opening. One shout in particular sounded like: "*Aaaaaaaggggghhh!*"

And another sounded like: "*Noooooowwwaaahh!*"

Two figures tumbled through the gap, which instantly zipped shut behind them. The falling figures crashed into several pine trees, and Siggy heard branches breaking. Birds took to the air. The shouts cut off abruptly.

Siggy looked at Martin, then at their hands. He flinched away and they both shook their fingers as if suspecting cooties. Siggy's whole body felt hot, but not in a way that had to do with pedaling against an invisible barrier.

"You saw that, right?" Siggy asked.

Martin raised an eyebrow. "I don't think that was science."

Siggy shook her head. "It's only science we don't know yet." Laying her bicycle on the road, she walked toward the forest's edge. The foliage was shivering. Trees rustled. Something powerful was moving through the wall of greenery, as if lost giants were stamping around.

"Sig! Stand back, willya?" Martin called. "They might be monsters! Or aliens!"

She ignored him.

And then, two figures popped out of the trees just down the road. One was dragging the other. The upright one was as long limbed and tall as Martin when he stood up using the pneumatic function of the chair, with a thatch of dark hair that resembled a wig. His face was greenish, with oddly square eyes. He—she—it?—was towing a limp individual who was so pale he was nearly luminescent. The one on the ground had a mop of gray hair with interesting red, glowing bits and a curling blond mustache. They were dressed in ill-fitting suits, with badly knotted ties and uncomfortable-looking dress shoes.

The wigged one released his load and turned. Brushing his hands on his legs, he straightened the badly knotted tie and smiled. "Excellent! A welcoming committee!" He removed his hair, bowed to Siggy, then returned it to his head. "Might you be the Show— er, Director?"

"*Mayor*," the not-quite-unconscious one on the ground groaned. His eyes fluttered open and were a funny shade of green-brown, with gold flecks throughout the iris. He clutched at his foot. "Marsh thorns, that *smarts*."

"N-no." Siggy's mind had gone quieter than she realized it could. Normally her head teemed with questions and thoughts and opinions and ideas, so fast she had a hard time taming them. Understanding scientific constants had been a way to throw up roadblocks of understanding and slow a few of her ideas down. But now as she stood in front of two people who had literally just fallen from the sky and *not* died from the impact, she was utterly without thought or roadblock. "You mean Mayor Neal?"

The bright one—who was without a doubt the most beautiful creature Siggy had ever seen—rolled his eyes. "Pah. Fine. Take us to your leader." He both glowed and glowered. "Or are you simple?"

Siggy snapped to attention; no one had ever called her dumb. "Mayor Neal is kind of not available. He—"

"Nerts!" said the standing one, bowing again. "Pardon my rudeness. I'm Malvous V. Hill, at your service. Down here, we have Finch-whose-True-Name-would— ow!"

Finch had flipped over and nipped Malvous' hand, hissing, "Watch your language!"

Then he rolled back over with a groan.

"Ahem." Malvous flapped his hand. "We're in need of a bit of assistance."

Siggy glanced over her shoulder. Martin hadn't rolled from the invisible barrier or inched closer. She wondered if he'd even heard all this. "What kind of assistance?"

"Isn't it obvious?" Sitting up, Finch gestured at his foot, which had bent at an odd angle. "My ankle is not behaving itself. I can't walk! I can't even fly— er, I can't even walk!"

No one can fly flitted through her mind, but she released it like a bubble into the skies.

"I can carry you." Malvous sighed, resigned. "We should be quite close to Seaview Haven."

"I do not wish to be carried, you millstone!" cried Finch. "I wish to know why this ankle is not instantly healing itself." He sighed dramatically. "I will never understand why you have been sent with me. You're completely useless."

Malvous set his fists on his hips. The cuffs of his white dress shirt rode up his forearms and a button popped off from the chest. "Understand that I'd rather be anywhere but here on your ridiculous *assignment*." He paused. "Also, I am the opposite of useless."

Finch rolled onto an elbow, and his head nearly disappeared into the oversized collar of his own dress shirt. Thanks to him, Siggy was learning a valuable lesson: beauty did not mean someone couldn't be a complete jerk. Or know how to dress themselves. "You, youngling," he said. "You are a girl, correct?"

Siggy folded her arms and frowned.

Finch shrugged. "Well, you are wearing trousers. And you smell like sweat."

"Everybody wears pants. Everybody sweats. I'm Sigfrieda Sommersday. Siggy." Her mind felt foggy, and her movements were slow. She gestured behind her. "That's Martin. And you could be nicer to your friend."

"Friend!" Finch sat up straight. "More like a pain in the—"

"I am a conscript," said Malvous. "I am here to assist. But by no means confuse this nuisance on the ground with a friend of mine. He keeps falling onto things." Clasping his hands in front of his waist, Malvous took a deep breath and released it slowly. "Ms Siggy, do you suppose you can assist us in reaching the town of Seaview Haven? We have business to attend with the Mayor to discuss your TROPE Town."

What was a TROPE Town? Siggy knew the words but had never heard them paired together. "Discuss what?"

"Fixing things!" Finch tilted his head. "Aren't there a few things broken here?" He gestured at the road beyond the barrier. "Like that?"

"Well, yes—" Siggy felt a strange wriggle of hope but didn't trust it. There was something suspicious about these newcomers.

"Well, then!" said Finch. "All is explained. Take us there. I require some form of cart or wheeled conveyance."

Siggy held her bicycle tight. "We don't have—"

"Hold up, hold up." Martin rolled over to Siggy. "Need a ride? I can help. For fifty bucks. We'll help you for fifty bucks. Otherwise, we're outta here."

"Martin!" Siggy flailed at him. "They're *guests*." She leaned closer and whispered. "And they're the first *guests* to show up in town in ages!"

"They're weird," Martin muttered. "Their suits don't fit right. Their shoes look brand new. And that one guy took his *hair* off. They're a mystery. They might even be"—his lips twitched—"*football.*"

It took a moment for that to register with Siggy. Martin definitely didn't mean *football.* He meant *magic.* But they'd never discussed this before. She hadn't realized the word was something other people couldn't pronounce right, either. "*Football* doesn't exist—" she said in a low voice.

Martin continued to whisper. "Well, they're not my guests. I didn't invite them." He turned back to Malvous and Finch, and at full volume said, "Fifty bucks."

"Sir," said Malvous. "I am not in the habit of carrying around herds of deer to parcel out for favors. But I can promise that if you help me with this fallen Unsee— that is, my assistant—"

"You're *my* assistant, dolt!" Finch barked. "I'm your *boss.*"

Malvous ignored him. "We will make it worth your while."

"I have gold," Finch spat through gritted teeth. He turned his perfect, shining face toward Siggy and Martin. "Will gold grease your wheels?"

Martin's eyes were wide, and he was already lowering his chair using the pneumatics and gears he'd added to it. His legs stuck out straight, supported by a series of smaller wheels. "Let's find out. Hop on."

With Malvous' help, Finch crawled backward and up onto Martin's lap. He rested against Martin's chest as though the young man was a chaise lounge. "Now, that's a proper response." Pointing down the road, he ordered, "Allons-y!"

And suddenly, they were off, leaving Siggy in the dust.

Chapter 8

Writer, Blocked

WINNIFRED ARROWMAKER, FORMER teacher, former wife, former author, former—well, former *everything* was how it felt these days—glanced at her watch. The children were late. They would have fewer than fifteen minutes with her before skedaddling to the Counting, and that was never enough time to accomplish anything.

Winnie was an accomplisher. Today she'd risen at dawn, cursing the fact that she had a hard time sleeping past dawn anymore. Her back twinged as she slid out of bed, and she had to sit on the edge of the mattress gathering herself for a few minutes. She did her daily stretches in positions that came with more grunts and groans and unexpected pains than they had when she was in her early fifties—and made scrambled eggs and fried tomatoes for herself and Siggy.

Shortly after that, the remaining children in town—all eight of them—had arrived for two hours of instruction. There were no longer enough young folk in Seaview Haven (or *Nowheresville*, as Siggy had taken to calling it) to hold official school hours, so the youngsters rotated among the remaining teachers' homes. Today, they'd discussed simple machines and physics, and she'd given them a pop quiz.

After what passed for school, Winnie had helped Siggy oil the chains on her bicycle before sending her off with Martin to 'do science,' whatever that meant. They'd left with sandwiches and cookies in their packs, and she hadn't expected to see them again until around Counting time—sundown.

A fairly typical day in these very atypical times.

But at what point did 'atypical' become, well, typical?

Was two years enough?

Eve, you better have a really good excuse when you finally show up, Winnie thought. *I charge $12 per hour for babysitting. You owe me about $105,000 at this point.*

Not that looking after Siggy was a chore. Winnie loved how much Siggy reminded her of Eve, and how part of her was getting to replay her own childhood by enjoying the world through the eyes of her friend's bright, sole offspring. Winnie just hadn't been prepared to be a mom all over again, and certainly not in the midst of the end of the world. Ever since she'd restarted her life on this side of the Veil, Winnie had leaned on her savvier friend to be there as they solved both the mysteries of the village and of middle age. With her gone, Winnie was unmoored.

Somebody's got to figure out what's going on in this place, Eve had said. *Neal's a lost cause. Sorry, but it's true. And the only way we're gonna save Seaview Haven, I reckon, is to get help from one of these other TROPE Towns. Not like SCN's answering our calls.*

Not like we know how to call them, Winnie had said.

That had been their last conversation. Eve had driven off with Hal a year ago, and nothing had changed since—only gotten worse in slow, inevitable motion.

Like watching snails in a marathon, Winnie had once told Eve.

Normally in this non-normal world, Winnie spent the Siggy-free hours of her day diving into a second round of routines—everything from tending to the garden, adding to the compost, taking a brief dip in the ocean, then lunch. Some reading. Napping. Groaning as her knees spoke to her when she slid off the old living room sofa. Then, having tackled nearly everything else in her life first, she would sigh and sit in front of her typewriter to stare at it. Or rather, stare at the paper curled into the platen.

Today, she'd written:

`DAY 704: I HAVE NOTHING TO SAY.`

But she forced herself to remain at the desk for an hour anyway. The page, which had been in the typewriter so long it would probably never uncurl again, was largely filled with a series of all capital letter lines just like that.

`DAY 590: WHAT IS THE POINT.`

`DAY 602: DAMNIT I MISS YOU.`

`DAY 635: THERE ARE NO MORE STORIES WORTH TELLING.`

By nature, Winnie was a storyteller. But writers aren't naturally adventuresome. They are bold in their settings and carefree with their plot twists and sometimes downright sadistic with their characters, but if you uprooted a real writer and planted them into the kind of story they wrote—in Winnie's case, mysteries and thrillers—they'd be positively lost.

Winnie had imagined she was different. Ever since Eve had introduced her to the beyond-the-Veil existence of TROPE Towns and the Seelie Court Network, she'd been Seaview Haven's resident private eye. The woman to call when circumstances took two left turns and the sheriff's office was baffled. Eve was smart and capable, but she knew her job in this T-Town: her office was *always* going to be left baffled. That was how this TROPE Town operated. Winnie was there to meddle. Uncover clues. Speak to shady characters with the bold fearlessness of the post-menopausal. Be utterly underestimated in part because of her age, in part because of her gender. (At least, in the books she wrote, and the movies Neal had made.) Occasionally, she'd even been caught up in a bit of danger, including getting locked in a root cellar overnight by a temporary 'guest star' transplant from the T-Town of Second Chance, a nasty piece of work sent in by SCN to up the ante in the mystery. Guests, visitors, outsiders, and transplants typically signaled trouble in Seaview Haven.

For fifteen years, Winnie had worn many hats in town. She'd been the nosy-but-charming teacher-turned-sleuth who'd helped solve 332 Seaview Haven-based crimes and mysteries. The crimes included robberies, blackmail, stalking, kidnapping, sabotage, election fraud, poisoning, arson, vandalism, and assault. Deaths were almost unheard of. According to SMD Neal Bartleby, who ran the town and directed the movies, their audiences—who were often semi- or fully-immortal—didn't understand the emotional weight of death, so the town avoided murders.

The ongoing *Seaview Haven Presents* stories worked in several ways. Sometimes, Winnie and Neal cooked up movie treatments together. Neal would cast, stage, and shoot the story using a host of embedded (and mobile) cameradryads, drone bees and birds outfitted in tiny cameras all over town. The stars were the village's residents, basically playing versions of themselves (with a bit of prepping and scripts). They all had clearly defined roles: The Pharmacist. The Grocer. The Bicycle Repair Shop Family. The Tea Store Owner. The Librarian. And so on. Afterward, Winnie turned each script into a cozy mystery novel. Sometimes, they did that in reverse—book first, then movie. However it worked, the novels were instant bestsellers among mythics, and the films drew enormous numbers of audiences—'eyeballs,' as Neal called them—to SCN.

(Winnie had never met any of her mythical creature fans, but she was tickled to learn that her catchphrase, "Looks like *somebody's* up to no good," was quoted regularly among viewers.)

But that was over. There had been no movies, no treatments, and no books for going on for two years. It looked as if there might never be any more again, either.

Winnie was left itching to solve something but also blocked. If she left the house for long, would she vanish like so many others? Where would that leave Siggy? The house? Her garden? No one knew how or why people and places were vanishing, but living in Seaview Haven these days felt like walls were closing in. In one way, they literally were—a strange, invisible barrier that extended into the sea had the town blocked off. Some said the barrier was inching inward. Before the barrier had been the strange disappearance of impossible objects that had raised Eve's hackles. But then *people* began disappearing, too; they'd walk into a room and when someone came looking for them, both the person and the room were gone. The town used to have two bookstores; overnight, one, along with its owner, vanished. The books stayed behind, piled in a vacated lot. It was all so random, so unexplained.

Writing should have helped. Winnie had been in the middle of editing her latest book, *The Case of the Vilified Vintner* when Mayor Neal had been taken out of commission. He'd gone into his house with an injury and hadn't been seen since. The house had remained intact, so Winnie imagined he was still in it, but maybe he was one of the disappeared, too. Without an SMD, there were no mysteries. No new movies. No new books. Winnie's words had dried up.

So after a full (if not exactly productive) day, Winnie looked forward to her brief time with Seaview Haven's younger set. Siggy and Martin would regularly stop by later in the day after racing around town, babbling about their adventures. Sometimes they brought along other children, everyone settling in for lemonade, using lemons plucked from Winnie's tree out back, and whatever sweet treat she could whip up with her dwindling supply of sugar. Working with children had always given Winnie life. Life with Neal had also given her life. Both of those things were gone now, and she had no idea why.

What've you got to hang out here for? Eve had asked Winnie fifteen years back, gesturing at her empty nest of a suburban home back on the other side of the Veil. *You rattle around alone like a rock in a tin can. Your kids are grown and in their own worlds. I can show you a new world, but you'll have to keep your mind open.*

You sure showed me, Winnie thought now. *Changed everything. I live in a magic village run by Seelie and solve mysteries and write books and make love to a fae creature. At my age! And now you're missing.*

The distant sound of whoops drifting from the road made Winnie's heart soar. She rose from the swing she'd been lounging in on the porch and fetched the lemonade pitcher from the refrigerator, setting it on a glass-topped wicker table along with a collection of mugs. On a second trip to the kitchen she returned with a bowl of ice cubes.

"Ahoy there, mateys!" Winnie called to an oncoming cloud of dust. She stood at the top of the stairs leading to her wraparound porch like a ship's figurehead, her long, blue smock billowing in the afternoon breeze. Winnie knew who she was and what she looked like: a woman in her late fifties (chronologically fifty-eight, but time was wonky on this side of the Veil), living alone, freckled, and thickset with formerly russet-brown hair gone silver.

Reading glasses perched on her head, holding loose strands in place. Neal had said her smile was enough to turn on hearts, and the wicked twinkle in her eye was sufficient to give him pause about handing over his own. Siggy once said she smelled like pencil erasers and peaches. All of that was true, but very little of it was how she imagined herself.

Winnie stepped down to the lemonade table, trying to make out what was coming through the dust cloud. Siggy, of course. Martin and his incredible chair. But Martin wasn't alone. He was carrying someone while a fourth, thin individual loped behind everyone. She only recognized half of the people approaching her house.

"Reporting for duty!" Siggy arrived first, setting her bicycle against the handrails of the steps.

Someone—something—hopped from Martin's chair as he rolled up, and Winnie nearly fell over.

"Siggy, what in the world—"

But Siggy was already gulping lemonade, handing a mug to Martin. Then the girl handed a mug to the tall newcomer and the angular-faced one who was now leaning on Martin's reconfigured chair, dangling one foot in the air. Everyone drank like they'd just come in from the desert.

"Siggy," she tried again. "Why are there people here I don't recognize?"

Martin lowered the cup from his face, grinning. A wet ring encircled his lips and nose. "This is Finch"—he pointed to the hobbled one—"and this is Mal Fuss."

"Malvous V. Hill," said the tall, thin one with strange green tint to his skin. "That is the finest lemon potion I have sipped in a hundred— well, in many years."

"It's all right," shrugged Finch, who had an unsettling glow around him and whose face made Winnie's heart contract the way it used to with Neal. "I could evaluate more clearly if I had more." He paused and squinted at her, then tossed the mug over one shoulder. Hopping over to the table, he lifted the pitcher and drained the rest away.

"Hey," Winnie protested.

"Hey," Siggy echoed.

Wiping his mouth with the back of his hand, Finch gave Winnie a tiny nod then broke into a smile. "Looks like *somebody's* up to no good!" he cried.

Winnie snapped to attention as several facts arrived at once: These were *newcomers*. In a town that hadn't had any for a year or more. They were *fae*. Neal had a brownie living in his house that resembled the green-faced one, which meant Malvous V. Hill was almost certainly a very helpful individual. The beauty of Finch, and the way his beauty clutched at her heart told Winnie he was almost certainly Seelie. They were badly dressed in poorly-thought-through disguises, as if they'd been trying to pass for humans. Finally, Finch recognized her. Had a *fan* breached the barrier?

"You know me," she said in a flat, careful tone.

"I do indeed!" said Finch, grabbing her hand and pumping it up and down. "Winnifred Arrowmaker! The sleuth of Seaview Haven! I've seen *all* your movies. We must speak of them later."

The brownie made a soft squeal.

Winnie met Finch's gold-flecked gaze and forced herself to remain calm. "I have questions."

"Excellent," said Finch. "But first, there is a disaster—"

"He has a foot issue!" cried Martin.

"More like an ankle issue," corrected Malvous.

"It's rather floppy," said Finch, holding out his leg.

Winnie took note of the limb. "That's a break or a twist."

"Curious," said Finch. "Lasting injuries aren't known to my sort."

"Your *sort*?" Siggy asked.

Winnie glared. The Seelie was on the verge of revealing several things the children were not permitted to know. "He means businessmen." Winnie gestured at their ill-fitting suits. "They're usually so healthy."

"Precisely!" chirped Malvous. "Important businessmen, on a visit to discuss business matters with the head of your town. We heal expeditiously."

"But not here," said Finch, frowning.

"A lot of things don't work the way they should here," noted Winnifred. "That is another thing we can discuss. I imagine there's a good explanation for your injury?"

"There is," said Martin. "But you're not gonna believe it."

"We are wasting time," said Finch. "Your lemon potion's got me going again, and we should be off. Point us toward Mayor Neal Bartleby's home."

Winnie stilled. "That's another thing that's broken. You'll have to wait a little long—" A bell clanged in the distance, and she flinched.

"Counting!" Siggy's eyes widened. "Miz Winnie—"

"Yes, yes." Given a new task, Winnie became a model of efficiency. "Siggy, you and Martin go as per usual. Quietly send Doc Mallard here once he's been Counted. Don't say why, just that he's needed."

Siggy nodded emphatically.

"Excellent." Winnie flapped her hands at the children. "Off with you, then!"

"But—" Martin wondered. "Do they... Count?" He gestured at the newcomers.

No! Winnie wanted to shout. "Not today." She didn't want to set off alarms until she knew what was going on here. One of the first rules of being a good sleuth was to gather clues and not get ahead of yourself. She nodded to the greenish one with a terrible thatch of hair. "Will you help me with your friend—"

But he was two steps ahead of her, lifting Finch as if he weighed nothing. He winked. "*My* sort are much stronger than we look, Madam Arrowmaker."

Siggy hopped on her bicycle. "Don't go anywhere!" she cried. "I have questions, too!" And she sped away.

Martin remained. "My gold," he ordered, holding out a hand to Finch. "You owe me."

Turning from Malvous' arms, Finch plumbed his trouser pockets and withdrew a gold disc, then flipped it in Martin's direction. "There. You've been reimbursed."

Martin pocketed the coin, adjusted his wheels, and raced after Siggy to the Common.

That left Winnie with two very odd strangers. Two mythic strangers, if she'd guessed right, plus an empty pitcher of lemonade and four upended mugs on the ground. "Dia dhuit," said Finch in Irish. "I guess I never thought I could get starstruck. But— wow. Winnie Arrowmaker. I really hate your character."

Winnie blinked.

"She solves everything!" Finch cried. "I'm always siding with the criminals, you see."

Malvous hefted Finch to cut him off, flashing a grin. "I have read each of your books, and I *adore* your sleuthing," he said, bouncing up and down on his toes. "The one where you had the dog solve the crime by pulling aside the sheet of the—"

"Cease!" Finch smacked him in the head. "You're making me queasy."

"Charmed." Winnie looked back and forth between them. "Clear me up on one thing first. Malvous, you are clearly a brownie. Finch, are you from SCN?"

His glow intensified. "I sure am! And I am *thrilled* to not have to disguise what I say because of the younglings. What a ridiculous rule that is."

"Why have they sent a Seelie here?" Winnie tilted her head.

The glow dimmed. "I am *not* Seelie!" he barked. "I am Unseelie!"

"Don't yell at me," said Winnie. "I have no idea what Unseelie are or do. But if it involves yelling, you can take it and go your merry way."

"As was my plan," said Finch. "Like I instructed earlier, point me toward the mayor's home."

"Not now," said Winnie, gathering up the pitcher and mugs. "The Mayor is indisposed. Follow me, and don't dawdle. You'll want bandages and a splint on that ankle as soon as possible."

She marched up the steps to her porch, hands shaky under their burdens. Not from a lack of strength, but a whole body quiver rising up inside. Newcomers. *Fae* newcomers. They could mean disaster. They could mean hope. They definitely meant change. Ideas skittered across her mind like pebbles on a lake surface. *I'm excited*, she thought. *Excitification. Not a word, but it fits.*

And on top of that: *Hey, looks like I did write something today. One new word.*

It was a start.

Chapter 9

The Game's Afoot

Crossing the Veil portal fifteen years earlier had been hard on Winnie's knees, and once in Seaview Haven they continued to act up.

"What I don't get is why they can't just *football* this kind of stuff away over here," she'd told Eve shortly after her sometimes-best-friend brought her across the Veil. "Why does someone have to have creaky, bad knees in a land of *football*?"

She'd made a face after saying that, hating the way word wards set up in Seaview Haven transmuted certain language into sports lingo. This was early on before Neal had lifted the ward on her and Eve. "And what is this about not being able to say certain words?" she'd continued griping. "It's so specifically weird."

"It's a rule from higher up than Mayor Neal can reach," Eve had explained, choosing her language carefully. "He told me once that they're still new at this T-Town thing. Only a hundred years or so. I know, I know—but if you're immortal, I guess time feels different. Anyway, they don't want us mentioning *football* or *referees* or all of that stuff on camera. Something about how their audience prefers to think the movies are our real life."

"I'm gonna take this up with management," Winnie'd said. "I have questions."

"You'll adjust, girl." Eve had smiled and caressed her pregnant belly. "You've crossed over into—"

"Was dragged into, you mean."

"Semantics. You'll love it here. You've got a sweet place in the world of the *referees* and Seaview Haven. We get to live inside a bubble, inside another bubble, and because of the movies they make with us they want to keep this world true to human life. So you're gonna feel pain sometimes."

"But where do I get aspirin? My cholesterol pills? My estrogen?"

The gold on Eve's sheriff badge had glinted in the morning light as they crossed Seaview Haven's common, a lush, well-tended park smack in the center of town. "There's a doctor. But *referees* prefer things to be uncomplicated."

Winnie had panicked. "No prescriptions?"

"Not exactly. Doc Mallard has this *football* potion called 'Medicine' that cures just about any ill you might have. He'll stop by, leave you with a few bottles."

"Jeez, Eve, this is veering into weirdland."

"Welcome to weirdland, then. Mythics don't get hurt, not for long, so they don't understand why we care about doctors, even though they know we need them. What they don't want is a lot of gross details. So, 'Medicine.' It'll help if you put yourself into the way they think."

"But you're going back to the other side when you deliver, right?" Winnie's head had spun for days over so many things she'd discovered after arriving in Seaview Haven, but few things had boggled her more than Eve's advanced pregnancy.

Eve had waved her away. "Nope. Doc Mallard. He's the guy. Potion or procedure for everything, even if they have to do *football* to make it happen. And the big stuff—don't worry about it. Nobody gets real diseases here, not unless they're part of the script."

"One more question."

"Shoot."

"'Doc Mallard'? For real?"

Eve had laughed. "Good thing he's not really a quack."

Looking back, Winnie sometimes questioned why she hadn't demanded to be taken home instantly. Everything about this place was eerily familiar yet totally alien.

But then she always remembered Neal.

"THE GOOD NEWS is that it isn't broken," Doc Mallard announced after examining Finch on Winnie's lumpy blue living room sofa.

Finch had never imagined his bones *could* break. What a ridiculous piece of engineering, bones snapping like twigs. Or snapping when you landed into a bunch of twigs. It was slightly appealing on an Unseelie level, but also foreign; Finch, like other fae, only dealt with pain in fleeting circumstances. "Sounds like there's a 'but' coming."

"Indeed. You've got a bad sprain." Doc Mallard dabbed perspiration from his forehead. He was the sort of mortal Finch found morbidly fascinating—large, florid, and nervous. During Finch's first experience among humans as a changeling, folks like Mallard had been the ones who'd chased him around, trying to *expel the demon baby*. Thus far, Siggy, Martin and Winnie had treated Finch like the proper superior being he was, but the medicine man only brought back bad memories.

Still, all of this was a waste of time. Until Finch could speak with Mayor Bartleby, he couldn't start evaluating the town. If he couldn't evaluate the town, he couldn't recommend it for cancellation. And if he couldn't recommend it for cancellation, he'd never get the assignment to tear it down—which would, of course, prove that he was an Unseelie with star quality. Worthy of being ranked higher even than Laurel and Hardy. Instead, he had to suffer through an examination by this sweaty, nervous human.

Winnie would have been a better choice, but she'd insisted she wasn't trained in caring for injuries. *Particularly Seelie ones*, she'd said.

Unseelie! Finch had barked.

There's that yelling again, Winnie had said.

Pouting, Finch had told her, *I liked you better in the movies.*

You hated me in the movies. You said so.

So he'd agreed to be seen by the village doctor.

Now, on doctor's orders, Winnie placed a pillow under Finch's foot and set a towel-wrapped bag of ice on the ankle. "Excellent," said Doc Mallard, who hadn't yet met Finch's eyes. He kept looking beyond him or at the ground. "Funny, I thought your sort healed on your own. I never treated a—"

"Unseelie," Finch pre-corrected.

The doctor looked perplexed. "Sure. Anyway, I'm not sure why it's not working—"

"Clearly this is another symptom of your falling-apart town," Finch said pleasantly.

"Possibly," the doctor allowed. "Are you here to work on that?"

"I am here to evaluate. Make recommendations, then adjustments."

"Why not just fix it?" Winnie asked.

Finch eyed her. In person, humans were more complicated than they appeared in streaming productions. Winnie was both like, and not like, her character in all the *Seaview Haven* movies Finch had watched. Getting a read on her was slippery. She was not a crone or innocent wanderer, and the child she was raising in her home was not her own. He could smell that much. Finch had decided to treat her like a new, as-yet-undefined cryptid.

"How did the injury happen?" Doc Mallard asked.

"In the most chaotic way possible," Finch said with satisfaction. "I fell from the sky."

Finch's lifelong teleportation glitchiness had led to hundreds of unsubtle entrances over the years, a failing he leaned into as Unseelie. It was that detail, along with his Hideous Deformity, that had convinced him the Unseelie way was the right one many years back. It was a great comfort to know how you fit into the universe, even if the universe needed some convincing of your essential nature. Fae secure in their identities just *fit* better in mythic society, were better able to get some of the more plum assignments from the Seelie Court and were less likely to be scrutinized as Exile-worthy. Seelie and Unseelie alike preferred clear-cut lines. Binaries. And, Finch suspected, they weren't the only species that did so. That belief helped him feel secure in his decisions to be *un*wavering, *un*flinching—Unseelie.

"*We* fell from the sky," Malvous huffed. He was sitting quietly in a corner, leafing through a book he'd found on Winnie's shelves. "Landed in a forest on the edge of town."

"You landed in the forest," Finch corrected.

"True. *You* landed on *me*. Then the younglings found us and here we are. It's not a great story." Malvous tapped on the pages of *Seaview Haven Mysteries No. 83: The Case of the Pulchritudinous Pomeranian*. "But *this* is a great story! It has the dog who—"

Finch waved him silent. "What can you do for me, Doc? Will this take more than a sun cycle to resolve?"

The doctor stood, knees clicking. "In typical cases, much more than a day. First, you've got to use RICE."

"Rice, I see." The Unseelie adjusted himself on the sofa. It was a strange piece of furniture, imbued with the quality of becoming more comfortable the longer he reclined in it, and he was starting to feel a tad sleepy. Not that Finch *needed* to sleep, but indulging in unconsciousness every few days refreshed his brain and body. "How many grains should I consume?"

Winnie's mouth quirked up. "That's an acronym: Rest, Ice, Compression and Elevation." She turned to the doctor. "I did raise two kids, back in the real world."

"Then get on with it." Finch waved at the humans. "RICE me. I have places to be."

"And the sooner he gets to those places the sooner I go home." Despite being entranced by the book, Malvous sounded very put-upon. His tone irritated Finch. What could be more exciting than tramping around the T-Town map with a potential dismantler on an SCN-sanctioned mission?

Winnie pressed her lips together. She was about to throw up another roadblock, Finch could sense it. At least in a T-Town like this, he hadn't had to go through the rigamarole of convincing the humans that he was *real*. The Guide had indicated that in most T-Towns, humans were aware of the purpose of their home, though in select instances those humans might choose selective, temporary amnesia about the fact that they lived in an invented, full-time movie set. So far, the mature humans Finch had met were fully clued in, though the younglings were just as clearly still under the ward of ignorance.

"Stay off the foot for at least twenty-four hours," said Doc Mallard, packing up his bag. "Use a cane or a crutch for two weeks after that."

Finch groaned. "Delays, delays."

"I've got something you can use," Winnie said. "Sooner you two vacate my house the better."

"Agreed entirely." Finch stared at the doctor, who had extended his hand, palm facing toward him, like an arrested slap. "Yes?"

The doctor shrugged and put the hand away. "I was gonna say, 'Pleasure to make your acquaintance,' but I'm rescinding the offer." He headed to the door and nodded at Winnie. "And don't worry about me. I'll keep schtum about them being here."

She nodded. "Let's avoid a panic until we hear from Neal."

After he was gone, Winnie turned to her guests, fists on her hips. "Guess I'm stuck with you for a day, at least."

Malvous, who'd draped himself over an easy chair, glanced up from his reading. "If we have to be sticky, there are worse places than this. It's clean and quiet here and we get lemon drinks and books."

"Don't get too comfortable," said Winnie. "I don't plan on hosting a brownie and an Unseelie forever."

Finch stared at her.

"There are no wards on me," said Winnie. "The Mayor and I spoke a lot. He trusted—*trusts*—me. But an *Unseelie* investigator? What is that? You look like an elf."

Finch made a disgusted noise. "No need to be insulting. I'm the same as Mayor Bartleby, if we have to discuss species."

"You're *nothing* like Mayor Bartleby."

"We definitely don't think the same." Finch rarely conversed with humans at all, except to yell at the streaming shows sometimes, and had never had a conversation like this before. He gestured at his bandaged foot on the pillow. "Unseelie are opposite to Seelie. We're cruel and capricious, hideous creatures, often deformed and ready for destruction. We push Seelie out of the way."

"But it's Seelie who sent you here."

Finch grumbled. "We let them do the boring work of creating stuff and maintaining it. Then we swoop in for the fun bits as needed."

"In my experience, you're both capricious, and sometimes cruel. But whatever you say, you're clearly not hideous."

Finch rolled his eyes and waved at his left foot, now hidden beneath a blanket. "Go ahead. I dare you. Examine my deformity. It's the smallest toe on the far left. But brace yourself."

Winnie swallowed and pinched the blanket to the side. Finch waggled his bare toes. "What am I supposed to be seeing?"

"There!" Finch indicated the spot. It was a point of pride, clear and undisputed proof that he would never be Seelie. "Or do you require your reading glasses?"

"She's probably blinded by the hideousness," Malvous noted, not glancing up from his book.

Winnie stared at the far left, smallest toe. "Finch, that's a freckle. If that."

Finch flicked the blanket back into place. "Truly an ugly thing in this world, I agree. It is my burden and my delight to bear as Unseelie. Normally I wouldn't subject a human to it, but you are brave, and you'd asked."

She stood, pressing her hands against her back. "Great googly moogly. First, a deformity does not make a person *hideous*. Or cruel. Or capricious. It might make things challenging. It might make you see the world differently. Some people might think it makes you more interesting. But it doesn't make you *Un*."

"Shows what you know," said Finch. "Humans are used to daily hideousness in a way we fae are not."

"Meaning?"

"The perfection of Seeliekind is total. No blemishes. No dimples, no scars, no moles, no asymmetrical features, no—"

"Personality," muttered Malvous.

"Seelie are breathtaking creatures, perfect and untroubled and simpering and boring," said Finch.

"Humans are far more like my type. You are all full of imperfections and fragilities. If I had as many spots on my entire person as you do on your face, Winnifred, I would—"

Something in Winnie's face cut him off.

"Well, I would think of you as one of us," Finch finished.

"I *like* my imperfections," said Winnie. "They're what make you human. Or, I guess, Unseelie. But in this case, Finch, I think you're deluding yourself—"

Finch held up his hand, cutting her off. "I will not be insulted in your own home."

The older woman put a hand over her mouth, as if trying to stifle something. "All right," she said after a moment. "You're hideous. But that doesn't explain what an Unseelie investigator does. Spit it out."

Finch wriggled his toes under the blanket. "Seelie constructors like your Mayor Bartleby—they are creators. The doers. Unseelie like me, we're the un-doers." A pause. "In most cases."

Winnie's eyes were bright and intent. "Then what are you doing in town? Are you here to 'evaluate,' as you said earlier, or help us fix things? Or is something bigger afoot?"

Finch took her hand. It was warm and plump and hideously freckled. "Yes! And… yes!"

Chapter 10

A Matter of Perspective

WINNIE LOWERED THE burner on dinner and carried a fresh glass of lemonade (with a bit of a kick) through the living room. She passed one fantastical creature sacked out on her couch and nodded briefly at a second who had draped his long legs across the easy chair Neal used to settle in after dinner. Both had abandoned their ill-fitting 'disguise' suits and now wore cast-off trousers and T-shirts from Winnie's to-be-donated pile.

Leaving them to their quiet, Winnie slipped onto the porch's rocking swing and gazed out over her front lawn. This view, this house, this life had been hers for nearly fifteen years. Her home was perched at the curve of Halibut Lane, on the northwest side of town, the ocean only yards from her back garden. The nearest home—another Arts-and-Crafts-style bungalow like her own, painted in earth tones instead of blues and mauves like hers—was the Sommersdays'. Had been the Sommersdays'. Maybe still was. A quarter mile away sat the next nearest inhabited house, the Terwilligers', where Halibut intersected with Turbot Trail. This end of the village was quiet, and people left Winnie alone.

She loved this soft, peaceful afternoon time. Everyone was out at the Counting, something Eve had instigated after anecdotal reports of strange goings-on in town became undeniable. Without Neal around, something about the town had gone on pause. Then property disappeared. Then people. A few people ran scared but never came back. Then the barrier had sprung up, and voluntary departure became impossible, even though *people* sometimes just vanished. The Counting had become something everyone, well, counted on. A daily chance for everyone remaining—or their appointed proxies—to gather on the common and acknowledge they were still here. That they could be seen. Since those early, nervous days the Counting had expanded. Now, when the weather was fine villagers lingered, had picnics, supervised the remaining children as they scampered around, and set up tables to trade goods or services.

Winnie opted out of Countings. She'd seen Havenites giving her odd looks, whispering behind their hands.

She knows Bartleby.

Why won't she tell us what's going on?

I've always been suspish of someone who likes mysteries that much.

Somethin' ain't right with her.

Can't trust writers. They make stuff up.

No one said those things to Winnie, but she could feel the words behind the silent stares. Her neighbors might not be spiraling into literal Shirley Jackson territory, but there was an undeniable vibe of Salem, Massachusetts, circa 1692. Winnie sensed she was a few weeks away from being accused of being a witch and perhaps had a season before someone took action. By then, though, there might be no one left to turn fear into outrage.

Last person in Seaview Haven, turn out the lights, she thought, realizing that person might be her.

The hardest part was trying to pretend this was all normal to the remaining children. Nearly every adult in Seaview Haven knew the secret behind the village—

that they were a fishbowl, a terrarium, a contained, created, elaborate movie set—but none of the kids did. They weren't allowed to know until they were *of age*, as Neal had explained. *SCN rules*, he'd said. *Not perfect but the alternative is not allowing children at all in a TROPE Town. Apparently, some of you mortals feel if the children are in on the whole plan that there will be Trauma, or Lasting Effects on Their Development.*

This was an area that both mortals and Seelie seemed to agree on. Human children didn't ask to come to a TROPE Town, nor were they invited. They came as part of a package (and given selective amnesia spells about their past), or they were born into the town in the natural course of things, like Siggy. Children were wild cards who might one day rejoin the real world on the other side of the Veil—and once there, they'd be magically restricted from even talking about their Veil-side experiences. In time, as with all mortals who crossed back over and stayed, the actual memories would fade until they were a generic blur.

Keeping them out of movies was a natural extension of keeping them in the dark. Children under eighteen were omitted from T-Town projects except as background, or incidentally. Fae considered groups of more than four children to be a 'herd,' a collective noun offered by centaurs, as Neal explained. If children absolutely *had* to appear in a movie, they could only show up in groups of four or fewer.

Hence the well-known Showrunner phrase: "Children may be in scenes, but not herds."

But children weren't stupid, they were just young. They believed in Santa Claus and the Tooth Fairy (not a real fairy, as Winnie learned) up to a point, then started getting nosy. Asked questions. Wanted to see other parts of the world. SCN's Guide said they were to be kept in the dark until they turned eighteen summers or finished their schooling. Wards were in place to prevent slipups, and parents who thought they could circumvent the fae learned the hard way that Seelie did not play around. Once youngsters learned the truth during a conversation with Mayor Neal, they were given options: return to the other side of the Veil and fend for themselves or stay in an appropriate TROPE Town and be subject to its rules, wards, regulations, and spells.

All of this was a balancing act, run by mythical creatures who had some godlike powers, but little godlike wisdom. Mistakes were made. Errors in judgment occurred. People got caught in the crossfire. In trying to create their own little worlds in TROPE Towns, Seelie at SCN had spent the last century learning just how danged difficult it could be to raise humans.

You're all such work! Neal had once said. *But we need you. Someone has to believe in us, and if audiences want to watch human antics, that's what we'll give them. Without eyeballs on our shows, we'd start to fade into nothingness. But there are a lot of fiddly bits we never anticipated.*

Children were a *fiddly bit*.

And for some reason, in the last two years the entire existence of Seaview Haven had also become a fiddly bit. Movies weren't being made. The Town had no purpose except to be the bowl in which all the people were living. And so it was crumbling, literally and figuratively. Winnie could see that much. What she didn't understand was *why*, *how*, or how the hell she was going to fix it.

This was one mystery Winnie hadn't been able to solve.

I am basically useless, she thought. She knew she was alone. Even her friends who hadn't vanished kept their distance. It was best to let Siggy be her town representative. It was Siggy who picked up supplies when they were available; most folks grew their own crops now and relied on the fishermen's catch to keep their bellies full, using the Counting or the grocery market to trade. It was Siggy who spoke for Winnie at the Counting. It was Siggy who gave Winnie purpose, and focus.

Siggy was saving her. If Winnie couldn't have Eve, the woman she'd been friends with on and off since middle school, and if she couldn't have Neal, there was always Siggy. Winnie had birthed and raised two children of her own, both of whom lived on the other side of the Veil and thought she'd relocated to a weird off-the-grid hippie commune. But Eve's daughter had been the child of her heart since the moment she'd first met Sigfrieda.

"WHAT IS UP with that name?" she'd asked Eve once mother and child returned to their Seaview Haven home after the birth. Winnie pulled back a small piece of yellow blanket engulfing the baby, who'd been born with a gorgeous puff of hair that cradled her head like a pillow. She was more richly dark than either of her parents, almost like volcanic glass. "Last I checked, there's not a lot of German in your family. Or is that Swedish?"

Eve had shrugged, never taking her eyes from the baby. "It means 'victory.' 'Peace.' It's a classic name." She paused. "And a damn fine Frank Ocean song, if you spell it a little different."

"I think that's 'Seigfried.'"

"Like I say."

Winnie started calling her Siggy, and Siggy she became. She quickly learned how to delight the baby, then the toddler, then the little girl. The child particularly loved making hand shadows with 'Miz Winnie,' who would come into her room and turn a lamp on its side, casting vibrant shadows on the blue painted wall. Birds. Dogs. Horses. Swans. One-eyed monsters that nuzzled up to you. The pair invented stories for their creations and spent hours finding ways to bend the light to their whims. Sometimes, Winnie sensed Eve and Neal standing in the doorway, watching.

One day, Winnie had fallen ill. Not very sick—no one got truly sick in Seaview Haven; real 'illnesses' were expressed in the movie plots. She'd had a cold and lay on a bed on the porch listening to the day and waiting for sleep to come. Siggy, then about seven, slipped onto the porch unnoticed and raised her small hands into the afternoon sun. The girl's thumbs touched, and her fingers were spread wide, fluttering.

"Ooh," said Winnie, waking. "What are you up to, you sneaky thing?"

"I made a bird," said Siggy. She held her arms up high, and the shadow created a flying eagle, or hawk. Her fingers flapped in and out as she swooped and swerved, eventually bringing the creature to rest against Winnie's blanketed leg. "See?"

Charmed, Winnie nodded and sniffled. "I do."

"And do you *see*?"

At first, she didn't. But the girl nodded toward the open space where her thumbs joined. The dip of her forefingers to her raised, connected thumbs made a 'W.' Winnie's eyes burned with joy, her throat closing. "Oh! Oh! Now I do. Siggy—that's lovely."

"It's a 'W' for Miz Winnie!" Siggy crowed. "A Winnie bird. 'Cause you're gonna feel better soon and fly up and away from here and be your old self again."

"I feel better already."

"Just one thing," Siggy added. "If you fly, you gotta take me with you."

Winnie wrapped the girl in her arms. "To the moon and back, Siggster."

* * *

Being stranded in this strangely collapsing little Seelie village with Siggy had kept Winnie sane. Without the girl to look after, she'd have been totally lost, totally panicked, and probably talking to herself by now.

Winnie stared into the distance as the sun lowered in the sky, lemonade glass empty. She sighed and turned to pick up the book she'd left inside—and jumped. An ice cube leapt from her glass and landed in her lap.

Malvous stood on the porch, hands clasped behind his back.

"Holy cats, Mal, don't sneak up on a body like that," she growled, dropping the cube back in the glass.

"My sincere apologies," said the brownie. "You seemed troubled."

"That's one word for it."

"How may I be of assistance?" He brightened. "Brownies are quite good at—"

"Helping. So I hear." She stared at his rounded, greenish face and thought of Neal's helper Felicitous Worrywart, who was more of a rosy shade, and wondered for the first time—might he be able to render *actual* assistance? Maybe he could help convince Felicitous to at least let her into Neal's house. Winnie had tried to gain access dozens of times over the last two years but had always left empty-handed. Malvous might have more luck. "Maybe later. Do you need anything?"

He shook his head and held up another of her books, No. 12 in the collection: *Seaview Haven Mysteries: The Case of the Reprobate Roofer*. "I find a great pleasure in reading, but I did have questions." His gaze slid to the rocker.

"'Course. Jump on up."

They swung back and forth gently, Malvous' skinny legs dangling, the toe of Winnie's flip-flop touching the ground. "Ms Winnie?"

"Winnie, please. Go ahead. You're not interrupting anything but my thoughts."

"Then I will wait until you pause your cogitations."

"You'll be waitin' a long time."

"Well." He paused for several beats. "What exactly is *wrong* with Seaview Haven?"

She laughed. "Easier to ask what's *not* wrong."

"Explain, please?"

Winnie took a long breath. This wasn't something she'd discussed with anyone in a long time. A whole town, living the same nightmare. She didn't know where to start, and knew there were things she wasn't privy to. Sure, she knew how the town worked. About Neal. About how he got hurt. But she was locked out now, same as everyone else in Seaview Haven.

Eve was the one she'd prefer to be talking to. Winnie missed her even more than Neal, sometimes. Evelyn Sommersday and Winnifred Arrowmaker had known each other since they'd connected in eighth grade. Winnie had been sitting in homeroom class, quietly reading *The Count of Monte Cristo*—the adult version, not some truncated thing for children, and yes, she was fully aware that this sort of behavior was why most of her fellow students had treated her as if she had a communicable disease—when a girl she'd never talked to before appeared at the side of her desk and pointed.

So how many people are in the Monte Crisco, anyway? the new girl had asked.

When Winnie read books, she fell into them. She was deep into the plight of Edmond Dantes, chewing on a cuticle as she worried about who was making those noises on the other side of his cell wall. She pulled herself out of the Château d'If prison and into the real world, mentally telling Edmond to hold on a second. She'd blinked at the girl on her right.

Eve Sommersday.

A new face in the world to Winnie, and one of the few Black faces in her class. Eve's hair had been bound up in two soft, thick braids that arced out over the sides of her head and wore a fixed, unsmiling look on her face. Winnie couldn't tell if she was being asked a question or accused of something.

Huh?

Winnie was not a master of conversation then, or now.

I asked how many folks are in Monte Crisco, Eve had said, sliding into the empty seat in front of Winnie. *If they're counting, they ought to know by now.*

Winnie blinked. That unsmile on Eve's mouth quirked up a bit. Then her own mouth was turning up. Out of nowhere this stranger was interested in her book, and her thoughts on the book, *and* she was making a smart person's joke *and* a pun all at the same time. Winnie needed to be fast and witty with her response.

Cristo, was all that came out.

Eve made a casual backhanded wave. *Shoot, I know that. I just finished reading this Stephen King book and it's also about a prison and he mentions Monty Crisco in it, so I thought I'd come over. But if you're busy—*

No! Winnie grabbed her wrist, realized what she was doing, and released Eve, apologizing. People near them in class were staring. *I meant—I never read Stephen King before. He's scary.* But then she heard what Eve had really said, and Monty Crisco tickled her mind, then deep in her chest. She started laughing. *Monty! Crisco!*

A moment later, Eve was laughing too, her braids waving like extra arms. That's all it was, an ordinary meet-Crisco.

Eve had been Winnie's go-to, baseline person in Seaview Haven. Eve was the reason she was here, and she was the reason Eve had been here. When sheriff's duties hadn't required her attention, Eve was always up for a jaunt to the beach or a round of picking peaches in Winnie's backyard, for building a birdhouse or gazebo, or just spending a quiet afternoon on the porch reading, eating jelly sandwiches, and drinking spiked lemonade before napping. Winnie longed for Eve's laughter to ring again through the house, but knew Siggy had it far worse. Her parents had driven away and not come back. The girl was made of steel during the day, but Winnie had heard her sobbing in bed at night.

Winnie didn't tell Malvous any of that. Instead, she casually enumerated the changes she could see in front of her. "The grass is long now. There are weeds. My gutter needs cleaning. There's a pothole down the road a ways. The tree next door used to shift location when the cameradryads were filming, but they're either hibernating or they have left, because it's been stuck there half on my neighbors' driveway, half in the yard, for the last eighteen months."

Malvous nodded, then stopped. "Those are bad things why?"

"Because they never used to happen here. They're just small things that explain the big, scary things. When things were normal—the Mayor used to tell me—the whole town was held together with spells and wards. Things to fend off entropy. You know entropy?" Malvous looked confused. "I'll show you a book later. Those spells made things consistent. Clothes didn't wear out. You didn't get gravel piling up on the side of the road. The boats had no barnacles. 'Least, not unless a family wanted it or it was part of one of the stories we were filming. I didn't get weeds in my garden, or mosquitoes to eat me, or my pipes to clog. All of those things are happening now. The Mayor isn't renewing the spells, and the whole town is getting worn at the edges."

She didn't add: *And I feel like I'm in the extended coda of a grand opera that has now finished its final aria.*

"We did see a rift in the road at the edge of town," Malvous noted. "Entropy."

"Entropy."

"But the other things seem small," Malvous suggested. "Not enough to warrant an, er, investigator from SCN."

Winnie nodded. "The biggest problem is this: the Mayor doesn't come out of his house anymore. Nobody answers when you knock. There are no more movies being made. Without him—without those stories—we're like an engine without fuel." She told him about the disappearing infrastructure, and the people. "I don't know where they go. All we know is they don't come back. It's like the town developed a sickness. Anyhow, that's why we count everyone in town, to know who's still here."

"And this doesn't happen to all TROPE Towns?"

"I'm not an expert in all TROPE Towns. I haven't heard of it happening before, and Neal never hinted that it was something that could happen." She sighed. "At least, when we were still talking."

Malvous nodded. "I myself have only recently learned that TROPE Towns were… well, constructed and scripted," he said. "I had thought the movies were showing us human reality."

"They are—they did—and they also didn't," said Winnie. "It's complicated. Reality is a soft concept around here, and I could do with a lot less 'real' right now."

They rocked a while longer.

"Malvous, what do *you* know about what's happening? About Finch?"

"Not much about the first," he said. "This is my first foray outside of SCN."

"Out of the entire building?"

He shrugged. "Brownies enjoy the insides of things. We live in pockets behind the walls. We have gardens at SCN HQ on levels 498 and 732. I linger there from time to time. This kind of outside is much, much bigger." He watched a ladybug scamper over his fingernail and onto the swing's armrest, then settled his hands in his lap. "But I will tell you everything I know, Ms Winnie. You are a great writer, and writers need to know everything so they can write about it."

Winnie's neck flushed. Neal spoke like that sometimes. Earnest lines like that had kept her in Seaview Haven all these years.

"So what are you two really doing here, then?"

Malvous hesitated. "The details of our purpose in town are best left to Mr Finch. I have been ordered to accompany him here, I believe, to temper his… natural instincts. You see—" and he launched into a strange tale of Finch interrupting Malvous' cleaning of Level 1037 at SCN HQ, then getting dragged into an executive meeting in a trash bag, then Finch using the SCN Guide to manipulate the Seelie in charge into allowing him to investigate a town that had been forgotten because it had been hidden beneath the executive's teacup.

"The entirety of Seaview Haven was a *coaster*?"

Malvous cleared his throat. "Maybe?"

She wasn't sure whether to laugh or throttle someone. Neal would have been ideal, but then a wave of missing him came over her again. The brownie was confirming some of her worst fears—namely, that Neal had flown the coop. That he wasn't just hiding out in his house for unknown reasons.

"So Finch is our new Showrunner? Mayor? Director?"

"Not at all." Malvous bit his lip. "He is still an intern."

That sounded both insulting and shocking, but Winnie

couldn't make the connection. Was Finch chaotic good or chaotic evil? "I'm still not getting it."

The screen door behind them scraped open. "Ugh, mortals. So dense." Finch hobbled outside, leaning on an old wooden umbrella Winnie had dug up from the basement, and sat in a wicker chair. His glow was at a lower wattage now, but a glint hopped around in his eyes. The red streaks in his hair danced with mischief. "Here I thought you, Winnifred Arrowmaker, had great insight into unknown, mysterious things, like myself." He patted his hair. "I am not here to run your town. Quite the opposite. I am here to report everything I see that is broken in your town. I will send in a report about the shameful, negligent behavior of your mayor."

Winnie leaped to her feet, ears roaring. "Neal is a wonderful person—er, Seelie. He is marvelous and warm and kind and generous and—"

"He's absent without leave," said Finch. "He doesn't even have the sense to report in at an Emergency All-Hands SCN meeting! Which is why *my* services are necessary."

"He got hurt," said Winnie, but she refused to share the details. It was too embarrassing. "He fell off the roof."

"*Before* the town was in trouble?" Malvous asked.

"Of course. It was... an accident," said Winnie. "Everything was fine before then. But then"—she closed her eyes, remembering their worst fight ever—"he wouldn't come out of the house. And *after* that is when things started getting bad."

Finch laughed. "Are you suggesting that Neal Bartleby's oopsie sent the town into this downward spiral?"

Winnie folded her arms.

"Cheeze, Winnifred, the more I get to know you the less esteem I have for your skills," said Finch. "Seelie—and Unseelie—do not suffer *true* injuries. If all this occurred before the town started disintegrating, Mayor Bartleby would have been back on the job instantly." He gestured at his bandaged ankle. "The fact that my own wounding is not instantly repairing is a symptom of a town that has been neglected by a careless Showrunner/Mayor/Director." He waved a hand. "Either he is malingering or missing. It makes no matter to me. It all goes into my SCN report, after which they will undoubtedly call for Seaview Haven's cancellation. Then I can get to the real fun."

"Which is?" Winnie was either having the worst ever hot flash, or all the rage she'd been suppressing for two years was about to unleash itself.

"Dismantling!" Finch's voice was filled with glee. "That's what Unseelie do! I told you this earlier. I am here to be in charge of undoing Seaview Haven! Of taking it apart brick by brick! Of, probably, sending every one of you back to the human world!"

Winnie wanted to smack the delighted grin off the Unseelie's face.

So she did.

Finch tumbled backward in the wicker chair, his umbrella cane clattering on the porch's floorboards as he crashed to the ground. He raised his hands as Winnie dumped melting ice cubes and vodka-laced lemonade on his head. "This is my *home*," she shouted. "How dare you come in here and—"

"You struck me!" Finch whined. "Mortals do not strike fae and live!"

Winnie grabbed the fallen umbrella cane and lifted it over her head. "Oh, yeah? Try me. I'm ready for round two."

"Miz Winnie!"

The hot flash dialed back a few notches, along with Winnie's fury, at the sound of Siggy's alarmed voice in the front yard. The girl had let her bike fall into the patchy lawn and now stood halfway up the stairs to the porch. Down in the front yard, Martin gaped at them. Winnie had no idea how much of all of that they'd heard—or seen.

"Miz Winnie, let me have the cane," said Siggy, and Winnie slowly released her grip. "Good. Got it."

Winnie loomed over Finch. Malvous crouched down next to him. "It's all provisional!" Finch mewled. "All provisional! Nothing is happening imminently!"

"Which means *what*?"

Finch sputtered.

Malvous stared up at Winnie, eyes wide in—was that admiration? "It just means he's here to look around. Assess. Investigate. Meet with your mayor. Decisions are pending!" said the brownie.

Siggy was trembling. "I thought you were here to fix things," she said.

"Well," said Finch from the floor of Winnie's porch. "Everyone has a different definition of 'fixing,' apparently."

Chapter 11

Super Soakers

RAIN THAT FALLS on a coastal town is more unpleasant than any other sort of precipitation, and in Seaview Haven it could be positively malicious. Chilly winds gusted with gusto off the harbor, blowing microscopic granules of salt seasoned with remnants of Kraken breath, and during storms, the entire town could smell like brimstone and flatulence.

Malvous stood in the downpour, soaked through to his underthings. Puddles gathered in his boots. He had to close his eyes each time a squall of wind blasted his face, all while clutching the umbrella Winnie had thrown his and Finch's way when she'd kicked them out of the house a few hours earlier.

Moments after that, clouds had clapped together, lightning shot from the sky, and the deluge began.

"Perhaps Mayor Bartleby left the weather settings on Monsoon," Malvous suggested, worrying at a cuticle. He'd started picking at his hands out of nerves, a behavior he'd begun as a crumb of a brownie but had largely eliminated with regular manicures. Yet after less than a day of 'investigating' with Finch, he was back at it. Sighing, he thought of Foxtacular and how much he'd prefer right now to be holding his fellow brownie's warm hand instead of a patched umbrella with a bent rib.

Because of his duty to be helpful, the umbrella was only sheltering Finch's head, not his own.

Finch was grumbling. The chunky spikes of his hair had curled over in the damp, and he sat on a tree stump while glaring at Winnie's house. Her home glowed with warmth, lights burning in several windows. A few minutes ago, Siggy had waved from a window in the front room but now the upstairs lights were illuminated, suggesting she was heading to bed. Winnie studiously ignored the soaked fae in the yard when she passed the window. Every time Malvous glanced at his undesired associate, Finch looked more constipated, folded tightly against his knees. His nose had turned nearly as red as his hair's highlights.

"This is all your fault." Malvous' words were garbled from the water blowing into his mouth. "We could be inside eating stew and reading books and curled up under blankets right now if not for you."

It wasn't polite for a brownie to address an Unseelie like this, but Malvous was out of patience with Finch, who had turned the brownie's life to pure caca.

"She's lucky I didn't give her warts," grumbled Finch. "Or send her to Second Chance."

Malvous shuddered; the TROPE Town for human offenders created content too raw for him to watch. "I question whether you could relocate a Main Character from a T-Town, Finch."

The Unseelie continued grumbling.

"What about doing something about this weather, instead?" The brownie's voice spiraled. "Isn't there a spell of Moisture Protection? Or Tarp Creation? At least one of us is starting to wrinkle." He held out his free hand, revealing puckered finger pads, and splashed in his boots. "What are you actually good at?"

Finch slid a golden gaze his way. "I'm good at getting you fired, Bro. If I want."

"I think not. I have a union. Besides, you're stuck here with me. If you could do anything, you'd've figured out a way that involves us not standing here all night, getting wet. Or in your case, mildly damp."

"Shut it, Bro. I'm thinking."

But Malvous wouldn't. "This whole town was built by Seelie constructor magic. You could *require* them to let us in. Or, here's a better idea. How about we stop staring at Winnie's house like you're going to unleash unholy vengeance and find an empty one to spend the night in? People have been disappearing. There'll be dozens of places to crash. But no. *You'd* prefer to sit on your hairy faerie derriere, looking like someone took away your toys—"

"*Enough.*" Finch leapt to his feet (or, rather, his good foot) so fast his head smacked into the top of the umbrella and tangled his hair in the ribs. There was a flurry of Unseelie and brownie fingers plucking at the patched cloth, attempting to untangle him. This led to the umbrella coming loose and being caught by a brimstone-stinking blast of air that flew it high into the branches of a tree. Drenched brownie and hopping Unseelie stared at it glumly, then turned to one another and started flapping their hands again, this time connecting against each other's face and head in frustration and fury.

But Malvous had the most to be furious about. He recalled an old tactic: if one curled one's fingers together to make a fist, one could—

The next thing he knew, Finch lay flat on the muddy ground. Malvous leaped on top of him and pinned his hands back. "Why does everyone keep *striking* me?" Finch cried, struggling against the brownie's grip.

(Brownies are much stronger than most people expect.)

"Because you deserve so many good smacks!" Malvous

shouted. "I had plans! I have a life! I have a hallway to keep tidy, or I won't have a job! Instead, the only thing that matters is you getting your own little town that no one wants you to destroy—and I don't know *why* you want to even do that!"

"Because I am Unseelie!" Finch garbled, swallowing rainwater. "I will be respected!"

"If you really believed that you wouldn't have to shout it all the cobweb-cornered time!" Malvous glared. "Hold it. That actually makes sense. Do you maybe *question* your Unseelieness?"

"Never!" Finch struggled again, uselessly. He spat out a mouth of water at Malvous, but gravity made it fall back in his face. He spluttered, then went slack. "I'm just not always very good at Unseelieness. I need more practice."

"Especially in portaling."

Finch closed his eyes. "That's none of your business, brownie. Now let me up."

Malvous kept his grip tight a minute longer. "You know, you could try helping. This town might just need a little nudge. But you'd rather pout outside a Main Character's house because she dared thwart you."

"I'm not *pouting*!" Finch said. "I've been trying to get that house to listen to me for an hour! It only rains harder when I try to get it to stop! And I did make a protective screen for us—but it was only as big as your nose! Which, to be fair, is pretty huge but not big enough for us to stand under!"

That explained the small piece of linen Finch had produced some time ago. It had unfurled in his hands but had only been the size of a handkerchief. They'd used it to repair a tear in the now-escaped umbrella, and no other cloth had appeared.

"Then you're as broken as this town." Malvous sat up and released Finch's hands.

The Unseelie shoved him, and the brownie rolled into the mud. "It's not me! It's Seaview Haven. The wards are weak, the magic isn't responding, and something or *somefae* is gumming up the system! It's not supposed to work like this!"

Finch folded his arms again and hunched into himself. Malvous was quite certain that the Unseelie wasn't crying, though it was impossible to tell with all the rain. But his crunched expression was the closest thing to misery Malvous had ever seen on a fae of any stripe, much less an aspiring dismantler. He was almost... human in his abjectness.

Malvous shivered at the prospect.

"Come away from the window, Siggy," said Winnie, gesturing. "You'll only encourage them, and it's time for bed."

Siggy held up a hand to the dark, soaked figures in the near distance, then lowered it when neither moved. It wasn't right that Finch had lied to them about fixing things, but it wasn't right to force them to stand in the storm, either. Rain wasn't typically this awful in Seaview Haven; bad weather tended to only show up to underscore some big event in town, usually when Director Neal was making a movie. But this was practically an ice storm—and an ice storm in July was *weird*.

"But they're just standing there!" Siggy turned away, sliding under her sheets.

Winnie settled in the chair next to her bed, resting her cup of tea on a side table.

Aside from the creatures standing outside getting wet, it had been a lovely evening. Martin had headed home the minute the rain began to fall instead of staying for dinner, missing out on Winnie's hearty vegetable stew with rosemary bread. There'd even been an icebox cake for dessert. Afterward, Siggy had done a bit of homework but had found it hard to concentrate. Her mind kept returning to the pair outside.

"They can go home at any time," Winnie said now as Siggy nestled against her pillows. "Use their little fingers and whisk themselves away. I'm not helping somebody who wants to tear down our home."

"Whisk their fingers." It wasn't quite a question, but Siggy didn't know anyone who could make themselves vanish like that. "Like *football*?"

"Like magic," said Winnie. She met Siggy's gaze, and a long, drawn-out pause made the room feel electric. "That is the word you're trying to say, isn't it?"

"Yes! But you can say it! Why can't I?"

Winnie sighed. She stared out the window, then down at Siggy. "There are things about Seaview Haven that you are not meant to know until you're older. I've always questioned how much sense that rule made. But our visitors"—she gestured at the window—"have thrown a monkey wrench in the works."

Siggy plucked at the blanket. "Maybe they will fix things," she said. "Finch said everything was 'provisional.'"

"Don't hold your breath." Winnie sipped her tea. "Don't you see? He *wants* to get in here and tear it all down. His 'report' is just going to boost that plan. He's positively gleeful at the idea of making us all homeless."

Miz Winnie was right about that, Siggy had to admit. But Finch wasn't really her concern right now. He seemed like a guy who could take care of himself. Siggy did worry about the soft-spoken, tall one. Malvous. Such weird names, such weird people. Why had they been dressed in suits and ties and bad mustaches and wigs? All day events had rushed by her and now the thoughts were gathering in her head. Malvous and Finch weren't like regular folks, even if she couldn't tell how. They reminded her of the eccentric Mayor Bartleby, who sometimes acted like he was running a carnival, and who always behaved like his secrets had secrets. But Mayor B had known how to make things happen. Every town meeting, he'd take a list of requests from Havenites and tell them the same thing: *I'll see what I can conjure up.*

Conjuring made Siggy think of *football.*

Sometimes, people got what they asked for. Farmer Ted got a pair of breeding goats, plus a pen and supplies. The grocery got extra lemons in the delivery so the Smarts could make their incredible lemon squares, and Miz Winnie's own lemon tree had been extra bountiful that month. Mostly you only got a little of what you asked for, though; Siggy had wanted a pony and ended up with a plastic toy horse. And Mr Zhao hadn't gotten a 'retractable rainbow,' just a rainbow-colored banner.

Without Mayor B, though, everything had stopped. The town had to make do with what they had, or what they could grow, or what they could harvest from the sea. It had stopped being Seaview Haven and started becoming Nowheresville. Now, Finch and Malvous were here. Actually dropped out of the sky. Something had shifted.

Siggy's questions were coming together. She wasn't a bit tired; her brain was fired up.

Winnie smiled. "Ready for story time tonight? What do you want to hear?"

The girl tapped her chin, trying to decide. This was their nightly ritual; Miz Winnie was a bottomless pool of stories—sometimes mysteries, sometimes ideas for books she wanted to write. The last two years, though, Siggy had mostly wanted stories that included her mama, and if possible, papa. Winnie didn't know much about Siggy's father, but she had so many Epic Adventures of

Evelyn and Winnifred. Hearing those stories was like running her hands over smooth stones or soft fur. The stories calmed her and helped her sleep. They put Mama in the room, almost, and let her dream about them. When that happened, it was like Siggy could be part of their story again.

Before Mama and Papa disappeared, Miz Winnie and Mama would tell their stories together.

Winnie didn't like me at first, Mama might start.

You scared me, a little, Miz Winnie would reply back.

From there, the stories could go anywhere, but they liked telling them in a back and forth way. Mama and Miz Winnie were so much fun to listen to that sometimes even Martin would stick around.

Mama's favorite memory was this: Miz Winnie, when she was in grade nine, brought Elspeth the middle school turtle mascot inside from the lake where she lived. Young Winnie carried her dripping into the classroom, the turtle's legs flailing. *Like she was trying to escape*, Mama recalled. *In the slowest way possible.*

That was a big deal for me, Miz Winnie continued. *The way I thought for a long, long while was you had to follow rules one hundred percent of the time, or horrible things would happen. I've gotten better in my old age.*

You're not old! Siggy insisted. Truthfully, Mama and Miz Winnie were pretty old compared to her, but it was a polite thing to say. Sometimes, Siggy knew, you had to tell a polite untruth.

We are and we like it this way, Mama said.

So what happened to Elspeth? Siggy asked.

Went back to the lake, said Mama. *But Winnie got suspended!*

To my eternal shame, Miz Winnie admitted. *But not unexpected.* She pointed at Mama. *This one skipped classes, turned in homework late, sassed the teachers—and nothing ever happened to her. She charmed everybody.*

I softened 'em up, Mama insisted. *Kept the bar low.*

Yeah, you always did make your own rules.

Miz Winnie's favorite memory was a little different. (It was also Siggy's favorite, but she never admitted it.) She talked about how she would hang out in her living room with Mama, listening to music on her father's stereo system. *We spent hours reading the lyrics*, she said. *Looking for deep meanings.*

You did, Eve contradicted. *I danced. Practically had to drag your butt up to get you to join me.*

Siggy would explode in laughter hearing her mother say *butt*.

The only message that mattered was 'get up and shake it.' Eve wagged a finger. *Let the music happen. Like getting wet in the rain. Or falling in a ball pit.*

At this point, Miz Winnie would always stand up and say, *Like this?* And then she'd kick a foot over there, throw an arm in the air, shake her head, and wiggle her behind. Every time, Mama and Siggy fell on the floor in hysterics. Then they would turn on real music and dance together. Exhausted and breathing hard a while later, they would flop on the sofa, or the bed, or in the front yard, depending on where they were.

That taught me to turn off my brain once in a while, Miz Winnie said while they caught their breath. *You have to let music, or dancing, or life just happen sometimes.*

Siggy had a revelation the first time she'd heard that. *Like the turtle,* she said.

Miz Winnie had been surprised. *Elspeth?*

Siggy nodded. *Yeah! Like, maybe she wasn't trying to get away from you. Maybe she was dancing.*

* * *

When Siggy failed to come up with an answer after a few minutes, Winnie realized something was up. "So you *don't* want to hear about me and your mama tonight?"

Siggy shook her head.

"Your choice. What would you like me to talk about?"

But even as she asked, Winnie knew: the fae. Over the years, Winnie and Eve had shared so much with Siggy: how they'd met, what they argued over, the fact that they were out of touch during college, their eventual reconciliation. But there were big parts of their shared story they knew better than to share—like how they'd come to be in Seaview Haven in the first place. Like the fact that Eve had *dragged* Winnie with her. And, of course, what Seaview Haven was.

Every adult in town knew the rules. But Winnie and Eve, thanks to Neal's dispensation, lived outside those rules. Siggy should have had to wait another four years to get the truth broken to her, when she was more mature and able to take it all in. Neal would tell her, probably with Eve in the room. But neither of them were available anymore. Now that outside fae had blown into town, the fragile wall SCN expected to be maintained was as cracked as the road out of town.

Winnie's stomach was doing flips. The moment was here. She could get up and walk out, feigning ignorance. But that was a lie. "All right," she said carefully. "Let's talk about something else. You look like you're ready to burst."

Siggy sat up in bed, more serious than Winnie had ever seen her. "Really?"

"You can ask me anything, Sigfrieda." Winnie set a hand over hers. The girl's fingers were cold. "I might not always give you the answer you want, but you can ask."

Don't lie to her, Eve had said a long time ago. *If she knows enough to ask, we'll tell her the truth.*

Siggy nodded. “Good. Okay. So. What’s Unseemly?”

“Say that again?”

“An Unseemly investigator. A brownie that’s not a dessert brownie. I heard those words. And why did Finch say he wanted to ‘undo’ Nowhere— I mean, Seaview Haven? It’s a town, not embroidery.”

Yep, this was the moment. Over the years, Winnie had omitted. Elided. Diverted. Misdirected. Never told Siggy an untruth and wouldn’t start now. Still, she wished they had more time. Around them, rain continued to smack into the house.

“I’m not supposed to answer these questions,” she began. “There’s a magic rule called a ward that says if a person is under eighteen, you aren’t to know certain things. Neal—I mean, Mayor Bartleby—has a special speech he gives to high school seniors. He’s the only one who’s supposed to explain things.” She swallowed. “But there’s something I realized before you were born.”

Siggy waited.

“The most important rule is to know when *not* to follow the rules. So buckle up, kid. This’s gonna be a bumpy night.”

The girl nodded. “I’m ready. But after you’re done, we’ll let Finch and Malvous back inside?”

Winnie’s jaw clenched. “When I’m finished, you tell me if we should.”

FINCH MADE A long, ragged noise, huddling into himself.

Malvous scooted over. He was going to have to take charge, odd as that sounded to a brownie. “We can’t sit here all night. I’m going to fall asleep and then the water will run up my nose and I’ll drown. Also, I’m starving. If we go up to Winnie’s house and ask nicely, she might let us in. I think she’s a good human.”

"She is not!" But Finch's voice wavered. "She hit me!"

"That wasn't… ideal. But try to think like a human for once—"

"Never!"

"And imagine how you'd feel if some yo-yo with spiky hair showed up and declared it was time to kick her out of her house and, by the way, her town was going to get tossed into the trash. This is her whole world! Can't you at least *act* like this isn't the most fun you've ever had?"

Finch let out a long, heavy breath. His cheeks were pink now, his hair flattened. "Well. Fine. I had thought this would be a lot more fun."

"We need her," said the brownie. "The town is in trouble—even the magic isn't magicking like it's supposed to. So just pretend to be halfway nice, even if you don't believe in it. You have to make a report, and you're going to need her help. Right now, we don't even know where Mayor Bartleby's house is. So, fake it until you make it."

Finch looked thoughtful.

"I think you have a lot in common, actually."

Finch swung back to fury and stamped his (good) foot.

"You are! You're both in the middle of a mystery. It's like one of her books. You both want to solve the mystery of Seaview Haven."

"Maybe you're not as dumb as you look, Bro." Finch was nodding. "But I don't think we want the same solution."

Malvous shrugged. "The point of a mystery is you don't know the solution because you don't have all the clues. And sometimes the solution isn't what you imagined, but what is needed."

Finch chewed on his lip. "I *need* things to turn out a certain way."

"But why?"

"Because it would… because then I could stop being an intern. And Laurel and Hardy would have to act like I'm important. Because they're big stupidheads, and—"

"Do you hear yourself? They're stupidheads and you want their respect anyway?" Malvous waved that away. Maybe all Unseelie were as chaotically inconsistent as Finch. "My point is that you and Ms Winnie could figure things out together."

"I already have a partner that I didn't ask for."

Malvous stood up. He wasn't sure why that stung so badly. He hadn't asked to be paired with Finch, either. But who was he to say 'no' to an EVVVVVPCTTAP? At least he was trying to make the best of their shared circumstance. "Fine," he sighed. "Stay out here and stare at a house. I'm going to talk to Ms Winnie. I'll get inside and you can sit out here and be a damp ineffectual Seelie rat—"

"Unseelie!"

"Here in the cold. No need to threaten me with firing, Finch. I quit."

Malvous sloshed his way toward Winnie's house. Arriving at the porch steps, he upended each boot, pouring out what felt like a gallon of rainwater. Turning, he caught Finch scrambling high into the tree where their umbrella had landed, then leaping from the branch with it popped open. The fae floated to the ground, landing on his good foot. Collapsing the umbrella, he used it as a cane to hobble to the house.

"Halt right there," Finch ordered. "Resignation not accepted. And I'm not quitting, either." He leaned on the brownie's shoulder. "Fine. I can pretend to play nice. What did you say a minute ago, bake it until—"

"Fake it!" Malvous rolled his eyes.

"Wake it?"

"Make it!" How could this Unseelie be so *dense*?

Finch reached over and pinched Malvous' cheek, hard. "I heard you. But you're almost as fun to rile as a human. I can fake it." He paused dramatically. "Until I *unmake* it."

Chapter 12

We Know This Much is Truce

SEELIE WERE NOT overly houseproud, which meant a TROPE Town mayor's residence was nothing special. Underground bunkers, crystal castles, or elaborate treehouses would only underscore the mythic-ness of any given SMD—so, accordingly, Neal Bartleby's home was a modest two-story Cape Cod, painted white with cobalt blue shutters and trim. There were a few surprising elements, though, for those who looked closely enough: a north-facing porch and a south-facing solarium, which received both sunrise and sunset light. No one questioned why. The backyard (which featured a badminton net) was enclosed by a ring of tall yew bushes, which did not permit egress or ingress. They might as well have been made of stone. And then there was the way the house did its best to keep outsiders away.

Winnie and her entourage of four (Finch, Malvous, Siggy, and Martin) strolled and rolled up to the house the morning after the rains ended. Martin had turned up at her house as Martin often did in the mornings for class , but Siggy had encouraged him to stick around once the lesson was over. Finch and Malvous had been allowed to sleep on the porch after they'd pleaded to be let in out of the rain. Winnie had tossed them some towels and went to bed herself, half expecting them to be gone in the morning.

Now they had arrived at Neal's house. Winnie hadn't been here in months. For a time, she'd come out every day, then every other day, then every week and month, but being constantly turned away by the house brownie had become painful. She felt like a stalker. And the house wards were of no help.

Those blueberries in my backyard need harvesting flitted through her mind like a butterfly on its third cup of coffee as they lingered outside the house. *Then there's that light switch I need attending to. And oooh! I just got a great idea for a plot twist, really ought to write that down.* Then: *Does my skirt have a stain?*

That nonsense was the house, protecting itself. All of those thoughts collided in her head, fixing her in place. *Focus,* she thought. *Focus.* But focusing wasn't working. So she grabbed her hair and pulled hard. "Ouch!" That cleared her head briefly, and she remembered what they were here for: to introduce Finch to Neal. To get Neal out of the house. Finch was going to make that miracle happen.

Then again… The fog rolled in again. *I could head back home and take a nap.*

"Miz Winnie?" Siggy tugged on her sleeve. "I think I left the door unlocked."

"Hey, that book on entropy, you were going to show it to me—" Malvous began to turn.

"I know! Let's check out the water tower!" Martin whirled his wheelchair around.

"Sure," said Winnie in a dreamy voice. "Sounds grand."

Finch snapped his fingers in front of her face.

The thoughts vanished.

"Ugh," said the Unseelie, rolling his eyes. "Humans. Brownies. Malvous, you should know better." He gestured like he was pulling back a curtain. "The house is warded. It doesn't want us bothering it. No wonder I couldn't find it when we arrived." He twirled his fingers and leaned to one side so far Winnie thought he would fall. "There. Found a hole." He drew his hands outward. "Just bite your tongues and go through." He gestured at Siggy and Martin. "Not you two."

Martin brightened. "Water tower, Siggster—c'mon!"

Siggy didn't move. She was pinching the thin web of skin between her thumb and forefinger so hard her eyes were welling up.

Winnie stepped through, intent on defeating the ward, then seeing Neal. Nothing else was holding her attention. Malvous trailed behind.

"*Football*," murmured Siggy on the other side of the ward. "It's all *football*."

"Hmm." Finch eyed the girl as Winnie and Malvous drifted to the porch. He turned to the house. "I guess this means some magic still works in this town."

"Maybe it means Neal is still inside!" Winnie clapped her hands together. She'd smartened herself up for this journey in anticipation of their reunion, wearing the purple shirt he so liked along with her flowered skirt. She practically sparkled. Neal was going to regret not coming outside to see her sooner. "He's alive!"

"'Course he's alive." Finch scaled the porch railing, ignoring the steps. "We fae are *very* hard to kill. He's just—well, I don't know what he's just, but he's definitely not dead. Probably not even in a coma."

"I wanna come in!" Siggy called out from the front yard. "I have *questions*, Miz Winnie!"

Winnie didn't doubt that. She'd done what she could to explain the fact of Seaview Haven to Siggy last night and fielded every question possible until the girl had literally dropped off in the middle of a sentence.

Why does anyone live here? she'd asked.

It's a near-perfect world. It's safe. There was more to it, but Winnie wanted to keep all of this complexity simple. *People are kind and they're not scared of each other.*

Except there are all those crimes you and Mama solve.

Most of those are made up for the movies, Siggy.

That had been another layer of the onion to peel for the girl.

But you didn't tell me why anyone leaves the real world and comes here.

And that had been the hardest question of all. *Life is very complicated beyond our borders. It's harder. There's no real magic. I'm here because your mama asked me to come. I was helping her, and she helped me.*

"Sig, c'mon," said Martin. "If you don't want the water tower, maybe we can go do science."

Winnie watched the two young people as Finch approached the house's front door. She knew Siggy's heart wanted to be anywhere but here; usually a day out with Martin was the only way that girl wanted to spend her life. But last night changed things for her. There was a split between them now, one Siggy couldn't even explain to Martin.

"They need me here," Siggy said.

Martin blew his long bangs out of his eyes in disgust. "They definitely don't. Fine. I'll go without you." He pushed the controller on his wheelchair so hard the thing shot down the sidewalk, kicking up a few rocks as he raced away.

Siggy stared at the ground.

"You can go," Winnie encouraged her.

"I can't," said the girl, in a voice that made her sound much older than fourteen. "I'll... wait."

And that was that. Winnie climbed the few steps to Neal's porch, grateful for the shade from the hot morning sun. Neal's bright blue door greeted them invitingly, and her heart ached. She'd come here so many times after his injury—*why* had he needed to grab that stupid Frisbee from the roof?—and been either distracted away or refused entry every time. She missed him fiercely all over again. They'd been such good partners, as writers and lovers, and then it was as if she'd been ghosted. She couldn't bear to imagine he was ill, but it was equally as unbearable to imagine him fully recovered and refusing to see her again.

Behind her, a bird twittered, and Winnie stared into a corner of the porch. A pair of sparrows fluttered around their nest, feeding bobbing, barely feathered heads. She noticed a patch of paint peeling from one of the porch posts. And down by her feet, one of the wooden planks had warped.

Clearly, she and the fae with her weren't the only things that had found holes in Neal's house wards. Things were falling apart here, too—right at the village's most important structure.

"You can go away, too," said Finch, glancing over his shoulder. His expression said, *The grown-ups are going to talk now.*

"Hell I will." Winnie gritted her teeth. In all this time, she'd never been inside Neal's home. Their love and working affairs had been conducted entirely outside of his house, more often at her residence. *Nothing to see inside*, he always said. *My house is a house. Yours is a home.*

Time for that to change.

Time for *anything* to change.

Finch shrugged, using his umbrella cane to gesture. "Malvous, do the honors."

The brownie raised and lowered the door's moon-shaped knocker three times in rapid succession. Everyone stood there, waiting. Birds sang. In the near distance, ocean waters ebbed and flowed. Winnie twisted her hands.

Malvous made to rap the door with his knuckles again just as the door opened. His fist connected with their greeter, who yelped.

"Trouser walnuts!" Felicitous Worrywart, Neal's brownie, rubbed his forehead. He was a wan shade of pink, and his ears stood out surprisingly far from his head. He moved with stiff and jerky shifts like a marionette, and his hair was wild. His clothes were frayed and worn, and a strange smell came from either him or the house itself that reminded Winnie of fried eggs. He frowned at everyone on the porch, but his eyes seemed glazed over. Every inch of his small self screamed *so very tired*.

"I do not respond to knocks on the head," said Felicitous. "I have enough of those already." Then he slammed the door.

"That went well," noted Winnie.

"How dare he!" Finch harrumphed. "I am here on *official SCN business!* Open up or I'll—"

"Knock again?" Siggy called out, still a few yards away on her bicycle, shading her eyes from the sun.

Finch glared at her. "I do have abilities, youngling." He glanced at Winnie. "And I am going to *use* them, whether she is here or not."

Winnie nodded. "Doesn't matter. I told her everything last night."

Finch straightened and gave her an admiring smile. "Well, then! All right! Welcome to the forbidden side of things, Winnifred Arrowmaker!"

Not like I have a lot of choice, Winnie thought.

The Unseelie puffed up his chest, crossed his arms, then lowered his chin. His hair spiked up taller and for the first time Winnie saw him as slightly worrisome—like a surprise spot of mold on your half-eaten sandwich. When Winnie was around, Neal almost never worked magic. He'd preferred to keep that aspect of himself on the down-low and be, if not human, then not magical. Only when he was making movies had he disappeared into the fae side of himself, ordering around cameradryads in trees and bushes, or barking at drone camera bees to swoop in.

At last, Finch seemed ready. Sparks jumped from his fingers, and he flicked them at the door. A jolt of lightning whizzed at the doorknob—and bounced off, nearly rebounding on its sender.

Finch flinched in time.

Freed into the world, the bolt shot past Siggy and smashed into a sapling next to the sidewalk. The tree quivered, shook, dropped its leaves, then disintegrated into a pile of wood chips.

"Your aim needs work," Winnie said.

Siggy's jaw hung open.

Finch stamped his (bad) foot, cried out and grew even more furious. "That's! Not! How! It's! Supposed! To! Work!"

"We get that a lot around here," Winnie told him.

"That was a charm." Finch glowered at the door. "The spell should have killed the wood. And this proves the ward is still *quite* strong here. We'll never get in now."

"Maybe ring the bell," Siggy called out, pointing.

All three on the porch noticed for the first time a large dinner bell hanging from one of the support posts. A sign above it read:

RING FOR SERVICE

Winnie couldn't explain why she'd never noticed it before.

"Useless suggestion," Finch growled. "A bell is insufficient to break a ward—"

But Siggy was already rolling over. Somehow, she'd beaten back the wards and was now grabbing the rope dangling from the bell's clapper. She tugged.

Clang!

The door opened to reveal Felicitous again. "Much better." He pressed his hands together and peered outside. "How may I help—" His eyes widened. "Do I spy a Bro?"

"You do—" And with that, Malvous was enveloped in a full-body hug as Felicitous threw himself at his fellow brownie.

"Oh, it's been so long!" Felicitous sobbed. "I haven't seen the community in *years*!" He released Malvous and dabbed at his eyes with a filthy apron corner. "I'm Felicitous O. Worrywart—"

"Malvous V. Hill, but—"

"Tell me everything!" said Felicitous. "Right here on the porch! Also, how did you get here? The town is sealed, I believe—"

"Ahem!" Finch was livid at being ignored. "Unseelie here! As I shouted a moment ago, I am here on official SCN business, and we are *not* about to start a gossip session!"

Felicitous straightened his tattered vest, then smoothed down his hair as Malvous introduced everyone.

"Ah, Ms Winnifred!" A spark of recognition came to Felicitous' eyes, and Winnie barely fended off another suffocating embrace. "Please accept my apologies for all the instances I declined to permit you entrance."

"You can make up for that now," Winnie noted.

Felicitous was shaking his head. "Alas."

"No alas, no alack!" Finch was nearly as crimson as the highlights in his hair. "Unseelie investigator here! Sent by SCN! To evaluate! I require admission!"

Felicitous stared at him. "Evaluate? You have portaled in from SCN to *evaluate*?"

"Yes! The town! I have a report to write and I demand to begin by speaking with your wayward Mayor!" Finch had begun speaking entirely in exclamation marks. "Show him to me now!"

"Ah." Every ounce of joy drained from Felicitous. "I fear Mayor Bartleby—"

"Is dead?" Finch leaned forward.

"Of course not."

Winnie's heart fired up.

"Stuck in a coma?"

"Eh, no."

Winnie's heart attained liftoff.

"Sleeping?"

"No. He rarely— no."

With each pointed question, Finch took a step forward, tapping the porch's floorboards with his umbrella. Now he was nearly across the threshold of the house. "Trapped under something heavy?"

"Well, sir, yes. In a sense."

"Explain," ordered Finch, then barreled on. "Because that might be the *sole* excuse for this falling-apart, no-good mess of a town. Has he no idea what's going on just outside his front door? This place is—" He waved his hand, hoping for the brownie to complete the sentence. When Felicitous failed to do that, the Unseelie sighed. "Then what is he up to?"

"He's typing."

The engine of Winnie's soul coughed and stalled. She looked at Finch. Finch looked at Malvous. Malvous looked at Winnie. Outside on the ground, Siggy was leaning forward, trying to catch everything.

"I didn't expect you to say that," said Winnie after a pause. "Exactly what is he… typing?"

"Everything." Felicitous' voice was more miserable than last night's rain. "And I can't make him stop."

* * *

CALLING THE INTERIOR of Neal's house a shambles was an insult to shambling things. What had once been an average human-designed dwelling of wood, plaster, nails, insulation, and inexpensive decorative furniture now looked like an elephant, rhino and wildebeest had spent the night discoing up and down the hallways.

From the moment the small party crossed the threshold, all seven of Finch's senses went on alert. Felicitous guided the visitors (minus Siggy, who was required to remain outside, sat on her bike fuming at being called a 'minor') around an obstacle course of disarray and through a stale funk of unwashed clothing mingled with the reek of rotten fruit. Chairs lay scattered in the foyer like a broken battlement wall. Paintings of bucolic farm scenes lay askew minus their painted inhabitants, who'd cleared out for cleaner, greener pastures. The Will O' the Wisps in the light bulbs buzzed sourly; a few had collapsed against the glass casings.

Winnie was able to draw her initial in the dust that coated everything. She held a sleeve to her nose, and Malvous looked stricken and twitchy.

"Oh, this is *wonderful* in here!" Finch crowed. He took a deep breath, then coughed. "Well, perhaps not *wonderful*, but deeply unpleasant. Which I like, being Unseelie and all." He felt shame that his own ramshackle cottage wasn't nearly as dilapidated as this place.

But then he wondered: if he liked this house just as it was, why was it making him queasy? Approximately forty-five percent of the Unseelie neurons in his brain were on fire, while the other fifty-five were deeply perturbed. Slowly, six of Finch's senses adjusted and he tapped into the underlying hum of the place. It vibrated with a discordancy of magic, like milk deliberately soured with lemon. There was a clotted heaviness to the spellwork in here that confused him. Fragments of magic lay scattered everywhere, but the thing that had shattered them was nowhere to be seen. It lurked in the corners with dark, pulsing power—something older and enduring.

Malvous gazed in horror as they trooped past the kitchen, itself awash in unclaimed pans, stains, and leftover jars of mayonnaise alongside opened containers of ambrosia. "What happened here, Felicitous?"

Before the Bro could answer, his waist crackled. A peremptory female voice issued forth: "Brownie. Where are you? Is this thing on? The Chardonnay is nearly empty—"

Felicitous snatched up a bottle of wine from the refrigerator and dashed out of the room.

Everyone watched him flee down the hall.

"I think I've figured it out," said Finch, and paused dramatically. "I sense there are *others* in this house."

Winnie gave him a slow clap.

"It is impressive the way he can state the obvious with such a profound sense of discovery," Malvous muttered.

"Hmph!" hmphed Finch. "I'm not here to evaluate the *Showrunner/Mayor/Director's* house! The Guide said nothing about how to—"

Felicitous skidded back into the kitchen. "Sorry. Heh. Left the radio on. Nothing to hear here."

Finch fixed his fists on his hips. "Brownie, you are not telling us everything."

"He's not really telling us anything," said Winnie.

With a fixed, tight smile, Felicitous waved them to a closed doorway. A strange, whirling sound leaked from the door's edges, ebbing and flowing. During the ebb, they could make out clicking sounds, followed by a metallic shifting and a ding! Then more clacking and whirling. "Master Bartleby is within," said the brownie. A tremble had come into his voice. "This is as far as I proceed, however."

"Mauve nonsense," Finch grumbled, leaning on his umbrella cane. "You're the Bro of the house. You're required to let him know that we are—"

"The last time I spoke to him he… he… *punched* me." Felicitous gestured at his left eye, which was more swollen than the right.

Winnie gasped.

"Not his fault, Ms Winnifred." Felicitous held out his hands.

Every step in this dungeon of a house made Finch uneasy, and angry—and not in a healthy, Unseelie way. His tummy tickled. His brain fluttered. It almost felt like fear. But what did Seelie—Un and otherwise—have to fear? They had created this entire invented universe. Nothing could bother him in Seaview Haven.

"He had every right to strike you," said Finch. "Just look at this place. I can find it homey, but a Seelie would see a proper disgrace. Now you're telling me you're slacking off and don't answer your boss' needs? That's going to require a whole other report to SCN HQ, and you'll be lucky if—"

Felicitous burst into tears again.

"Oh, stop with the greeting and the bleating," said Finch. "You're a grown—"

Malvous set a hand on the Bro's shoulder. "Leave him be! Don't you see he's *terrorized*?"

Slowly, Felicitous gathered himself. Reaching behind a sideboard he pulled out a flat piece of plywood. A handle of masking tape had been affixed in the center. "Now"—*sniff*—"if you're going in"—*sniff*— "you may want this."

Winnie slid the shield over one hand. "One thing at a time. Felicitous, why don't you and Malvous unearth some tea in the kitchen?" Her words were reasonable, but her voice shook. "We'll talk more after Finch and I see what's happening with the Mayor. Yes?"

The brownies nodded in unison.

It didn't happen often, but Finch found himself impressed. The human's stomach should have been as off-kilter as his own, yet he smelled no fear on her. Only determination. She was a rock in the center of a raging stream; she was trying to throw a lasso around whatever creatures must have invaded this house. Finch knew quite well that humans had no ability to work spells—but her firm, determined tone worked like magic on Felicitous.

"I'll take a tea." Finch nodded. "Eight sugars. No milk."

"Are you certain?" Malvous asked. "I believe I should be the one to go in—"

"I don't even know why you're here at all," Finch said. "You *quit* last night."

Malvous stood straight, asserting dignity. "I shall remain until this task is complete. If not for you, then for Ms Winnie." He set a careful hand on Felicitous' back. "And I certainly would not leave a fellow Bro in distress." He turned to the other brownie and guided him toward the kitchen. "Now, show me where we can find what you need..." His voice trailed off as they rounded the corner.

"Stupid brownies," Finch muttered. "Didn't even give us a key to the room."

"Oh, can the attitude." Winnie's voice was sharp and impatient. "Let them be. Here you are, barging in like you think you're Queen of the May—"

Finch held up a hand. "Winnifred, do not use that name. The May Queen is one of SCN's top executives and she should not be invoked in a trivial—"

Winnie barreled on. "You act like you're owed something. Well, get over yourself. I don't know much about brownies, but I do know that if they can't take care of houses or folks in them, they get a little crazy. Neal said having a brownie helper was like having an assistant who knew what you needed before you did. You parading in here, barking orders and making the staff cry fixes nothing and shows me just how small and unimportant you are."

Finch flushed. He opened his mouth, but words failed him.

"Next." Winnie let her anger dial down a notch. "There's no keyhole. This door is not locked." She curled her fingers around the doorknob, took a deep breath, and pushed. The whirling noise gasped from the room's interior. Raising the shield, she nodded at the Unseelie. "Are we clear?"

Finch would have to have words with SCN. For now, Winnifred was useful, so he would make use of her. But a human who didn't fear Seeliekind was a dangerous being. Her feeling free to speak to him like this made the case that this village was on the edge of collapse even more evident. He held his tongue. After all, if she was going in first, she could be *his* shield.

"Are we clear?" Winnie repeated.

"Fine." He gritted his teeth. "Good. What are you waiting for?"

And with that, they pushed their way into Neal Bartleby's office.

Chapter 13

Not His Type

NEAL'S EXCUSES FOR refusing Winnie entry into his house over the years were legion. The water was only running boiling hot. He'd developed an infestation of mice. He'd been using the bed for a hamper. The toilet smelled of onions. All of his lampshades had gone missing. A hobgoblin was studying in the basement. Felicitous was *in a mood.* His list had the vague ring of someone reading from a 'Red Flags to Avoid in a Roommate' article from *Teen Vogue*, minus the hobgoblin. And the excuses were blatantly untrue. For a time, Winnie came up with all sorts of wild theories about what was on the other side of that front door—including that maybe there was nothing but a blank void in there.

She hadn't even considered that he was harboring a small cyclone.

Using their backs, shoulders and behinds, Finch and Winnie pushed harder against the heavy wooden door, finally making it wide enough to squeeze through one at a time. The force on the other side of it was tremendous, as if they were fighting a monster made of air. But with several heaves, they slipped through the narrow opening and cringed as it slammed behind them, snapping Finch's umbrella cane in two.

"Ant flatulence!" Finch swore.

Winnie, setting a hand over her now twinging back, could barely hear him. They were in the center of a storm. Sheets of paper swirled in the air, smacking into her face. Batting them away like insects, she gawped at the room. On the one hand, it was an office: four walls, windows, desk. On the other, it was like no office she'd ever seen. A *tree* sprouted from the floor in a far corner, long branches meandering up to the ceiling, where green diamond-shaped leaves fashioned a foliage canopy. The floor was swallowed by discarded paper, used pages balled up, flattened, or shaped into airplanes and other origami figures. The mess rose to her knees.

Finch was distracted by his broken umbrella cane. Grumbling at the two pieces, he fitted them together and spat on them, then ran his hands over the broken place until they had knit together and transformed into an actual cane. "There," he sighed with pride, holding it out. "Crow darts, that feels good. Check this—"

Winnie grabbed his head and turned it to the room. She had to ensure he saw the most obvious sign of weird—the tiny, violent windstorm at the center of the office, sweeping the paper into the air and giving it a good swirl before spitting it out again, where it added to the ever-increasing mass at their feet.

Then Winnie saw him. Felicitous hadn't been spinning a tale; Neal was typing.

He reminded her of a gargoyle, hunched into a comma shape and nearly still as stone. Only his hands moved, fingers flying over the keys of a typewriter perched on a stack of crates before him. He hadn't paused at the sound of the door slamming or the umbrella cracking or the Unseelie investigator swearing. He looked for all the world like Winnie expected she did when she was deep into a draft of one of her books: the rest of the world vanished; only the words on the page existed.

"Wonders never cease." Finch had to raise his voice over the keening of the cyclone of paper. "Seelie can write?"

"He's doing more than that." Winnie pitched her voice lower, uncomprehending. "He's glowing."

Glowing was a fae thing, of course. Fae glowed the way humans gave off body odor. But Neal's glow was wrong—a pale, sickly green aura, as if he'd been irradiated.

The glow was wrong. Neal was wrong. Everything here was wrong.

» **Need your help.**

Fifteen years ago, Eve's plea to Winnie came through as a text message.

Winnie hadn't known what to do. She'd paused the movie she was watching and stared at the three words on her phone's screen. After years of estrangement, she and Eve had recently gotten back in touch, commenting on each other's social media posts, sending links to articles, sharing brief messages. Rarely, they spoke on the phone.

But then Eve had dropped off the map. No responses, no comments. Winnie's heart had torn all over again.

» **Need your help.**

Based on the time stamp, Eve's previous message had arrived nine weeks earlier. Nine weeks of silence in which Winnie assumed she'd done something awful. Again.

Her phone chimed again.

» **Found a door. Meet me.**

Two minutes after that, a set of GPS coordinates.

Winnie had stared at the numbers for a few seconds before pasting them into Google, then coughed out a laugh—Lakeforest Shopping Mall. Eve and Winnie's unofficial clubhouse in high school. They'd eaten their weight in junk food, shoplifted a couple times from the record store, and watched their first R-rated movie in the theater. But Lakeforest had been shuttered for nearly a decade. The last time Winnie had walked there, most of the stores were holding Final Closing sales or had turned into pop-ups with no official names. The place echoed with uselessness and smelled like old frying oil.

Eve's summons was ridiculous, mysterious, and unsettling. But it landed in Winnie's ears like a megaphone. She could have ignored it. The message was a joke, obviously. It conformed to no rules she understood. Yet as Winnie knew well, playing by the rules guaranteed you *nothing*.

» **Found a door.**

Whatever that door was, Winnie was sure it didn't lead to the old JC Penney's. Eve wouldn't text for just that. The words were few, but just enough to tickle Winnie's innate love of mystery. She jumped up from her couch and drove to the mall as the sun began disappearing behind the trees. It was the time of day some called the gloaming, the magic hour.

Unsurprisingly, the mall was desolate. But it was also a haven for vandals; it took Winnie only a moment to find a door with a shattered lock. Using the coordinates and her phone's flashlight, Winnie wound her way through the empty corridors until she reached the former Bloomingdale's entrance. Just outside the store, in a common area, a nook of ripped sofas and dead plants were stationed next to the stilled escalators.

That was where she'd found Eve.

Her old friend stood next to the one still-living tree in the nook. And it wasn't just not dead, it was flourishing. Green leaves spread in all directions, blocking the escalator. High above, a skylight had broken, and water dripped in from the roof.

Winnie hurtled toward Eve, feet clomping on the tiles. She might have fallen ass-over-teakettle and bumped her head, but the linoleum was firm beneath her boots and her legs felt stronger than they had in years. But then she slowed, for two reasons. One: The only living tree in the forgotten mall, the one directly next to Eve, was glowing. Two: Eve was pregnant. Easily six or seven months along. Eve, who amid the chirpy public posts about her apparently very interesting life as a security guard, had confided in Winnie that she would do anything to have a child.

The glowing tree next to Eve pulsed softly, like a heartbeat.

Eve held her arms out in anticipation of an embrace, but Winnie kept her distance. Eve dropped her arms and her smile faded a few degrees. "There's an explanation."

"I bet there is." Winnie prepared to run in the opposite direction. Mysteries were fine inside the pages of a book, but less so when they stood in front of her. When Winnie wrote a conundrum, she could be the one who untangled it. But the real world was hard. Illogical.

"They want you, Win." Eve's breath caught. She was on the verge of tears. "They want your stories."

Winnie glanced around, expecting that they were being secretly filmed. "Right. Is it *Jackass* or *Candid Camera* that's paying you five bucks to pass on the message?"

Eve's jaw hardened. Her eyes were bright and wet. She curled her arms around her distended belly. "All you gotta do is come with me. Staying is an option. But please, meet with them?"

"Them? Who's 'them'?"

Eve let out a long breath. "Okay, this is a little hard to swallow. Remember that poem from Mr Davidson's class? About going up the airy mountain and then down into a rushy glen?"

It was a long-ago memory, but certainly Winnie recalled William Allingham's words; she'd had to explicate that funny little poem in high school. *We daren't go a-hunting, for fear of little men*, came the next line. "Are you on something, Eve? You're not saying you've been off with the fairies?"

"Actually," said Eve, "I am. And I have."

In time, Winnie learned that Seelie Court Network executives had sent *her* their 'memos' first. But they'd communicated the way fae often did—with initials carved on a tree branch. Musical tappings at her door. Apples on her car hood. But Winnie wasn't personally whimsical. Her flights of fancy and imagination were for her stories. She'd tossed the tree branches back into the trees, blamed her neighbors for a new doorbell chime, and gave the apples to some neighbor kids. Then she went back to her life of structure and rules.

Frustrated, the executives had approached Eve—the one person in the world who knew Winnie best. Eve was an open wound of need. She was turning forty, didn't even have a boyfriend, and solo IVF had failed her. She'd answered the Seelie version of text messages and gone beyond the Veil. She fell in love with the world being offered, tumbled for a human already living there named Hal, and accepted the bargain: `Deliver the writer, and you will deliver your fondest wish.`

Once Siggy was on the way, Eve sought out Winnie.

But while standing in that shuttered shopping mall, Winnie hadn't known any of that. And in that moment of seeing her next to a pulsing, glowing tree while impossibly pregnant, Winnie had a moment of panic. But then she'd realized: this was *Eve*. She took her friend's hand, and they pulled one another into a firm—though not too tight—embrace, the big belly of future Siggy sat between them.

"Hold on," Eve had whispered and reached into the glowing tree.

They'd fallen into the pulsing light, into the unmistakable smell of salty air. It wrapped around their bodies and pulled them in. Winnie hadn't even had time to cry out before they'd landed, softly, on a patch of sand. Air had rushed out of Winnie's chest, and she gasped for it back, stretched flat on the ground and staring up at a perfect blue sky. Eve lay next to her, also winded. A warm salt breeze caressed Winnie's cheek as waves crashed nearby. Eve, who still held her hand, gave it a squeeze.

"We're here," said Eve.

Winnie gripped that hand in return, hundreds of questions racing through her mind. "Where is 'here'?"

A shadow had fallen across her face as a figure craned its head over Winnie. He had a perfectly symmetrical, elfin face framed by joyful black curls. He glowed a warm orange-yellow shade, like a sunset. "Greetings, Winnifred Arrowmaker." Neal Bartleby had smiled. "You have arrived in Seaview Haven. We've wished for you."

NEAL STILL GLOWED today, amid all the madness of his office, but that sunset hue was gone. Even at this distance, Winnie could feel that something was very wrong with him.

Finch beelined for the tree, running his hands up and down the trunk. "Fantastic. All right. He's got a word tree in here. That explains all the paper." He plucked a sheet from the air and squinted at the words, clucking. "Nope, I take it back. Seems like Seelie really *can't* write."

Winnie didn't care if Neal had crafted the finest words ever put to paper. She only wanted to know if he was well. Wading with careful steps through the paper, she approached him from behind. His clothing was exponentially more shabby than Felicitous', nearly falling off his body. Each time Neal pistoned one arm forward or back she caught his knobby elbows poking through the sleeve. His once sleek black curls were a tangled mass and threaded through with large swathes of gray. And he gave off a muddy odor.

We're self-cleaning, he'd once said before joining her in the suds of her bathtub. *The whole bathing thing is…* And he'd shrugged. *Some enjoy it as a hobby.* Later he would design a special desk she could use to write in the bath, and painted it purple. *This is a hobby I could take a shine to, though.*

Even when he hadn't bathed, Neal had always smelled wonderfully, like fresh laundry or Nilla wafers.

Not now.

"Yum!" Finch yelped, though his expression looked pained. "Smells like boiled cabbage and just-turned bologna! My favorite. Ish." He gazed around, voice softer. "Funny. My head. It's like… ideas are there. So many *ideas*. Maybe I could do a still life painting of boiled cabbage and bologna sandwiches."

Winnie turned to bark at him to get his act together, but in that moment Finch slipped, tumbling into the waves of paper. He disappeared beneath the discards, only his cane poking up. After a moment, his gray-red head popped out of the waves, and he puffed out his cheeks. "This room is a bloody minefield!"

Winnie reached Neal. His skin had always been a rich shade of cream with a slight whiskey tint, but now it was sallow and gray. His unblinking eyes gazed out glassily, hollow on the inside. He yanked out the sheet of paper from the typewriter's carriage, stared at it for less than a second, then cast it into the air. Another sheet of paper materialized in the carriage and Neal resumed typing. His fingers poked at the keys, which no longer featured any numbers or letters on them. They'd been typed clean.

"Neal," she said as gently as possible amid the ongoing roar.

Finch backstroked through the paper, emerging on the opposite side of the typewriter to face the Showrunner/Mayor/Director. The Unseelie leaned in, squinting, then knocked Neal on the head twice with his cane.

"I'm Finch!" he shouted. "Sent from SCN to evaluate your TROPE Town! Can I have a moment of your time?"

Neal kept typing.

Winnie flailed at Finch. "Back off!" Finch snarled but held still. He cocked his thumb to the side and Winnie waded in his direction.

"Look," he pointed. "Look close."

"I am," she growled. "I've been doing nothing but looking close. What is wrong with him?"

"He's under a spell. And it's a good one. Stronger than anything I've ever seen."

Some of Winnie's anger faded. "A spell? What kind?"

Finch shrugged. "Can't tell, exactly. It's personal, specific, and direct, though." He leaned in, as if sharing a confidence. "And if my guess is right, it's making him type a lot."

Winnie threw her hands in the air. "I have eyes, you nitwit! But he looks terrible. How long has he been doing this?" She gasped, realizing. "Not… not for almost two years?"

"Could be." Finch's tone was curious and clinical. "I've never seen a Seelie this broken."

Winnie's eyes flooded with tears and her throat tightened. She should have been here before now. Barged past that brownie. Braved whatever needed to be said to Neal. Started on a quest to get him healed. If she'd been as heroic as the protagonist she pretended to be in her stories, she'd have taken care of business—fearlessly.

But Winnie had never been heroic, exactly; she'd always known she was reasonably ordinary. Getting older hadn't helped; it was as if with life experience, she knew how to flinch before the blow landed. She understood consequences that came from risk-taking, and that wasn't just a metaphor. She was afraid to take physical risks because an injury could turn into something she'd have to live with for the rest of her life. And emotionally—she'd been able to avoid taking chances for many years, wrapped in a safe cocoon ever since Neal had climbed into her bath and kissed her for the first time. She didn't like these facts about getting older, but it was hard to always push yourself again, and again. So easy to let those muscles atrophy.

Neal's absence had been tangled up in so much. After years of feeling connected to him, and that they were on the same page personally and professionally, he started changing. He proposed they take her stories, and his movies, in a new direction.

Monsters! he'd begun declaring. *Actual monsters on Turbot Trail! I insist!*

They'd argued about that constantly. And amid their fighting, he'd gotten a bad knock on his noggin, and disappeared into his house. She'd been too prideful to chase him down, to have the fight she felt was brewing.

He'll let me know when he's ready for my next story, she'd decided. *I won't run after him.*

Then her rationale shifted. *He's just mad at me because I got him injured.*

Then she began to get frightened that she was about to be dumped and fired simultaneously. *If I don't talk to him then he can't tell me my time in Seaview Haven is up and I have to leave.*

All of it had added up to inertia. Winnie was good at inertia. But months had passed. Neal hadn't been seen anywhere. The town started to crumble. People vanished. Eve left and didn't come back. Winnie preoccupied herself with Siggy. Time rolled on, a wheel careening downhill, and it kept going whether you paid attention to it or not.

Still, seeing Neal now, her heart hadn't just been broken. It had been pulverized, leaving only dust particles. What if he really had been spellbound here the whole time?

And if so, how had it happened?

Winnie swallowed. Thought of her fictional self. *What would Detective Winnie do?*

"So how do we break the spell?" Winnie asked.

Finch tapped his fingers on the cane's head. "That'll take some doing."

"But you're Unseelie! Can't you just un-do it?"

Finch's cheeks flushed.

"Please don't say this is above your pay grade." Winnie's heart pounded. She kept stealing glances at Neal, hoping for some recognition.

"It— I—" A piece of paper blew into Finch's face, and he peeled it away. "It's not—" He swallowed.

"Spit it out, Finch! Don't make me wait another two years for an answer."

The flush deepened and he seemed to be controlling himself with great difficulty. "This is not a fae spell." He rubbed his face. "This is more powerful than that. More powerful than something our top Executive could fashion. I am a spectacular being, but even I have no way of reversing it." As he spoke, his fingers absently folded a stray sheet of paper into an origami unicorn. "And maybe it's not as specific to him as I thought. It's getting in *my* head now. I gotta exit."

Winnie looked at Neal, who still typed away, oblivious. They were invisible to him.

Finch was wading to the door, batting away paper with his cane.

"Finch!" she shouted at him. "What kind of spell is more powerful than a Seelie's?"

He was tugging on the doorknob and called over his shoulder. "A *godspell.*"

Chapter 14

Skin Magic

WINNIE FELL TWICE that first day in Seaview Haven. First, when Eve pulled her through that portal. Then, when she'd first laid eyes on Neal Bartleby. He'd reached out his hands to help both women to their feet simultaneously, and the moment Winnie had made contact a bright warmth spread down her neck all the way down her body, a sensation she hadn't felt since she'd been married.

She'd gotten to her feet, then cried out. "My knees!"

Neal had laughed.

I'm too old for this, she'd thought. *I'm too old for him.*

But she hadn't been. Over time, she learned about Seelie, TROPE Towns, and why her stories were critical to Seaview Haven's—and SCN's—success. By then, she understood that her initial impression (that Neal was barely thirty) was off by a couple centuries.

"You were a writer before you got here," Neal said early on while they walked around the village. Everyone greeted him, some more warmly than others, then raised eyebrows at her. "She was a writer," he told the townsfolk.

"I am a writer," she corrected each time.

"You're *our* writer," he added. "If you wish to be." Then he explained how they planned to make movies of each of her books—past, present, and future.

Back in what Winnie still thought of as the real world, that kind of attention was like hitting the lotto repeatedly. Hollywood paid big for adaptations, even ones that never got made. She could be the next George R.R. Martin. Or Gillian Flynn. Or that woman who wrote wizard school stories, then lost herself down a dark rabbit hole. Or even Stephen King. (In fact, her first story written wholly in Seaview Haven was called *Seaview Haven: The Case of the Malicious Monty Crisco* in honor of Dumas, Eve, and King.) Winnie had done acceptably well for money in the real world, but having her mysteries made into movies proved they meant something to people. Even if those people were mythical creatures.

"Really?" She'd had to step away from Neal; he'd radiated heat in a way no man ever had around her. Just standing next to him was like being in a permanent hot flash.

"Indeed!" He'd raised one eyebrow, then another. "You and I will be writing the fabric of this town, you see. Your stories will be about"—he'd gestured at the locals—"them. Loosely. You'll weave mysteries, and we will make them happen. Or mysteries will happen, and we will make movies and books about them. Our audience *loves* human mysteries!"

Winnie hadn't known what to do with herself. So she'd leaped into the air.

Neal leaped with her. Then he'd taken one of her hands between both of his own. He was so pale and slender, yet there was enormous strength beneath his touch. "Can we begin?"

Winnie took two days to think it through. She wanted to be the person who grabbed such an opportunity with both hands; this was the adventure she never knew she'd been seeking. But she had questions.

"You'll live next door to Eve, unless you want to live

somewhere else," Neal had answered. "She'll be your partner-in-solving-crimes. Your stories will create the reality of this town—well, your stories and my magic. You'll write exactly what you already were writing back home—mystery and suspense. Nothing gruesome, though."

"No problem," she said. "My cozies rarely have dead bodies."

"A relief. Our last resident writer became enamored with chalk outlines. And autopsies. Yick."

"What happened to him?"

"He… left."

For Seelie, 'leaving' was as easy as pushing an offending human through a portal and shutting the door behind them. For humans, 'leaving' was more complicated. Time ran differently on the fae side of the Veil than it did in the real world; returnees might have been gone five years but look *younger* than when they'd vanished. And they couldn't even explain things properly; back home, permanent wards prevented them from discussing where they'd been or what they'd done, and slowly those memories would become dreamlike and distant. Leavers were advised to claim amnesia if people wondered where they'd been.

"Plus, they don't leave empty-handed," Neal said. "Gold payments, maybe a bit of remnant magic like the ability to open tins without an opener."

"Consolation prizes," said Winnie.

Neal had folded his arms. "We think being here is the big prize."

Winnie had mirrored him. "Well, you'll just have to show me, then."

"Is that a 'yes'?"

Still, Winnie had hesitated. Of course she was going to say 'yes.' She would have a purpose, a house, and a beautiful Seelie collaborator hovering over her shoulder. She was magic to *him*, and he needed her. It was intoxicating. But before shaking on the deal, she had requirements.

"The people in this town—they're here voluntarily?" she asked. "They're not compelled or required to be in your 'movies'?"

Again, he'd taken her hand. Every time Neal did that, she found it harder to let go. "You are a kind soul, Winnifred Arrowmaker. None of our other resident writers ever asked that."

She'd fought melting under his touch. She wanted to stay strong. But with every passing hour, it became harder. "Answer my question, Mayor Bartleby."

He gave her a small smile. "Humans compelled to do things often do them badly. Or it feels false. Viewers can sense this. There is one TROPE Town where humans who violated fae rules are sent. It's called Settle. Some call it Second Chance. Here, we only take those who want to come and only keep the ones who want to stay. But being in the movies—well, you don't have to be a *star* to be in our show, as the song says, but you do have to be willing to be on camera. Otherwise, you may as well be a Leaver."

Winnie had wondered what constituted a fae violation but held her tongue. If she stayed, they'd have plenty of time to discuss the finer points of a TROPE Town as a fae detention facility.

"I have family," she continued. "I won't vanish from their lives. I have to close up my house, put things in storage. And I'll need to see them. Twice a year is fine. I'll tell them—" She'd paused. What would she say?

Eve, who had no family to speak of back home and had married Hal after getting pregnant with Siggy, had offered a suggestion later. "Communes are a fine excuse. Not a cult, though. Don't let them think you've gone off the deep end. You just want to live off the grid, which isn't exactly a lie."

Neal's eyes had twinkled. He knew he'd made the sale, and Winnie knew he knew it.

After that, they worked closely together every other day, then every day. Eve gave Winnie space when Neal was around. But Winnie and Eve had a special place in Seaview Haven's population. They were the stars in the movies, and there were no wards on what they could say or do. Neal trusted them both enough, and Winnie didn't plan to violate any fae rules.

The trust she'd developed with Neal became an intimacy, and within a month that intimacy became physical. Soon, Winnie couldn't believe there was a time she didn't know, or love, Neal. Sometimes she would stare at him from a distance, moon-eyed as a teenager, his carved features etched into her heart. He would take her hand as they watched the sunset—the same color as his glowing skin—and she felt his pulse against hers. Winnie made shortbread with tiny chocolate chips for him to snack on as he read her drafts, and he swooned over the gift.

And whenever she passed behind him in a room, Winnie got up on tiptoe or gently bent down to kiss the back of his neck. He tasted like that sunset, drizzled in chocolate.

"Mmmm," he'd always sigh. "There's magic on my skin."

Clack clack clack, *type type type—ding!*

Paper *crrrrching* out of the carriage.

Crumpling sound, or not. A moment's pause, then—`clack clack clack.`

Winnie couldn't bear seeing Neal in that zombie gargoyle position. So he'd been godspelled. What did that mean? What should she do with that bit of insanity? Meanwhile, all around them the miniature cyclone of pages whirled and spun with the noise of an engine, spilling paper around the room and deepening the mess.

Finch was acting squirrelly, even more so than usual. He'd wanted to leave the room, but Winnie had refused to follow, and he hadn't been able to open the door himself. Now, he scanned several pages Neal had discarded and handed them to her. "They're not *all* incoherent," he called above the roar. "Though there is a lot about monsters in here."

That came as a fractional relief to Winnie. That meant Neal was still in there, focusing on his monsters. But pain followed and she remembered all of their arguments over his unexpected interest in introducing unseen creatures to the town's mystery vault. Kraken footprints. Wendigo antlers. Selkie skins. All of which would turn out to be fake but would shift the mysteries a little. Make them scarier, particularly to mythic audiences.

I've been at this for a hundred years, he'd said. *I'm tired of all the forged check scams and gaslit spouses and stolen sturgeon mysteries.*

True, they had gone to the same wells a bit too often. But as Winnie understood it, introducing the supernatural, even fake supernatural, went against everything SCN wanted. *Besides,* she'd added, *I'm not going to start writing episodes of* Scooby-Doo.

Neal hadn't known what that meant.

Finch snapped his fingers in front of her face. "Return to me, Winnifred Arrowmaker." He waved another sheet of paper with one hand and held his head with the other. "Even if we locate something in here worth reading, finding the next page or the before page will be impossible. Nothing connects. Besides, my head is thumping."

"Mine too, but you don't hear me complaining. And

who cares what he's writing! Look at him!"

Finch blinked. "Yes. Broken. We've established that."

Winnie was torn between wanting to burst into tears or smacking the Unseelie again. She pushed both aside. Her head whirled, but she found that by keeping a focus on Neal, she could think straight. Or perhaps just a bit crooked. "Who casts a godspell?"

"Gods, of course."

That was as creepy as anything Neal had proposed. Winnie had been aware for nearly fifteen years that fae and mythical creatures existed, but she'd never given much thought to actual godlike entities. She'd never known they were even part of TROPE Towns. Why would a god care about a silly invented village?

"Let's move him," she said. "Make him stop typing."

"You go right ahead and do that." Finch folded his arms. "He *punched* a brownie, remember."

"He won't hit me."

"Maybe, maybe not," said the Unseelie. "But I'm going to watch. If the spell attaches to you, too, then I'll know what happens."

"You're rotten, Finch, you know that?"

His glow heightened. "Thanks!"

Winnie stared at Neal. She was going to have to risk it. Better to be in the madness with him than outside and terrified. She reached out a hand, only to be blocked by Finch's repaired cane.

"On second thought," he said, "we can't fix this if you're locked like him. Best not."

Furious, Winnie yanked the stick from his hands. Finch stumbled backward into the paper. She pressed the end of the cane against Neal's shoulder and gently poked. Then she pushed. Then she was leaning against it with all her strength. Her back sang and her knees strained. She pressed so hard she was canting to one side.

Neal did not move.

Nor did he stop typing.

"Argh!" Winnie prepared to throw the cane away.

"Ahem." Finch held out his hand and she helped him to his feet. "Godspells do not respond to violence."

Winnie stared at Neal. Early on, she'd wondered why he needed her at all. *What's up with having me here?* she'd asked. *I always thought magical creatures sat around making up poems and telling stories all day.*

Yes and no, the Seelie had told her. *Music, poems, we do dabble in those areas. But whatever we create is so threaded with magic that it's hard to say if it's any good. Fae-written tales go nowhere and say nothing. This is why we like listening in on humans. You're fascinating. Your words are clear, bright, and magic without being magical. It's a gift.*

Now, Winnie lingered on the Seelie's gray skin and flat, saucer-sized eyes. He barely blinked. But his fingers kept moving, cracked and stained pink and scabbed as they were. If perfection was the definition of being Seelie—as Finch insisted—then at some point, Neal had become *Un*.

It was too much. Winnie's tears spilled over. There was nothing more they could do here, not now. They'd have to leave him in this stinking room of unfinished tales and impenetrable poetry. Of monsters on the page and curdling dreams. Of incoherence and chaos.

"Fine," she sighed. "Let's go."

Handing Finch the cane, they took careful steps away from Typing Sisyphus. Finch hop-stepped to the door and set his hand on the knob. Winnie prepared to open it with him, casting one last glimpse at Neal. He was so hunched and wild haired, bony, and stuck. His long curls draped over his shoulders, leaving a lone patch of exposed neck.

"One sec." Winnie hurried back to Neal, crouched down, and brushed her lips against that exposed area, as she had so many times before. "I miss you," she whispered. "Come back to us."

The typing paused.

Finch removed his hand from the doorknob.

Neal turned his head a degree, then two. Winnie curved around his body, trying to meet his gaze. His eyes were no longer flat. There was recognition in those dark pools, along with joy—and fear. Neal opened dry, parched lips and spoke.

"Cuidigh liom."

The light faded again, and he turned back to the typewriter.

`Click click click`—*ding*.

"Neal? Neal?" Winnie's heart had soared and now plummeted again. He was in there. Somewhere. He'd spoken something—Irish? Gaelic? She'd never learned much of it. "Say it again!"

A hand landed on her shoulder. Finch was back. "He's gone."

"But he *spoke* to me!"

Finch nodded.

"What did he say?"

"'Cuidigh liom.'"

Winnie imagined shredding the Unseelie into pulp-sized pieces. "I *know* that! What does it mean?"

The Unseelie's face was grim. "'Help me.'"

Chapter 15

We Are Not A-Mused

FINCH HOBBLED OUT of Mayor Bartleby's office in a state of shock, hop-pacing and muttering to himself. "A *godspell*!" he cried, grabbing at his hair. He'd heard of such things, but never seen one, though they were known to be exponentially more powerful than a cantrip or curse. And what did it mean to lob a godspell in fae lands, much less one that laid low a Seelie SMD?

"It could mean *war*!" he said. "Destructive, shattering, forever war!"

Unseelie should *love* that kind of chaos, but it only gave Finch a more intense headache.

Behind him came a soft sob. Winnie was leaning on the wall, the heels of her hands shoved into her eyes. Her cheeks shone.

Humans are always leaking water, he thought. Yet his heart clenched at seeing his greatest love-to-hate Main Character upset. Finch withdrew a scrap of linen smeared with garden soil from his pocket. He blew on it and gave it a shake, turning it merely gray. "Quit sniveling, won't you?" He shook the makeshift handkerchief at Winnie. "It makes me uncomfortable."

Winnie looked at the cloth, then used her sleeve to clear her face. "This is my fault. I'm why he was susceptible to a godspell."

Finch sniffed at the refusal of his perfectly mediocre handkerchief. "Doubtful. You are a fascinating person in the movies and utterly frustrating in person, but you are not a god-attractant."

"Stupid Frisbee," she said, almost to herself.

Finch raised an eyebrow. "Freeze bees? Tell me more."

Winnie's cheeks were pink and her eyes puffy, but the crying was over. "*Fris*bee. It's a… curved disc. You throw it around."

"Is it offensive?"

"For fun, Finch. You ever heard of fun?"

"Unseelie are nothing *but* fun. Even if we are the only ones who think so." But was that true? He *had* enjoyed climbing up on the TROPE Town Map and showing up the EVVVVVPCTTAP. That had been clever, not fun. Born of desperation. He *had* enjoyed his raucous times laughing at SCN shows with Agatha by the lake, while they got pissed on cherry wine and shouted at the moon. But he'd spoiled all that.

And for what? So he could be here with too many ideas whirling in his brain, next to a crying human? Finch pushed that aside. "So this fritz bee attacked Mayor Bartleby."

"No. We were playing Frisbee and arguing," she sighed.

"Do those activities usually comingle?"

"They're not supposed to." She told him how the SMD's focus had wavered in recent years. How he'd nitpicked her stories, even the ones that drew many eyeballs to their movie versions. Neal insisted on variety. He'd attended an SCN-sponsored series of Rapscallion University seminars and come back buzzing with ideas to reshape the mysteries they told in Seaview Haven. He wanted monsters. Winnie wanted status to remain quo.

At first, it was the only thing they'd ever argued about. Then it became the thing they argued about most. Then it was the thing they did nothing *but* argue about, even while trying to blow off steam by throwing a Frisbee.

Shapeshifter dolphins in the ocean! Neal had shouted, hurling the disc at her that fateful afternoon.

Winnie had whoofed as the disc thudded into her chest; it had been thrown with more power than Neal usually used. She tossed out a more Seaview Haven idea as she threw it back. *Lost keys under the car leading to accusations of infidelity!*

Harpies raiding the grocery store! Neal had returned the disc with such strength that it bruised her wrist.

Watch it! Winnie had said, throwing it back. *What is up with you?*

You never even consider my ideas! he'd cried, and this time his throw whizzed at Winnie so hard she dove to the ground. The disc lodged in the dirt a foot away, wobbling in place. *You act like you're the only one who can write a story in this town!*

Winnie had yanked the disc out. *I am!* she shouted back at him, though that wasn't entirely true. *You don't know how! What, you're gonna hire* Eve *to grind out your crummy ideas?*

Maybe I will! he'd growled back. *She takes direction!*

That had hit a sore spot in Winnie she didn't want to explore, and she'd hurled the damaged disc with all the oomph she could muster. It soared high and above Neal's head, coming to rest on his rooftop. *You're an idiot*, she'd said.

At least I can throw a Frisbee!

"Who won the game?" Finch asked now.

"Nobody. Neal insisted on going up there to get it down."

Clearly the work of a simple retrieval spell. Finch kept hoping this story would get interesting. Actually, he suddenly had many suggestions for how to improve it, the ideas stomping in his aching head kept feeding him options. "Let me guess: he flew up there—"

"He got a ladder."

"Whatever for?"

Winnie took a deep breath. "Neal liked to be *not fae* around me. He liked the challenge of playing human."

Finch recoiled. Neal Bartleby had gone native in his own T-Town. *That* would go into the final report, for certain. "So he ascended the ladder—"

"*Stormed* up the ladder. Acted like I'd done it on purpose. Maybe I had. Anyway, when he glared at me my eyebrows grew an inch."

A bright light burst inside Finch, and he spun in a circle. "Stop there! I know how this ends. Picture this: He got up on the roof and picked up the angry fritz bee. It attacked him. Winnifred Arrowmaker produced a wand—proving she was a witch this whole time—and zapped the creature. In the scuffle, Neal Bartleby—disguised as a 'human'—tripped and hit his head—"

"Finch. Stop."

But he couldn't. It was like the ideas were pouring out of him. His head felt better for letting some of them out, but his brain was on fire. He was telling a story. He was *creating*. It felt good, and it felt ooky, and a few degrees satisfying. But Seelie and Unseelie alike did not *write* stories of any quality or depth. Typically, they only spewed out basic ideas based on all of the stories they'd ever read, which wasn't the same thing as creating a story. Yet here Finch was, patching together a story from bare bits that Winnie had thrown his way.

What are you doing? He shook his head. *You are here to prove just how Unseelie you are, and instead you're fixing umbrellas and starting stories! You keep going this way, and you'll never get the chance to tear apart this town. You might even get Exiled for being so fake.*

"What happened next?" He gritted his teeth.

"Well, you were right. A bit. He threw the Frisbee down to me and tried to look superior and then he tripped and—" She closed her eyes for a moment. "Fell into the decorative shrubs. Hit his head and got knocked out." She braced herself against the wall again. "Felicitous took him inside and wouldn't let me in to visit. Until today, I hadn't seen him in almost two years."

And that's what comes from pretending to be something you're not, a voice inside Finch piped up. *You get knocked on the noggin and a godspell wanders in to show you what's what.*

Finch sighed. "Winnifred, you are not responsible here. A godspell doesn't need a bump on the head to pin down a Seelie. No, something else has kept him in here for these two years. There has been an Intervening Incident."

Winnie stared at him.

In the silence, Malvous appeared in the hallway and cleared his throat. "Finch is correct. Much as I hate to admit it. There was an Intervening Incident."

Neal's brownie peered from behind Malvous. A scent of fermentation, sugar, and butter wafted from the kitchen. "And it's still intervening," said Felicitous.

"Where?" Winnie was at full attention.

Felicitous gestured deeper into the house. "Thataway."

Winnie raced down the hall.

SHE GOT TEN steps, just far enough to hear muffled voices from behind one of the doors lining the dim hallway, before getting jerked backward. Her purple blouse strained, and a button popped off. Flailing, she fell and landed in Malvous' arms.

"So very sorry, Ms Winnie," he said, holding her fast. "There are things that must be discussed first."

"I want to intervene on that 'Intervening Incident'!" she cried. "You can't stop me." Winnie raised a fist, but Malvous' squarish eyes were so full of concern and worry she felt it would be like striking a child. Breathing heavily, she stopped fighting back. "You must let me fix this."

"You cannot fix anything without the correct tools," said Malvous, gesturing at the kitchen. "Please."

With everyone in the kitchen, Felicitous passed around mugs of Chardonnay. Finch paced around the table, slowing his steps only to shove freshly baked shortbread in his mouth. He left a trail of crumbs in his wake. "Oh," he sighed in ecstasy. "That's the stuff. Tamps down the brain whirling *just* enough."

Effects of shortbread on fae aren't often the subject of scientific studies, but it was well known on the fae side of the Veil that the biscuit was a powerful Seelie calming device. Winnie had prepared batches at least twice a week for Neal, adding in her special addition of chocolate chips. Neal would often eat so much he'd fall into a stupor. *I wish shortbread worked on me like that*, she thought now. But, no. Winnie knew she had to be alert, capable, and heroic for her spelled Seelie. Neal needed her. She could fall apart later. She pushed aside the Chardonnay and the treat.

"Felicitous has been explaining the situation." Malvous took a seat next to her. "But first, how was it in Mayor Neal's office?"

Winnie stared at her hands. She yearned for Eve—solid, sensible Eve. Her best friend would have ideas or solutions or at least be a shoulder to cry on. But Winnie didn't have Eve. She was stuck with three marginally competent mythical creatures. For the first time since coming to Seaview Haven, she felt homesick. "Awful. Finch says he's been godspelled. What does that even mean?"

"Not what. Who." Felicitous sipped Winnie's rejected cup of wine.

"The house guests," clarified Malvous.

Finch thrust a fist into the air. "I *knew* there were others in this house! I said it first! I get credit!"

Winnie shook her head at him, then turned back to Felicitous. "You have house guests? And they did this to him? Who are they?"

Silence.

Neal's brownie piped up in a hushed, quivering voice. "Muses, Ms Winnifred. Muses who debauch and consume and invite *more* guests and play badminton at midnight and who refuse to leave—" he gasped.

Malvous slid a paper bag to the brownie, who took long deep breaths from it.

Winnie waited for the other shoe to drop. "Wait. You're serious. *Literal* Muses?"

Both brownies nodded.

Finch leaned across the table, waving a rectangle of shortbread. "That explains a *lot*."

"No, it doesn't!" Mythical creatures were one thing. But there really were gods mixed up in the TROPE Town 'verse? That was almost too much to handle. "Why would Neal invite them here?"

"He didn't!" cried Felicitous. "Never would."

"Muses and Seelie rarely mix in healthy ways," said Malvous. He looked pale and poured another teacup of Chardonnay before knocking it back. "But I think this time, Neal did invite them here. Two years ago. Indirectly."

"Explain," ordered Winnie, barely restraining herself.

Chapter 16

The Wrong Stuff

So Malvous explained:

Bros work hard. They play hard. They drink hard. And, given the opportunity, they hold hands hard—which Malvous was still working on doing with his crush Foxtacular at the time this story took place, two years before he was dragged to Seaview Haven. On this night, he and Foxtacular had gathered at The Clocked Out, ranked the No. 1 Bro Watering Hole for three years running by *Bro Bar Biweekly*—which made it a popular hangout for brownies and non-Bros alike.

At this stage in their relationship, Malvous and Foxtacular were still in the 'Oh, you're here! What a lovely coincidence' stage of things. Both had recognized that they came to The Clocked Out at the same time, once a week, and sat at the same booth, sipping the same fruity cocktails sprinkled with roasted cricket legs. It was another bit of coincidence that drove them closer. They shared careful small talk, thighs nearly touching.

("Good grass stains, Malvous," Finch interrupted. "This isn't Romance Story Hour. We have an emergency in a falling apart town and a set of *Muses* in a room down the hallway. Get on with it.")

Malvous had been considering inching a hair closer to Foxtacular when a lull in the room permitted them to overhear a most curious conversation coming from the next booth over.

"Another round!" Janus raised their voice and waved around the bar. "For everyone!"

A cheer went up among the customers. A grumble went up among the bartenders. Janus always drank for free in Bro Bars, and liked to share the wealth, though it dismayed the establishment owners.

"Thanks, man!" Foxtacular waved at their booth neighbors.

"Thanks, *god*," Janus pointed back at him. "But I forgive you."

Turning bright red, Foxtacular leaned toward Malvous, squishing him against the booth divider. "Did you hear that? Janus forgave me! And did you see—I think they're sitting with that *Tune in Tomorrow* Showrunner Jason Valentine! We're in the presence of greatness!"

Barely able to breathe, but still happy to be this close to his high-haired co-worker, Malvous decided to go with the conversation. "Who's the third one over there?"

"Dunno." Both brownies peered at the other guest in the booth, a Seelie with thick dark curls, high cheekbones, long pale hands, and a perfectly unblemished complexion. He was complaining through a sloppy drunkenness. Malvous would have preferred to share confidences and whispered delights with Foxtacular, but it was hard to surmount Bro celebrity enthusiasm.

"She's being such a *human* these days," the unknown fae slurred, knocking back a glass of uiscie beatha. It definitely wasn't his first. "Doesn't understand you gotta shake things up. Same old same old stories for the last hundred years in my T-Town. The monsters are due on Mackerel Street!"

"You're the SMD," Jason said. "Stamp your hooves to get her attention, if necessary."

"Don't got hooves," the curly-haired Seelie slurred. "Bet I could write *everything* without her." He wiped his face and held up his glass; the bartender gestured at him and the container magically refilled. "Been doing this longer than her. She's not so great as she thinks I think she is."

"Human writers wear out," said Jason. "That's why I treasure our werepanther at *Tune in Tomorrow*. Her prehensile tail can churn out five scripts simultaneously. In your case, a replacement may be in order."

"I love my human," the Seelie sighed. "She's special. But I am Seelie, and she ought to be seeing *me* as special. After all, my ideas are pure *magic*. My *outlines* have received Endless Awards. Why else would SCN put me in charge of its most-watched mystery-series-set-in-a-small-seaside-village movie franchise?"

"Clearly for your magical ideas—" began Janus.

"Precisely!"

"—though little else," the god ended.

The fae squinted. "I try! I just get stuck sometimes," he said. "It never comes out on paper the way I see it in my mind."

Janus shook their head. "Quite a unique ability you Seelie have. You can recognize an excellent concept but have the unique inability to see it to completion. Apparently, gods and Seelie have more things in common than anyone admits."

"So diplomatic," said Jason, tapping his pink concoction against Janus' glass. "This is why you're the god of executive producers, among everything else."

Foxtacular inched even closer, and Malvous' heart thudded as much from the proximity as the lack of oxygen. It was titillating and suffocating at the same time.

"But I could do it!" the Seelie declared. "I just need time to prove it to her. Seelie can learn. What I really need right now is a quiet space and proper inspiration.

That's something else I learned during my seminar at Rap U."

Janus finished their drink. "Interesting. What if I could provide you with what you required?"

Jason shook his head. "Look at you, just itching to make trouble."

"Moi?" Janus' expression was wicked as they pressed their fingers into their chest. "How dare you."

A centaur clopped into the bar and caught Jason's eye. The Showrunner waved, sliding out of the booth. "I'll be back in a few. 'Scuse. Gotta see a man who's a horse."

With Jason gone, Janus slid around the booth toward the unnamed Seelie—who was, as Malvous realized much later while standing in his wrecked Seaview Haven kitchen, Neal Bartleby. "I could send a few important personages like myself to goose along the process," said the god in a conspiratorial tone. "To assist with turning your unique, special, grandiose ideas into scripts. I mean, I haven't seen them in a couple dozen cycles, but we are old pals."

"Who?"

"Muses."

Neal flinched. "Yikes. Why would you use a Molotov cocktail to light a cigarette?"

"Maybe I like burning eyebrows away?" Janus held up a hand. "Joke. Seriously—think of it like an experiment. Gods love experiments, you know—take it from me. And these women, they're the best. Completely not a problem; they know how to sit there and look cute. Mousy. Real pushovers."

"Funny, that's not what I heard," Neal slurred.

"You'd be surprised. Now, if you make friends, you can probably tell them to turn up the volume or whatever on their inspiration ability—that'll help squeeze the good stuff out." The god paused. "That metaphor needs tweaking. Anyhow, I'm sure it'll be *fine*. I mean, you already have the ideas, yes?"

"Plenty! I've even written them down in notebooks." Neal tapped on his near-empty glass. "Was Winnie's idea, actually." The Seelie's leg was bouncing up and down so hard with excitement it shook Malvous' and Foxtacular's booth.

"Simplicity itself. Put the Muses up in your guest room and let them inspire you. Focus on creating just one useful story, show it to your writer, and she'll collapse in gratitude. All you have to do is provide wine and snacks to the Muses, and it'll go smoothly. Trust me, I know how to handle females of all species." They glanced to one side, tapping their chin. "Oh! And set up a badminton net out back. You can't catch Muses without a proper net."

"That's all?"

"That's it. Easy peasy on your kneesy."

Neal finished his drink. "I'm in. Time to prove I've got the right stuff."

"The right *monstrous* stuff," Janus laughed, and they raised their glasses for a refill.

NOW, FINCH STARED at Malvous with something approaching admiration. "Well, you've proven to be unexpectedly informative."

Malvous beamed.

"So the Intervening Incident is actually nine Muses," said Winnie.

"Four, mostly," said Felicitous. "Sometimes more. Sometimes they invite guests."

"And they've been here since—"

"The day after the Frisbee altercation."

Winnie closed her eyes. She could still see Neal tumbling from the upper roof, then bouncing off the porch covering on his way to hitting the ground. Hearing the noise, Felicitous had raced out of the house, scooped up his boss, and shut the door behind them both. And for the next two years, Winnie had been cut off from Neal. "You should have let me in," she told him.

"But I couldn't!" Felicitous exclaimed, saying that Neal had given explicit, if dazed, instructions to bar Winnie from the house until he recovered. *I don't want her seeing me like this*, he'd said. *She already doesn't think much of me.*

"That's not true!" Winnie protested. "I've been worried to a frazzle!"

"Is that like a Fritz bee?" asked Finch.

Winnie cut him a glance that, had she been magic, would have sealed his mouth forever.

As Felicitous noted, there hadn't been any time to deal with the Neal/Winnie drama because just hours after the Seelie's knock on the head there was a second knock, on the front door. "Janus!" the brownie recalled. "They greeted me, and then the Muses strolled in and ignored me one hundred percent. They were so beautiful, but so haughty. Janus ordered me to 'Look after them in all matters' and how can you tell a god 'no,' especially since Bros owe Janus so much—so I said I would. Janus left. The Muses stayed."

Neal went to bed and did not wake up, leaving Felicitous to be run ragged trying to attend to the sudden influx of house guests. On the second morning, the Muses demanded to meet the Seelie of the house.

How inconvenient, Calliope had said when presented to the unconscious Neal, who lay still as a corpse in his bed.

How convenient! Euterpe had countered. *This way, he won't bother Us.*

Maybe We should godspell him, just in case, Clio had suggested. *Keep him from interfering.*

This is a gal-cation, sweet sister, Calliope had said. *No need to exert Ourselves unnecessarily.*

Curious, Thalia had pinched the Seelie's nostrils shut.

Please do not obstruct Mayor Neal's nose, Felicitous had said as diplomatically as he could. *He needs to use that.*

Calliope had bent down to Felicitous' level. Her natural aura was so bright he had to shade his eyes. *Good, dear brownie. We are very patient and easy to work with. You'll hardly even notice We're here. Let the sleeping Seelie lie and rustle Us up some cucumber and butter sandwiches, a few bottles of wine, and point Us to the nearest swimming pool.*

But I need to report to SCN! Felicitous had insisted. *Seaview Haven cannot tell stories if Mayor Neal sleeps!*

Clio had grabbed one of Felicitous' ears and pinched it. *No one is contacting SCN. Janus has convinced Us of the value of a gal-cation, and We plan to take full advantage of Ours. That means We are in OOO mode. This whole house is in OOO mode. In fact, this whole town should be in OOO mode.*

I could effect an invisible barrier, Thalia had suggested. *To enforce the OOO.*

Later, if needed. Calliope had patted her sister on the head. *Let's see if We can enjoy Our downtime while making the least amount of effort.*

Does being OOO mean you're inviting ghosts? Felicitous had asked, trying not to have his ear pulled off.

It means Out of Office, Euterpe had giggled. *Silly brownie*

Be honored that your home has been graced by Our Presence, Calliope had said. *We are exhausted and need beauty rest and relaxation. We are overworked and underappreciated. SCN can survive Our brief sojourn into OOO mode. Obey Us and all will go well for you, your Seelie, and the entire town.*

It was the most beautiful threat Felicitous had ever heard.

Now, having related those first moments with the goddesses, Felicitous was worked up and sweating. "I did not 'hardly notice they were here.' I noticed it all the time! I had four—sometimes nine!—goddesses who wanted to play and eat and do karaoke and have friends over! They made a mess and slept in every bedroom and ate everything in our cabinets and refrigerator. I started clearing the grocery shelves to get the rest. They drank most of the wine cellar, then wanted cheese and spanakopita and baklava and fish and—" He rattled off a long list of everything the Muses had desired, all of which corresponded to the things the town gradually ran out of.

"And this was not so difficult because for a time we were still getting deliveries from SCN," Felicitous continued, getting worked up again. "But then Mayor Neal failed to make supply lists because he was sleeping, *and* the Muses were keeping me hopping with cleaning and fixing and making and brushing of hair. I lost track of the days. Then one of them thought it would be fun to barrier off the town and supplies dwindled to *never* and *nothing*. Your arrival this afternoon was opportune—it is their daily naptime. I get few other hours free in a day. The Muses laughed when I mentioned our beloved union rules."

Winnie felt for the brownie and set a hand over his. But she couldn't spend too much time on sentiment. Neal needed help. "Mayor Bartleby did wake up, though. Eventually."

"After seven sun cycles," said the brownie. "One week. Opened his eyes and yawned and said, 'That's quite enough of that nonsense.'"

"Slacking off!" cried Finch. "Of course that's what he was doing."

Winnie resisted a fresh urge to smack him in the head. "What did he do next? My guess is either he tried throwing them out on their toga'ed behinds, or somehow entered into a holy alliance that backfired."

Malvous and Felicitous clapped their hands together in delight. "No wonder Ms Winnie is a storyteller!" Malvous cheered. "That is precisely it!"

"Which part?"

Neal had known the Muses were there, or at least he felt them while unconscious. *I was lost in my dreams*, he told Felicitous. *Stuck in a forest of voices overlapping with other voices. It was like trying to listen to several choruses at once. Nightmarish. But then I realized: all that noise meant the Muses had actually arrived! So I forced myself out of that forest and opened my eyes and now it is time to get to work!*

With that, he had grabbed a mug of fresh tea, a handful of shortbread and went forth to meet with the Muses.

Mayor Neal, perhaps you should wait, Felicitous had scurried after him. *They are not what you think they are.*

Nonsense. They're pushovers. Janus said so. All I have to do is present my grand plan, and they will help. Passively. That's all I really need. And in a few hours, I will be one of the first Seelie ever to have written a proper story! *It will contain monsters! It will impress Winnie! Won't that be fun?*

He'd arrived at the sliding indoor doors that led to the living room. On the other side of the door someone was singing a karaoke version of The Scorpions' 'Rock You Like a Hurricane.' Neal had pressed his curls down, handed the empty mug back to Felicitous and brushed the crumbs of shortbread from his hands. *How do I look?* he'd asked his brownie.

"I told him he looked mayoral," Felicitous said now. "I couldn't very well say 'like a lamb to the slaughter.'"

Once Neal had passed inside the Muses' room, Felicitous waited for three hours on the other side of the door. He'd been afraid to leave, but more afraid to knock. Eventually, he went to make more food for their guests. And the next time Felicitous located his boss, Neal was in his office, hunched over a typewriter. A tree had sprouted in one corner.

Exit, Neal had waved at him, his voice faraway and not quite his own. *I am becoming... a writer.*

Nothing had been the same since.

FINCH RUBBED HIS temples. "Stupid Seelie. Walked right into his own godspell."

"But he should have been able to leave," said Winnie. "Something must have gone very wrong when he met the Muses."

"Can't see how it could have gone right," said Finch. "First off, godspell or no, Muse influence or no, he's never going to be able to complete a story. It's like trying to drink from a firehose, all that inspiration coming your way at once. Whatever they're doing to him, it's never going to produce an actual story."

"But who judges that?" Winnie looked around the room. "Who gets to decide?"

Felicitous looked at his hands. "The Muses, I suppose. Every so often a page he's typed on magics itself through a wind tunnel into the living room. It flutters onto an enormous pile of paper in a bin in one corner. In spare moments, a Muse picks out some pages to share with the room. There is usually a lot of laughter then. Mostly, they ignore the pages, which after a few days spontaneously turn into small ice fragments, which the Muses scoop out to keep their beverages cool. For that reason, they call it a—"

"Slush pile," said Winnie. "Hilarious."

The fae tilted their heads.

"That's called sarcasm," she told them. "All right. So what we have here is a Seelie with an ego too big for his common sense, who's somehow convinced the Muses to toy around with him. He has a task he can never complete. And because of this insane confluence of events my town is vanishing. Just perfect. If he ever gets out of that office, I'm going to have to kill him."

"Ms Winnie!" Felicitous yelped. "I won't allow that!"

"Cool your jets," said Finch. "Not like she could anyway."

Winnie stared down the hallway. She was thinking about Neal's plaintive request for help. Bullheaded and idiotic as he could be, it hurt her heart to imagine him trapped. She was going to have to do *something*, but the only idea she had was to go to the source. To approach the Muses.

Felicitous' waist buzzed and hummed, and he started as if he'd been goosed. "Oh, chopped liver and chopsticks. It's Wine o'clock." He grabbed a bottle of Moscato from a nearly empty cabinet and stumbled against the kitchen table. "Oooh, weee. I am pixilated." He spoke into the speaker. "On my way, your worships!"

Winnie snatched the bottle, holding it by the neck like a club. "Let me. I have things to discuss with the Intervening Incident. Excuse me—your *house guests*."

"Don't go, Ms Winnie," said Malvous. "You shouldn't even let them know you're here. They may be beautiful, but they are not very nice."

Righteous fury surged in Winnie. "Well, I can be a two-ton bitch too, if necessary. Particularly in the face of no-count Muses."

"They're goddesses." Finch set a hand on Winnie's shoulder. "They are more powerful than all of us."

"Don't be so sure." Winnie headed to the hallway. "Where am I going?"

"Follow the singing," said Felicitous in a small voice. "Post naps they celebrate and sing."

Winnie glanced between Finch and the brownies. "I'm doing this alone?"

Malvous was trembling, but he got to his feet. "Certainly not! Of course I will assist!"

"Don't even think about it." Finch poked the brownie in the shoulder. "Your place is here."

Malvous shrugged him off. "You're not the boss of me!"

"I literally am!" Finch shoved the brownie.

A moment later they were flapping hands at one another.

Winnie rolled her eyes, then cocked her ear for singing. "Never send a Seelie to do a woman's job."

"*Unseelie!*" Finch cried, as one of Malvous' hands connected with his ear. "Ouch! You—"

The last thing Winnie heard before she aimed for the loose Muses was the sound of breaking crockery.

Chapter 17

No Accounting for Them

WHEN MUSES SING, there is almost no sound in the universe equal to it. Even if they are singing 1980s hair metal tunes. And though there is no sound in the universe equal to it, that doesn't mean the singing is *good*.

All of this made finding the Muses easy for Finch after Winnie had departed. Once he and Malvous quit swiping at one another, he straightened out the pinstriped vest he wore over the secondhand T-shirt Winnie had given him, fluffed out his red-tinted hair and grabbed a bag of corn chips labeled Snack-Ems. Then he limped down the corridor, straight into screechy, off-key strains of 'Every Rose Has Its Thorn.'

"Stay back!" he shouted at Malvous, jabbing in the air with his cane and simultaneously wishing his conscripted assistant would disobey.

Malvous said nothing, standing near the kitchen exit with fists on his hips.

"I mean it! I've got this!" Finch continued shouting. "Don't make me warn you again!"

Malvous did not move.

Fine, thought Finch. *I'll go alone. I've already survived an onslaught of Muse inspiration in my head, and you don't see* me *hunched over a typewriter. Even if my head feels like it's full of potato peelings and scrambled eggs. I just need to get enough information to add to my report. And maybe I should make sure Winnie is all right. She is a Main Character, after all. That's all that matters.*

He wasn't sure how much of that he believed.

A tiny part of him suggested: *You could just tell the Muses to leave. Imagine if you got them out of Seaview Haven and the town* stopped *falling apart. Wouldn't* SCN *appreciate that* more?

Shut up, brain, he ordered. *Unseelie don't fix things. We break them.*

He found Winnie standing in front of a set of barn-style sliding doors. Her eyes were wide. "You came."

"Meh," he said. "Didn't want to get flapped to death by Malvous." He rubbed his temples. "And someone has to speak with the ladies. Aside from them, I'm the closest thing to a functional god in this house—"

Winnie snorted. Then she laughed. She bent over, gasping for air.

"It's not *that* funny." Finch puffed up, indignant. "I am magical!"

Winnie righted herself, hiccupping once. She set a hand on the door. Finch expected her to barrel inside, but the outrage that had powered her down the hallway moments earlier was gone. "Look, Finch. I talk a good game, but I'm terrified," she said. "I have the strangest feeling in my stomach. It's like being hungry, but also heartburn."

"Understandable."

"Why are they *doing* this to him? Who decides when he's written a proper story, anyway?"

Finch shrugged. "We'll get that information. But not until one of us opens these doors." He gave Winnie a stiff pat on the back, possibly the first time he'd ever consciously reassured anyone.

"I shouldn't have been so dismissive," Winnie said. "Maybe we could have had monsters on Mackerel Street.

But… I get paranoid. What if someone else is the better writer in the room? Did I ever tell you about this fight Eve and I had once?"

"You're stalling," said Finch. Now he was getting rattled. "Tell it to the Muses."

The music on the other side of the door paused.

Behind them came soft tapping. Finch and Winnie turned. They saw Siggy in the window of a bedroom across the hall, drumming her fingers on the pane. Their eyes met, and she waved, then made a bizarre gesture with her hands. Her thumbs touched, and fingers drew wide. Then she fluttered her hands away.

"What is that strange child doing?" Finch wondered.

Winnie wiped at an eye, mimicking the gesture. "A Winnie-bird," she whispered, folding her fluttering fingers over her heart. Siggy cupped her hands and dragged them backward, implying they should leave the house. When Winnie shook her head, Siggy's shoulders slumped.

Finch closed the door to the spare room.

Eddie Van Halen's solo guitar wrangling declared that the next song had started—Van Halen's 'Hot for Teacher.' Finch's trembling hand hovered over the Muse room's door handle. For once, he had no idea what was about to happen—which was kind of exciting. A world of ideas had woken up behind his eyes, and the longer he lived with it the better he could filter the strange imagery. He was getting comfortable with it. He thought of Neal, tormented in his office, possibly with the same whirlwind inside his head. Why was Finch able to cope? Could it be that Unseelie processed Muse inspiration better than Seelie?

Once upon a time in a land far away, he thought, and bit down hard on his tongue. *Stop it!*

"Concentrate," he said, then grabbed the handle.

The door slid open at that exact moment, dragging Finch to the side.

"Felicitous! At last!" A plump woman in a purple tracksuit and a French braid of long hair greeted them. Her name, *Euterpe*, was embroidered on a top left pocket. "Goodness, you're not brownies."

"An excellent observation," said Finch, regaining his balance. "I am, in fact—"

"Corn chips!" The Muse lurched at the snack bag in his hand. When she spotted what Winnie carried, she lurched with the other hand. "Wine!"

Neither Winnie nor Finch released their property. "We want to come in!" grimaced Finch, holding tight.

The goddess pulled harder, emitting musical notes unrelated to the karaoke. "Muses only!" she groaned. "Release the Snack-Ems!"

Winnie and Finch exchanged a look and let go at the same moment. Euterpe stumbled backward into the room, thumping against the sofa, giving them a split second to limp/stride inside. The doors slammed closed, and the Muses stared at the newcomers. The newcomers stared at the Muses. A long, drawn out silence was filled only by the karaoke instrumental version of 'Hot for Teacher.'

Finch gazed around the room. One Muse, standing with a limp microphone in her hand. Euterpe, peeling the foil from the top of the wine bottle, a busted-open bag of Snack-Ems littering the floor. Two more Muses sprawled on a C-shaped, oversized couch. Small side tables dotted the room, topped with vases filled with flowers, snack bowls, and at least one odd-looking black box. The far wall was dominated by an enormous flat-screen television so old it wasn't even powered by water. On the screen several animated humans were passionately playing instruments, with lyrics superimposed over their faces.

All of the Muses were dressed alike, in velour tracksuits of different colors. The plush fabric shifted around their bodies as if it never touched their skin. Their striking, lovely faces were similarly bright, and they all had wavy or curled hair that rippled like forest streams, despite the headbands, braids or barrettes holding it back. Between the cascading tracksuits and waving hair, each woman appeared to be moving even as she held still.

Finch had never been this close to a Muse, much less four. He was thankful he'd had about an hour in this house to process the word and image salad in his head because now, here, in their presence that whole effect had doubled, maybe trebled. He felt as though thoughts were running out of his nose, his ears, his eyes, his—well, everywhere. All the shortbread in the world would barely take the edge off this.

"Gosh, brownies are getting scruffier by the day." The singer in blue put down the mic and headed over to Finch and Winnie. The other Muses huddled together, whispering.

Winnie stood unmoving, as if she'd been hit by a block of wood.

"Not a brownie," insisted Finch. "Unseelie! And my name is—" Forgetting himself, he spoke his True Name.

Winnie started as her hair sprouted patches of lilac and twisted around on itself. "Hey! Ouch!" She grabbed her scalp.

"Whoops." Finch made a small gesture at her head. The twisting stopped, but the color remained. "Er, I can be Finch in the presence of humans. Which she is. Obviously. I'm from the Seelie Court Network and I need—"

"A human! In the walls of this house!" The Muse in blue's embroidered name read *Calliope*. She assessed Winnie with a quick up-and-down glance. "You must have enormous fortitude to have breached the wards, the gates, the guards—"

"Felicitous let us in," said Winnie.

Finch cleared his throat. "She's not important right now. I'm from SCN and I have been tasked with—"

Winnie bumped him with her shoulder. "I am *very* important! I need to ask you all about—"

Calliope held up a hand and their voices cut out. "I'm delighted you are here," said the Muse, taking hold of Winnie's hand. "Over there are Clio and Thalia—" She pointed to the Muses on the sofa. "Clearly you've met Eutie. The Others should be around later." She tilted her head. "Now, allow Me to guess who—"

"That's Winnifred Arrowmaker," said red-suited Clio, scooping up cards she'd been playing solitaire with. "Can't You *smell* the writer in her?"

"I showered just this morning," said Winnie, feeling dazed again. "You four are *breathtakingly* lovely."

"Oh, she's darling." Eutie's voice trilled a happy tune as she wrestled with the wine bottle.

Calliope took a long, deep sniff of Winnie's neck. "Ah, You are correct, sweet sister! Ink. Metal. Wood. Graphite. And"—she took a second deep breath—"vodka with lemonade!"

Pop! The cork came free. The Muses applauded. Calliope peered at Winnie like one might a slice of chocolate cake. "You're the Seelie's pet writer!"

Winnie blinked. "I'm nobody's pet. And Neal and I are—"

Thalia made kissing noises. "We know. We've read his dreadful poetry. Your name comes up all the time in his awful, incomprehensible writing. But now that you're here, you can tell Us more! Coherently! You must have *wonderful* stories!"

"*Ladies!*" Finch shouted, climbing up on the couch. "A moment of your extremely valuable time!"

"Yeah, yeah, We heard you." Clio glared at him. "SCN. Evaluation. So what?"

Finch sputtered. "Do you not know what is going on in Seaview Haven? Or any of the TROPE Towns?"

"Ugh, boring." Eutie poured wine for everyone. "We don't go out, except into the backyard. Anyone We want, We bring here. Who wants to wander around this dopey made-up little village, anyway?"

"It's falling apart!" Finch gasped. "And it's probably falling apart because of *you*!"

"Halitosis and hog feathers," said Calliope, guiding Winnie to the sofa. "We aren't bothering anyone."

Finch slid to the ground, clenching his fists. He'd get them to take him seriously. Raising his hands, he gestured at the television and sent it a tiny spell. It flipped off. He shot a glance at the Will O' the Wisps shining in the lights, and they blinked into darkness. The room dimmed. For good measure, he gave himself a personal glow-up and radiated warm brightness into the room. "Now, as I was saying—"

Clio snapped her fingers, and everything came back on again. Finch dimmed. "Stupid little parlor tricks. Are you going to get on Our nerves like the last Seelie who walked in here, little fae?"

"He's not Seelie," said Winnie. "He's nothing like Neal."

Several Muses giggled.

Calliope handed Winnie some wine. "Doubtful, but if so, it might be a good thing. Now, on to more interesting topics. Winnifred, you are the most creative, talented, prolific writer in this entire village. Possibly on this side of the Veil. You are a welcome breath of fresh air, a creature We barely need to inspire to turn out good stories."

"Goodness." Winnie's voice turned soft as a marshmallow, and she took a sip of the wine. Whatever moxie she'd had earlier was fading fast under the lavish attention of the Muses. She took a quick, deep breath.

"It's very kind of you to say, but I'm here to talk about Neal."

"Oh, bother," said Calliope. "That fae needed a time out, so We gave him one."

Finch kept his volume just shy of shouting. "This T-Town is falling apart. It needs to be restructured or eliminated. I am here to make a report." He tilted his head. This time, he would make them *truly* see what power he had. Closing his eyes, he summoned a spell of removal, of empty places. He would take all of them to a green, blank Veil field—

The spell launched.

Grass sprang up under his feet.

The room remained the same.

Everyone was staring at him again. Finch coughed. "I meant to do that."

Rising from the couch, Clio set a hand on his shoulder, cutting and shuffling her deck of cards with one hand. "Finchy, Finchy, Finchy." She steered him to the sliding doors as Calliope stroked Winnie's hair and the two spoke quietly to one another. "Let's have a little chat."

At the doors, she lowered her voice. "Don't waste your spell energy here. Surely you know that Seelie are"—she held up the deck of cards—"a full house in the poker game of immortal power. Strong hand, not strong enough. Not when playing with goddesses. We're a straight flush, every time. We *are* the house. And no point in trying to bluff Us. You can't win."

"I'm not trying to *win* anything." He folded his arms. "But you lot are making trouble. You can't just bind up a SMD in a *godspell* and not expect it to cause problems in his town. Or that it won't get back to SCN. Because that's totally going in my report—"

Clio's grip on his shoulder tightened. "Now, why would you want to do that? We're having a lovely time here. You're not looking to get godspelled too, are you?"

Finch licked his lips.

"I sense We're already in that little brain of yours, rattling around. You're just *itching* to get some of those stories out there, aren't you?" Clio made a soft chuckling sound. "The thing is, you *are* just like him, Finchy. Do you know why Neal Bartleby is stuck in that room?" She paused dramatically. "He stormed in here and made *demands* of Us. Insisted We help him write a story. That We show him how a Seelie could finally, after all these centuries, write a tale that would put humans to shame. He said it was Our *duty* to serve him in his own town, and in exchange he'd have snacks and beverages delivered. He was quite insistent, and quite obnoxious, about it all. Even if We weren't on gal-cation, We couldn't tolerate that kind of attitude."

The grip grew tighter, and Finch's arm was starting to go numb, but he couldn't move. "Callie was going to banish him to Hades for a few seasons, but the rest of Us—well, mostly Me—thought it was more fitting to give him *exactly what he wanted*. You've heard of the quaint human theory that if you put a monkey at a typewriter for an infinite number of years, he'll produce anything, including the works of Shakespeare?"

"Would that be in English, Greek, Gaelic or Ape?"

Clio batted him on the head with the deck of cards. "Well, We're giving Neal exactly that. He has to stay at that typewriter until he writes a decent story, and We'll stay here until that happens. I love a good game, and Neal was the one who set the rules on this one. He's getting bombarded with whatever passive inspiration We give off, and all of Us have infinity to wait. Anyone who can't last that long is a mere mortal."

Finch squirmed. He thought about Winnie. Siggy. And lemonade. Of using RICE on his ankle. "Your game is messing up the entire T-Town system, though. They really need you at SCN."

"If Our brief break from Our agreed-upon Muse Central duties causes this TROPE Town system to crumple, then perhaps the whole construct of Seelie entertainment was never going to last. You all had a good century or two's run."

"It's not a quick break, though. It's been two years."

She laughed. "How ridiculous! Two years is *nothing*. A T-Town is *nothing*. They are all flashes of light in the vast universe of time. We are barely getting started."

Finch's face was red hot. He'd never felt so insignificant, so unmoored.

Clio leaned in closer. "One last piece of advice: stop fooling yourself. Go home. Plant a new garden. Make amends with your witchy friend—"

"How can you know—" Finch stared at her in horror.

"Goddess of memory." She tapped her chest with the deck of cards. "Think I don't know *your* timeline inside and out? Put away your grand delusions. Be who you really are. Lean into that. Most of Us can see right through you, anyway."

With that, the doors slid open, and she gave him a gentle shove. They latched quickly behind him, and he was back in the hallway.

Finch stared at those closed doors, as lost and confused as Winnie had seemed moments earlier before they'd entered. The endless churn of notions, thoughts and ideas in his head seemed quiet compared to what he'd just been told. He'd gone in there with a righteous assignment from SCN, packed full of pure intent and energy, and prepared to lob spells. He'd been jonesing for a battle—or at least some kind of clarity. Instead, they'd done the worst thing to him possible.

They'd dismissed him.

Finch slumped to the floor. Even the whooshing ideas in his head were no comfort. A moment later, the singing started up again, and he recognized a new voice joining in.

Winnie's.

Chapter 18

Cards on the Table

TIME PASSED. WINNIE sang karaoke song after karaoke song. Drank a bottle of wine. Consumed her weight in Snack-Ems. Wrote down several ideas for future novels in a notebook provided for her. Every time she thought she should really get focused and talk seriously about why she was there, another diversion popped up. She'd say to herself, *Get on their good side. You don't want them to leave you forever, do you?* And then she'd succumb again to the attentions of the Muses, which were pretty damn impossible to ignore.

After a difficult-to-approximate amount of time, she collapsed onto the couch alongside Euterpe and Calliope and pushed away yet another glass of something fizzy and alcoholic. "Whew," she gasped. "I might require a nap."

"Lightweight." Calliope poked her arm.

"Crash anywhere," said Clio, who was now playing poker with the remaining Muses and Terpsichore, who'd arrived when Winnie wasn't paying attention. They were using jelly beans to wager. "Felicitous will bring whatever you need."

I need Neal. I need you to leave.

But she didn't say those things. Instead, Winnie stared at the ceiling, watching the Will O' the Wisps spinning, glowing. How had this happened? What was she doing here on this exceedingly comfortable sofa, alongside actual *Muses*? When had it gotten so dark outside? Half drunk, half sleepy, she blinked at the ceiling as Calliope began combing her hair with a light, practiced touch.

The Wisps spun some more. They flitted around in their own little bubble world. They fluttered like wings.

Like fingers making shadow puppets on the wall.

Like Winnie-birds.

Winnie sat up, all the blood rushing to her head. "Ooof," she said, as Calliope's comb got stuck in a knot. "You ladies have been distracting me!"

"Done Our best," said Clio, pushing forward three jelly beans. "Call," she told her fellow players. Glancing over a shoulder, she said sourly, "Now you're going to be boring again."

"Guess so," said Winnie, trying to center herself. Being in a house occupied by Muses was like being a kid again, spinning around and around until dizziness knocked her to the floor.

Feels like taking drugs! Eve shouted when they'd done that during recess one afternoon.

How'd you know? Winnie had shot back.

Eve had deadpanned, *I never told you I've been hooked on phonics since first grade?*

Eve could always come up with a great line, or a great idea. She could have been a writer, too. Sometimes, Winnie felt a little guilty about that.

But—not now. She had to get her mind straight, not linger on what might have been. She knew she shouldn't be enjoying too much time with these Muses; they were holding Neal captive! Siggy relied on her, too. And probably the whole of Seaview Haven. Winnie looked around the room and frowned. "When did Finch leave?"

Calliope and Euterpe shared a glance. "The silly spark-headed fae?" Euterpe asked. "Ages ago."

"Days!" chuckled Calliope.

Well, that couldn't be true. They were having fun with her again. All the more reason to speak up. "Calliope."

"Callie, please!" The Muse tilted her head and smiled indulgently. Winnie almost thought she was going to get her cheek pinched.

"About Neal Bartleby."

"Told you!" cried Clio. "Here we go."

"Please release him from whatever game you're playing," said Winnie. Thinking of him trapped in that whirling dervish of an office sobered her quickly. "It's been so long. I miss him. I need him."

Callie stroked Winnie's face with the back of her hand. "Aww, poor Winnifred. I feel that. I truly do. But…" She gestured across the room at a small, matte-black box on a side table between the sofa sectionals. "Well, it's rather out of Our hands."

Winnie had seen the box earlier and thought it might be a humidor or hold wine bottles. She hadn't given it any thought. But now, she noted that it vibrated gently without disturbing anything on the table. It even seemed a bit blurry. "What's out of your hands? That's just a box."

"Just a box!" chirped Euterpe. "Hardly! It's the best box in the world! Pandora's Box™!"

Of course it is, thought Winnie. "I think that one's been opened already. Humanity's been cursed a long time."

"Oh, you," Euterpe flapped a hand at her. "This isn't the *original* Box, of course. Pandora went on to make a *killing* trademarking the name. PB Inc. puts out a new color out every year, and tastemakers on ArachneWeb go bonkers to acquire them all."

"What do you keep inside, then?" But even as she said it, Winnie had suspicions.

As one, Calliope, Euterpe, Clio, and Thalia leaned together and sang, "Got a wish? Got a prayer? Put that curse behind a wall! Anything you want, anything you own—Pandora's Box™ holds it all!" They giggled behind cupped hands. "Everyone knows *that* jingle!"

Winnie looked between the Muses, and the box, and back again.

Clio lifted the box and set it on the coffee table. "G'head, Winnifred. Open it up."

Winnie lay her hand on the edge of the box. It was surprisingly warm, and the vibration increased the moment she came in contact with it. "This isn't a trick, is it?"

Callie shook her head, and for the first time she looked a little resigned. "No, it's quite exactly what it seems to be. That's part of the problem."

Another problem? Winnie couldn't seem to get to the bottom of the troubles in Seaview Haven. With gentle fingers, she lifted the lid and a glowing, purple neon interior sent light into the room. The color shifted to blue, then green, then orange. But amid the color-shifting glow was the real surprise: a roundish, loose ball of pale yarn that twisted around itself like entangled snakes. It held its ball-like shape and position within the box, touching none of the walls. It was ridiculous, beautiful, and terrifying, all at once. "Wait. This isn't… the godspell?"

"Say hello," said Clio.

"To the—" Winnie blinked. "Hello, um, Godspell. Pleasure to meet you."

The glowing yarn pulsed once, then a second time.

Calliope lowered the lid and returned the box to the table. "As you intelligently surmised, that is *the* godspell We have recently woven. At first it seemed enormously exciting to create—none of Us had knitted in eons. But it was the best way to complete Our agreement with your Seelie. He contributed a few threads as well. This way, Our desires became entangled. Humans still use ink and paper to complete contracts—well, this is Our version. And once woven, the godspell will not release its weavers until all contributors are satisfied."

"*Truly* satisfied," Clio underscored. "Godspells know when you're cheating."

Euterpe nodded. "Fake a resolution, and you only make it *more* entangled."

"The Box is for safekeeping," said Clio. "Seemed like a good idea at the time. Mayor Bartleby asked for something from Us, in exchange for leaving Us alone on our gal-cation. We said We'd depart after appreciating a proper story, written by himself."

Calliope glared at her sister. "And now We're as entangled with this bargain as he is."

"Hoisted with Our Own petards," said Thalia. "A most unusual sensation. "

"The duty to complete is in his court," said Calliope. "Or, rather, office."

"But he *can't* complete it," said Winnie. "It's like if I made you a bet to keep me locked up until I could hold my breath for a half hour. It isn't about being willing. Or talented. Or even inspired. It's not physically possible."

Clio chuckled. "You might be right there, mortal. We've made wiser decisions before. But wine was involved, and he'd also kind of ticked Us off."

"A pinkie swear would have sufficed!" said Winnie.

"Clio likes to flex Our powers when She's angry," said Calliope. "Errors were made."

Realization dawned in Winnie. "So you all *can't* leave here? Not until he delivers?"

"Our other sweet sisters can come and go as They please," said Calliope. "They were not here when the deal was struck. But We four... well. Our gal-cation is stuck in a somewhat *permanent* status."

"At least We've got lots of wine," said Clio.

"That was the problem in the first place," said Calliope.

Felicitous knocked, and the door slid open. He wandered in silently, delivering hot towels, more wine and sandwiches with their crusts cut off. He met Winnie's eyes briefly but said nothing. She did get a hot towel, and wiped it across her face, feeling immediately fresher. After that, he offered everyone shoulder rubs, his strong fingers kneading them all like loaves of bread. No one addressed him directly, and he never spoke a word.

Calliope stared at Winnie as if she were trying to perform a new, curious trick. Winnie decided to try another tack. "Doesn't so much free time get repetitive?" asked Winnie. "What do you do all day?"

"Oh!" cried Thalia, putting her feet up on the coffee table. "We do *everything*. Melpomene, Erato, Polyhymnia, Urania—they come over frequently and we have oodles of grand ideas. Like—Talent Show! Remember that?"

Calliope nodded enthusiastically. She explained that some weeks ago, each sister had summoned their greatest, still-living modern inspirational success story. Joining them in the living room had been a Puerto Rican poet, a Ukrainian scientist, a Nigerian author, and a country rock guitarist from Nashville. The humans had stood side by side, disoriented and awed. Some were still in their pajamas. They'd been required to demonstrate their expertise, and the sisters voted on which Muse had done the best inspiration. Then the people were sent home.

"That night, they all imagined they'd had a very vivid dream," Thalia continued. "Isn't that fun? It's all fuel for the fire, NBD."

Goddesses, not humans, Winnie had to remind herself. *No better than aliens who nest in your stomach and hug your face. They don't have human consciences. Or hearts.* That was the big difference between them and the one Seelie she'd known. Neal had both heart and conscience.

"What We haven't done lately," said Clio, scooping forward her winnings, having cleaned out her sisters of their jelly beans, "is heard a great, original story. We had hoped the Seelie would have one for Us by now, but..." She shrugged, looking at the slush pile. "That's why We're so pleased you're here. *You* will know stories We haven't yet been told. You must!"

Winnie shook her head. "Oh, don't look at me. I'm no Scheherazade. I wrote some mildly successful books back home, then got spirited here. I haven't written a word since Neal's been... gone. But you five inspire *everything*. How can you not know every story ever written already? You inspired all the ideas."

"A common misconception," said Calliope. "Inspiring is not *doing*. Generating ideas is not *storytelling*. We do not dance or sing, at least not very well. We do not write anything worth reading. There is a heavenly spark within each of Us that, in contact with all creatures, causes different reactions. Humans are wonderful receptors and projectors—you absorb Our inspiration and distill it into something uniquely your own and make it special. This is in part because you are aware of your own mortality. There is a tragedy lying in wait for each one of you, but you go on. You *live*. You *create*. You *exist*."

Finch had said something like that about Seelie while they were in Neal's office.

"You can tell Us incredible stories that We have never heard before because you are human," Callie continued. "We have invited you here to stay with Us for that reason."

Winnie didn't recall getting an invitation. "And if I do?"

"Then We will celebrate you!" Calliope tossed her hands in the air.

"And if I don't?"

The doors to the living room slid open. "You may, of course, depart at any time," said Callie.

"I won't. I can't—not without Neal."

"Excellent. Because We won't ask you back after that."

The doors slid shut again. Clio leaned over her sister, toward Winnie, and fanned out her deck of cards. Instinctively Winnie took one: the Jack of Spades. "Stay, but don't waste your life on waiting for him," she said. "Seelie can only be receptors. He knew that going in. But your main squeeze got a bright idea that he could be more. I think he was jealous of *you*. He wanted to be at least as good as you are with his words, because you denied him a story. Pretty selfish of him, if you ask me."

Considering the results of Neal's insistence on provoking the Muses, Winnie almost agreed with her. But her heart tore to think that she was the cause of all of this entanglement. "Oh, I don't know."

"What magic did you ask him for?" Clio asked.

"I-I didn't." It had never occurred to Winnie to ask. "And I don't think he would have given me it, anyway."

Clio fanned out the cards again. This time Winnie chose the Queen of Hearts.

"There you go," said Clio. "Try not to stay too hung up on him. Hardly any writers—human or otherwise—get to stay in any TROPE Town for more than a handful of years. Fae get bored quickly, even the good ones, and they live by whims. The minute you're more trouble than you're worth, you're out. He'd have replaced you soon enough."

Each sentence landed in Winnie's gut like a stone. Yet that couldn't be the truth. In a soft voice, she said, "I think I'll take that nap now." She curled up on one end of the sofa, turning her back on the Muses.

"Excellent," said Calliope. "Anyone for midnight badminton?"

Chapter 19

Pardon the Interruption

SIGGY STARED AT Finch. The fae lay face down and motionless among the living room sofa pillows. He had one sock off and one sock on. His red-streaked gray hair was both matted and flattened. He smelled like burnt toast.

Outside, summer bees hummed, and birds twittered in the afternoon stillness. Deeper in the house, Malvous was cobbling together dinner, which Siggy was not anticipating. In the days since they'd returned from Mayor Neal's house without Winnie, the brownie had done his best to keep things running smoothly, but meals were not his strong suit. Anyone who considered tomato chunks slathered in mayonnaise and marshmallows a palatable main course had a lot of learning to do.

He didn't have a lot to work with, Siggy understood. Winnie's garden was picked over; her collection of home-canned vegetables and jams was nearly depleted. Malvous would open the refrigerator or wander out the back door several times a day in the hope that something new had appeared but usually came back swearing his own brand of swears.

"Jackfruit tootsies!" was Siggy's favorite, but she rarely smiled at it. Everything felt ten times scarier without Winnie around.

Folding her arms, the girl twisted her mouth up, and down.

"And he's been like this how long?" Next to Siggy, Martin ran a hand through his hair. He'd rolled in a few minutes ago and was expected to stay for dinner. Siggy was grateful he was here and decided that it was time to bring him into the circle.

Assuming he would believe her.

"Since they got booted from the mayor's house."

"Five days? Cheeze. How's he not dead?" Martin tossed a pillow onto Finch. "Or is he?"

Siggy had a lot of explaining to do. "He's not. His kind don't die, I don't think. Anyway, he doesn't stink like a dead thing."

Martin was silent for a moment. Then: "Y'know, it's been that long since we saw each other. Five days is a lot."

"I know. Sorry. I was hiding out." The day she'd lost Winnie, Siggy had sat for hours outside the mayor's house, mentally flicking away the small urges it sent at her to leave. They'd felt like someone poking her brain. *You have homework! Martin's out there! Take a nap! The house is on fire!* But she'd battled every impulse because each minute she expected Miz Winnie would walk out that front door with Mayor Neal. And if Winnie's house burned down or monkeys took over running it or homework went undone, those would be challenges. But Siggy had priorities.

After several hours of waiting, the door had opened, but only Finch and Malvous had stepped out. They'd conferred a long time on the porch. Miz Winnie had been nowhere in sight. The last Siggy had seen of her was when they'd caught each other's glances through the window and made Winnie-birds together. Now it was as if the house had swallowed her.

Malvous had informed Siggy that Miz Winnie had been *detained.*

Finch had been strangely quiet.

Siggy then spent several moments uselessly pounding on the door and ringing the bell, but no one had opened it again. Malvous had guided her and Finch back to Winnie's house, where Siggy had raced to her room and had a proper crying jag. Mama and Papa had driven off and left her behind. Now Miz Winnie was lost to her, too. The inside of her chest hurt so much she wondered if she was having a heart attack. But the next morning she woke up alive and hungry and a little angrier about everything. She continued to attend the Counting, telling everyone Miz Winnie was around but had a cold—so none of her students would come by—and she was resting up.

Martin had never bought this story. While Siggy hid away in the house, he'd roll into the shade of a nearby tree and read a book until dinnertime, then wheel away. Siggy would see him outside and want to tell him everything, but where to start? The parts she knew (about what Seaview Haven really was, who Finch and Malvous really were) required words she couldn't even say. The other part (like why Miz Winnie hadn't come out of the mayor's house) she didn't understand.

So Siggy watched him outside her window, heart heavy.

Then this afternoon, she'd realized he was pining for her the way she pined for Winnie, and waved him in. Martin had wheeled up on the ramp outside Winnie's door and they'd sat on the porch for a while.

Five days is enough for anybody, he'd said. *Whatever's going on, you gotta deal me in.*

Everything is going wrong, she'd said. *And parts of it don't make any sense.*

Then tell me the parts that make sense.

Not a lot of them do. But that gave her a place to start. She told him what Winnie had told her—at least, the parts she could tell. When she couldn't use the right words, she found ways to dance around them. *Seelie* wasn't allowed in her vocabulary, nor was *magic*. But then she had a bright idea and pulled out a piece of chalk. Paper was too hard to come by, so she drew on the wall what she wanted: magical creatures with wings and wands, transforming frogs to princes and all the stuff that came out of the books they'd read as kids. Then she'd pointed at Finch and Malvous.

Finch and Malvous are referees?

Sort of. Different kinds, but yeah. You're close enough.

And when we say football, *it's actually a real thing? It exists?*

Now you're getting it.

Martin had taken things surprisingly well. He'd blinked a lot. Rolled up and down the porch. Then come back to her. *Look Sig, after everything we've seen these last couple of years, I'm less shocked than you'd think. I knew there were things we couldn't science out, no matter how hard we tried. What's that line from Shakespeare about there being more things in Heaven and Earth—*

Than are dreamt of in your philosophy, Siggy finished. There'd been a sparkling, charged moment of silence between them, and something inside Siggy turned over. Martin shone to her more brightly than ever.

So she'd had the courage to tell him more. About Miz Winnie going into Mayor Neal's house, ignoring her at the window, and not coming out. About how according to Malvous there were Greek goddesses called Muses in there, playing games. At last, Siggy brought him over to Finch, who had remained on the couch, unmoving and unspeaking, since they'd left the mayor's house.

"When he gets up, I bet the pillows stick to him," Siggy said now.

Martin prodded the Unseelie with his cane.

"Mmph." Finch spoke to the cushions.

"That's the most you'll get from him." Siggy folded her arms again. "I tried yelling at him, tickling him, putting his hand in warm water—"

Martin snickered. "He wet himself?"

"I don't think *referees* go to the bathroom. Or have to eat." She sighed. "At least Malvous is here, so I'm not totally alone."

"I can't believe Miz Winnie left you."

"Apparently, she's 'looking after' the Mayor. But I don't think Malvous really knows, either."

"The Mayor still needs a nurse? And oh, yeah, Miz Winnie's not a nurse!"

Siggy shrugged.

Martin shook his head. "This is stupid. Somebody has to do something about Nowheresville. It'll be year two soon and people are *mad*. Like, they used to be scared, but now they're scared and angry. There's not enough food, even from the stuff people are growing, and there aren't as many fish to pull in. Cap'n Roberts said at Counting that he's been hearing a 'glug glug' sound out in the Bay."

"The Kraken?" Siggy felt sick. That was all Nowheresville needed, a giant sea monster rising up to smash things.

"More like in the bathtub after a wash. Water going down the drain."

Siggy chewed a nail. "All I know is Miz Winnie is in the house and isn't coming out. Malvous makes it sound like she might be under a *stadium*."

"Not an actual stadium."

Siggy shook her head and pointed at the wand doing a transformation on the wall: *a spell*. She'd tried writing forbidden words once, but the letters had reconfigured. Pictures seemed to stick, though.

"Because that would be heavy," said Martin. "A whole stadium and all."

For the first time in days, Siggy laughed.

Martin laughed back. Then he said, "You should make that noise more."

Siggy stared at the wall because it was too hard to look at him. The funny moment faded and all she actually knew was that Winnie had chosen Neal—and whoever else was in that house—over her. Over the town. Her chest hurt again, and she knew she would have more angry dreams tonight.

Martin rested a hand on her shoulder. "They could break my arms, and I wouldn't leave you all alone, Sig."

His touch traced sparking heat across her body like fractals expanding. *Oh, jackfruit tootsies*, she thought. *I might love this idiot*. Not that she'd ever say those words. Too embarrassing. Plus, he would definitely laugh. "So—" Her voice cracked. "I don't know what happens next. Do we tell people everything? Or keep quiet? Did you tell Big Dad Dean anything?"

"Not a good idea. He'd just tell the rest of the town."

"Miz Winnie can't have her cold forever," though.

Martin thought about it. "People might not ask. They're pretty caught up in their own stuff these days. If anybody asks, we can just say she's helping Mayor Neal get well." He turned to Finch and gave the Unseelie a poke. "What about him? Does he move at all?"

"Not really. And he was worse when he first got home." Five days earlier, Finch had locked himself in the bathroom and moaned, banging his head against the wall every two minutes. When no one had intervened, he'd moved his pity party to the living room and fallen on the couch, bewailing his uselessness. Finally, Siggy had told him she needed to study, and could he keep it down? Since then he mumbled into the cushions every so often, alternating with an occasional gigantic sigh. She'd started using him for a pillow.

Siggy felt stuck, about all of it. She'd been scared so long she almost didn't know what it felt like *not* to have the weight of the world on her shoulders. But being scared all the time wasn't exactly scary. Scary stuff became a dull roar in the background that slipped into a mental filing cabinet, one whose drawers could pop out at unexpected moments. At those times, Siggy would have to stop and remember to breathe. Mostly, though, she drifted through the days.

"All right," said Martin. "So if the *referees* in this game are going to take a back seat, it's going to be up to the real heroes to figure the next part out. Us."

Finch mumbled something into the pillows.

Siggy's insides felt like they were melting. Martin was so sincere, so real in that moment—there was no joking in him. His deep-set hazel eyes even had a flicker of fear in them, which was the last thing she wanted for him. "I'm only fourteen," she said. "You're fifteen. We're not supposed to have to make these hard decisions."

"True. But I'm fifteen and you're fourteen. We're old enough to handle tough stuff. You with me?"

Siggy nodded so hard she thought her head might fall off.

Martin leaned closer. He smelled so much better than the burnt toast odor Finch still gave off. They leaned together, drawn like magnets, alongside the prone Unseelie on the couch. Siggy was closer to Martin than she'd ever been before. She could see soft fuzz on his upper lip.

Just then, Malvous' face popped up from behind the couch. "Soup's on!"

Nuts, thought Siggy.

* * *

MALVOUS CARRIED A bowl to the table, his nose tickling with the aroma of warm nuts, garlic, and Parmesan cheese. Then he returned to the stove and decanted a pot of roasted crickets into a bowl. They clattered with a delicious sound.

Siggy would probably hate this meal—she'd turned up her nose at everything he'd made thus far—but as a Bro in a strange land, he had to wing it. This afternoon, Siggy had brought home eggs from the post-Counting market, so he'd used what was at hand. Maybe it was right, maybe not, but either way, terrible culinary skills were not his fault. Malvous' major had been in Hallways, Ceilings and Baseboards. Kitchen Wizardry was one of his weaker areas.

The table had a guest tonight: Martin, who sat next to Siggy with a kind of electricity bouncing between them. "I see Mr Finch is not joining us again," Malvous said, reaching into the bowl of hot food and scooping out portions of eggs topped with peanut butter, garlic, and cheese. He crumbled up a few crickets and sprinkled them on top.

Martin goggled at the bowl. "Is that—"

"It is!" Malvous cried, delighted to show off his skills to a newcomer. "Eggs à la peanut butter. The insects are an unusual accompaniment for humans but for Bros they are complementary—" He stopped. Both younglings' faces had crumpled. "I thought you liked both eggs *and* peanut butter!"

"Not together!" Siggy pushed her chair back. "Martin, you like mayonnaise sandwiches?"

"I guess," he said. "Is there any un-cricketed peanut butter left?"

Malvous' stomach sank. He was as bad at being a Bro in this house as Finch was at being Unseelie in this town. His lip quivered and he made an unintentional whimper.

How had he gotten here? A little over a week ago, he'd been happily mopping his floor at SCN and dreaming of nothing more grandiose than holding hands with Foxtacular. Now he was stuck in this odd T-Town doing human child-sitting with the most annoying Unseelie investigator ever. Oh, he liked Siggy well enough, nearly as much as he liked Winnie, and for a brownie who'd had almost no human contact before, he felt that he was being pretty brave. But they were so strange to him. He had a life back home—a life he couldn't return to until Seaview Haven was fixed.

Or ended.

Meanwhile, Malvous missed his little cubbyhole in the wall behind the 227th floor's dragon-fueled boiler room. It had always been warm and cozy, and he could chat with the fire-breathers on the other side of the wall. He'd put his feet up, resting in a chair made for the shape of his irregular body and read a book. Sometimes he visited The Clocked Out to meet friends, or 'run into' Foxtacular.

Truth was, Malvous could be home in an hour. All he had to do was get Finch to portal him out. Or he could brave the walls of Winnie's house, which in theory should lead him to any other location a brownie resided, and thus guide him home. But he didn't know if they worked the way other walls outside T-Towns did. He could get lost.

Still, that wasn't the only reason Malvous remained. Abandoning a task and a fae would be tantamount to quitting his SCN job. He'd lose access to the entire SCN building and his cubbyhole. And the boiler room dragons. And Foxtacular. He would have to stick things out.

But Finch was making things drag out. Days of doing nothing on the sofa was grating on Malvous' soul, and he was losing patience. Someone was going to have to kick that Unseelie in the behind, but much as he wanted to move on with his life, Malvous questioned whether he had the fortitude to be the one to do it.

"Siggy, please sit," he said. "I would like to apprise you of a few things." He cast a glance at Martin. "Do you think your friend should—"

"He knows," said Siggy, setting the bread loaf and a variety of toppings on the table.

"Who knows what?"

"Martin knows about *football.* And *referees.* And *stadiums.* And whatever dumb sports words I have to say instead of talking about the real thing," said Martin, slathering peanut butter on the bread. "At first I thought Siggy was telling me a big joke, but she's not all that funny these days."

"Hey," said Siggy.

"Don't take it personal," said Martin. "Nobody 'round here is. If it makes you feel better, you're still funny-looking." He grinned, and Siggy felt it down into her core.

"Indeed," said Malvous. "Well, I can't say I approve, but these are extraordinary times. Knowing that, Siggy and Martin, this is the situation. I—"

Siggy stared at him. "No! Wait. Please don't leave. I'll be all alone—"

Malvous patted her hand. "Goodness, girl. I'm not going anywhere. Certainly not until Winnie comes back." *Wait, what did I just promise?* "I was going to say that we must get Finch off that couch and out into the world, doing his duty."

"He's just going to try and get the whole town torn down!" Siggy blinked away tears, embarrassed to be so emotional in front of Martin. "Besides, I've tried everything. He doesn't move."

"Then we will have to think of everything else," said Malvous. "A second problem is the emptiness of Winnie's garden. I don't have supplies, and all of us in this room must eat, even if it is optional for Finch. Where do you normally procure edibles?"

"Grossinger's—the grocery store," said Martin. "They used to get new supplies delivered every night." He thought about it, shaking his head. "Never asked how or why they arrived. But I guess it's more *football*."

"The Counting's a good place to trade, but we don't have a lot to share," said Siggy.

Malvous had found the need for the villagers to keep tabs on one another a sweet, if pointless, gesture. Humans could be quite Bro-like at times, particularly in groups. "And no one has questioned Winnie's absence?"

"She never goes to Countings," said Siggy. "And the students think she's had a cold. But I told Martin we should just say she's helping Mayor Neal now." She stared at her sandwich and pounded a fist on the table. "So many secrets. I hate it."

Malvous sighed. "I do wish Winnie hadn't told you so much. You would be happier."

"No, I wouldn't!" said Siggy, pounding again. The bowl of crickets jumped. "I have a right to know! Too many people I love are disappearing. *I* don't want to disappear. I don't want *Martin* to disappear. But I can't do anything about it!"

Malvous wrapped his arms around Siggy, rocking her the way his mother had when he lost control. "There, there," he said, imitating Mama Hill. "We are not going to tear down Seaview Haven. We will get things fixed. I don't know what they will look like when they are fixed—but they will get fixed."

And where did that promise come from? I can't keep doing that. But for the first time, Malvous thought, *Foxtacular is going to have to wait*. The realization made him sad, though not as sad as Siggy's tears. He held the youngling until she sat back down.

"Now," Malvous continued. "One calamity at a time. What is our best chance of obtaining more supplies?"

"The Counting," said Martin. "Guess you can raid the last of Miz Winnie's jams and jars. And most houses have *something* saved up. We could also raid the empty ones."

"No stealing!" Siggy sniffed. "But growing things takes time. It's not like you can start the season *now* and expect to eat in a few days."

Malvous gazed out the back window at Winnie's garden. Having someone handy with expertise in gardening would be beneficial. Someone who could work a little magic on a plot—

The brownie shot up as if someone had punched him in the back and grinned so wide his teeth appeared to fill up his round face and squish his squarish eyes shut.

"Yikes!" cried Martin. "That's terrifying."

Malvous ignored him. "Siggy! I've just had the most fantastical idea."

Chapter 20

Plant Yourself into a Corner

MORNING CAME. FINCH awoke to a playlist of voices in his head.

Put away your grand delusions. Stop fooling yourself.

You're such a floofy lightweight.

Muse removal? Seelie rescue? Pah! Your spells don't even register among those goddesses. You couldn't write a stupid report, not if your life depended on it. And it might!

Where'd all the stories in my head whoosh to? I might have, maybe, kind of liked *them. A bit.*

A pause. Then the whole playlist started up again.

Finch cracked open an eye. Something was different. His back was tender, and his head ached. His feet were chilled. The room felt taller, somehow.

He was on the floor.

I fell off the couch?

Wondering how that hadn't woken him up, Finch squirmed up to his elbows and winced at their soreness. The likelihood that he'd rolled off the couch, landed on his back, and his bad foot had strategically landed on a pillow was slim to nonexistent. Flailing into a seated position, he grasped for the couch, but his fingers only met air.

I've shrunk!

Actually, the couch was gone.

Everything else in the room looked in order, though. Narrowing his eyes, Finch crawled to an armchair, pushing out the lounge lever so he had a footrest. It would have to do until he could figure out how to bring the couch back. Normally, Finch would have been ecstatic to have accomplished an Unseelie disappearing spell in his sleep, but all he felt was resignation. His goal now was to return to the ongoing pursuit of the greatest amount of inertia possible. Maybe if he slept long enough, he'd become a stone.

Stones didn't have to care about reports, or stories, or floofiness. They didn't care if they failed or succeeded at anything. They didn't have to think about the Seelie Court, or Exile.

Fae didn't get depressed, did they? Not like other mythics, he was sure. Dragons were in therapy all the time. There had been a goblin clan embracing Jungian dream therapy to conquer their fears. But, no. That wasn't this.

Everything that should make Finch happy didn't anymore. He was the Unseelie who failed to fail, which was not the same as succeeding. He'd fallen into Seaview Haven with such grand plans, aiming to position himself as the one to eventually disassemble the entire town. Yet somehow, he'd gotten off the path. He'd lost a Main Character to a gaggle of goddesses that had flicked him out of their room like a bothersome bug. Meanwhile, he still had to deal with an unhealing foot. He was such a failure, even his *body* was letting him down. Finch felt neutralized.

Can't say 'useless' without 'you,' he thought.

For the last several days, he'd pondered the situation between bouts of sleep, each ponder leading to deeper ponderation, nearly reaching full ponderosity. He knew what he had to do: march around the village, take some notes, write them up and turn them in. But what would he say? If he revealed the meddling Muses were the source of the Showrunner's absence, he risked their retribution. Even if he didn't care about that, the explosive report would likely lead SCN to push him out of the way and escalate matters. They'd send in the big, experienced guns—Laurel and Hardy. He'd be ignored all over again, marching home without the support of Agatha and bringing an existential crisis in his baggage.

What if Clio was right? What if he'd been deluding himself all along? What if he were just a lousy... Seelie?

Impossible. I have a Hideous Deformity.

What he didn't want to face was the truth: That on the Unseelie/Seelie spectrum, he was neither fully chaotic nor entirely creative. He sat smack in the middle. He was—Finch shuddered—utterly *ordinary*.

Be who you are.

Finch would rather die first.

Finch squinted into the sunlight streaming through the window. He made a few calculations based on its angle and realized he had been out on the couch much longer than he'd thought. He'd erased a full five days from his life by simply not moving. It was the Unseeliest thing he'd ever done.

He wondered if he could do it again.

Finch woke again, back on the floor. Now his hip sang and his shoulder felt as though he'd rammed it into a wall.

The armchair was gone.

Ugh, I'm sleep-casting.

Yet, throwing spells in your sleep wasn't really a thing. Magical creatures weren't known for being somnambulists, much less ones that conjured unconsciously—though a few had night flatulence that could cause other creatures to disappear from rooms. But there was the fact of missing furniture. Finch was running out of places to park himself.

Malvous appeared next to him. "Morning, Mr Finch."

Finch started.

A second face popped into view: Siggy. "You have to get up now."

"Make me."

"We encourage you to rise," said Malvous. "I would prefer to stop relocating furniture."

"You moved the— you—" Finch cried. "Why?"

"Because we need you." Siggy grabbed his hand and tugged.

Finch tugged back. "Give me that."

"No." She pulled harder.

Malvous took up Finch's other hand and they dragged the existentially crisising Unseelie into a seated position. Finch put up no further resistance. Fighting took energy, and he had little in reserve. Who knew so much rest might make him weaker? He allowed them to hoist him into a standing position on his good foot, leaning on Malvous' shoulder because his cane was also missing. "The moment you two stop tormenting me, I'm going to bed."

"As you like." Malvous began guiding him to the kitchen. Siggy trailed behind. "This way, first."

"Hold up! I'm injured."

"Really?" wondered Siggy. "You've been off that foot for a week."

Finch ground his teeth, setting some weight on the bad foot. It wasn't back to normal, but he felt no shooting pains. "Ow!" he cried anyway. "Ow, ow, ow."

Siggy shook her head. "You are a terrible actor!"

"Simply awful." The brownie unlatched the back door in the kitchen. "But I suspect he may have hidden talents. There's something you need to see, Mr Finch."

The fae hop-stepped behind him, exaggerating his limp whenever one of the others turned around. Passing through the kitchen, he caught a whiff of rosemary bread. His stomach twisted with hunger. Grabbing half of the loaf from the table with one hand and a wax paper wrapped stick of butter in the other, he began alternating bites from each as he maneuvered through the back door. A warm morning greeted him as he took in Winnie's backyard for the first time, squinting into the sunshine.

"Tah-dah!" said Malvous.

It was a yard. Or really, it was a garden. A sad, picked over patch that looked as if a Smash had recently been held on it. A small fuse lit in the back of Finch's head that focused his attention. Handing the loaf to Siggy and the melting butter to Malvous, Finch hopped down the deck steps and into the greenery. Once there, he took stock: a patch for vegetables, one for herbs and flowers, two rows of mature fruit trees, berry bushes engulfing the back fence. A pond with a couple of fat orange fish.

He picked an overlooked berry from a bush and rested it on his tongue, then bit down. Ripe and luscious, if small (he'd grown accustomed to his overgrown versions) it wasn't bad-tasting. He plucked and ate a second, then a third—and the oddest wave of homesickness crashed over him. He missed his own patch, his own trees, his greenhouse, and trickling stream. Why had he ever left home? Why was he aspiring for greater things?

"Miz Winnie called this her 'pride and joy.'" Siggy gestured around the space. "She spent hours here every day, growing stuff."

Finch sneered. "If she's proud of *this*, maybe she can

give me Unseelie lessons. This place looks like it's been picked over by wild animals."

Malvous cleared his throat. "It's been picked over by a single, not very wild *brownie*. Me. While you've been in a champion sulk, some of us had to take on boring chores like cooking, eating, bathing, tidying up or, you know, trying to figure out what happens next with Winnie stuck in the mayor's house."

"Brownies aren't supposed to give lectures," said Finch.

"And Unseelie aren't supposed to sleep all day. Siggy and I are at our wits' end and also running low on food. You can't harvest forever, even in a T-Town that isn't falling apart." Malvous wandered through the garden rows behind Finch. "When I met you, I knew two things instantly: you were terrible at portaling, and you knew your way around a garden. You had dirt under your nails and berry stains on your teeth."

Finch turned pink. *Can't even hide my hobbies right*, he thought, and a bubble burst inside. "It's too embarrassing for words! Unseelie do not *garden*! We do not *build* things! We do not *create*! We wreck gardens. Urinate on the trees. Add more gophers. Prune bushes into sticks! It's *embarrassing*!"

"You spend a lot of time yelling about who you are," Siggy observed. "Miz Winnie always said, 'don't "should" on yourself.'"

Malvous' mouth twitched. "Maybe not every single thing you do in your life is 'supposed' to be Unseelie, Finch. You're not a single purpose T-Town. Maybe you've got some Seelie in there."

"Don't make me invert your lips," Finch snapped. "Seelie are ninnies. Boring. Think they're better than every other fae. The world is theirs because they can make it. I wouldn't admit to being Seelie even if I *was* Seelie, which I certainly am not."

The brownie sighed. "Then take the long view. If you want to be recognized as a useful SCN employee, you will have to submit a report on Seaview Haven. To do that, you will have to see Seaview Haven. You might even consider it part of your job to recover the Main Character of this town, and even the SMD."

"And you can't do any of that from the couch," Siggy said.

"I am beset on all sides by nagging nincompoops!" Finch cried.

"I will ignore that," said Malvous. "You fell off a horse back at the mayor's house. Get back on and ride it."

Finch faced the remnants of the garden. His stomach churned in a pleasant way. It was almost like the way his mind had whooshed from all the Muse influence. For the first time since he had crashed out on the sofa, the voice playlist in his head was merely murmuring, not shouting. He almost felt peaceful. "So what does this have to do with anything?"

Siggy offered up a pair of worn garden gloves. "This garden needs help. We have to harvest whatever's left, compost the leavings, and prepare for fall vegetables. Malvous and I have to keep eating and we're running low on food. The farmer's market isn't reliable. But Malvous says this is your thing, kind of."

Seeing the hopeful looks on Malvous and Siggy's faces, he made a discovery that took his breath away. *They don't care what brand of fae I am. Or if I'm good at being a fae. Or if I'm a dragon. Or a goblin. What they need right now is a gardener.* And for good or ill, sometimes both, he was quite excellent at working the earth. Finch glanced around to ensure no one was looking and nodded. "Fine. But I want a shovel. And a hat. No gloves. Seeds. Where's Winnie's shed?"

Siggy shone bright as the summer sun. "Side of the

house!" She clapped her hands together. "Thank you, Finchy! Thank you!"

A knot inside Finch loosened and he felt unexpected delight. It was hard, agreeing to help. To see something that was broken and actively try to repair it. Unseelie did not do that. He was badass. Born to hinder. But he did like Siggy and did not like the idea that she might go hungry. He had to start somewhere, and at least with gardening he knew he wouldn't screw it up.

Probably.

All he had to do was hope word didn't get back to the SCN Execs.

But even that almost didn't matter. All the despair he'd woken up with was being washed away by eagerness to get stuck into the soil. To speak with it. To find out what it had to offer.

"All right, you talked me into it." Finch hobbled to the shed with the youngling. With the *young woman*. "But if either of you breathe a word about me doing this, I will set the entire patch on *fire*."

Chapter 21

Meta Fours

WINNIE PAUSED AT the bedroom door, listening for sounds of movement. Everything was quiet in the house—no swish of velour tracksuits, no clatter of coffee mugs, no pitter-patter of goddess' feet hurrying around her.

Delightful.

Maybe they thought she was sleeping in. Last night, she'd dragged herself from the couch amid the squeals of delight issued by the goddesses playing Blindfolded Badminton in the backyard, then stumbled off to the closest bedroom to collapse on an extremely fluffy duvet. She'd needed that rest; Calliope, it seems, hadn't been kidding at all when she'd said that Winnie had goofed off with them for *days*.

Had no idea I had that in me, she thought.

But Muses had a way of being uniquely distracting.

Her stomach made burbling noises.

Hush, she thought. *I'm trying not to be intercepted on the way to the kitchen.*

Days wasted in frivolity with the Muses, while Neal typed his heart out and Siggy faced up to having another adult abandoning her. Winnie couldn't stand it.

Remember, Winnifred, stories in the morning!

You'll have tales to tell Us!

We haven't actually read any of your mystery books before!

So many demands from the Muses last night. She'd become the newest, shiniest thing in the permanent gal-cation, which was simultaneously wildly exciting, extremely draining, and anxiety-producing. But it did give Winnie ideas. All that attention was like requesting a shot of tequila and getting a glass the size of Pittsburgh. Winnie had ideas for centuries now. But that wasn't what the Muses desired. They only cared to hear a story they didn't already know.

Winnie had those, as well.

The bedroom door flew open, and Winnie narrowly missed getting clocked on the head. Spinning away, she fell against the mattress. Bright-eyed and grinning, Euterpe ("Call me Eutie!") launched herself onto the bed and offered a mug of tea. (The fact that the tea hadn't splashed all over creation was just another instance of selective deity physics.)

"Morning, sunshine!" Eutie said. "Your audience is assembling, and you haven't even had breakfast!"

Winnie rolled over. Eutie was the least bossy of the sisters and seemed to understand mortal needs, like regular meals and occasional bathroom breaks. She appreciated that. But with a single Muse in the room, Winnie's head was starting to fill up with ideas again.

In the normal course of things, Muses had to be awakened. But in this house, they awakened *you*.

"Eutie, any chance you can turn that passive mode to off?"

The goddess rested her head on the covering inches from Winnie. "Alas, my lovely one. This's as meek and mild as We get."

Winnie sighed and accepted the tea.

"Now, for your first story today—" the goddess held out a paperback book. "We want to hear your seventh Seaview Haven mystery—*The Case of the Jealous Janitor*!"

Winnie peeked over the sheets. She hadn't seen that cover in years. "You do understand this is not exactly a life-altering, mind-blowing text. And you could read it to one another."

"But it is!" Eutie waggled a finger. "Your reading to Us is like a very fine wine—it's a direct distillation of Our valuable inspiration." She leaned closer, giving off scents of pine trees and cumin. "But remember: you *must* be useful in this house, or My sweet sisters will tell you to depart!"

Winnie understood her purpose now. She accepted the book and fanned through it. "It's been ages since Neal and I typed this thing up. It'll be like reading it again for the first time."

Eutie tilted her head. "Yes, indeed! You always spoke your stories aloud, then the Seelie typed them up. This explains how he got his Delusions of Ideas."

"He did contribute, though!"

"Which likely gave him Delusions of Grand Ideas."

So this is my fault, she thought. *In about eight ways, this is my doing.* "Look, if I read to you all a bit, can we then spend time talking about how to solve the godspell issue?"

The Muse scrambled from the bed. "Yes! Or, at least, we can *talk about* talking about it." She bounced to the door. "Get clean and fed! See you in the living room!"

She darted away.

Once dressed, Winnie stumbled to the kitchen. Was there a good German word for her mixed emotions this morning—existential dread and extreme excitement? She had to stay in Neal's house. She had to be here to help free him. But was she only being stubborn and unrealistic? What, after all, could a human do to a spell woven by goddesses and a Seelie?

Approaching the kitchen, she caught rich scents of

pancakes and bacon, then heard a bustling. Stomach still a-rumble, she turned the corner, calling out, "Hey, Felicitous, we got any more of that bourbon maple—"

There was someone in the kitchen. Not a Felicitous. Not a goddess. A someone who was chugging the last bits of bourbon maple syrup directly from the bottle.

"Hey, stop that!" Winnie barked. "I need that for—" The serving dish Felicitous had set out for breakfast was bare save for a couple crumbs and a lone rainbow sprinkle. "My pancakes."

"Not anymore you don't!" The maple syrup-drinking, pancake-stealing (Winnie assumed) person tossed the empty syrup bottle back into the refrigerator and swiped their mouth on a leather-jacketed sleeve. Whoever it was—Winnie started thinking *guy*, then *gal*, then *whatever*—was tall and slender with an aquiline nose and a head of wild twists that were not quite locs and not quite braids. They looked like a biker in faded jeans and white T-shirt, plus that leather jacket, which featured a dozen enamel pins festooned across the chest with slightly off-kilter slogans like *Subdue the Dominant Paradigm* and *Inspect Pronouns* and *Workers of the World Untie.*

"Mighty tasty, though," said the biker. "Rainbow sprinkles on pancakes! Wonders never cease."

"Who are you?" Winnie crossed her arms. "What are you doing here? Did the Muses invite you?"

"Janus. Call me Jan." They tapped the pronouns button. "They/them. Which is more true for me than some." They turned their head, and an eye peeped out from beneath the tangle of twists. It winked. Janus turned back around. "Haven't seen any wandering Muses around here, have you?"

Winnie shook her head, trying to get her bearings. Fifteen years of Seaview Haven had not prepared her for a god in the kitchen. "You ate my breakfast!"

"Most observational." Janus was the picture of delight. "I suspect you are the local writer!"

"Some say so. Winnie."

"Excellent." They wrapped an arm around her shoulders, pulling her close. "I've been giving this writing thing a go, and I have questions."

Winnie's memory of ancient Roman mythology was as good as her knowledge of ancient Greek mythology, which was to say she had no idea whether Janus was known for wordsmithing. "I didn't know you wrote."

"Now I do. A bit. I'm good with beginnings and endings. The middle parts are sticky. With the ladies gone from SCN I've been using their offices. Did I mention that writing was hard?"

Winnie pulled a bunch of grapes from the refrigerator. Better than nothing. "Not everyone has to be a writer. We need more readers."

Janus nodded. "An *excellent* point. I am learning so much from you already, Winnie. But I'm not ready to throw in the tarp just yet."

"Towel. You throw in the towel."

Janus snapped with recognition. "Of course! See, I've been writer-curious for a few centuries, and now felt like a good time to give it a thrust. Or is it a stab? Or a shot?"

"Many things are used." Winnie's initial awe at having a new god in the room faded, leaving her to realize that their presence might be an opportunity. "You know the Muses?"

"Sure!" They tossed popcorn from a bowl into their mouth. "Callie's my gal, mostly. Good to see them on a break. A lot fewer computers getting tossed into windows with them away from SCN, and it's been so amusing to see the executive Seelie dashing about in all sorts of frantic ways. But it has been a minute or two. I keep wondering why they haven't come back yet. The cafeteria won't be serving ambrosia for much longer."

"Apparently," Winnie said carefully, "they *can't* leave."

Janus gaped. "Balderdash! There's nothing a god or goddess can't do. At least, I don't think so." They tossed some more popcorn. "Hey! Let me read you something I wrote."

"Actually—"

Ignoring her, they fluttered their hands. A piece of paper with curled corners and tea stains appeared in the air, hovering. Janus grumbled as if a piece of popcorn had lodged in their throat. "I hear it's a *great* idea to start your stories with a lot of throat clearing," they said.

"Inaccurate."

"I'll make a note." They rustled the incorporeal paper by waving at it. "Once upon a time." They gave a long, dramatic pause. "The End."

When nothing else came, she held up her hands. "That's it?"

"Told you I'm good with beginnings and endings. Those are pretty spectacular."

"If you say so. Don't quit your day job."

Felicitous darted into the kitchen, arms full of dirty dishes. He clattered them into the sink, muttering to himself, and turned the hot water on full. Then he flipped the spigot off and whirled. "Mx Janus!" he cried, flinging his arms around the god. "This is an *amazement*!"

Janus returned the embrace warmly. "Oleander sends her best," they told Felicitous. "At least, she did the last time I saw her. I'm sure her best is still quite good, though."

"They thought your pancakes were delicious, and we're now out of maple syrup," Winnie said, inching toward the doorway.

Felicitous deflated with a sigh. "Ah. Well. I'll forage for more if I can find the time. So many things need doing—"

All of the light that had burst from the brownie upon seeing Janus drained away.

The god frowned. "Felicitous, are you the lone Bro in this household?"

He nodded.

"Serving one Seelie, one human, and nine Muses?"

"Mostly just four Muses. Sometimes nine. Sometimes their friends. Winnie has only been here six days."

"That is about twelve union violations!"

Felicitous only looked more worried. "A Bro can handle anything!"

Winnie patted his shoulder. "He's doing his best. But everybody's gotten a little stuck around here, and nobody's sure what steps to take next. The town is falling apart. None of us have any idea what to do against a—oh, maybe I shouldn't say."

Janus leaned forward. "Spill."

"No, a spell." Winnie paused. "A godspell, actually."

Janus listened intently as Winnie related what she knew about the current situation, and the god said nothing. Mid-sentence, though, Felicitous' portable speaker crackled.

"Send Our writer!" Eutie chirped in the speaker. "We are eager to hear about jealous janitors!"

"On her way," gulped Felicitous, turning wide puppy dog eyes on Winnie. "Miz Winnie should hurry."

"I'm going," said Winnie, giving one last look at Janus. The god was now staring thoughtfully into the refrigerator's icemaker. She shook her head. *Gods, fae, mythics—impossible. No wonder people become atheists*, she thought. "I'm going," she said again, louder.

Janus started. Their face was stony. "Winnie Arrowmaker, you wait here. I should like to greet my… friends."

The god strode down the hallway with a stiff gait and unbending confidence.

"Janus is a friend to brownies," Felicitous whispered. "They look out for us."

Winnie wondered if that care applied to humans—or Seelie.

The door to the living room slid open, then closed.

Joyful greeting sounds filtered through the doors, followed by loud voices, rising voices, and complete shouts. A crack of lightning followed by a boom of thunder made Felicitous grab Winnie's arm. Then all went quiet, and if Winnie strained, she could make out sounds that might be murmurs. Several minutes later, the doors rattled and slid open. Janus beckoned them over.

Could they have defeated a godspell? Winnie wondered. *Maybe it's all over?*

Janus stood to one side and Calliope came forward.

"This has been a fascinating discussion," the god said.

"Ahem," said the Muse. A high pink flush in her cheeks made her appear simultaneously frazzled and lovelier than ever. "Heartfelt apologies for asking too much of you."

"Oh, that's all right—" Winnie began, but Callie waved her off.

"I refer to the brownie." She crouched down to Felicitous' height. "I had always imagined that brownie enthusiasm and capability was infinite, but now I comprehend that not all brownies are up to the task of running a large household."

"But I am!" Felicitous went from hope to panic in an eyeblink. "Mx Janus must have… misunderstood!"

"Calliope," said Janus. "This is not what we discussed."

"No, no," said Calliope, resting a hand on Felicitous' thin shoulder. "You deserve a nice, long break, so we are going to send you back to the Bro Employment Pool where—"

"Clueless," Winnie muttered. "Cruel."

Overhearing her, Calliope shot Winnie a fiery look that stripped at least half of the ideas from her head. Winnie felt like someone had sandpapered her brain.

Felicitous had gone a sickly gray-white. "No, no, no!" He stamped his foot. "I can do this! I will work ever so much harder!"

Janus' not-quite-locs twisted around and for a moment all four of their eyes glared at Calliope. "Another moment of your time, my dear." But there was little warmth in that tone. "Excuse us—again." They slammed the doors shut. This time, there was no lightning, no thunder, just godlike quiet.

Winnie guided the brownie back to the kitchen and set water on for tea. "Felicitous," she said. "Janus will fix this. You're not going to be sent away."

The brownie sniffled. "Ms Winnie is sure?"

"I'm not sure of anything these days. But Janus feels like an ally." She sat next to the Bro, sipping from her own mug. "And going forward, don't worry about taking care of me, all right? I can make my own meals."

"Maybe." The brownie half smiled. "Anyway, you can't stop me."

No noise came from the hallway. Anxious, Winnie tapped her fingers. "Felicitous, have I really been here for six days?"

"Seven nights, six days."

Somehow that was even more astounding than losing five days to frivolity. Seven nights felt ridiculously long and absurdly short at the same time. "Do you have any idea about the outside world? Is Siggy all right? Is the town even still there?" She conjured up the girl's face, picturing her wiggling her fingers at the window—and then she was gone.

Felicitous refilled their mugs, then began wiping down the spot-free table. "Siggy is bringing more fruits to the market after Counting these days. So that suggests your garden is beginning to flourish again. And—"

"That can't be. We were practically at bare earth."

"Then perhaps someone is using special soil nutrients."

That's one way of putting it, Winnie thought, realizing it was likely Finch exercising some kind of magic. *He strikes me as someone who's got a lot of spare… fertilizer.*

"You saw her, then?"

"Briefly, Ms Winnie. I try not to be overly seen, as townsfolk connect me with Mayor Neal and start asking so many questions. I get in, I get out." Felicitous stared off in the distance. "But I might have heard her say Malvous is taking care of things."

Winnie was relieved but also disconcerted. A brownie and an Unseelie now in charge of the most precious person in this village to Winnie? It was time to stop wasting time. Winnie stood up.

"Where are you bound, Ms Winnie?"

She didn't know. Was she really going to walk out the door and chase after Siggy and that Unseelie weirdo? If she thought a quick check-in might work, and that she could return to the house unnoticed, she would risk it. But Callie had been clear: she wouldn't be *asked back* if she vacated now. Yet she felt she was letting Eve down by not having eyes on her daughter. And why was Finch revitalizing her garden? Wasn't he supposed to be critiquing Seaview Haven? Why hadn't he submitted his report by now and gone home?

That's not your story right now, she thought.

Winnie had to triage. Siggy was doing all right. That left Neal and the Muses to deal with—if only she had an idea where to start. The only thing she did know was that telling stories all day to goddesses was a waste of time. It wouldn't defeat the godspell; nothing she could read or write would help now.

Felicitous placed a toasted bagel with butter in front of her. She knew it would be delicious but couldn't summon the will to take a bite. "Felicitous, I'm lost."

"Ms Winnie is right here in the kitchen." Felicitous wiped the table.

"What I mean is they want me to tell them stories. They want me to be their play buddy. And when I'm with the Muses, I want that, too. But that's not *right*. I'm not here for my own gal-cation. It weighs on me, what's happening to Neal in that office. And then we start talking about Siggy and my garden and—" Her throat tightened. She was frustrated enough to want to cry, but not out of sadness. "What do those Muses think they were doing, making that godspell with Neal? You can't insist on a great story."

Felicitous paused in his cleaning and rested his hands on the back of a chair. "Mayor Neal used to tell me about your stories. How he went into your house and you spoke them to him and he typed them up." He paused. "He said you knew where stories came from. Your gut, he said, then your head, then through your mouth and then onto paper."

Accurate, though it makes it sound like I coughed out a hairball, she thought. But something was missing. "There's nothing about the heart in there."

"Heart is not involved?"

Of course it was. It might sound treacly, but when Winnie was with Neal the world burst with brighter colors. Corny things felt true. His hand in hers was a puzzle piece that had found its mate. Winnie had had a full, complete life on the human side of the Veil—but nothing felt as right as when she and Neal were composing the next story. Neal wasn't *a* Muse, but he was *her* Muse. She'd never felt more herself than when she was with him. Of course that had showed in the writing—in the writing they *both* did together.

"What if—" She hadn't dared to imagine this before. "Maybe... I could—" she stood up again. "Maybe he could *type* a new mystery... that I create?" It sounded so simple. But would it please the Muses if she was involved?

It might work. It's worth a try.

Felicitous waggled his head noncommittally. "That is how you did things before. But inside Mayor Neal's office, it is hard to think straight. Or leave." He stared out of the kitchen, down the hallway toward the office with the swirling vortex of paper. "Do you wish to do this thing?"

Winnie nodded. Her stomach gurgled again, this time with excitement. "I think I have to do this thing."

"Well, then that's decided." Felicitous slid from his chair and set a hand on her forearm. "But remember what they say about the care and feeding of Muses." He paused. "Or maybe it's just what *I* say. But here it is: Never ignore a Muse. Never bore a Muse. Surprising a Muse, though, is a tremendous joy."

The idea wasn't so much a lightning bolt as a slow dawn. An absence of darkness. Then colors. And, at last, the heart-stopping sunrise. Winnie's head cleared. She wolfed down the bagel. And when every sesame seed was gone, she grabbed Felicitous' hand.

All her writing life, Winnie had been a methodical outliner of stories. She knew exactly where each scene would go before she wrote her chapters. Some people were 'pantsers,' starting with only a vague idea of where the tale was going and how it might end up, and she'd never understood that way of thinking. Until now. In this moment, she very much wanted to fly by the seat of her pants, spinning out words to a tale she knew inside and out until it felt right.

She heard a click in her mind. A loud one. And with that, she knew exactly how to tell the story she was supposed to tell. To please the Muses. To untangle the godspell.

But not just *her* telling the story. Her and Neal.

"Felicitous, you're a genius." Winnie leaned forward and kissed him on the forehead. His rosy color turned deeper pink. "Can you help me into Neal's office? Now? We're going to write a story for the ages, *together*."

"Should be a story for the Muses, not the Ages, Ms Winnie."

"It can be both. Will you help me get in?"

"Of course! Bros always help!" He tossed the dishrag into the sink and clapped his hands. "But getting out may be… difficult."

Excitement jolted through Winnie, and she felt more awake than she'd been in months. This might not work. But it also *had* to work. Either way, she'd get to see Neal again. "I'll burn that bridge when I come to it. I need to get in there before all the gods and goddesses finish their discussion, or they might distract me again."

She started to pull Felicitous to the hallway, then stopped.

"No," she said.

"No?" he asked.

"I can't do this alone."

"Oh!" Felicitous turned very pale pink. "I, Felicitous… will try… but—"

"No, dear brownie," she said. "I wouldn't subject you to that room again. But I need the proper tools. How long will it take you to make a fresh batch of shortbread—with chocolate chips?"

Chapter 22

Plants, Shoots, and Leaves

FINCH DIDN'T DO things halfway, Siggy noticed. Once committed, the Unseelie became a dervish in Winnie's backyard, accomplishing more there in an hour than he'd done in almost a whole week during his Seaview Haven 'investigation.'

As Finch enigmatically explained, working in the garden was the equivalent of singing in the shower. *No one who matters is paying attention, so I can really belt it out.*

Siggy took offense at being called *nobody who mattered*, but she couldn't stay mad long. What he was doing was spectacular, and on the second morning she joined him in the garden as an assistant.

"Fetch more compost," he barked. "Use the wheelbarrow."

She kept waiting for him to use his magic. (She couldn't say the word, but she could at least *think* it.) But so far, Finch was being extremely unmagical about the garden. "Can't you just say 'abracadabra' or 'alakazam' and make the wheelbarrow roll itself?" she asked, wiping sweat from her brow.

"First you tell me to get off the couch and do something, and now you want me to sit back and wave my hands?"

"Or a wand."

"Hmph! I'm nobody's performing seal. Or monkey. Or troll."

Siggy looked away. "I guess I thought you could speed things up." Miz Winnie had once read her a poem about an apprentice who got chores done faster by making a broom haul water in a pail. Things went wrong, but only because the apprentice was new. A small part of her had been wishing Finch could do something similar. She had a hankering for fresh corn.

The Unseelie leaned on his shovel handle. "When I started gardening, I did it by sitting on a chair behind my house. I shot out enchantments all day. But there's no single spell that orders the ground to 'grow stuff.' It's a hundred little spells. Consumable food is fiddly. The soil has to talk to you, tell you what it needs. You feed the soil and *then* you have to ask the sun where it plans to send beams so you can put the seeds in the right place. Maybe it's a little like—" He smiled a bit. "Writing a book. Use a spell and sure, you might get words on a page and a cover and a spine, but who wants to read that?"

"*Football* is more complicated than I realized."

He blinked at her, confused, then rolled his eyes. "Enough with that word ward. That's something I'm happy to destroy." He snapped his fingers. "That's better."

"Wait—so I can say *magic*?" Siggy covered her mouth briefly. "And *Seelie*? And—" She bounced up and down on her toes.

"Don't let it go to your head," said Finch. "We've got work to do. Now, if you wanted straight-up magic plants, I could spell some hungry grass or a fern flower. Those're ephemeral, so they're easy. Full of magic, but nothing else. I could weave 'em just like that." He tossed aside a handful of dirt.

"Actually, I'm kind of interested—"

"But I'm not going to. The real stuff, the food you're going to put into a living creature means you have to do it the hard way. Either we do it like this right now, or I spend a lot of time weaving little spells to get you a mandrake. One single mandrake. Or yarrow. Or a tomato, they're not too complicated. But magic food doesn't feed you. It puts magic in you and that's not healthy in the long run."

Finch knew a lot of things, but apparently he'd never showed them off. Before now, he'd been rude and bossy and dismissive—but here in the garden, he just felt passionate. Siggy was surprised to find herself *liking* him now that he was being helpful. "Because we need calories."

"Among other things."

A deep cough interrupted Finch. Malvous stood on the back porch with a tray of lemonade and glasses. "Less chatting, more digging!" he called. "That garden won't plant itself!"

"Exactly what I was saying," said Finch, and after a brief drink he and Siggy returned to the yard.

Siggy felt incredibly contented. Hot and sweaty, dirty, and tired, but contented. She'd felt the opposite when she'd first come to live with Miz Winnie. Back then she'd been resentful, angry, and sad about having to live with her mother's friend, even though they'd always gotten along well. Miz Winnie, meanwhile, was also surly and hurt and sad, and for a time Siggy thought it was because of *her*. It took ages before she realized they were both sad and furious for the same reason: they missed Eve.

But they didn't talk about it. Miz Winnie had lived alone for a long time, and on her own schedule. She moved from task to task and did things because they needed doing, not because she had a particular deadline. For a time, Siggy was fine with being waited on hand and foot. Her meals were always ready, her bed was always made, her clothes always clean. But slowly, having everything done for her, around her, or despite her felt like being ignored.

By then she wasn't furious or scared one hundred percent of the time. Maybe more like 88.2 percent. The pity parties she'd thrown for herself were down to maybe every other week. Miz Winnie picked up on the change, and about two months after Mama and Papa vanished, her new guardian had announced that Siggy's 'freeloading' days were over. She'd make her own breakfasts and lunches, clean up her room, and take on chores. At first, Siggy had moped and groaned and slouched through her tasks, feeling simultaneously put upon and finally seen. Then one day she'd woken up with a big idea to make pancakes. She'd never done more than boil eggs before then. She found a jar of sprinkles for ice cream in the pantry and added them to the batter. Soon, she learned to like making meals, especially baking bread. Miz Winnie showed her how to keep the sourdough starter fed, and how to use it to make loaves.

Siggy had been like a chick emerging from an egg. For so long she'd been in a dark, cramped place, but every day since her change of attitude she'd become brighter, more herself. That was why she put so much faith in gardening for Finch. He hadn't lost his parents (Siggy wasn't sure Unseelie *had* parents) he'd lost his confidence. For Finch, confidence seemed to be everything. A person, a fae, could stay on the couch all day. SCN shows were always on, even if they showed a lot of reruns these days, but at some point a body got tired of being useless.

Miz Winnie had been a sink or swim teacher when it came to gardening. She'd handed Siggy tools and pointed at trees that needed harvesting or pruning. Gardening hadn't been as wonderful as baking bread, though, and over time Siggy started biking around town with Martin and some of the other kids. They took notes about the changes in the town and the way the world seemed to be disintegrating, all in the name of gathering information for Siggy's science experiments.

Every science experiment had been derailed, though, since Winnie explained things to Siggy. She was annoyed with herself for not questioning the nature of the universe she lived in, though, long before that. But Siggy had grown up on this side of the Veil, and the idea that the world was full of small villages separated by big forests, and that each village had kind of its own theme, or flair—well, that was normal because it was all she'd known. Siggy had watched her mother and Winnie in TV movies all her life. That was normal for everyone too, wasn't it?

Nope, Miz Winnie had said. *Where I come from, most people don't live like here. This town is how it is because that's what some Seelie creators thought it should look like. Same for the other T-Towns—you'll visit them someday, probably. Like, we have one big metropolis over here—La Ciudad Grande—but on the other side of the Veil there are dozens. Hundreds. Here, small towns of varying sizes are just more manageable. So says Mayor Neal, anyhow. Havenites used to be able to visit any of them they wanted, except Second Chance, which is a whole different kettle of fish. But Seelie only made a* version *of how human civilization works. On the other side of the Veil, where only humans live, it's bigger. There's more variety. Things are more random. Life isn't scripted by the mayor and his trusty writer or filmed by birds and bees and trees. And magic is a bunch of tricks.*

Siggy was still wrapping her head around it all.

"I miss Miz Winnie." She upended the wheelbarrow filled with compost where Finch directed. "And my mom. And my dad."

"They're around. Someplace." Finch spread the compost over the beds.

"Really? How come they're not *here*, then?" She gestured. "Or standing in the road right outside the barrier?"

"For one thing, there is no more road there, probably," said Finch. "That rift in the pavement I saw when I arrived is only getting bigger. According to the SCN Guide, when T-Towns stop producing new content, they start to break down. People getting shut out, or being spirited away, is all part of that. Looks like your folks got caught up in the changes."

"But are they okay?" Until now, Siggy had never pictured her parents being in pain. Now, she imagined them stuck between two boulders, or buried underground.

"Should be. Probably they're in another T-Town right now, trying to get back here. But nobody gets in until we've fixed things, one way or the other. That's why I'm so important."

"But you want to tear it down! Not fix it!"

Finch raised an eyebrow. "I never said that. But even if I did, I'm not permitted to do anything yet. My spells have limited functions. For now, I can only gather details for a recommendation. I am not tearing anything down."

"You want to, though."

"'Tis my nature, girl."

Siggy folded her arms. "This from a guy who loves *gardening*."

"Shut up." Finch turned his back on her and began digging somewhere else. "I don't *love* gardening. Not more than a little bit."

"Well, you must love it more than writing your report, because you haven't even started that!"

"I am aware."

Siggy returned to the wheelbarrow, grumbling. But as she pushed it around, moving soil and compost, she was thinking hard. *He hasn't even seen the town*. How could he write a report about a town if he hadn't seen it? What if he just needed an enthusiastic guide? Or two?

"Come here, girl." Finch kneeled on the ground and Siggy scampered over. He yanked a few potatoes out of the soil and set them in a bucket; each was as big as her fists balled together. "I'll show you some magic."

She dropped down next to him and Finch plucked the gloves from her hands. He pointed to a hole in the ground. "Go ahead, shove those fingers all the way into the dirt." He joined her. "Now, just listen."

"I don't hear anything."

Finch gave the briefest toss of his head and lowered his gaze, focusing on her for a second. "Now you can. But not with your ears. Listen with your skin."

A tickling tremble curled around Siggy's fingers, and she yanked her hands out, examining them for worms. Nothing. She slid them back into the hole and thought about listening with her skin. Her body. The tickle returned, this time as a faint drumbeat running up and down her wrists like a burbling stream of water. She could almost taste it on her lips, this cold, clear sensation like murmurs or tiny kisses. "What am I 'hearing'?"

"The earth speaking to you. That's what I feel when I'm working outdoors. The plants, the dirt, the seeds, they tell you what they want."

"Then I think this part needs water. I keep picturing my arms in a stream with little fishes trying to nibble me."

"Interesting interpretation. Hand me the hose."

They doused the patch with water, then each pressed a finger against the dirt. There was no sensation, tickle, or murmur. "Good enough." Finch's voice was soft and kind, almost dreamy.

Siggy stared at her spread fingers. "Can I keep doing that?"

Finch gave her a look. "You're not getting magic powers, girl. Just a little boost that wears off."

She felt warm all over, almost like when Martin set his hand on her shoulder. Siggy's throat tightened, and she wrapped her arms around the Unseelie. He stood like a pole against her but waited a good solid minute before pushing her free. "You smell like dirt," he said.

"Hey."

"No, it's a good smell. But don't go attacking me again. You act like that, I'm not going to share any further enchantments."

That night, the garden underwent a second bloom. Vegetables sprouted, the trees pushed out new fruit and the berry bushes positively sagged with new offerings. Siggy carried the bounty in panniers attached to her bike to the farmer's market after every Counting, eagerly bringing back home all the things they had run out of: eggs, village-milled flour, sugar, lamb sausages, loose tea, soap, salt.

During one of her trades, Mr Zhao, who ran the bicycle repair shop, winked at her. "That Winnie's pulling out some new tricks. Never saw peaches so late in the season."

"Yeah, incredible," said Siggy. "Like *football*."

Mr Zhao gave her a strange look.

Rats, she thought. She was back to being censored. Finch's boost had worn off.

Siggy didn't stick around long at Countings and tried not to chitchat beyond making her trades. Keeping her mouth shut meant she didn't have to lie so hard about where Miz Winnie was—she's in the garden! No, wait, she's helping Mayor Neal! No, wait, she's still got a cold!—or that things weren't normal in her house. She saw Martin every day as he rolled around Counting and the market, and he came over for a few words, but they never talked about big stuff. He always waved and said he had to get to dinner with Big Dad Dean and rolled off.

That confused Siggy. Martin was the closest thing she had to a confidante in town. He knew the truth about Seaview Haven. And they seemed to have been on the same wavelength about figuring out what was going on in Nowheresville. But ever since that night when she told him how the town worked, he always acted like he had to be somewhere, anywhere else than standing with her.

And Martin had always been there. He was a rare permanent fixture in her world. They'd known each other since they were five and six, when he'd smeared finger paint on her face in class. Later, he'd apologized with a droopy handful of dandelions, and she'd shown him how to 'pop' their heads off with a thumb. Martin sprinkled salt on cucumbers and ate them like candy. He had the world's greatest flop of asymmetrical hair that grazed one eye and shifted when he blinked. But over the last few days, it was like she didn't know him.

A few days after the garden started blooming, she'd had enough. Siggy blocked his path as he tried rolling away from the market. "Stop in the name of the law," she said.

"What law?"

"Siggy's law." She put her hands on her hips, thrust out her chest, and gave him an imperious look. "You're in violation."

"C'mon, Sig, I probably need to get home—"

"Dinner won't be for hours yet. Stop running—I mean, rolling—away from me. Don't do this to us."

"Do what?"

"Act like I smell bad."

"You don't! I don't!" But he wouldn't look at her face.

"You're acting all weirded out 'round me. Is it 'cause of what we talked about at the house, or what?"

He stared at the ground and mumbled, "'Or what.'"

"So, it's not like you don't believe me any more about Nowheresville?"

"'Course I do. Also… well, Big Dad Dean said you're right. Look, I couldn't keep everything a secret. It was too much not to talk about. I did some drawing for him like you did for me and then he nodded and gave me a hug. I can't remember the last time he bear-hugged me like that. But now he knows what I know. Which you know. I just had to know it really was the truth."

"I wouldn't lie to you!"

"I know it." He still looked squirrelly, though.

"So, if it's not about *all that*, why are you avoiding me?"

Martin stared at her, and she held his gaze. Her toes curled in her shoes. Suddenly, she was afraid she already had her answer. Maybe she wasn't the only one who couldn't stop thinking about what almost happened that night she'd told him about Nowheresville. That moment they'd had by the sofa when Finch was passed out. How close they'd gotten before Malvous interrupted them for dinner. Would everything have changed if they'd kissed? Did she even want everything to change? The whole town was changing. Could she handle more?

He half shrugged. "Aw, don't make me get into it, Sig. You know I like you."

He wasn't even touching her and that fractal warmth shot through her again. "I like you, too," she said in a quiet, small voice, then brought something out of her pocket. "Here. Was saving this for you."

Martin accepted the ripe, soft plum and grinned. "Whoa, Winnie's doing some serious *football* over there."

"Finch, you mean."

"Finch!"

"He woke up and now he's like this gardening powerhouse. He's actually kind of… tolerable now. But Miz Winnie's still"—she glanced over her shoulder and lowered her voice—"AWOL." She scuffed her toe in the dirt. "Thing is, the garden's doing great, but Finch isn't supposed to hide out in the garden. He's supposed to be writing his 'report.' Which none of us want him to do, but… well, I started having this idea."

"I'm all ears."

"Always thought they were pretty gigantic." Siggy jumped on her bicycle, glancing around. She wasn't sure if people were watching them or not, but best to be sure. "C'mon over to the water tower. Nobody'll be there now. I'll tell you all about my big idea."

Martin's face lit up. "Race you there!"

"You're on!" And Siggy pedaled away.

Chapter 23

Heads, Quartered

"STRAIGHTEN UP," THE Unseelie known as Laurel told their partner. "And put those digits away. She'll be here in a second."

At the other end of SCN's 925th floor hallway, three figures rounded the corner and briefly paused to don Muse ray-banning sunglasses.

The Unseelie on Laurel's right, often referred to as Hardy, continued knotting their fingers. "Think we'll get the go-ahead?"

"Tricky," said Laurel. "Seelie get *touchy* if they think they're being second-guessed."

Not that that's what Laurel felt they were doing here. It's just that this assignment already had an auditor—if that's what one could call Finch, the floofiest of Unseelie. But this was an emergency situation that was emerging quickly, based on the tip Laurel and Hardy had received the day before, and protocol was too *Seelie* for this moment.

So they'd invited the EVVVVVPCTTAP herself to join them right here, in front of Muse Central.

Laurel felt ready to boil over. They'd been on low simmer since the All-Hands Meeting almost two weeks ago, when Finch had snatched up Seaview Haven. Only Finch could've found a rule in the Guide that was so obscure even an inexperienced UDIP intern could exploit it, leaving him with the plum assignment of auditing a whole TROPE Town. Sending Finch to Seaview Haven upset everything Laurel revered about SCN. They'd had stomach pains ever since.

But the truth was, the only thing worse than Finch screwing up the assignment would be if Finch succeeded in completing it. There was no way Laurel would stay in an organization that would reward *that* sort of 'Unseelie.'

Maybe be patient, Hardy had urged. *Worst comes to worst, he shows back up and the town needs dismantling. We'll get it from him then.*

That had been the plan. But then an inside tip had arrived, and they dispensed with patience.

"The EVVVVVPCTTAP loves us," Laurel insisted. "We have an eyewitness. It's all gonna swing our way."

Hardy had hopelessly entangled their fingers now. "Hmm. Another nice mess I've gotten myself into. Remind me what we're doing here again?"

Laurel rolled their eyes. *You may be my fae-sib from another mother, but you are not good with the details*, they thought. Hardy was more a big picture Unseelie. A blunt object in the long game. Laurel ensured they portaled to the right place and swept up the crumbs, tea leaves, stray buildings, and leftover organisms in whatever location they were sent to unmake. The yin-yang of their personalities made them formidable. A decade ago, they'd even gotten complementary tattoos: *I'm with them* scrawled in Gaelic, followed by arrows that turned in whichever direction the other was standing, like compasses.

"Just follow my lead," Laurel said. "Think Finch. Think Seaview Haven. Think time to take out the trash."

Their intended target glided down the hallway, flanked by her two elf assistants: Right Side Assistant and Left

Side Assistant. As was fashionable among SCN executives, she was floating a few inches above ground. Aside from keeping the marble tiles pristine, the move demonstrated expert spellwork and made her seem even more graceful.

Laurel spelled themselves a few inches in the air. "C'mon," they hissed at Hardy. "Follow her lead."

Hardy tried their own levitation and shot to the ceiling, smacked their head, and fell into Laurel's arms, just as the entourage arrived. "Whoops."

The EVVVVVPCTTAP fixed the Unseelie with a royal gaze. "I have arrived," she announced. Butterflies encircled her head. "Make this worth my while. And good gracious, put on your ray-banning sunglasses! What are you thinking?"

"All will become clear in a moment, your Executiveness." Laurel inclined their head respectfully. "We have information about the failing TROPE Town of Seaside Haven."

ɮ— turned to Right Side Assistant, who murmured something low. "Ah, yes. The Unseelie intern we sent there has not filed a report. But he still has several sun cycles to complete. Make your point."

Laurel stood straighter. Finch still had time, but virtually all of the Unseelie auditors had reported back in, and several towns were slated for cancellation due to their dilapidated appearance and lackluster content. But there had been no *cause* determined as to why so many towns were in dire straits.

"We have reason to believe that the source of the TROPE Town problem is based in Seaview Haven, and that UDIP intern Finch has failed to report in about *that*." Laurel felt their stomach unknot a tad just from saying the words.

They had ɮ—'s full attention. "Explain. And then explain why we are *here*."

"I can give you both answers at once." Laurel stepped aside from the office's main entrance, gesturing into the high-ceilinged, rounded room known as Muse Central. Every desk was empty, every computer turned off. The most startling feature was nine stacks of unanswered paperwork that, rather than toppling over, had towered to the ceiling, swooped back down again, then up and down several more times like a rollercoaster track.

ꝫ— lowered her sunglasses and gaped, wandering into the room. "The Muses are *gone*? *Again*?"

"We got a tip!" Hardy skipped behind her.

ꝫ— waved Hardy aside. "They can't still be on a coffee break. Or at lunch. Have they quit? Were they kidnapped? Are they dead?" Butterflies fled her coif.

Right Side Assistant and Left Side Assistant floated over to her, gesturing at phone records that indicated ꝫ— herself had checked in with Muse Central and been diverted multiple times. "Well, I can't be expected to remember *every* call I make," she spluttered, and waved at those assistants. "This lapse is clearly *your* fault."

The assistants disappeared mid-protest.

"I sent charts to your office yesterday," said Laurel. "There is a direct correlation between the drop-off in creative output in T-Towns and the Muses' believed exit date. It appears they've been gone close to seven hundred sun cycles."

ꝫ— stared around the room in silence, taking it in. A few more butterflies fluttered away.

"Of course, I'm sure you have alternatives for creative inspiration," began Laurel.

"Hah! Inferior to idiotic to nonexistent!" ꝫ—'s voice rose higher. "If we'd had better options, why would we make accommodations for *deities*?" She spoke the word as if it tasted like rotten fish.

Laurel was unsurprised by this reaction. Everyone in Muse Central at this moment was well acquainted with the ego and power struggles between fae and gods, but the more riled up ꜩ— got right now, the quicker she was to send in her best and brightest to attend to matters in Seaview Haven.

Hardy held up their hands, waggling their freed fingers. "Untangled! Phew!"

Or maybe only *some* of their brightest, Laurel decided.

"You mentioned a tip," said ꜩ—, eyes narrowed. "Please tell me that it provides information as to the location of our Muses."

"Naturally," said a voice in the doorway. "They're in Seaview Haven."

All heads turned to find Janus holding a cardboard to-go box.

"Janus?" ꜩ— gasped. "What brings you to this side of the Veil?"

Janus waved the box, and a faint olive oil scent drifted into the room. "Your cafeteria, mainly. The spelt-and-salt cake is *divine*, and I know divine." They tossed the box onto a desk and strolled over to the fae. "But I also wanted a proper office. For writing. And playing Minecraft."

ꜩ— narrowed her eyes. "This room is meant for Muses, Janus. It is not a recreational facility for every god and goddess in the firmament."

Janus shrugged. "Be more gracious, fae. It's thanks to me that your"—they waved at Laurel and Hardy—"destroyers even have a clue about what's going on."

"Janus is your informant?" ꜩ— seemed ready to spiral again.

"I merely told them that Seaview Haven had a Muse infestation. Suggested they'd want to look into it."

The day before, as Laurel and Hardy had enjoyed lunch, a passenger pigeon had arrived on their table.

Ech, unsanitary. Hardy had tried batting it away.

Hold up, Laurel had said, pulling a small strip of paper from one of the pigeon's legs. The bird flew away. The message had said: *Come to 925 now. Your Muses have been out lounging in Seaview Haven, sipping wine, singing karaoke, and tormenting the locals—including a brownie I rather like and a human who's* brutal *with her writing critiques. – Janus*

Once they met up with the god, Laurel had wondered how a human could dare say anything against the scribblings of a god.

She said not to quit my day job, Janus had admitted.

What is your day job? Hardy had wondered.

Being me.

Laurel had to concede that it was an accurate job description for a god.

I felt you all ought to know, Janus had concluded. *I was the one who'd urged them there in the first place, so it's up to me to repair the damage.*

But if you're sending us, we'll be repairing the damage, Hardy had said.

Gods work in mysterious ways.

Now, ꝫ— gave Laurel and Hardy a searing look. Crooking her finger, they all tromped to the opposite side of the room as Janus finished off their spelt-and-salt cake while leaning on a desk. "I do not approve of all this god-mixing," she said. "But clearly things cannot go on. If we continue to delay, we are facing the end of the entire network. Possibly the Veil! We'll all fade into obscurity!"

Executives traditionally had to have things spelled out for them, Laurel had learned. They addressed ꝫ— as if speaking to a youngling. "The situation may be even more dire. The Muses are now *unable* to return. A godspell is in play that cannot be unwoven until the SMD of the town creates a story that passes muster with them."

ꜩ— went pale. Then paler. She nearly disappeared. Then she took a deep breath and whirled around. "All right. This information does *not* leave this room. What do we know about this Unseelie intern and why he has not reported back?"

"That he's barely Unseelie," said Laurel. "That he likes to *garden*. That he was an unfortunate choice who tied your Executive hands to get him sent to the village in the first place. For all we know, he has fallen in with the Muses. He may be conspiring to bring down SCN. He may be the most dangerous creation on this side of the Veil."

ꜩ— clasped her hands behind her back. "Based on your assessment, he's either a traitorous intern who's the greatest existential threat to all Seeliedom or a complete incompetent. Which is it?"

Laurel worried they might have oversold the hype.

"Maybe he's all those things!" said Hardy.

The executive looked the pair of them up and down. "Recommendation?"

"Someone—or perhaps two someones—should go investigate the investigator," said Laurel. "Find out what the delay is. Look into disassembling a godspell, which we all know is extremely fiddly business."

"But who could I send?" The Executive was calmer than before, though still agitated. Her coif was relaxing back into its style, and butterflies were making tentative forays of return.

"Send the Unseelies, for my sake!" Janus called from across the room.

ꜩ— whirled, mouth agape.

Janus shrugged. "Acoustics are amazing in this place. I heard everything."

"This is irregular," said ꜩ—. She called up another memo and scribbled with her invisible stylus. "Done. Go. You two will look into the status of Muses in the T-Town of Seaview Haven and confront this pseudo-Unseelie gardener's relationship with them."

Laurel gave a small bow, barely disguising their delight. "And if Seaview Haven *does* require elimination?" This was the whole aim of the meeting. The moment when they erased the point of the interfering Finch once and for all. He was an affront to all things Unseelie and could not be permitted to take charge of Seaview Haven's cancellation. They would un-make it. They would un-dream it. Correctly, without sentiment or remorse.

"Well, of course then that would be *your* job," said ꜩ—. "I trust the both of you, explicitly. Well done, my perceptive dismantlers."

Despite being Unseelie, Laurel and Hardy were not immune to a Seelie compliment. It washed over them with the satisfaction of a mud bath.

"You're welcome!" cried Janus.

ꜩ— ground her teeth. "Thank you as well, Janus."

"My pleasure." They tossed the last piece of cake into their mouth and leaned back in their chair, content.

Laurel rubbed their hands together. This was going to be *fun*.

Chapter 24

All Around the Town

IMMEDIATELY FOLLOWING BREAKFAST, Siggy hefted on her backpack and called to Malvous. "Going biking! Around town! With everybody!"

She didn't have to report to Malvous, exactly, but it was a reflex. The brownie, who was settled in the living room recliner with a science book Siggy had recommended, a cup of tea, and a bowl full of—were those *grubs*?—on a side table, gave a small wave. "'Everybody' sounds like a rather large affiliation."

"I mean, including Finch."

Malvous raised an eyebrow, though not his gaze. She swore she heard a tiny sigh of relief. "He's all yours."

Finch didn't have to be asked twice; he was already out front, boasting to Martin about how he'd turned the garden around.

"—sound pretty proud of yourself," Martin was saying as Siggy hopped down the porch steps. "I had a plum from the backyard that blew my mind."

Finch flushed. "Yes. Well. Keep that kind of thing under your hat."

"But you *are* pretty good at gardening," Martin insisted.

"Be careful," Siggy intervened, pulling her bicycle around. "Finch might not be the greatest Unseelie on earth, but he'll get a rash if you tell him he's good at making stuff."

"So cruel for one so young." Finch threw his hands in the air. He was able to walk almost normally now and gave off a healthy aura. "But I will forgive you. I have so much to be pleased about today. I am starting my *evaluation* at long last, and I have two able minions—"

"Assistants," said Siggy.

"Friends," said Martin.

"Two *whatevers*. Now. Where is my wheeled conveyance?"

Martin gestured at his chair. "It'll cost ya another gold piece if you want a ride."

"No, no," Finch said. "I spent fifteen minutes yesterday practicing on Winnifred's bicycle and now I know how to ride. I will travel as the average humans do in this village, so as to better blend in for my evaluation."

"You might want to dim that glow a little, then," Siggy said. "You're gonna blind folks."

Finch dialed things down to the level of a healthy tan, or an advanced pregnancy. "Accomplished. Let's get critical!"

Siggy pushed off first, prepared to give Finch the grand tour. Convince him that Seaview Haven was still a good place, even if it was suffering. It was the only thing to be done at this stage, and she was glad Martin was on board with her big idea. If Finch had gone off wandering on his own, who knew what trouble he might get into. She also couldn't be sure. Was it better for the adults of Seaview Haven to know who, and what, Finch was? Or would that fire them up even more? Martin kept telling her what his remaining dad told him—the town's mood got darker and harsher every time more folks went missing, and less food became available. Big Dad Dean worried it could tip over into something more than grumbles and mumbles.

Well, it was going to be up to Siggy and Martin to show Seaview Haven at its best. But she had no idea what that would look like anymore.

He'll see it needs some repairs, she'd told Martin. *And he'll see we need our mayor. But no way does it need tearing down.* After that, Finch could make his report and go home. If Malvous wanted to stay, that was fine. She liked him being in charge of the house; he paid attention while also giving her plenty of room. But Finch, he was like a bug bite she couldn't scratch. Even if he was pretty to look at.

What if he reports that Nowheresville has to be erased? Martin had asked after they'd settled themselves up on the water tower, overlooking the town. *What if he wants to scrap everything? Where do we go?*

It's a risk, she'd admitted. *But Miz Winnie has this science book. Talks about something called 'entropy.' Everything in the world's always falling apart, slowly. So Seaview Haven has always needed fixing. But we had Mayor Neal. Without him, I think Nowheresville might have become entropized too long. Maybe we're all falling off a cliff. Maybe it can't be saved. But we can't sit around here and watch it deflate like a leaky balloon.*

A leaky balloon off a cliff, Martin had snickered.

You mix your metaphors, and I'll mix mine, she'd snapped back. *Whatever happens, it might not be Nowheresville, but it might be Somewheresville.*

Sommersday for Somewheresville, Martin had said, and her heart beat faster. *Some folks might think limbo is better than nothingness.*

Not me. I want my mama and papa back. I can't wait for stuff to change. Don't you want your other dad Will back?

Martin had reddened. *You ask the dumbest stuff sometimes.* Then he'd taken her hand and she'd gone about the same shade.

But they hadn't kissed, and they hadn't talked about kissing. For right now, that was fine with Siggy.

Now, they headed toward town. The day was cool for summer, the slightest nip in the sea air suggesting fall was heading their way. All Siggy's life, the weather had told her things. September's chill meant jackets and classes. December was snow, sweaters, snowmen. April, back to jackets and umbrellas. July meant bathing suits and shorts. But in the last two years the weather had been as unfocused as the town. It snowed in June. February had a heat wave. Nothing to rely on. Siggy was exhausted with having to think about the town falling apart every day. A town should just *work*. All this worry made her feel like a boring grownup, and she didn't want that yet. She wanted to not be in charge all the time.

We deserve better, she thought, glancing at Martin. Behind her, Finch was pedaling while standing up, mouth open in delight, gray hair with those dancing red streaks whipping around in the breeze. *You better give it to us, Finchy*, she thought at him.

Off in the distance, the mayor's house peeped over a hill. They should take a wide left to avoid the entire back of it, but Siggy slowed. Then she stopped. No. They couldn't do this. Not yet. She had to check on Miz Winnie.

"Be right back," she said. "Wait here."

"Sig—" Martin began, but she was pedaling furiously toward the house. No one would answer the door for her, not if she rang the bell for an hour. But maybe she could find Winnie in a window again. Make her Winnie-bird hand gesture. See that she was at least *alive*.

Abruptly, she stopped moving forward. Her wheels spun, but it was as if she'd come up against another invisible barrier. Finch swooped around her on Winnie's bicycle and halted. "Come away," he said, his voice soft and kind. Almost unrecognizable. "What is inside that house is not your story."

"But—"

"You have a job to do. A job you promised me," he said, and circled around her again. "You are my tour guide. So, guide me, Sigfrieda."

Her heart was so heavy, she couldn't move.

Finch backed up, blocking her view of the house. He closed his fingers around hers on the handle and turned them both away. Siggy's legs hung limply for a moment, then she fitted them back onto the pedals. Somewhere in the distance was Martin, but as she touched the Unseelie all she could focus on was his face. His absolutely annoying, but astoundingly beautiful, face. She gave in. She let him pull her back to where Martin waited.

"What was *that* all about?" Martin drummed his fingers on his chair. "Were you trying to do magic?" He paused. "Hey. I said *football*. Aw, rats."

Finch licked his finger and poked briefly into the air. "Word wards continuing to decay," he muttered, scribbling with his finger. Then he made a swirling motion. "For the report."

Siggy barely heard him. She made a Winnie-bird with her hands, flew it to the sky, then crashed it toward the ground. "Just wanted to let Miz Winnie know we were here. Thinking about her."

"She knows," said Finch. "Rest assured."

Siggy blinked at him. This was like that moment in the garden, when he'd been a real person to her, not a puffed-up bug bite of a creature. "Thanks, Finch. Sometimes you're not such a rotten egg."

"Ach!" Finch threw his hands in the air again. "You're such a meanie."

Martin looked at her intensely. "No leaving the pack, Sig. You keep us on track. Yeah?"

Siggy's instinct was to fight. To tell him, *You don't get to order me around, Martin Timmlerwicz.* But he wasn't ordering, exactly. This was something else. "Gotcha. My head's on straight again. Promise."

"Speaking of promises," Finch shouted, "I have been promised an adventure. Allons-y!"

They rode off again. Finch was right: She had a different story right now. And it was taking them to the heart of Nowheresville.

AS THEY TURNED onto Main Street, Finch caught up to Siggy and Martin, whooping. "This bye-cycling is marvelous!" he cried, passing them both. "This must be what flying is like!"

Siggy grinned. This Finch she was starting to like a bit. "Guess your foot's a lot better!" she called.

"Still Hideously Deformed, thanks," he said, and shot forward. "Bye-bye-cycle!"

Main Street was reasonably empty. Most people couldn't drive their cars anymore (no more gasoline) and, of course, the population of Seaview Haven was significantly depleted. That was good for pedestrians. Excellent for bicyclists.

Terrible for bicyclists who weren't paying attention.

Martin, whose chair ran on electric and solar, paralleled with Siggy. "That Finch is a nutcase."

Up ahead, a small group of children, not expecting cars and certainly not expecting an adrenaline-fueled magical creature barreling their way, chased each other across the road. Siggy recognized them immediately: the three Zhaos, all under ten, all town terrors. Their father's bicycle repair shop, Cycle-ology, had been on the corner of Main and 5th as long as she'd been alive. The Zhaos were one of the few intact families in town. None of their loved ones had vanished—yet.

Hearing his name, Finch glanced over his shoulder with a wave, then turned back to pop a wheelie. He approached the intersection as the youngest of the Zhaos paused to pick up a lost coin.

Everything happened quickly.

"Penny," said young Yulong, crouching down.

"Finch!" Siggy shouted. "People!"

"Fibrous oxides!" Finch screeched a curse and launched both himself and the bicycle *into the air*, front wheel still held aloft in the wheelie. He cleared the squatting boy with a fraction of an inch to spare; the air from his rear tire ruffled the boy's hair as it passed. But Yulong was so startled he fell hard on his knees, then onto his hands, and started howling.

Finch landed and curved around. By then Siggy and Martin had reached Yulong, and his siblings had doubled back. The kid was clutching his knee with one hand, howling, and holding on to the penny with his other. There was a surprising amount of blood.

A few onlookers paused at the flurry of activity.

"Stars and feathers!" Finch released his bike. It fell in the road, but he just stood there, staring.

"Gimme," said Martin, dropping his chair into the recumbent position. One of the boys' brothers handed over a T-shirt and Siggy helped Yulong onto Martin's lap. They wrapped the shirt around the knee and Martin raced toward Cycle-ology, meeting Mr Zhao as he raced out of his shop. Siggy ran with her bike the few feet to the store.

"Baba, I fell!" Yulong wailed, then held up the penny. "But, money!"

The other boys stood around, looking scared and guilty.

Finch approached, then paused outside the door.

"Who caused this?" Mr Zhao glared at his sons. One pointed at the other. The second pointed at Yulong. Then they both pointed at Finch.

"Purely unintentional—" Finch began, but Mr Zhao was focusing on his son. He peeled away the T-shirt. "Yulong, this is deep. We will need Doc Mallard, and probably stitches."

The boy wailed.

Mr Zhao looked at Martin and Siggy. "Stay here. I need to call." He raced back inside.

"This what you mean about breaking things?" Siggy flared at Finch. Why was he always a disaster?

"Certainly not." Finch had come a few feet closer. His hair was tousled and awry, the red streaks sparking gently. He limped into the store, advancing toward the boys with a faraway look in his eyes. He was glowing brightly again and almost seemed to be sleeping with his eyes open. He kneeled next to Yulong.

The other Zhaos reacted to Finch the way Siggy had that first time: wary but fascinated. Finch was clearly the strangest stranger they'd ever met.

The Unseelie spoke a few words of Mandarin to Yulong, who had paled, and the boy's mouth fell open.

"We speak English, mister," the oldest boy managed.

"Excellent," Finch reverted. "As I said, Master Yulong, this injury will be painful for some time. It is messy and will take many sun cycles to heal. Do you like it that way?"

"No!" the boy shouted. Tears streamed down his face, but he wasn't sobbing. He almost seemed in thrall to Finch.

"It's gonna leave an awesome scar, though," Yulong's brother said.

"Ah, excellent." Finch grinned up at him. "Big gnarly thing. I have a notion." He turned back to Yulong. "Allow me to turn you into the toughest-looking youngling in town?"

"Yulong," said the boy. "Not 'youngling.'"

"What if we could skip all the hurting and blood and stitches?" asked Finch, his brightness pulsing gently.

"He's not going to *remove* that kid's leg, is he?" Martin whispered.

Finch glared. "What do you take me for?"

"An *Unseel-feree*," said Martin, and looked confused. The word ward continued to weaken. "A *referee*, I mean."

Finch turned to the boy again. "What do you say, Master Yulong?"

The injured child nodded mutely.

"Then give me your hand."

The young Zhaos looked at Siggy, then Martin.

Siggy bit her lip, unexpectedly hearing her mother's voice. *You're not always going to know what the good choices are,* Eve said in her memory. *Make the best one you can in that moment. Feel it in your gut and your head. Then, jump. No regrets.*

"It's okay, it's okay," she murmured to herself.

"Glad *you* think so," said Martin.

The boy placed his hand in Finch's. "Now," said the Unseelie. "Since you were going to get a scar anyway, what do you want it to look like?"

Yulong frowned. "I dunno."

"Of course you do." Finch closed his eyes briefly. "A fox? A lion? A—"

"Dragon!" the boy burst out.

Finch's dreamy eyes widened and he placed all four of their hands over the wound. The fae released a breath and nodded. "And, done."

A pause, and their hands came away, revealing a bare, blood-smudged knee. One boy handed over a wet wipe and Yulong cleared the area. Everyone inched closer. The knee was no longer bleeding or even sliced open, but it did have a two-inch scar shaped like a snaking dragon with clawed legs and a roaring muzzle. "I felt you would want a lóng, rather than a wyvern," Finch said, using a word Siggy assumed was Mandarin. "Correct?"

Before Yulong could answer, the scar moved. Cocked its head back and made a tiny, but audible, *roar*.

Finch's eyes lost their glaze, and he shook his head.

"Whoa," muttered Yulong.

"Radical," whispered Martin.

Finch's glow dimmed slightly and stopped pulsing. "Hmm. Where-where was I? He blinked at the knee. "That is quite incredible, young man."

"You just did that, Finch," said Siggy. "That was… that was total magic." Her eyes flew wide hearing the word.

Finch stood up, bemused. "Aw, anyfae could have. Done and dusted. Easy and peasy. But I didn't quite *know* I was doing it until it was done." Worried, he rubbed his face. "Don't tell anyone."

"Too late." Siggy watched Yulong run to the back of the store. "You can't keep something like that quiet. I guess this answers just how much of a disguise you were planning to use today."

"I didn't *choose* to do it." Finch was frustrated. "This is deeply disconcerting. I do not like *helping*."

Yulong was in the back, pointing at his scar, then at Finch. "He fixed it!"

"You can't prove that!" shouted Finch, and he dashed out of the shop.

Mr Zhao ran after him, followed by the others. The shop owner grabbed Finch's shoulder. "I didn't ask you to do this. I owe you nothing for it. Neither does my son."

"On the house!" Finch shouted. "But don't go *telling* people, for crispy critters' sake. You'll ruin my reputation!"

The shop owner stared at him.

"I love it!" Yulong was already running around again, followed by his brothers.

"Your kind never does anything for free," said Mr Zhao. "Tell me the price."

Finch folded his arms. "I am not the creature who brought you and your family here. I'm barely part of the Seelie Court. There is no exchange for this service. I just enjoy making scars."

One of the brothers wheeled over Finch's abandoned bike. "You dropped this, mister."

"I'll bring you all plums at the Counting tomorrow," said Siggy.

Mrs Zhao emerged from the shop and Yulong ran to her. They hugged. She wore a fragile smile and had a smudge of bicycle oil on her cheek. She gave Finch a long look up and down. "So you truly are one of *them*."

Finch bowed. "In a fashion, I am."

Mrs Zhao nodded briskly. "Well, it's about time."

BACK OUT ON the sidewalk, Siggy kept turning to Finch. They were walking their bikes for the moment. "Why'd you do that?"

"I got carried away," said Finch.

"Twice," noted Martin.

"Twice," agreed Finch. "I will be less… reckless on my conveyance."

"But aren't you all about unmaking things?" Siggy asked.

"I unmade the injury." But Finch still seemed stunned by his own behavior.

"And made something else," Martin noted. "Something that *roared*."

Finch pressed his lips together. "This town is affecting me," he said. "I'm not sure I like it."

"That's right," said Siggy. "You've been forced to garden. And forced to help a kid. It's really rough on you." She leaned closer. "Maybe you're not as Un-*referee* as you think you are."

"Gah!" Finch flinched away. "One more outburst like that, and this tour is *over*."

"Then what's your report going to say?" Martin asked.

"I will make things up!"

"Your bluffing is as good as your acting," said Siggy. "C'mon. Grossinger's should have something for lunch. I'm starving."

She and Martin were a full block away before Finch thought to get on his own bike. For a moment, she wondered if he was about to turn back home and flop on the sofa. Instead, he barreled toward them and shot right by—again.

"What're you waiting for?" he hollered without turning around. "We've got a job to do!"

Chapter 25

No Guts, No Story

THE MISTAKE WAS waiting for the chocolate chip shortbread.

Winnie was geared up to storm Neal's office and recapture their personal magic, and write a story with him. She even knew what that story would be. Passive Muse influence had heightened her creativity to a peak, and it was just about asking the right question in her mind. *What untold story can I write to blow those Muses way? Ideally, blow them all the way back to SCN—or even Olympus?*

And it had come to her. She'd even gotten Felicitous revved up. But there was one doubt: How could she dampen the assault that had made Neal a near-zombie? How to turn off that tap, just long enough for him to listen to *her*?

Shortbread. Chocolate chip shortbread. Memories of Neal sitting on her sofa, blissed out on the latest batch, mug of tea in hand, while she drank in his chiseled features and dark curls, flashed through her mind. He'd always been most open to collaboration after a shortbread feast. So, while there were few tools she could take into his whirling nightmare of an office, chocolate chip shortbread was a necessity.

Felicitous had none. Not even plain shortbread was available. Between Janus and the Muses, they were completely out. He didn't even have any butter in the house, which meant he had to go to the post-Counting Market, always a tricky exercise. "Havenites give me strange looks," he said. "Like they have upset stomachs. But I *must* go. So I try to look small and not-brownie like, but it is a bit of danger every time."

"Would they hurt you?"

Felicitous opened his mouth, then closed it. "In the past? Never. Now… well. Havenites are scared. Put hands up at mouths and talk behind them when I approach. I worry."

"I know the feeling." Winnie understood what it was like to be too closely associated with the Seelie part of this town, which was why she'd stopped going to Counting a long time ago. What Havenites thought they might be able to *do* about it, she had no idea, but they weren't going to be passive forever. "Well. I can do this without the shortbread, but it will be a *lot* harder—"

"No!" Felicitous insisted. "I have a disguise. It works, a bit. But Market will be this afternoon. Can you wait?"

"No waiting!" Brownie and human turned, finding Eutie standing in the hallway, fists on her hips. "We are not accustomed to waiting."

Winnie's anger flashed. She wanted to shout, *You have eternity! What's wrong with a wait?*

But then the anger faded. She could simply *tell* the Muses what she planned to do. They were all tangled together in that glowing yarn ball of a godspell in the other room, weren't they? She glanced at Felicitous, trying to ask with her eyes whether they should let them in on the new plan.

Felicitous shook his head, slowly.

Better to beg forgiveness than ask permission and be told no. Winnie didn't like that phrase; it encouraged sneakiness. True, the little she knew about the Muses suggested that things could go much worse for her if they disagreed with her idea. But she didn't like being sneaky. She was going to have to try honesty, first.

"Eutie," said Winnie, "I was thinking of doing something *other* than reading to you all just now. Something that might help with our mutual problem in that Box. See, if I went into Neal's office—"

A minor chord sounded. Eutie grabbed Winnie's arm and curled herself around it. "Absolutely not! That is the most dangerous place in the world for Our writer. I won't hear of it. Neither will My sisters." Her voice dropped to a whisper. "My sweet sisters would never admit it, but We could not pull you back! Your escape before was perhaps because you were so new to it; the spell did not know how to hold you there. But if you venture into that office again, there is every chance you will *become* part of the godspell, Winnifred. And We cannot permit that."

Winnie's resolve faltered. The Muse on her arm made a lot of sense. She was going to have to come up with some other idea.

"Market opens at the gloaming," said Felicitous.

His voice ripped her out of Eutie's spell. The fact was, permission or no, they were out of butter. She was going to have to postpone her trip to the office. And part of Winnie (the part she wasn't proud of) was relieved at having an excuse. Neal's office scared her. Maybe another idea would come along while she read about jealous janitors to the Muses.

"All right," said Winnie, nodding slowly. "Let's have story time."

THE SCENT OF freshly baked shortbread and melted chocolate reached Winnie's nose a full minute before Felicitous' knock sounded that night. Her stomach rumbled, but she couldn't pay attention to that. She had a bed to stuff.

Another idea had *not* struck Winnie during her morning reading for the Muses. Nor did another one come along when they went swimming that afternoon. And by the time night came, and the Muses headed out to the ocean to revel with their sister beneath the Perseid meteor shower, Winnie was without a better option.

Truth: Going into Neal's office wasn't a good or bad choice. It was the only choice.

At the sound of the brownie's knock, she darted into her darkened bathroom.

Felicitous peered around the door, carrying a container of the tantalizing shortbread she'd asked him to prepare. "Miz Winnie!" he called in alarm. "You're not sleeping, are you?"

Score. Winnie realized her ruse would be effective, even to the casual eye. "Nope!" she called from the bathroom, and the brownie jolted in surprise. Shortbread flew into the air, but the brownie moved so fast he caught every piece before a single crumb landed on the floor.

"Impressive," she said.

"Miz Winnie," he said, clutching his chest. "This is no time for hide-and-seek."

"We're not doing that, and obviously I'm not going to bed." She set a calming hand on his shoulder.

"Then who is *that*?" He poked at the bed. A lumpy shape rested beneath the duvet.

"Pillows. Old trick from when I would sneak out of the house as a teenager." Actually, it was Eve's trick. Winnie had been so boring she'd never thought of it herself. "In case the ladies came home and want to check up on me. I didn't want anyone getting in the way of our plans."

"They are not suspicious of you," said Felicitous.

"Because they think I'm helpless. I'm a mere human."

The Muses were kind to her. But they were kind in the way a person was kind to a favorite pet. If a golden retriever had hopes and aspirations, would their owners know they existed? "I'm a toy to them. But I like you. You've made this whole experience bearable. You are an extremely good brownie."

Felicitous beamed. "Brownies have a number of skills that go unappreciated," he said. "So, are we going to the office now?"

Taking a deep breath, Winnie steeled herself. She knew she might not emerge for a very long time—if ever—if her plan didn't work. On the other hand, if it did, she and Neal could be free in hours. Of course, that had been Neal's assumption before he became part of the godspell, too.

She nodded. "Onward. Though I'm dreading trying to open that door." She'd been thinking about how it took all of her and Finch's combined body weight to gain entry to Neal's office that first time.

"There is nothing to dread."

Winnie stared at him.

"We are not going in the main entrance."

"Felicitous, last I checked that room only has one entrance. Or do you mean the windows?"

The brownie pressed on the wall to her room and a three-foot high space materialized, revealing darkness beyond. "No windows. Follow me."

"Wait—that's always been there?" Winnie had heard of jib doors in old country mansions but had no idea one existed in her room. And this was so *small*. Brownie-sized, even. She waved a hand in the area, feeling a cool breeze on the other side. Her fingers brushed an inner wall, meaning the space was barely a foot wide.

"This is where I live," said Felicitous. "No, not in your room. But brownies live in the walls of houses. Once we spend any sleep cycle in any structure, we have access to the interior walls. Outside TROPE Towns, we can even access any structure in which a fellow brownie resides by following their paths, though there is a permission issue to enter the interior—" He cut himself off. "Never mind. This will be tight, but Miz Winnie is not so large for a human. I will lead us to Mayor Neal's office and open an exit there."

It was astonishing. Winnie vowed to think about this in greater depth later. "Why is this better than pushing open Neal's office?"

"Muses sense when that door opens. If his godspell breaks, they will be aware instantly. They are far away now, at the seaside, so perhaps the connection will be very light. But this way no one knows what you are doing. Except Felicitous. They will discover the truth, of course, but this purchases you time."

"Eutie said they can't get me out."

Felicitous shrugged. "And you have stuffed your bed. Precautions are wise. Cover your tracks even if you don't know the Minotaur is following, brownies say."

Winnie kissed the top of his head. "Not only are you a good brownie, you're a genius."

Felicitous turned a deep rosy pink. "This way." He disappeared into the doorway.

Taking a deep breath, Winnie followed. The opening sealed shut behind them.

WINNIE DIDN'T KNOW a lot about how houses were built—her entire experience came from one summer watching a hunky contractor build a second wing onto the family home when she was fifteen—but she knew that for the most part, houses did not come with sixteen-inch-wide corridors between main and exterior walls. Felicitous' ability to conjure a second, narrow world on the other side of the wall left her speechless.

It almost helped her forget that she got claustrophobic in tight spaces.

When the space became a small, *dark* space with no obvious exit, Winnie felt her heart lock up and her brain go on hold. She gripped Felicitous' shoulder like the edge of a cliff as they wound through narrow corridors, ducked when he said to duck (thwacking her head once when he forgot to), then got down on her hands and knees when necessary. The last bit triggered a small panic attack; Winnie took long, deep breaths and thought of open, grassy fields while inching forward in that insanely tight space. She began to imagine it all coming to a point where she could no longer fit and being unable to reverse to return to her room.

"I had no idea," she gasped, wanting to fill the emptiness. "Was this built into the house?"

"The space will appear when the correct brownie is near," Felicitous chanted as if reciting a charm. "Every house, every building. It is just *there*. Brownies must have someplace to live. One day, perhaps, Miz Winnie would like to see my quarters."

"Not tonight, though."

"No. There is a Plan in motion."

Winnie kept trying to think of things to say, but the darkness was starting to get to her. Then she could wait no longer. "Are we there yet?" she squeaked.

Felicitous paused for a long moment, and the answer came without his saying a word. Winnie heard a hum like a storm raging outside a window that grew louder with each step. They halted. "Yes. Now we are here."

A new doorway opened in front of them, also three feet high. Winnie winced at the brightness of the room beyond. The cyclone of paper still swirled over Neal's typewriter, and her heart caught. He was hunched in the same spot he'd been in before. The only difference now was that more paper filled the floor, and the word tree had grown larger and leafier. Winnie had never found a tree threatening before, but this one gave her goosebumps.

Felicitous handed Winnie the plate of shortbread and raised his voice over the whirling howl. "I must clean up and keep watch." He held up a thin book. "This door will be held open for you, for when you are prepared to depart." He stepped back to gesture her into the room, and immediately Winnie was enveloped in noise and wind and flying paper. Felicitous propped open the door with the book and gave Winnie a small wave. Then he let the wall slide shut, with barely an inch to reveal there ever was a door. It was merely a three-foot-high dark stripe against an otherwise blank wall.

Winnie turned to face the storm. Her gray hair swirled above her head like the branches of a tree. She laid a hand over the shortbread.

And she began wading through the thigh-high stack of discarded paper, toward Neal.

Chapter 26

Without Pier

LIKE MR ZHAO, Mrs Grossinger took a beat upon seeing Finch. Unlike Mr Zhao, her smile remained broad and wide as she escorted her visitors around the mostly empty store. She clearly knew how to recognize a fae when she saw one. "I believe you all are part of the biker gang that made things interesting just a few minutes ago on Main," she said in Hungarian-accented English.

"Word travels fast," said Siggy.

Mrs Grossinger gestured at one of the other Zhao kids, who was scooting out the door with a paper sack of pre-made sandwiches. "Is difficult to keep anything hush-hush in a town that keeps shrinking."

"Madam," said Finch, "while I appreciate the lust for sensationalism more than most, it would be beneficial to everyone if you did not characterize us as a 'biker gang,' an affiliation that often suggests—"

"Lighten up, Finchy," said Martin, sipping on a bottle of punch. "I kind of like the idea of being a gang, though maybe something more focusing on the *wheels* than the *bikes*."

Mrs Grossinger guided them toward the back of the store. "In any case, many greetings to you, our bright stranger," she said. "I anticipate greatly the changes you may bring to our town."

Don't hold your breath, Siggy thought.

The small, plump woman pulled back a curtain to reveal the storage area, which was barer than the store. Some of the only items in the back room were a stack of empty sacks and some equally empty barrels. "Our supply system has always been quite clear. At night, I make list, list goes in sacks and barrels. Morning, sacks and barrels are full, list is gone. No more, now."

This had never been a secret to Siggy. Growing up in town, it was just one more thing she'd come to accept as How Things Worked. Only after Miz Winnie had explained things did she realize it was more *football*, and that on the other side of the Veil probably supplies didn't follow a wish list.

"These days, storeroom holds leftovers from Counting Market, and we repurpose and sell," said Mrs Grossinger.

Finch ran his hands over a stack of the cloth sacks, now neatly piled on a table. Siggy kept a close eye on him, while Martin remained in the store and ate his lunch. "These are what the food arrived in?" he asked.

"Once," said the owner. "I keep, sometimes use for laundry, then wash and return. Perfectly good sacks."

Finch opened a sack and took a long, deep whiff as if evaluating its vintage. When his head emerged from the fabric, he'd gone sleepy eyed and distant, like he had when attending to Yulong. Taking a step back, he interlaced and inverted his fingers. The knuckles cracked like popcorn. Then he picked up sack after sack, blowing a puff of air into each before discarding it on the table. Every three or four, he gave his head a toss but never lost the sleepy-eyed look.

"What *is* he doing?" the grocer asked Siggy under her breath.

Siggy had an idea but was afraid to speak it aloud. Too fanciful. Too hopeful.

Finch finished with the sacks and did the same thing with the barrels. Then he coughed. The faraway look in his eyes faded. "Right," he said. "Go forth and put your lists back in tonight."

Mrs Grossinger's eyes widened. "Are you... our new Mayor?"

Finch shook his head. "I would not presume! Mayor Bartleby is still... in residence."

"For all the good he's done lately," the store owner muttered. "Then what are you doing here?"

Finch seemed dazzled. "Looking around, my good merchant." He pointed at the sacks. "Weren't those on the table a moment ago?"

"You tossed them down," said Siggy. "After you blew into them."

Finch turned pink and stamped his bad foot. "Ouch!" he cried, hopping up and down. Then he stamped his good foot and pounded around the back room before storming through the curtain again, swearing. "Musk noodles!"

Mrs Grossinger hurried after Finch and wrapped her arms around him. He went stiff and unyielding, his fingers splayed wide. "You are, indeed, a magical creature." Her eyes widened, hearing what she'd said. "My goodness. These are forbidden words to us."

Finch wormed out of the grocer's grip, muttering his version of swears, then limped out of the store.

"And you, young Sommersday, you know who this *referee* creature is?" Mrs Grossinger sighed. "Ah, well. Back to usual."

"I do!" said Siggy. "I am ahead of my time. I've been let into the secret club. But the whole Things We Can Say aspect seems to flip back and forth. Look: Magic! Seelie! SCN! *Football.*" She cringed. Well, the word ward was loose for a few seconds there.

"Is good enough for me," said Mrs Grossinger, picking up the phone. "I must make some phone calls now. While the words can come to me. Good day."

Siggy found Finch outside with Martin. The Unseelie was pacing in circles, muttering to himself.

"What's up with him?" Martin gestured.

"Finch might've just fixed our food issues," said Siggy.

Martin lunged toward the Unseelie, who backed up. "Come no closer, youngling!" Then he grabbed his hair. "I did it again. I fixed something. I didn't want to, but I also truly *did* want to. Oh, this is madness."

"I mean, maybe?" said Siggy. "All I saw was you breathing into some sacks. Maybe nothing got fixed at all."

Finch blinked several times. "That would be a relief. Always look on the dark side of life, I say. Being—"

"Unseelie, I know," said Siggy. "You've mentioned."

Finch shook his head. "I am not a glitch. My *deviances* are about me, not your town. Your weakening word wards are symptomatic of the town crumbling like your roads. Chaos looms. So why aren't I more excited?"

Behind them, Mrs Grossinger carried a paper sack to Siggy. "Is present for you and your 'biker gang.'" She winked at Finch. "And note inside for Winnifred." Quickly, she kissed Finch on the forehead and dashed back into the store.

Siggy opened the bag. It was full of sandwiches and cookies, and she handed one to Martin.

"That woman is a menace," said Finch. "She knows nothing about me."

"What's the note?" Martin asked Siggy through a mouthful of cookies.

Siggy crunched the top of the bag in her hand, then tossed it in her bike basket. "Not here," she said. "It's for *Miz Winnie*, remember?"

Martin winked at her.

Finch held a sandwich but didn't take a bite. He stared into the distance and let out a long breath. The dreamy look was returning. "I wish to see the ocean. Now."

THE DOCKS SIGNALED the edge of town, the end of the world. Siggy and Martin led Finch out onto a pier, skidding to a halt just before they would have ridden directly into the ocean. In the distance, several trawlers and other small craft dotted the horizon as the ocean slapped and lapped against the pilings.

"Well, Finchy, you're delivered," said Martin. "What's so important about coming all the way out here?"

"Finchy?" Siggy laughed.

"Maybe 'Finchmeister,'" Martin grinned.

"Mr Finchella?" Siggy giggled.

"Younglings, do cease attempting to make my name adorable," said Finch. "I am not, and never will be, 'cute.'"

"Finchmeister it is," said Martin. His eyes met Siggy's, and the laughter trickled away. She took Martin's hand and gestured for him to lower the chair. He turned it recumbent so they could both dangle their legs over the edge of the pier. Siggy wasn't sure what, if anything, today had accomplished in terms of Finch evaluating the town, but she'd gotten a good look at Martin and seen him in ways she never had before.

"You were kind of heroic earlier," she said. "Racing to help Yulong. Like, no hesitation."

Martin looked at her with soft eyes. "You were there, too. Immediately."

Finch plopped down next to them. "A most curious day indeed. We have learned that wards are failing all over Seaview Haven, and that individual residents show up for their work. They are living their lives. They are prepared to repair bicycles, make sandwiches, and conduct phone conversations. All pointless activities in a crashing world. So how is it that humans go on when they are quite aware that their world is falling apart?"

Siggy felt irritated; she'd have liked a moment alone with Martin. She snapped, "Aren't you paying attention? What should they do—lie in the dirt and wait for rain? 'Cause gosh, world's done, who cares, blah, blah. Some of us are trying to make things better. Like dragging a cranky Unseelie all around town."

"Nobody's happy to be in Seaview Haven these days," said Martin. "But it's not like we can leave. There's this song my dad Dean plays a lot lately: 'When the World is Running Down, You Make the Best of What's Still Around.' Says it all, to me." He lifted his chin. "What's in the bag, Sig?"

"We ate the sandwiches," she said.

"No, the other thing."

Siggy remembered the note from Mrs Grossinger. "Maybe we shouldn't read it. It's not for us."

"Not like Miz Winnie's gonna read it any time soon. If you like, I'll read it. You can say I insisted."

Siggy fetched the bag from her bicycle basket and pulled out the note. It was handwritten on half of an old ad for the grocery store, a rare piece of paper in town. It said: *Clouds gather. Tonight. Time to plan.*

"Well, that's not ominous or anything," said Martin. He took the note and read it again. "Mind if I keep this? I think Dad Dean should see it. He's had a few *thoughts* lately."

"Like?" Siggy asked, and let him put it in his pocket.

"Oh, like the walls are closing in. Like, people feel it more now. They're worried help isn't coming and want to shout. Make things better. And now Finch is here. I think they're starting to have hope, and Dad Dean says hope can make people impatient for change."

"I do not wish to be a harbinger of hope," said Finch, but his tone suggested otherwise. "Yet, I do find myself revisiting several moments from today. I had not realized what it might feel like to *fix* a thing instead of wanting to *break* it. It is a very different sensation for me. Perhaps—" He cut off, turning around.

Siggy followed his gaze. Two tanned individuals in matching white outfits were lingering at a lamppost at the opposite end of the pier. They were staring at an upside-down fold-out map, glanced up, then turned back toward town.

"Newcomers," whispered Siggy.

Finch had frozen in place.

"Folks you know?" Martin asked.

"Unclear," said Finch. "Not something I will look into right now." He turned back toward the ocean, restless, as a trawler sailed toward the dock. "I will have to make a report," he said after a long moment. "It is inevitable."

"You're *not* going to tear down this town," Martin declared, and Siggy had never heard him so emphatic. "I'll drown you first."

The trawler pulled in alongside the pier. A man hopped out, lashing it to the cleats embedded in the wood.

"Hah," Finch laughed. "Shows what you know. I can't drown."

Siggy wanted to push him into the harbor. "So after everything you saw in town today, you still think you want to tear this place to pieces?" She recalled all the smaller stops they'd made through town, bending back one finger for each instance: the shop owners, kids on the playground, women gathered in a café laughing, several men kicking a soccer ball, a radio station playing tunes while a couple danced in the street, another couple moving furniture. The town wasn't healthy but didn't deserve to be taken into the woods and shot.

When she finished, Finch had no reply.

Men in heavy orange coveralls disembarked from the trawler, hauling buckets of fish. Siggy noted Martin counting: one, two, five, seven. "Pathetic haul," he said. "Dad Will always said they should take in ten times that much every day."

"Think you can do better, sonny, come out w'us next time," growled one fisherman. He was about Miz Winnie's age and sported a sun-bleached beard. "Wait—you're the Timmlerwicz boy?"

Martin raised the recumbent chair. "Sorry, Cap'n Roberts. Didn't mean *you* screwed up."

Roberts sauntered over, appraising Martin and eyeing his companions. "You're Eve and Hal's girl, if I'm right." He gestured at Siggy, then squinted at Finch. "You're new. An' I know every soul in this town."

"He's a visitor," Siggy explained for what felt like the millionth time. "From… SCN. Know what I mean?"

The captain's eyebrows shot up in surprise. His fellow fishermen came over, windburned and tired, damp in the hair and coated in a slick of fish guts. "Did she say—" asked one.

"She said it," said another. "SCN. Network. Seelie. Whoa. Guess things really are changin'."

"Go away for three nights, come back to this," said the captain. "Get cleaned up, fellas. Maybe we oughta hash a couple things out at the Rum Runner, if we're able to really talk about this stuff now." The men muttered and cast sharp glances over their shoulders at Finch before returning to the boat.

Finch seemed gleeful. "Look what you started, Siggy! Now everyone knows the word wards are failing, too!"

"You. Punk hairdo." The captain pointed at Finch. "What's wrong with this town?"

"Well, I've been sent to find out," said the fae. "But I believe you know the answer to that writ small—namely, things don't work here like they used to."

"You don't need to tell me," said Captain Roberts. "You got spells, enchantments, whatnot?" He gestured with his yellow cap. "Well, we can't barely sail more'n a mile out these days. Not enough fish to pick up no more. Plus, there's this *draining* sound. Glug-glug everywhere."

Finch folded his arms. "I'll think about it."

Roberts turned red. "You little—" he grabbed a crowbar and made to swipe at the Unseelie. Martin rolled away and Siggy ducked. Finch raised a hand, and the tool turned into an eel. In surprise, the captain dropped it, directly on to Siggy's head. She squealed and hurled it into the water. Then she jumped up and faced off with the captain.

"Look. I've wanted to do something like that with him a couple times, too. But you can't just go whacking the resident *referee*." She made a face. "He's a little drained now. Weak. That's probably the last magic of the day. All out of wands, if you know what I mean."

"Hmph." Captain Roberts backed off. "Maybe we oughta be using that Seelie for *bait*. Like to see him on the end of a hook."

"Unseelie!" Finch shouted, and dove into the water.

Siggy whirled.

"He jumped! Right in!" Martin pointed. "Minute you called him 'weak' he got mad, real fast."

Her smile was sly. "Good thing he's never heard of reverse psychology before. Learned that one from a cartoon."

Captain Robert raised his binoculars to scan the horizon. "Can that thing swim?"

"Well, I don't think he's going to kill himself because Siggy insulted his wand capacity," said Martin.

But Finch was nowhere to be seen.

The three of them maneuvered from one side of the dock to the other, squinting as the sun lowered in the sky. The water had gone dead calm, with only tiny eddies here and there—and no bubbles. Siggy strained for that glug-glug sound the captain had referred to. What if the ocean was broken, too? What if it was a giant bathtub and was draining out all the fish? Maybe the world didn't end with a bang, but with a glug.

"There!" Captain Roberts pointed, still staring through his binoculars.

Several hundred yards out, the harbor had begun to roil like a pot on a burner. The glassy surface was shifting, small crests dancing across its surface. Bubbles rose and exploded. Foam spread. Then a spout of water spewed into the air and continued spouting. Then someone was climbing the spout. When the someone reached the top of the burbling water, a second spout nearer to the dock rose, and the someone leaped to the top of that second spout. Then a third. And a fourth. Until Finch, who had lost his shoes and socks somehow, reached the pier and leapt. He crashed into Siggy and Martin while the captain darted out of the way. Everyone was covered in seawater and foam. Finch spat out a glob of seaweed and peeled a starfish from his head, flinging both back into the water.

"Done," he said, like he had more than once that day.

"What was—" the captain spluttered.

"What did you—" Martin began simultaneously.

Finch held up a hand. "Listen."

Siggy heard water sloshing against the trawler. The sounds of the Rum Runner crowd in the distance. Gulls in the sky.

"Gone!" cried the captain, astonished.

Siggy understood immediately. No more glug-glug.

The roiling began again far out in the water, a chaotic splashing and gurgling beneath the waves. Siggy peered over the edge of the pier, goggling. The water was teeming with fish. Large ones, small ones, all kinds.

"Never underestimate an Unseelie," said Finch. "I do not *run out*."

The captain dashed to the Rum Runner, summoning his shipmates. "Fellas, put down your brews—we're goin' back out!"

"So what did you do?" Siggy asked.

Finch leaned on an elbow, still dripping. Self-satisfaction radiated from him like heat. "Bit of a blurp with your local Kraken. She was amenable to assisting me in the plugging of a hole."

So there really *was* a Kraken! And it was female! Siggy wished she'd been able to see it.

"What fills up a big sea hole?" asked Martin.

"A very big sea plug." Finch spoke as if Martin was a toddler. "Couple of old sunken ships, sand, seaweed. And Kraken, eh, sputum."

"Spit?" asked Siggy.

"Precisely. Quite gummy stuff, that."

"And naturally, you speak Kraken." Martin sounded just a shade annoyed.

"I am versed in over one hundred and twenty species' dialects," said Finch. "The Kraken was pleased to converse with someone who knew her sounds. It said life had become dull—not enough sailors to intimidate or whales to consume any more. I promised if she could help me plug that hole, she could postpone coming up on land for her next meal. Which would have been in about six hours' time."

Siggy and Martin straightened.

"So you see, you two owe me. I have *saved* this town." He heard himself and his smile vanished. "Crusty crawfish. I am helping my way out of a job. A career. My *life*, probably. This has to stop."

"Does it?" asked Siggy. "What's the worst thing about being a failed Unseelie?"

Finch sat up and wiggled his toes. "I don't think I know any more," he said quietly.

"If it helps, I don't know if you're a very good Seelie, either," said Siggy. "But who cares which one you are, anyway? I once had parents. Now I don't. Martin could walk once. Now he can't. Miz Winnie promised to never leave me behind, and she did. Things change. Stuff happens. Why isn't it possible to just be a Finch? What's wrong with being unique?"

Finch stood and walked around in a circle, fluffing out his drying hair. He no longer had a limp. "Where I come from, it's important to know these things. Seelie are one way. Perfect. Unseelie are the other. Imperfect. The ones in between are not seen as being very useful, or important. And then there are those like me who are just bad at everything."

"I would disagree," said Siggy.

Finch came to a hard, sudden halt. "Oh, no. No, no, no." He reached down and caressed his small, left, bare toe. "This can't be!"

Siggy and Martin leaned over. The fae's feet were remarkably human, if somewhat pale and wrinkly for having been in the ocean. "What are we looking at?" asked Siggy.

"It's… not there!" Finch's voice broke. "My Hideous Deformity! It's… gone!"

Then he fainted.

Chapter 27

Visiting Hours

FELICITOUS COULDN'T RECALL the last time the house was this empty and quiet. It almost felt like freedom.

He was distantly aware of the whirling hum within Mayor Neal's office, and of course he made a certain noise while scrubbing out the shortbread pans. But right now, it was as if stillness covered his brownie self like a faux Yeti fur coat. The Muses were down at the ocean, communing with the stars, and he daydreamed that the local Kraken might take an interest in their delicious, well-stuffed presence.

I wonder what happens to a godspell if half of the party gets gobbled up?

That wasn't very Bro-like thinking, but Felicitous' hospitality hormones were depleted after two years of caring for the demanding siblings.

He held up a cleaned shortbread pan and considered it. *Guess I'll need at least one more batch,* he thought. There was a single pan left at the cracked-open door for Ms Winnie should she require reinforcements, and the Muses would undoubtedly be peckish after returning from their night journey. This, assuming the Kraken didn't come calling. Fortunately, shortbread with chocolate chips could also be loaded with any number of soothing spices, including ones that would encourage long, deep naps.

Those were the ones he would save for them.

After sliding a fresh pan in the oven, Felicitous made tea and sat on a barstool at the raised kitchen table, his short legs dangling. Closing his eyes, he savored the relative quiet again and sent good thoughts Ms Winnie's way. And Mayor Neal's. He didn't hold out much hope for success, but what else could he do at this point?

Prior to the Great Muse Invasion, Mayor Neal's house had always been too big for a single Seelie and brownie helper. They'd barely used it. Neal was either in his office working, out roaming the town, or visiting Ms Winnie. He could be gone several nights in a row at her home, which freed Felicitous to indulge himself. After ensuring the house was dust and smudge free, the brownie might take a dip in the pool, read a book in the backyard, or craft his personal favorite snacks. (The ones with nutmeg and cattails, primarily.) But he'd also craved the company of fellow Bros, and pre-GMI, he spent his evenings visiting pals in other T-Towns, using the in-house corridor network. So long as a building had a Bro in it, he could at least knock to see if they were around. For a time, he'd dated a Bro working on the long-running reality TV series *Tune in Tomorrow*. He and Oleander were just friends now, but she was a sassy, resourceful brownie who'd taught him much about dealing with mortals.

When GMI descended, he'd lost all that free time. There was always something the uninvited guests wanted. He couldn't even risk taking off tonight; he'd promised to keep an ear out for returning Muses and remain alert in case Ms Winnie needed help.

Not that I have the least clue what to do if she calls for me, he thought. *But helping is what we do*.

Yet he'd failed to be helpful enough to keep Mayor Neal from falling into the mess everyone was in now.

Felicitous and Mayor Neal had been partnered for decades in Seaview Haven. The brownie had seen the Seelie creator through scores of movies and more than a few resident human writer and law enforcement officer pairs. The SMD had a gentle soul but also experienced sharp mood swings. Over the years, Felicitous learned how to handle his occasional dark, sudden passions. They cropped up most often when the Mayor was in Showrunner mode, tangled up with an edit, sweating over a script, or obsessing about a particular shot. He turned sour if they ran out of his favorite tea. True, brownies could turn themselves into a tea-like concoction in a pinch, then reconstitute shortly afterward, and Felicitous often volunteered himself as a substitute if Mayor Neal was so inclined, but he'd never had the offer accepted.

Can't afford to wait for you to get yourself back together, the Mayor had said once. *And no, I don't want to know what that entails.*

For some months pre-GMI, though, Mayor Neal had been uncharacteristically prickly. He and Ms Winnie had not seen eye to eye about the nature of her new mysteries, a sign Felicitous noted often presaged a given writer's departure. But Ms Winnie? She'd been so special to the town and to Mayor Neal especially. Felicitous hated to hear them argue.

Why can't she see things my way? the Mayor had blustered. *Even if they're just a 'hoax'" She keeps saying she doesn't want to write 'Scooby' stories. What is a Scooby? Does it fit in a breadbox?*

Felicitous hadn't known how to answer that.

Then had come the Frisbee incident. Felicitous had heard Mayor Neal tumble from the roof and raced out to ensure there was no injury. At first Felicitous had been worried; the Seelie appeared unconscious. But the moment he picked him up, Mayor Neal had barely fluttered his eyes and whispered, *Take me in. Don't let her see.*

Felicitous had been startled. *You're not injured?* he'd whispered back.

'Course not, you silly brownie. I'm Seelie. Now, don't let her in behind us.

Felicitous had done so, feeling awfully rude to Ms Winnie. Once indoors, he'd been given fresh instructions.

I'm going to take a long nap, Mayor Neal had said. *I have to come to some decisions about the future of our town. About who will be writing our stories.*

Mayor Neal! Felicitous had been scandalized.

Tell anyone who asks that I have a grave head injury and can't be seen. Not even by the Doc.

For the first time, Felicitous had judged his boss. *That's not very kind.*

Hmph. Let her stew for a few days. She loves a mystery, so let her wonder what happened. And when I recover, I bet she'll be fine with a few monsters in town.

Hating to do it, Felicitous nevertheless followed orders. Ms Winnie's worried, pained face was so hard on him that he'd started getting stomachaches, so he'd stopped answering the door when she came by. The only thing that made this new situation tolerable was that he was certain Mayor Neal would be back to himself soon.

But then the GMI had arrived, Mayor Neal had woken up with his grand idea to write a story, and the Muses and the Seelie had created their godspell to ensure it would happen. They would get their escape from SCN, and Neal would arise in triumph, possibly negating hiring any more human writers in TROPE Towns, ever again.

This seems unwise, Felicitous had told him. *You don't know what will happen. And I thought you liked Ms Winnie.*

Of course I do. I just don't like needing to need *her. Seelie are above that. We have mastered so much of the creative arts. It's time one of us figured out how to write. I mean, how hard can it be?*

You're leaving me alone with all of them! Felicitous had tried one more way to keep Mayor Neal from what he was certain was a mistake. *That's a lot!*

They won't be here for long, he'd assured Felicitous.

Mayor Neal had been wrong—on all counts.

THE RICH, DELICIOUS scent of browned butter filled the house as the oven dinged, indicating the latest batch of sleepy seasoning-laced shortbread and chocolate was ready. Felicitous removed the pan and set it on a trivet to cool, inhaling deeply.

The bell outside the house rang.

Felicitous stopped inhaling and half turned.

It was the middle of the night. Obviously, it wasn't Ms Winnie. Siggy and her friends would be tucked in bed by now. Malvous might have tried the corridor access method; it was something Felicitous had not discussed with him, but that would be a knock. So it wasn't Malvous. The townsfolk should be well-warded away. Might the wards have finally shattered? Anything was possible now in Nowheresville.

Seaview Haven, he corrected himself. *Past, present, and future.*

One possibility was left, though what the Unseelie investigator might want at this hour was a mystery. Felicitous pulled the front door open, preparing to inform Finch that it was too late, go home, Ms Winnie had things under control.

Not Finch. Instead, Felicitous faced two strangers. They had overly tanned faces and looked almost identical, except that one had shimmery platinum hair and the other's was a deep cobalt blue, and one was tall while the other was portlier. Four large, dark eyes burned into Felicitous, and he knew instantly that they were Unseelie. They even *smelled* like Unseelie, that mix of potato peels gone bad and dirty laundry.

"How may I help?" he asked, turning on full butler mode.

"Greetings," said blue hair, offering a card that read:

SEELIE COURT NETWORK
DECONSTRUCTION DIVISION
CALL ME LAUREL
THE OTHER ONE IS HARDY

"We are with SCN, and we are reconnaissancing," said Laurel.

"My sympathies," said Felicitous. "Is that painful?"

Laurel ignored him. "We are taking over the evaluation of this town from a rogue Unseelie investigator called Finch. He is derelict in his reportage. We've followed him all over town today and observed him doing the most extraordinary Un-Unseelie things."

A cool tingle of warning spread through Felicitous. "He's not here."

"We didn't expect so." Hardy placed a hand on the door. "We decided to talk to your SMD first."

Silence. Felicitous swallowed. "He's… engaged."

Hardy chuckled. "Been that way a long time. Didn't even show up to an All-Hands Emergency meeting. Bad form."

"Well, ah"—Felicitous had never been good at thinking on his feet—"come by in the morning and I'm sure things will be different." He crossed his fingers behind his back. "Really. I'm certain." He was trying not to sweat, unable to imagine what might happen if these two were in the house when the Muses returned. Or if they interrupted Mayor Neal and Ms Winnie. Either possibility felt as likely as the other, and both felt like big trouble.

"Different from the last two years?" Laurel took a step forward, but Felicitous didn't budge. "Really, now. We'll only be a moment. We must speak with him before journeying back to the Network."

Felicitous gripped the door more tightly.

"Fine." Hardy flapped their necktie. "The hard way it is."

The two Unseelie shoved the door open with a mutual heave. Felicitous shoved back. For a moment, neither gave ground. Then the visitors glanced at one another and released the door simultaneously. Felicitous stumbled, and they redoubled their shoving. The door flew open, knocking the brownie backward.

And they were in the house.

"Interrupting the Showrunner's writing process is ill-advised," Felicitous cried, scampering after them. What would Oleander do? Maybe give them a chance, but not a full chance. He needed a diversion. Snapping his fingers, he thought he had it. "Knock first! If he responds, then of course you may have your meeting. If not—"

Laurel raised an eyebrow. "A Seelie has a *writing process*?"

Hardy sniffed the air and rubbed their belly. "Do I smell… shortbread?"

"He does. Have a writing process, I mean." Despite his best efforts, Felicitous was now sweating. "Of a kind. And yes—I just made a batch."

"If he's writing, why is this town in such need of attention?" Laurel scratched at their blue hair.

"There's been a hiccup in new content," said Felicitous. "He hit his head after a fall. Slow recovery. But now he's back on the horse."

"He's horseback riding?" Hardy's brow knitted, but their attention was directed toward the kitchen.

"No, he's just writing."

Laurel jabbed a thumb at Neal's office door. The whirlwind sound was unmistakable. "Listen." They pressed their ear on the door. "What is that noise?"

"Writing." Felicitous made out the sounds of keys clacking and carriage returns through the hubbub and hoped that was a good sign. "As I say, the Showrunner's writing process is unique."

Laurel stepped back from the door as Hardy disappeared into the kitchen. "All right," the blue-haired Unseelie allowed. "I suppose SCN wouldn't want us to interrupt something creative." They set their hands on their narrow hips. "We can speak with him later. Now, do you know the whereabouts of a dysfunctional maybe-Unseelie investigator called Finch?"

"I can draw you a map." Felicitous was nearly woozy with relief. "But it is late."

"I'm not tired," said Laurel. "Hardy?"

Mumbling came from the kitchen. Brownie and Unseelie followed the sound and found Hardy face down in the still warm pan of shortbread. "Mx Hardy!" Laurel cried.

The Unseelie glanced up, face flecked with chocolate. "This is really not bad."

"Another fine mess," Laurel sighed, pulling the tray toward them. They picked at the crispy shortbread corners and popped a few crumbs into their mouth, but within seconds was grabbing at every wedge not imprinted by Hardy's face or teeth and shoving it into their faces. Hardy pulled the tray toward them; Laurel responded by grabbing it. They growled. Then they laughed.

"We'll just have to have *more*," Hardy grinned.

"Indeed," Laurel agreed. "Brownie, another batch, quickly. If we must wait, we will wait with shortbread."

Felicitous reached for the butter. Then the chips. Then his seasonings.

Down the hall, the typewriter continued to clack.

Chapter 28

Taking the Biscuits

WINNIE FELT BOTH terrified and ridiculous simultaneously, an emotion she dubbed *terridiculous*. Living in an invented town on the magical side of the Veil for a decade and a half had prepared her for many wonders, but nothing came close to this.

The noise in Neal's office was like a trash truck grinding waste. She was attacked by flying paper that left behind tiny slices in her skin. Even the word tree seemed to have it in for her, waving its branches to hinder her progress. Every instinct urged her to go *back into the wall*, which was a nightmare of its own.

And no one was coming to help.

Living in Seaview Haven all these years had been like settling into a cushioned retirement. Everything Winnie had wanted was in arm's reach, and then some. But her personal magical experiences had been limited to portaling from one side of the Veil to the other, and experiencing Neal's occasional, whimsical eccentricities. She'd gotten used to him keeping his magical self hidden. Once in a while, he'd dazzle by slapping on the bass or whipping up a levitating angel food cake or typing so fast his fingers were blurs. And she'd watched him communicate with spirits in trees and hum with bees to get the right camera angles in the movies. But those things aside, her life here had been remarkably *human*.

Birds? Bees? she'd asked early on. *Trees?*

Dryads live in the trees. Or shrubs. Sometimes in houseplants. Camera-dryads, see? Then we can get pixies to mount these teeny-weeny cameras for the birds—

Did you really just say 'teeny-weeny'?

What? Is it supposed to be 'weeny-teeny'?

That had been the first time Neal had made her really laugh. Who wouldn't fall in love with such a being? Winnie put up no resistance. Magic Seelie Neal became Showrunner/Mayor/Director Neal, then Neal in a shockingly short span of time. And finally, 'my love.'

'My love' was who she saw now, hammering on the typewriter keys like a soul doomed in hell. His clothes were even more worn than a few days ago, his curls longer but less buoyant. No facial hair—growing it was an option for fae. His full face was gray and mottled, his eyes vacant. He'd become the machine.

Hey, Neal. I know you're a little preoccupied, but I have biscuits and how about we write a story?

It was the dumbest idea ever. But it was the only one she had.

She prepared to say his name, but a piece of paper slapped against her mouth. She pushed it aside, swallowing the word. That hadn't worked before. Only her touch had made him sit up and take notice. Wading through the paper surrounding Neal, she cleared a small space on a table next to him with a sweep of her arm. She set the plate of shortbread down, circling around to his back, to the pale patch of skin where his hair divided and his neck bent to the work. Leaning over, she kissed him on that patch again then set her hand on it.

The typing slowed.

Then it stopped.

As before, Neal turned. Blinked.

Keeping her hand against his neck—*I cleared that space when I kissed it before. There must be no spell on it now*—Winnie curled around him and wafted a piece of shortbread in his direction. She recalled him dipping the cut pieces into his tea, making a game of how long he could hold it in the liquid before it crumbled. Shortbread had been the first thing Winnie had learned to make for him, and they always kept some around for whenever the mood struck.

Winnie wafted some more.

Neal pulled his hands from the typewriter and straightened one agonizing inch at a time. His fingers remained curled like a crone's, held in typing pose. A fat tear rolled down from one eye as he unbent one finger, one knuckle, at a time. At last, his head turned, and he was looking at Winnie. Seeing her.

She hoped.

Winnie wanted to throw her arms around him and hug and hug and hug. Then she wanted to drag him from the room, but heard Finch's warning. Hugging might not be violence, but dragging definitely was. Besides, they had a task to complete before anyone left this room. She held his gaze. "It's me!" she projected above the cyclone. "Can you see me here?"

Neal's head bobbed up and down, slow as a dream. How much of him was in there? How much could he understand? How much time did they have before the godspell reasserted itself? No way to know. Time to dive in.

"Neal, the godspell will never let you go if you can't give the Muses a story they like. I don't know if even I can impress the Muses enough to untangle the godspell. But maybe we can do it *together*."

Did his eyes flicker? Was the light coming on inside? Was he trembling against her touch or was she quaking against his? Winnie thought of the dark corridor in the wall again. She stared at the slightly open crack and thought about that tomblike crawlspace. Going in there again would be like burying herself alive. It wasn't an option.

If I leave now, we'll both wither away in this house while Seaview Haven completes its transformation into Nowheresville and Finch gets what he came for, she thought.

Neal's fingers curled again. He turned to the typewriter. Winnie's heart sank as he began typing. Clack, clack, clack. She felt sick. Of course she had no magic of her own. She couldn't break a godspell. What could she possibly do?

Neal's lips moved and he whispered something.

Winnie leaned in.

Sounding like the March wind on a metal roof, the Seelie whispered again, "Read."

Read?

Winnie looked at the paper he'd typed on. It wasn't nonsense. It was a whole sentence, of whole sense.

`Did you cut your hair?`

Winnie barked a laugh. Two years with no communication and the first thing he'd noticed was her bobbed haircut.

"I had some free time," she said. "Wanted to doll myself up for you."

`Ha, ha,` he typed. `I hear you. I see you. Smell you. Smell chocolate, shortbread.`

"I want to kiss you," she said. "I want to hug you until next year. But—" She decided not to get into the fact of Finch just yet. No need to worry Neal unnecessarily. "But I might get tangled in your godspell. I'll save everything for when you're out of here."

`XXXXXXXX OOOOOOOO.`

Winnie's eyes burned. "I kiss you with all the letters I

have, too."

`You are so brilliant. I only wish you'd been here sooner. But this will do. What is your idea?`

Wiping her face dry, she gathered herself. "We always wrote best together. So, if I dictated a story and you typed it, I think that would satisfy the Muses."

Neal's fingers twitched, but he didn't type for a long moment. Then:

`Can it have monsters?`

"Neal!"

`A joke. But the story they want has to be... incredible. Beautiful. Amazing. Something they haven't heard before. Your books and stories are wonderful and make perfect SCN movies but...`

"They aren't great." It stung, but it was true. Neal had always been honest with her.

`They are great to ME. Muses have different requirements.`

Winnie sat on the step next to him, breaths shallow and rapid. She massaged the small place on his neck where she'd laid her lips, and where she felt she now held him tethered to reality. He was so smooth, not a freckle on him. He'd loved counting the tiny marks on her body, kissing each mole, each scar.

`That's a cherry angioma, those are stretch marks`, she'd pointed out. He'd claimed they all tasted different. Her heart ached for those thousands of moments with him, small things that had nothing to do with him being Seelie or immortal or mayor or her being human or widow or writer. They spent time being themselves with each other. No one's definition, just their own. They'd shared their stories.

Now, Winnie recalled the click she'd heard. The moment outside of this room when she'd known what story they would tell. Her body whooshed with warmth like a hot flash, but far, far better. An idea flash. "Neal, I know the story."

Slowly, he turned to her again. The cyclone above the typewriter swirled and swirled and she watched it turn. She felt ready for battle. `I will be a cyclone, too`, she vowed.

"You know this story."

His eyes danced. They were full of sparks. He had the same idea. *Yes.*

Winnie loved him. "Ready?"

Neal's fingers flew once more.

`Always. But first—shortbread, already!`

Chapter 29

Connecting the Dot

FINCH'S DREAMS WERE full of Winnie's garden, where he wandered through rows of pumpkin and squash. He gathered their blooms in his hands, plucked for frying up later. He cackled at the idea of drowning flowers in oil and masticating them between his teeth. He ran his hands over the curly vines and re-oriented a pumpkin or two that was out of place. His bare feet squished in the soft soil, a satisfaction even more profound than orienting the pumpkins. He stood and stared at the setting sun, colors as vibrant as one of his blossoms.

When he glanced back down, the garden was in shambles. In that split second everything had gone to rot and been smashed or been smashed and then gone to rot. His guests crept through the rows, faces atavistic and malicious. Boggarts, trooping leprechauns, fauns. A scorpion man, a ghostly dybbuk. They rolled in his garden like pigs in mud, or dogs in—

"It's what ye wanted, no?" Agatha stood next to him, her familiar rasp startling. "All this work, done to bits. Guess you're a proper Unseelie after all. Doing that woman's garden dirty like you did mine."

Finch dug his toes deeper in the soil. He couldn't let her see that his Hideous Deformity was gone. All he'd done for so many years would be nothing if he didn't have it.

He'd worked so hard, aimed so low, he'd sucked up to so many Unseelie over the years and thrown away anyone who showed him actual friendship—all to prove that yes, he was badass. That yes, he was cool. That he could take pleasure in destruction, stink, and waste.

But in the dream, the pleasure was gone.

He wasn't a bad Unseelie; he was a terrible Seelie. He was nothing of any importance. And if he was sent to Seelie Court over his fakery, the only thing he'd be able to say in his defense was, *It seemed like a Hideous Deformity at the time, your Worships.*

Next stop: Exileville. Which was not a TROPE Town. It was the human side of the Veil.

I don't want to lose everything, he thought. He liked his house. He liked whatever friends he might still have. He even, just a bit, liked Seaview Haven. A sickness, all these warm feelings toward the world.

"Go away," he said in the dream, half to Agatha and half to the interlopers in his garden.

"You're the one who went away," laughed Agatha. "Forced yourself into the SCN 'verse. How's that going for you?"

His hands felt heavy. He was now carrying bottles of elderberry wine and bog whiskey for the smash. He'd meant to pour them out for the revelers, who now watched him with narrow, beady eyes. They were thirsty. They were hungry. "Party's over," he shouted. "Go home."

Laughter bubbled out of Winnie's garden from the gathered guests. They slapped each other's backs, their mirth like the stink of the Forever Swamp. Then they closed in, stepping on the remaining stalks of tomatoes. Strawberries broke open, oozing between their bare toes. They climbed the fruit trees and hurled whatever was left in the branches at the ground and each other. They were chanting.

"Floofy. Finch. Nobody needs you. Floofy. Finch. Nobody needs you."

Just what Laurel and Hardy had said at the Smash.

Finch stamped his foot, reiterating that everyone had to leave, or there would be consequences.

"Oh, Finchala." Agatha sidled closer. Her own basket was full of just-plucked berries. Her face made him think of Siggy, for some reason. "Don't listen to them. Never change your stripes. Or your dashes. Or your dots."

Finch summoned his powers. He glowed. His hair threaded with more red streaks. "Depart!" he bellowed. "I demand that you—"

An apple bonked him in the head.

A fistful of blueberries pelted his face.

Then they pounced.

STARTING AWAKE, FINCH clutched his chest and gasped. A darting glance around the room revealed he was back in Winnie's house, on her couch. A blanket covered his legs. His dream was in tatters, and all he could remember was being pelted by fruit and seeing Agatha. She'd told him not to change. Not to get confused.

It was morning, according to the light streaming in the room. Early. He'd been asleep for a long time. The last thing he recalled was swimming in the ocean with the Kraken (who'd blurped that her name was Terri), plugging up a drain with twisted sea wrecks, then surfacing to find—

Finch yanked the blanket from his feet. He wore soft gray and white fleece socks. He tugged the left one off and wiggled the toes. His smallest one had a tiny, dark dot on it—just like before. Maybe even darker.

Oh, he thought, oddly disappointed. *Oh*.

The previous day glowed bright and clear in his memory. All the places they visited, the people they met, the snacks they consumed. What he remembered best was that strange urge that had taken him over not once but multiple times to fix what seemed broken and mend what was injured. How, every time he gave into the urge, his foot felt better. The feeling had been like hunger descending, not based in his gut or head but somewhere between his ribs. Each instance had tightened his chest, and he felt compelled, as if by a finely woven spell, to take action. It hadn't been so much about making Siggy happy or even the human who required assistance. No, the urge came over him more strongly when he was told *not* to take action.

And once it was all over, he felt more powerful than ever. More powerful than when he'd participated in his Smash parties. More powerful than when he'd danced on the TROPE Town map in the SCN conference room. He'd been drunk on the strength of his magic.

Then he'd seen his bare feet on the Seaview Haven pier, still sparkling with wet from the ocean, and discovered his Hideous Deformity had vanished. That he had somehow become—well, perfect. That would not do. He just *couldn't* be like those idiots at SCN, glowing and preening and hovering down the hallways.

Apparently, that last part had just been a nightmare. He wriggled his toes again. The dot was back. Nothing to worry about now, he was as he'd always been—a terrible Unseelie with weird Seelie tendencies he'd have to hide for the rest of his immortal existence. Sighing, Finch lay back against the pillows.

Muted voices drifted in from the kitchen: Siggy and Malvous. They were discussing breakfast (pancakes in a strawberry sauce) while Siggy related the tale of the fish returning to Seaview Haven's waters and Finch's collapse.

Finch sat up on his elbows, shielded by the couch's high back side.

"I did think all along it was a mark and not a freckle," Malvous said. "Fae are so *averse* to proper baths, as if it's below them to imagine they attract dirt. But we're the ones who tidy up after them, and let me tell you—"

"So, what sort of being is he?" Siggy was speaking through a mouthful of pancake. "If you're not Seelie or Unseelie—"

"Maybe he's both," said Malvous.

A long silence. "Maybe," said Siggy, "he's just a Finch."

"I like that," said Malvous. "But I must ask—why did you re-apply that blemish?"

Finch froze.

"He got so upset when he thought it was gone," said Siggy. "Martin had a pen on him, and Finch was out cold. So I just, um, made a dot. We can tell him later if you think that was a bad idea."

Memory washed over Finch, and he returned to his changelinghood outside Copenhagen. He'd been the newcomer in a human house early on, before he learned how to return through the Veil. There, he'd had a human 'brother,' an older child who saw Finch more clearly than his parents. To him, Finch wasn't *different*; he was probably not human. Rather than outing Finch to the world, the brother—Rasmus—had devised pinches, slaps, hair yanks and even bites that went unnoticed by their parents.

Rasmus did have an artistic side, though. Paper was rare and expensive in those days, so he procured a long-lasting dye from the seamstress and, in one of his torments, drew on his 'brother.' Finch became tattooed with dye, covered in crude drawings of human genitalia, animals procreating and swear words in Old Danish. The dye lingered a very long time, partly because that was its nature but also because Finch abhorred a bath.

In time, he'd learned how to find the portals that would lead him back through the Veil, as all young fae put on Changeling duty had to eventually. He escaped Rasmus and vowed to never take a bath again. He was too traumatized—by humans and by being dunked in sudsy water. Over time, the sun faded the dye away on his body... except in one spot. A spatter on the small toe of his left foot remained. Sometimes, like after Finch's annual Smash events, it seemed darker. For decades, whenever he glanced at it, he recalled all those miserable years among ridiculous, cruel mortals, pouring all his bad memories into that one spot.

Which, he reflected now, might be why it lasted so long.

Over the centuries, he let those early memories go. Containing hundreds of years of memories was only possible if you could concertina them up once in a while. Some things went into deep storage.

But Siggy's admitting that she'd *drawn on him* brought it all back.

And bringing it back reminded him that he hadn't been born with the Hideous Deformity.

Under his breath, Finch let out a long string of curses in his native tongue so foul that, even though he couldn't see it, the bread he'd baked yesterday turned moldy. Directly outside Winnie's house, two birds began flying upside down. And in her garden, every worm tied itself into a knot.

When he finished, Malvous was speaking as if nothing had happened. "—baffles me, Siggy. If he's Unseelie he'll be aiming to tear down this tattered but lovely little town. He will make up reasons even if they don't exist. He's very invested in this, for reasons I don't entirely understand. Yet, if he's Seelie, he could fix everything. Perhaps."

Siggy said nothing for a long while. Dishes clattered. Finch peered over the edge of the sofa just enough to see her moving around in the kitchen. "So you think I did make a mistake."

Malvous guided her back to the table. "It is not a Bro's place to tell anyone if they have erred. I am only expressing confusion."

The girl drew circles on the table with her finger. "Mama told me once you can't change people. You take them how they are. She said Miz Winnie and her once had kind of a fight, only it wasn't a fight where anybody got beat up or where there was yelling. They just didn't see things the same. And when it was done, Mama said she had to decide if this different way of seeing things was worth losing her friend over."

"Do you know what it was?" Malvous cocked his head.

"Not sure. Something to do with writing. Mama said she made some kind of decision and never brought it up again and neither did Miz Winnie. Mama says the friendship was more valuable than one disagreement." She blew out a breath. "I started thinking about that. How you can't change folks. They gotta want to change themselves. So, if Finch has to think he's some kind of big awful destroyer, maybe it's not important if he's got a dot or not. We saw what he did in town. What he can do." She looked up. "But maybe none of this will matter. If Miz Winnie can't get Mayor Bartleby back on his feet, Nowheresville is gonna completely fall apart with or without Finch. Maybe I won't get to see Mama or Papa again." Now she was sniffling. "So really, who cares about a little old dot?"

Finch bent over his bare foot, staring at the toe. An excellent point the youngling was making. Who did care about a dot? Back home, everything he tried to do managed to disappoint those around him. But in Seaview Haven, he hadn't quite disappointed everyone. He'd made a youngling boy stop crying. He'd brought food back into the town. He'd stoppered up a hole. He'd made a bunch of humans a little happier.

Happier felt better than disappointed.

And that had only been one day.

Imagine what I could do with a second. Or a tenth. Or a thousandth. People weren't all that different from fruits and vegetables when he thought about it. All right, they were, in fact, very different from fruits and vegetables, when he continued to think about it. But there were things in common.

Finch sat up and stretched. Glanced down and noted his trousers were missing. The only thing he had on was one of Winnie's sweatshirts—green, with a tree growing out of a book on the front. *Oh, right. I swam. I got wet.*

Standing, he tottered out to the front porch and blinked into the sunlight. Another hot day was coming. Maybe they'd make lemonade. He might ask Malvous to show him the recipe for ice cubes. *Making* something was starting to take on a different meaning to him. There were so many ways to *make*. Maybe he could find one of his own.

Behind him, something stirred and groaned. Finch whipped around. Laurel and Hardy, who he'd last seen at the All-Hands Emergency Meeting many days ago, but who he was pretty sure had been tailing him around town yesterday, were curled up in Winnie's porch swing. They blinked awake and winced at the sunlight.

This was a terrible sign. Finch braced himself, mind scrambling.

"Ugh." Laurel squinted. "My head."

Hardy rubbed their temples, then rubbed Laurel's. "Gonna require tea," said Hardy.

"Stop yelling," said Laurel. "Whoo, been a while since I had a proper shortbread hangover." They raised a hand to shade their eyes. "How many pans did that brownie give us?"

"Six?" Hardy made a dry smacking sound with their mouth. "Yes. Tea. Gallons of tea."

Finch cleared his throat, and their heads whirled. Blue hair fell into Laurel's face and Hardy burped. "You two lost?"

Laurel tossed their shoulders, then tossed their head. More hair fell over one eye. They looked like they'd had a very rough night; gorging on shortbread would do that. Everyone knew Bro shortbread contained subtle, undocumented powers, so it was a real rookie mistake. But where had they gotten Bro shortbread from? Malvous wouldn't have sneaked out here to feed them.

That meant they'd met Felicitous. Which meant they'd been in the mayor's house. The not-good signs were starting to accumulate.

"Not lost." Hardy brushed crumbs from their chest, shoulders, and hair. A tiny chocolate chip nestled on their cheek. "We've been watching you."

"I guessed." So it had been the two of them lurking on the pier. Finch had also sensed they were behind trees and lamp poles during the day, too, but his glimpses had been so fleeting he hadn't put it all together. "Why?"

Laurel rolled their eyes. "SCN sent us, you twit. Because you haven't sent a report in."

"I still have time! There have been… complications."

"You had a duty to report the minute the SMD had been detained by Muses."

"I wouldn't say *detained*—" Finch scrambled for ideas. "Also, I injured my foot. There were delays."

Laurel waved their hand. "That should have healed in minutes—"

"But it didn't. Heal. The town is mixed up." Finch's hands were fists, and he wasn't sure how much to say.

Excusing himself would let them know how much the town was wrecked. But the truth was neither he, nor Laurel, nor Hardy, could fully fix or tear anything down right now. Even if they didn't care about SCN permission. With the Muses here, nothing worked quite right, including magic.

"Beyond repair, clearly," said Laurel. "Beyond your paltry capabilities, anyway."

"Enough." Hardy held up their hands. "Tea. Lots of it. And we will talk."

"We're talking now. Let's just get to it."

Laurel smirked. "I would prefer to carry on this conversation inside. Ideally, after you put on some pants."

TEN AWKWARD MINUTES later, Laurel and Hardy were gathered on one side of Winnie's kitchen table, slurping down their second pot of tea as Malvous tidied up. Finch had located a pair of oversized trousers in an upstairs closet and was cinching them around his waist with a belt. He nearly tripped twice before pulling up a seat at the table and rolling up his cuffs.

Siggy had refused to leave the room and now stared at Laurel and Hardy with a combination of fascination and distaste. They gave her a similar look back. "I renew my objection to the youngling mortal's presence," Laurel stated.

"Renew all you like." Finch poured his own mug of tea. "She lives here. And her name is Siggy."

"So you're what real Unseelie look like," she said. "From SCN."

Finch winced.

"Clearly, a prodigy," Hardy noted dryly. "And why can she even speak of these things? Isn't that warded *and* constrained by her years?"

"Welcome to Nowheresville," Siggy said. "Nothing works right. About seventy-five percent of the time I can say words like 'magic,' too."

"Gorse bobbins." Laurel goggled. "Worse here than I imagined." They raised a hand. "I will erase this from you now."

A broom smacked the Unseelie in the head and everyone turned. Malvous glared. "You lay so much as an *illusion* on this girl, and I will sic every Bro I know on you. My contacts say you are only here to evaluate Finch's evaluation."

"Reconnaissancing the reconnaissancer," Hardy muttered.

"Not unlike circling the circumference," Finch said.

"You have no more granted power to Dismantle than he does," said Malvous, still wielding the broom.

Wide-eyed, Laurel held up their hands and backed down. "Let's start again. We are here as much because of the delayed report—"

"I had a fortnight!" Finch screeched. "I am not late!"

"—as the lack of response from you about the Mayor, Muse and godspell entanglement. That should have sent you back to SCN *instantly*. Did you fail to recognize the potential danger? Aside from the danger SCN faces due to the lack of fresh content?" Laurel leaned forward.

"Give the creature credit," said Hardy. "They did discover—probably—at least *why* this is happening to TROPE Towns."

"So it's everywhere?" Siggy asked.

"It's most terrible here," said Laurel as if speaking to a very small child. "The big bad Musies are imprisoning our very own Seelie SMD with their outrageous divine godwork—"

"Not quite accurate," said Finch. "If I understand right, it was a mutual decision. SMD Bartleby wasn't aware of all the consequences."

"Neither were the Muses, it seems," said Laurel.

"So unless SCN has a plan to de-infest a T-Town of both goddess presence *and* a working godspell, I'm not sure what you think I should've done. I think we have to rely on Ms Winnie's storytelling acumen," Finch said. "The godspell can't be reasoned with, cajoled, guilted, bought off, or turned off. You all have wasted a trip."

As he spoke, the bronzed tan drained from Laurel and Hardy's faces, and their latest mugs of tea cooled on the table. They held unnaturally still for a long moment, then bent to one another. Their whispers were so low that Finch couldn't make out the Gaelic. At last, they straightened.

"We have come to a decision," said Hardy.

Finch folded his arms.

Laurel leaned forward. "We are hereby assuming control over Seaview Haven. Finch, you will return to SCN HQ immediately and report to the UDIP coordinator. We will complete our own evaluation of this sinking ship, then speak to EVVVVVPCTTAP ɮ— to obtain emergency Dismantlement orders. The SMD's brownie will be sent back to the employment pool; the humans will be reverted to their homelands beyond the Veil. We will remove the town around the obstacle, rather than waiting for the obstacle to begin functioning properly."

"No!" Siggy cried. "You can't take our town! Finch is learning to make things better!"

Hardy's face darkened with disgust. "Eww."

Laurel continued in a firm, officious tone. "The UDIP will deal with *intern* Finch's identity crisis in due time. Sending you here, Finch, has only delayed the inevitable. The way is clear. These things are facts."

"There is no need to blow everything up!" Finch insisted, surprising himself with his ardor. It didn't matter that these two were his mentors and—if all had gone well—future supervisors. They were idiots and they made him angry. "The fix may not be simple, but it is far better than tearing down decades of TROPE Town history and magical architecture. We only need to have patience and wait for the human—"

Laurel clapped a hand on the table so hard it rattled. "Silence! We understand you now, imposter. You thought you could pass under the radar, but you've been the butt of jokes since you started working at SCN. You're the fae who has to *prove* himself with Smash gatherings to cover up your failures. Then you finally get the gumption to claim a real job—this one—and you can't complete it because you hurt your little foot. Then you have the audacity to help the citizens out. You're a disgrace to Unseeliedom and I'll be thrilled to see you—"

Finch leaped up. His trousers nearly slid off his narrow hips. He grabbed at the belt. A wild fury raged throughout his body, and he thought of Malvous swatting Laurel with the broom. That was a fireable offense, if the Unseelie filed a report. Laurel was right—and Laurel was wrong. Everything was both right and wrong. He'd been right, and wrong, but more wrong than right.

I'm sorry, Agatha, he thought. *You had every right to dismiss me. Just like the Muses did. I'm going to figure out how to do better.*

Recalling his grand moment on the TROPE Town map, Finch stood on his kitchen chair, nearly clocking his head into the overhead lamp. He batted it to one side, and it swung back and forth like a pendulum. "I'm not going anywhere. The reason I'm terrible at being Unseelie, and I didn't figure this out until today, is—" He clomped a bare foot on the table. Their mugs splashed out tea. The lamp came very close to his head. "This!" He pointed at his ex-Hideous Deformity/current pen mark.

Laurel and Hardy flicked their gaze at his feet.

Finch leaned down and rubbed the pen mark out.

The Unseelie tilted their heads and exchanged a glance.

The lamp continued its back swing arc, clocking Finch in the head and knocking him off the chair. His foot remained hooked on the table. "Ooof," he said.

Everyone leaned over to look at him on the floor.

"Thank you for trying to protect me," he told Siggy, pointing upward. "But let's be honest. I'm not a bad Unseelie. I'm a bad Seelie." He took Siggy's outstretched arm as she helped him to his feet. He leaned toward the Unseelie investigators. "But guess what? That still ranks me above you two. Hear me? Turns out I'm a Seelie creator! I'm here to garden and fix stuff and I'm all out of gardening!"

His breaths came heavily, but his head was light and airy.

Siggy applauded wildly.

Laurel and Hardy looked chagrined for a moment. Hardy raised an eyebrow. "Well-played, Seelie," they said. "But you're not official anything until the Seelie Court declares it so. So, if you're not Unseelie, you're *nothing*. And we only take orders from the EVVVVVPCTTAP."

The Unseelie dismantlers rose from their chairs. "Thank you for your hospitality," they nodded in unison at Malvous, then Siggy. "This has been most educational." Together they headed for the door.

It couldn't be that easy. There was a catch.

"Where are you going now?" Finch demanded.

"Back to the mayor's house," said Hardy.

"No!" Siggy cried. "Miz Winnie is handling it!"

"Hush, mortal." Laurel glared. "We came here to do our job. And you all"—they gestured around the room—"will stay out of our way."

As they stepped over the doorway, they twirled their

hands in a mirroring, intricate pattern, fingers mere blurs. Then they slammed the door behind them.

The door vanished.

Then, so did the windows.

Then the rest of the *house* disappeared.

Leaving Finch, Siggy, and Malvous standing in a vast, empty, gray-white *nothing*.

Chapter 30

Chapter and Verse

WINNIE AND NEAL stayed up all night, writing the story.

Their story.

Truthfully, it might have been finished in one draft, or two, but after the first draft, Neal balled up the pages and tossed them aside. He ate more of the shortbread Winnie brought; it tamped down the voices so he could focus.

Then, he typed:

`I left some things out.`

In the next draft, when he reached the part about tumbling from the roof while getting the Frisbee, he added in that he'd employed some dramatic fakery in the aftermath.

`I did hit my head. But Seelie are quite tough and I let Winnie think it was much worse,` he typed in the story. `I wanted her to have my monsters. It was selfish. But then the Muses came and my little spell in bed turned into something I had a hard time waking up from. But I started it. I put myself in this room because I was holding on to monsters.`

After reading this, Winnie stomped around the paper-stuffed room, ranting and wailing even louder than the small cyclone above the typewriter. During her tantrum, Neal slid back under the godspell and was compelled to type again, but the draft became just page after page of apology and self-deprecating abject misery, all in capital letters.

Slowly, Winnie had calmed down. Neal had been a dope. No question. But what he'd done was so *human*. As was confessing it. It came from a real place, not a fictional or fantastical one. Good stories had to do that. The best ones even hurt a bit. For Neal to dredge that up and come clean was like admitting he was a fraction beneath one hundred percent Seelie. Less than perfect.

Briefly, but only for a second, Winnie thought of a less-than-perfect Unseelie out there in the world.

In the next draft, Winnie 'fessed up, too. How she'd worried about losing her place in their relationship. Their partnership. She needed to be the writer, the one with the great ideas. Not just because Writer was how she saw herself, but because she feared Neal might decide he didn't need her. That it was time to replace his resident writer. Clio had told her: *The minute you're more trouble than you're worth, you're out.*

`I couldn't do this without her,` Neal typed after she told him of her fear.

```
Any old writer we dragged in here
wouldn't be close to what the
movies—I mean, what I—need. I pledge
that Winnifred Arrowmaker isn't going
anywhere, not until she wants to. I'm
not interested in monsters anymore,
anyway.
```

They'd looked at one another then, hearing his last sentence in more ways than one. They both had monsters, in a way. They'd both hung on to them far too long. And sometimes, letting them go was the hardest thing of all.

They put the finishing touches on the story they wrote together (the third draft) as the faint blue of dawn crept over the horizon, lighting up the trees outside Neal's office. Not that he paid attention; the moment Winnie zipped the final page of the final draft out of his typewriter carriage, another page appeared. But this time, he didn't continue typing.

They held the draft together. Winnie's hands trembled as they clutched the pages she and Neal had created. She wanted to believe that the story they had written, the straight facts of it all, would be enough to entrance their audience all on its own. Just the facts, ma'am. They put heart into it, and truth, and revelation. What more did a Muse need to find the story wonderful? Surely, this would disentangle the godspell.

"Ready?" she asked him.

Neal nodded.

They released the draft into the cyclone. As far as Winnie understood it, that would send the pages to the paper pile. It would go directly to their audience.

"I have to leave," she said, realizing. "They won't know it's there if I don't show it to them." *I also have to rescue it before it becomes slush.* Her hands quaked from lack of sleep, and she felt crispy and otherworldly, like when she'd pulled all-nighters in college. It was a feeling of existence out of time, where you moved through the world but didn't feel of the world. A different kind of Veil.

Neal's hands were already returning to the keys as the godspell reasserted itself, but with great effort he pulled one hand around to his neck. Touched the bare spot. Winnie bent down and gave him another small kiss. Then she slipped through Felicitous' brownie door.

* * *

"What a delightful surprise!" Calliope slid open the doors to the living room, swishing inside. The blue velour of her tracksuit rippled around her, an effect that never ceased to entrance. The Muse's dark curly hair hung loose around her shoulders and Winnie gave her a wide, fixed smile. "Are you eager to begin reading to Us again?"

"I am." Winnie hurried past the other three Muses present, over to the thick stack of papers in the bin in the corner. She gave a quick eye to the Pandora's Box™ containing the godspell as she moved, wondering what would happen when the godspell untangled. Or broke. Or exploded. "I believe Neal has sent through a new tale that I'm planning on reading."

Thalia sat up straight, curious. Eutie jangled and made a small chirping noise. Clio rose and followed Winnie over. "That's not how this works," she noted. "We want to hear *your* stories. Nothing that's come through that funnel—"

Winnie turned, holding the draft. Her feet were unnaturally cold from standing in the slush. "Do you all *want* to be in this house forever?"

The Muses stared at her.

"What makes you think We do?" Clio asked.

"I've actually been thinking about Our office lately," Eutie said, her notes minor and soft. "I miss My plants."

Thalia nodded enthusiastically in agreement.

Felicitous opened the sliding doors just then and set up an elaborate silver samovar and tea mugs on a tray. He produced a plate of shortbread, cut into finger-length rectangles then noticed Winnie at the back of the room. His mouth trembled and she gave him a brief nod. He departed without saying a word.

"Tea!" said Calliope.

"Shortbread!" said Eutie. "Now We are properly arrayed for Winnie's story."

"Neal's story," said Winnie, holding the draft and taking her place in front of the television, which was off. "And mine."

Calliope paused in sipping her tea. "And *yours*?"

"We were up all night," said Winnie. "And this—" she held the draft aloft, "is our story."

Calliope kept a steady gaze on Winnie. "How clever." She leaned forward, resting her elbows on her knees. A small smile emerged. She looked like a hybrid of indulgent mentor, tiger, and disco running coach, thanks to that ridiculous tracksuit. "I am intrigued." She touched Eutie's hand. "You—We—may be back in Our offices sooner than imagined."

"Huh," said Clio, arms folded. "I'm keeping My expectations *low*."

The room crackled with anticipation.

Now or never, thought Winnie. She cleared her throat and began, "*The Case of the Spellbound Showrunner*. By Winnifred Arrowmaker and Neal Bartleby."

Chapter 31

Cloud Busting

Felicitous hadn't planned to go on another grocery run, but there was no good option. Making five batches of shortbread in one night had taxed even his emergency backup supplies. Those nosy Unseelie had eaten, demanded more, eaten that, and still demanded more. By the time they'd stumbled out of the mayor's house in the middle of the night, they were truly pixilated with the stuff. Felicitous had hoped one might fall off a pier on the way to Winnie's.

A goddess surely could have waved her fingers and restocked the shelves with her powers. But that was not the Muse way, and Felicitous was too cowed to make the request. Over the years they had made particular delicacies arrive on his doorstep—lobster, caviar, quail eggs, ninety-two percent dark chocolate—but never once had they asked the house brownie to make up a list of needs.

So on this morning, of all mornings, Felicitous had to go grocery shopping. He wanted to wait to see if Ms Winnie's story put an end to all of this nonsense. Perhaps the Muses would truly love it and then find their way out of town so life could begin again, but he had no idea how long the reading might take, if it would do the job, and even if the Muses would leave once the godspell was dispelled.

But from almost the moment Felicitous stepped from the house, he sensed something was *off*. For one thing, a few citizens appeared to be setting up picnics, or at least chairs, just outside the warded boundary of Mayor Neal's home. Ten or twelve Havenites clustered in groups, facing the house and whispering among one another. Several had dragged large coolers. A few were drawing on cardboard; a few others stapling that cardboard to long wooden poles. Their eyes followed him down the path and into town, and every time he got close enough to hear their whispering, they always hushed up.

The nearer he got to town, the stranger things became. Someone's voice was amplified and echoing, and there were many more mortals buzzing around on the sidewalks than he was used to. Veering toward the shouting, Felicitous peered down Anchovy Avenue to find an older man with wispy hair, wearing a cardigan despite the heat, barking into a megaphone.

"I heard one of the Strangers *ran down a child* in the middle of Main Street last night!" the old man shouted. "Creatures like *that one*,"—he pointed at Felicitous, who looked around to see who the man was talking about before realizing it was himself—"are a *menace* to us all! My heart can't bear this kind of news!"

Now Felicitous recognized the speaker. Mr Alexis, owner of the town's one used bookstore. He'd always been cranky and cantankerous, and the brownie had long wondered why he was in town at all.

You need some not-so-nice people in the mix, or you never get conflict, Mayor Neal had explained. *Every TROPE Town has to be seeded with Malcontents, Pot-Stirrers, and Misanthropes. They can leave whenever they like, yet almost none of them do. They live to be problems, which makes for good movies.*

Felicitous wasn't sure he fully understood, but that was not part of his job description. The brownie thought about trying to explain himself, and that clearly he knew nothing about someone hurting a child, but when he approached Mr Alexis, several Havenites gave Felicitous narrow-eyed looks of disapproval. Maybe even anger. At least one stood up, as if he planned to charge.

"We can speak our minds now!" Mr Alexis continued. "They can't take our words away anymore! Seaview Haven is breaking free of Seelie control, and we like it that way!"

"Oh, back off, you old coot," said Ms Zhao. "He didn't run him over! Get your facts straight!"

Felicitous backed away. Something was definitely different in Seaview Haven. No one held demonstrations here. No one acknowledged that Seelie, or 'creatures' existed in town. The word wards were no longer merely weak—they were shredded. He feared what that might mean for the wards around the mayor's house.

Whirling, he scurried to the grocery, hoping to at least get some basics before someone could do more than glare at him. He had his hand on the store's door when someone shouted, "You there!"

The brownie turned slowly, raising a shoulder up in case he needed to shield his face. One of the town's children, sitting in a wheeled mechanical chair, waved his hand and rolled over. "Felicitous, right?"

"Yeeeeesss," said the brownie, holding his empty sack close. "Who wants to know?"

"Martin. Siggy's friend." Then he seemed to be at a loss.

"Well, Martin, it has been a pleasure. I am going shopping now."

"Don't think so," said Martin.

The door opened and nearly knocked Felicitous over. Mrs Grossinger, her face aflame and holding an odd yellow ball, stood in the doorway. "Oh! You! Not that horrible *Unseelie* from yesterday."

"He's Felicitous," said Martin.

"Not in my books," said the grocer.

"I'm only here to pick up a few things!" Felicitous tried to ignore the awkward, uncomfortable vibe he was getting. "Not many! Going home after."

"It didn't work," said Martin. "Finch tried to fix the food supply and, uh—"

Mrs Grossinger grabbed Felicitous' free hand and smacked the yellow ball into it. The sphere was cold and solid, but also slick and oily. "You tell your friend Finch that yeah, we got a delivery. A big one."

"Huzzah?" Felicitous wondered.

"One hundred pounds of frozen butter! In round balls!"

"And?" Felicitous rolled the ball around in his now-greasy hand. He could use some of that butter for shortbread, but he was quite low on flour.

"And nothing!" Mrs Grossinger looked like she wanted to throttle him. "That is all! I told everyone to come by this morning, that everything would be fixed! They all think I'm a liar now!"

"I kind of hoped there might be cereal," said Martin. "Only butter. Not even milk."

In the distance, Mr Alexis droned on, addressing the disappearance of people. Of how the magic creatures must be involved. That this town was not what it seemed, and they'd made everyone lie to their children to live here. Felicitous wanted to cover his ears. Those things were not *true*, but they were also not false. Unsure what to do with the butter ball, Felicitous dropped it in his bag and tipped his hat. "I will see what can be done," he told the grocer, who was breathing heavily.

"Oh, there are things that can be done," she said. "And they are being done."

Felicitous swallowed. He turned to leave and found Martin still behind him. "Why is all this happening?"

Martin shook his head. "Been happening for a while, but you know, sometimes, my dad says, there's a tipping point. People've been scared. Then they got angry. Then Finch showed up and they thought he was fixing stuff but I don't think so. Siggy and I went all over town with him yesterday and he did some amazing, good things, but this morning none of them are as awesome as they were yesterday."

"He is a terrible creature," said Felicitous. "What is worse than false hope?"

"I don't think he was faking them out," said Martin. "I was there. He *meant* to do good, for once. He was proud of it. But this town—nothing works right. So maybe even Finch magic is broken." He took a breath. "I think you should come with me, though. You're the only bit of magic I can find in this town right now, and there's kind of a magic emergency."

Felicitous liked being called 'magic,' but had never heard of a 'magic emergency.' "Of what kind?"

"Just follow." Martin began rolling toward the edge of town. "Or do you want a lift?" He gestured at his lap. "No charge."

Felicitous did not like using humans for conveyance. But this was an emergency. Adjusting his hat and shouldering his grocery bag, he took hold of the back of Martin's vehicle and clung on tightly. "Lead on, Mr Martin. I am here for the emergency!"

THEY CAME TO a halt at the end of Halibut Lane, just off the intersection with Turbot Trail. It was one of the citizen neighborhoods, with the houses reasonably close together, unlike Mayor Neal's. Felicitous knew a few of the homes: Doc Mallard, the Sommersdays. And then there was—

An enormous gray cloud enveloped the space where Winnifred Arrowmaker's home should be. Neither dissipating nor growing, it just hovered. There was no indication that a house had ever been in that spot.

"This is unexpected." Felicitous jumped from the back of the chair and pressed his fists on his hips. Martin had diagnosed this situation accurately: it was magic. Clouds didn't come for visits on a random afternoon, though a few could be talked into becoming chairs if you worked inside SCN.

"Told you," said Martin. His skin was drawn tightly over his face and his eyes were red, as if he were having an allergic reaction. "I came out this morning to see how Siggy and Finch were doing and found… this."

"Did you touch it?" the brownie asked.

"It made my hand wet."

"But you didn't try to go inside, correct?"

Martin stared at the ground. "It kind of freaked me out. I-I didn't want to disappear! Siggy might be in there, but—"

Felicitous held up a hand and met Martin's eyes. "Deep breaths, youngling. Deep breaths." When the boy seemed less panic-stricken, he rested a hand on his shoulder. "You did the correct thing. This is quite powerful behavior."

"Do you think Finch did it?"

For a second, Felicitous considered that the Unseelie might have. Maybe his various magic attempts that were turning up botched all over town had swallowed Winnie's house. But—no. That made no sense. Not when you knew about two other, dangerous Unseelie who had just arrived in town. "Not Finch. I am reasonably certain. But… I think I know who did this, in any case."

"So what do we do?"

"Um." This brief grocery trip had gone awry. "I don't have answers."

"Miz Winnie needs to know!"

"She does," said Felicitous. "But she is in the middle of a very delicate project just now. I will alert her the moment she's free." *By which time perhaps all of us may be free*, he thought. "I must return to Mayor Neal's. You should go back to your home as well, Mr Martin." He glanced around, swearing he could hear distant voices chiming together. "Seaview Haven is not a safe place today." He tipped his hat and began to hurry back to the mayor's house.

"You're not going to do anything?" Martin called after him. "Nothing at all?"

Felicitous glanced over his shoulder, still hurrying. He was almost running, now. "What may look like nothing is really very something!" he shouted. "Trust me!"

BROS EXCELLED AT many things in life, but running was not one of them. While their arms were long, their legs tended to be on the stubby side. They usually waddled with great alacrity rather than truly ran. (The first, last, and only Bro 5K had ended after twelve hours, when all participants fell asleep on the ground before reaching the finish line.) But Felicitous did the best he could. While he didn't know what he was supposed to do after reaching the mayor's house, he knew that was where he had to be. So he moved as fast as he could, at top waddle-run speed, his sack filled with nothing but a butter ball bouncing against his thigh.

As he approached the house, though, his strides slowed even more, until he was walking in slow, measured paces. The number of Havenites who'd been lingering outside the mayor's house had grown exponentially in his short absence, and they'd stopped milling around in small groups. The locals had finished working on their cardboard posters stapled to wooden sticks and were waving the contraptions around.

Answers, now! read one in bright red and blue pen.

Where's my daughter? questioned another in wobbly handwriting, words surrounding images of a young woman.

Save Seaview Haven! shouted still a few more.

A single one was positively incendiary: *Seelie Go Home!*

The gathering was still gathering steam, so only a few people were shouting anything. There was just a lot of grumbling and bad mojo floating in the air. Felicitous sensed what was coming. Oleander had shared her first-person account of the historic sit-down protest by the brownies of *Tune in Tomorrow*. That's what this felt like, with a lot less sitting down. But could you protest Muses? Could you force the hand of a godspell?

Felicitous doubted it.

The fact was none of these people knew anything about the goddess infestation. They were still assuming Mayor Neal ran the village. He was the source and target of their anger.

Maybe I should explain things, he thought, imagining himself on the porch, borrowing Mr Alexis' megaphone. It wasn't Mayor Neal's fault, after all. But what if they listened and demanded to speak to the Muses? In the middle of Ms Winnie's story? That would never go well.

Lifting his chin and shouldering his bag, Felicitous prepared to head to the porch, but a hand brushed his arm. "Wait. Wait."

The brownie turned. The older boy, Martin, had followed him here. "Mr Timmlerwicz, you really should not be here."

Martin ignored the warning. "I just wanted you to tell them inside that they'd better do something, and fast.

Those protestors aren't going to stand around yelling forever."

"They're not yelling very much now."

"They will." Martin inhaled deeply. "What I mean is, more folks are coming soon. Mr Alexis has them all riled up, and I think they've got a lot of bags of butter."

"That seems like an odd thing to carry."

"Frozen butter balls. They're going to throw them."

"That's nice. A game of catch?"

Martin threw his hands in the air. "As *weapons*, Felicitous! They want to get Mayor Neal's attention! And some other folks are coming with bottles of home-brewed moonshine!"

"A bright idea," said Felicitous, still not quite understanding why frozen butter would tempt Mayor Neal outside, particularly not when he was in the thrall of a godspell. "They can drink heartily after they finish their complaining."

Martin groaned.

Ahead of them, the chanting had begun. Signs bobbed up and down. A few citizens shot dirty looks at Felicitous and Martin. "C'mon," the youngling said to Felicitous. "We should get away from these people." He started rolling around the side of the house, toward where yew bushes ringed the garden.

Felicitous hesitated.

Then a ball of butter clocked him in the shoulder.

Chapter 32

Here's Where the Story Ends

WINNIE AND NEAL's story was not a novel. Granted, the important parts were all in place: heroes, heroines, mystery, surprise, romance, friendship. Love blossoming where no one expected it. Words like magical beings, turning from thought to ink to paper to movies. Beautiful.

But as ever, things had to go wrong in the story. Lovers separated. Best friends vanished. Worlds falling apart, disintegrating. It was all true, every word. Winnie and Neal wrote of their shared romance, how their fears and monsters had broken their bond. There was even one big risk, where they said they, like their town, had been put under a spell that must be broken, or all would be lost.

At the end, Winnie sagged into a chair and closed her eyes. Weeks must have passed. Months. Years. Once again, time had fallen off the track and lost its meaning.

There was a long pause in the room. No applause, no sighing, no whispering. Also… no anger. Surely the Muses had recognized the story's truth and seen themselves if not as villains, then antagonists. But for a long time, there came nothing.

"And?" Calliope's voice cut through the quiet.

Winnie opened her eyes.

"Yeah," echoed Clio. "That can't be the whole thing."

"I do believe it is." Eutie's voice was a twitter of soft, low notes. "For now. How very brave!"

`We should make something up,` Neal had typed. `They won't be satisfied with this.`

Winnie had disagreed.

`The power is in leaving the story open. If we tie things in a bow, it'll just be wishful thinking. We have to keep this true. What makes this work—if it works at all—is we stick to the truth. They always say write what you know.`

So there was no end. Not even a 'The End.'

"Winnifred," Calliope leaned forward on the couch. "It is a good story. A very good one indeed."

Her heart soared, then dipped. 'Good' wasn't the adjective she wanted. Needed.

"I thought it was pretty great," noted Eutie. "Even without an ending."

Clio shushed her.

"Kind of smart to work with that Seelie," said Thalia. "That's definitely the best thing *he* could ever write."

Calliope made clucking noises. "We do like this story, Winnifred." She gestured at the Pandora's Box™. "Would you like to open the Box to see if We liked it enough?"

Winnie looked at all of them. No, they hadn't jumped up and down like she'd hoped, but did someone have to faint with joy? Neal had written a story. Most of them had thought it was quite good. That should be the end.

Yet she knew it wasn't, and her heart broke. Winnie turned to the matte black Box on the side table and gently opened the lid. The godspell spun its glowing yarns, shading from green to blue, to purple.

A single tear dripped down her face and into the Box.

The yarn paused in its spin. The glow held fast.

Then it began moving again.

"That was curious," said Calliope.

Winnie wiped her face and slammed the lid. "Curious? Curious?" When she'd sat down a minute ago, the floodgates to exhaustion had been threatening to burst. Sleep clawed at her. But in this moment, all that fled. A white-hot flame of anger forced her to her feet. She loomed over Calliope, imagining her eyes were as red as Finch's hair. For a second, she expected flames to burst from her mouth, then decided she didn't care. "What do you want from me? What does that stupid *spell* want from me?" she exploded. "How about some guidance, for once? It's not like you're out there doing the work! You all sit around like you made the world, sucking the life out of my town and the man I love—"

"Seelie," Clio noted.

"And do *nothing*! Clearly if I was inspired by any of you, I'd've been able to give you what you want by now. Maybe Seelie can't write stories, but I know I can. I've done it! People—mythics—love my work. I can write. I can do this! It's not my fault that you and that thing in the Box can't see it! Maybe your inspiration just... stinks!"

Winnie huffed and puffed. Every Muse was scandalized, except Calliope. She stood, straight and tall, and pushed a bit of hair from her face. Every inch of her seemed to flow, to hover. She grew taller, larger in front of Winnie until she assumed, well, goddess proportions. Then she offered her hand. "Come with Me, Winnifred."

Winnie was afraid to accept. If she took that hand, would Calliope throw her out of the house and eliminate her from being able to free Neal? She glanced around the room. Only Eutie had any sort of lightness to her; the others might as well be statues. But Eutie, who had brought her tea and bounced on her bed to wake her, who'd always giggled and had music in her voice, gave her a small, encouraging smile. The Mona Lisa would have been proud.

So Winnie slipped her hand into the goddess' own. It fit like a toddler's into her father's. Calliope closed her fingers over Winnie's and led her to the French doors that overlooked the garden. Pulling one open, she bent down to exit and drew Winnie into the fresh air and sunshine. For the first time in what felt like forever, Winnie felt warmth on her skin. Heard birds twittering in the skies. The lush grass tickled her ankles. She took a deep breath and felt, if not serene, then calmer.

Somewhere in the not-so-far distance she heard the murmur of voices but couldn't make any of them out.

Calliope led her across the hedge-enclosed garden, past the badminton net, beyond the rose bushes and to a wooden bench with a decorative metal frame that sat beneath a thick oak tree with broad, spreading branches. It was cool here, and it afforded a lovely view of the entire garden and back of the house. The goddess lowered herself onto the bench and moved to one side, gesturing for Winnie to join her. After a moment, Winnie sat. She was still furious, and frustrated, but the exhaustion of no sleep was calling to her again.

"Winnifred," said Calliope after a moment. "Do you have any idea why We are here?"

Winnie bit her tongue, but wanted to say: *Because you overstayed your non-welcome at a Seelie's home and then made a stupid deal with him that you can't get out of?*

"Slightly accurate," said the goddess. "Not entirely."

"I didn't say— how—?"

"Goddess." Calliope touched her chest. "True—We, I most particularly, wanted a break. But do you have any idea why this town was chosen? Why We are *here*?"

"Because… Janus told you about it?"

"Janus, dear Janus. They brought Us to this room at SCN and revealed the TROPE Town map. They pointed out several excellent locations where We might choose to spend some of Our infinite time. Los Esposos has lovely mountains surrounding it and some very interesting residents. La Ciudad Grande clearly has all the entertainments a city could offer, and some already great writers. Swee'ton—My goodness, We would never have stopped eating kouign amanns. But I chose Seaview Haven, a reasonably unremarkable town, aside from your ocean-dwelling folk, because it spoke to Me. Yes, it had a pool. Yes, it had a badminton net. But I could *feel* you at a distance. I felt you and the great story you inhabit. I also felt the problems that were brewing between you and your Seelie, even if I wasn't aware of their source. You've done quite well for yourself as a writer who writes... well. Capably. Enough. Most writers are like that. They go to the limit that gets them noticed, stop, and say 'that'll do.' Those are all good stories. You are a *good* story writer. And what you read Me this morning, it was so very close to being Great. Even if it was written with a Seelie. Even though you not-so-subtly meant for *Us* to learn a lesson from it, or some such hooey."

Winnie focused on her hands. Calliope waited until she looked up again.

"The thing is, I also felt the presence of something *else*. Something Great. Greatness that was buried within you, but greatness you had also helped bury in someone else. And I thought that if this town held *two* writers who at least had some measure of Greatness in them, something I could help surface, then that would make this visit worth it. That would be inspiring... to *Me*. Working at SCN has been a time-filler. There's a really good cafeteria, but it lets Me stay at My desk and inspire the masses, when I could be inspiring the individuals. Maybe We'll go back, maybe We won't. But I wanted to have a chance to kick a little writer ass one-on-one again. See what happened."

Winnie did feel like her butt had been kicked, thoroughly. But what she was really trying to do was parse through everything the goddess was saying. *Greatness that was buried in you, but greatness you had also helped bury in someone else.* Did that mean she had inspired someone once? She had buried a little bit of inspiration in… one of her students? But wait—Calliope had inferred this person was already in Seaview Haven?

"Those aren't quite the right questions," said Calliope, standing. She rested a hand on Winnie's heart. "You do have this in you. A Great Story. But the great story isn't always full of tropes We've seen before. You believed that if you told Us the story about the love of your life, that it would soften Us up. That We would declare it Great. And truth, what you've made happen between yourself and that snarky, self-important Seelie is remarkable. But there is another story in you, a place you avert your inner gaze from when you happen upon it. Where perhaps you are *not* the put-upon hero. I can feel it in there. *That* is the story you need to tell. *That* is the story, I believe, that will have Us cheering and will untangle that damnable, stupid godspell We wove."

She turned and headed toward the house.

"But—" Winnie began.

Calliope glanced over her shoulder and lay a finger across her lips. With her other hand, she mimicked writing. Then she disappeared into the house, closing the French door.

Winnie was alone.

SHE SAT IN the garden for a long time, listening to the world. She plucked a blade of grass and shredded it, then plucked another, and another until she could shove her frustration and weariness into a compartment and mentally lock the door. Next, she tried focusing on the clues the Muse had—finally—given her. She sat so still a small bluebird landed on the armrest of the bench, then hopped over to rest on her hand.

Bluebird of happiness, she thought briefly. *When was I last… happy?*

Happiness was a transitory thing. It didn't exist as a permanent state of being. Contentedness was a steady state of pleasure. Happiness came in spikes. Closing her eyes, she returned to what she considered her mental lily pads: the best and brightest, the greatest hits of her life. She'd had a lot of decades, and there were quite a few hits. They stood out as bright memories among the fog of the rest of her daily life, places she'd returned to and relived enough times that they traveled with her through time. Her children were in some of them. Meeting her future husband in another. Falling for Neal—more than one was with Neal.

But not every memory was bright and pleasurable; some of the lily pads were uglier, curdled, and mixed with things she didn't want to think about. *A place you avert your inner gaze from*, Calliope had said.

These other memories were fights. Failures. Mistakes. There had been a time when she was much younger when she'd thought writing long love letters to her crushes would make them See the Light and fall for her. Despite what movies insisted, they did not. There was a time, also when she was much younger, that she'd occasionally stolen things. Small things, nothing of real consequence. She had just enough conscience to hate the objects, to consider them tainted. She'd returned some, in secret. Those were things that she'd done. That she owned, forever. Those lily pads made her cringe. But in understanding this thing about herself, she'd felt she learned a greater lesson: That she always had to face herself in the mirror. That she could never again do something that she could not later look at and be proud of. She would have no regrets.

It was easier to avert your gaze.

What had she buried in someone else? And what if it wasn't... inspiration at all? What if she'd been the opposite of inspiring?

Getting closer.

The voice wasn't her own, but it wasn't Calliope's either. Strangely, it sounded a lot like Eve.

Winnie opened her eyes and took in the garden. The distant sound of voices felt closer now, and a bit louder. But she still couldn't make out words. Was there a party going on in town? A party so loud she could hear it all the way out at Neal's house?

The hedgerow on the side of the house began rustling. Bustling, even. A mechanical whirr came from the other side of the bushes and slowly a head, then a face, then shoulders emerged over the top of the leaves. Martin. Winnie imagined him standing in a cherry picker, the kind electricians used when working on the overhead wires.

"Miz Winnie!" he called out.

She couldn't go to him. Her heart broke. She tried to speak. No words came out.

He thrust his hands in the air, thumbs together, fingers waggling. Siggy's signal. Siggy's hand puppet. "Siggy taught me this!" he said.

Her heart soared.

"She said it's a 'W' for a Winnie-bird!"

Winnie watched him but still couldn't move.

"I don't know if she can see me," he said to someone on the other side of the hedgerow. He listened to an answer, then turned back. "Felicitous says you're in the middle of an important project. But you need to know there's important stuff happening out here, too. You need to be here."

New urgency surged through Winnie. She had to get out of here. She had to figure this final Muse mystery out—and now. Eve had been gone for too long. Siggy was not allowed to vanish, if that's what had happened.

Holding up her arms (Winnie could apparently do that much) she answered Martin's signal back. She made a shadow puppet in broad daylight, fluttered her fingers… and became the Winnie-bird.

And in that instant, she knew just what her Great Story really was.

To GET TO Neal's office for Round Two of Writing the Great Story, Winnie had to go through the living room. Two of the four Muses sat up at attention. Clio kept playing solitaire, and Thalia was napping.

"You have it," Calliope said. "I can tell."

"Oh, I believe she does!" Eutie's voice sang.

"Believe it when she reads it," Clio had said.

"I still have to write it," Winnie insisted. "This has to be the one. I-I should be outside." She hadn't gotten details from Martin but felt it in her chest: she was needed, by many. She'd fought for Neal as hard as she could, but if this didn't work, would she lose Siggy? Lose her chance to help the town?

"Of course," Calliope said. "Go. We will wait. We are good at waiting, particularly when there are snacks."

Winnie hesitated, then walked over to the side table between the couch sections. "The thing is, I can't just impress you all. I have to impress"—she opened the Pandora's Box™—"the godspell, too." There it was, still spinning and glowing and doing its magic, yarn-like thing.

The idea had come to her out in the garden. She'd thought about the way the godspell had briefly hesitated when she'd let a tear drop into it. How it had responded, then gone on godspelling. Maybe the story she and Neal wrote hadn't been the right one, or maybe she hadn't truly been part of the bargain. Winnie was going to have to join this ridiculous, terrifying, awesome godspell.

All the way, she'd thought. *Or nothing at all.*

Now, she looked at Calliope, expecting that the goddess could hear her thoughts. The Muse glided over and joined her at the Box. "A fascinating concept," she said. "It irks Me to say this, but I don't know if this is a wise idea. I am unaware of such a thing being done before. If your story is *not* the one to impress Us, you will be locked in here, too."

"Aren't I already?" Winnie asked.

"Not in the same way."

Clio fanned her cards and leaned back in the sofa. "The mortal has a point," she said in an almost respectful tone. "Deal her in, Callie."

"There is much to lose," said Calliope.

"That's only true when there's a lot to gain," said Winnie. "What do I do?"

There was a hairpin in Calliope's hand. "Contribute your essence. As with all good bargains, essence is—well, essential." She made a nervous chirp. "Goodness, I must be anxious. I'm making terrible puns."

Winnie held out her hand. A small prick from the hairpin and a drop of blood fell into the Pandora's Box™. Immediately, she felt different. Her mind felt seized. Examined. Then the story was flowering in her head, a story she'd already lived, but needed to tell once more.

"I'm going in," she said.

And left the living room.

Chapter 33

Outside the Box

ALL AROUND WAS nowhere and nothing. Void. Empty. Everything a pale beige-gray color. Had Pantone attempted to name the shade of this plane of existence, the nomenclature team would have expired from boredom before coming up with one that truly captured how nondescript it was.

Siggy realized it was the precise color of Doc Mallard's office walls.

"It's Nowheresville," she gasped. There was nothing beneath her feet, yet she wasn't falling. If she reached down to touch the solid surface of the nothing, her hand kept going, past her shoes, into more nothing.

Malvous stood nearby with his arms folded and squarish eyes wide. His body vibrated, as if he'd been plugged into a faulty socket.

Finch, on the other hand, ran away as far as he could, making squeaking noises and flailing his free hand (the other was employed with holding up his pants). He ran so far in one direction that without ever veering right or left he looped around and arrived back at Siggy and Malvous. He halted, bewildered.

"Huh." He blinked. Then he took off in another direction.

"Mal?" Siggy turned to him. "Where are we?"

The tall brownie shook his head. "As you say: nowhere."

It almost hurt to look at the nowhere, because there was, well, nothing to focus on—not even a light source. And while there was more space in every direction than she'd ever experienced, the lack of an exit had her feeling oppressed and closed in. Her throat grew tight, and goosebumps rose on her arms.

Despite not having veered left or right again, Finch returned to where they stood, but from the opposite direction he had just run away in, and abruptly stopped. He was breathing hard, his reddish-gray hair limp against his scalp. "This is not good," he admitted.

"Did they"—Siggy forced the words out—"unmake all of Seaview Haven?"

The mythics exchanged glances. "Doubtful," said Malvous. "You can't erase an entire town with the wave of a hand."

"Besides, they don't have authority to do that yet," Finch said. "Which doesn't explain where *here* is."

"'Here' is 'Nowhere,' as Siggy observed," said the brownie.

Siggy's hands gripped into fists, and she trembled. "We have to get out of Nowhere, then." She whirled on Finch. "Can't you *fix* any of this? Should I start telling you *not* to fix anything, so you'll fix it? Tell me!"

Finch stared at his nails. "I don't think that matters. Laurel and Hardy were right. In an official sense, I'm also nothing. Smack in the middle of nowhere. The apex and the nadir of… nothing."

Siggy was exasperated. A moment ago, Finch had seemed ready to take on the world. He'd rubbed out his dot and claimed himself. It had been inspiring. Now he was back to being the creature who'd moped on the couch for more than a week. Siggy might not always be sure of herself—she often thought her legs were too skinny and her head was too large and she was not very good with numbers—but even she didn't turn on a dime the way Finch did.

"Stop it," she told him. "Seaview Haven would be crumbling if you hadn't dropped in."

Malvous cleared his throat.

"And you." Siggy managed a faint smile for the brownie. "The town was being eaten by entropy. We were all sinking into a big hole and nobody was coming to rescue us."

"Neither was I, to be fair," said Finch. "I was here hoping to report back that this place needed wrecking. By me."

"But it still would have changed things. Miz Winnie says change is usually scary, but that you don't get a butterfly until you get a caterpillar. Or a cocoon."

Finch perked up. "I kind of like that, being a butterfly. Problem is, you need a hornet, and all I am is smothered in silk."

"That is how we started, you know," said Malvous. "Who could forget the hungry silken trash bag?"

Finch made a disgusted noise.

"I did not want to come," the brownie continued. "I was dragged here. All I wanted to do was clean up my hallway and go hold hands with—" He paused. "Never mind. The point is, I am so happy I visited Seaview Haven. Whatever happens next, Mr Finch has shown me the importance of getting up on a table and pointing out the things no one else has noticed. He discovered Seaview Haven beneath a foolish executive's mug of tea. He claimed it, even if he was the worst fae to do so."

"Now, wait a minute," Finch tried to interrupt.

"Every Seelie and Unseelie in that room had either not noticed that one of its so-called important T-Towns was decaying or were too afraid to point it out. As a Bro, I understand rules are for a reason. But what's important to know is when it's time to think"—he glanced around at the beige-gray nowhere—"outside the box."

Siggy was fascinated, but unable to shut out the empty forever that surrounded them. "But there is no outside of this box! There is no box! I feel like when you pull a turtleneck over your head, and it gets stuck! It's hard to breathe, almost!"

"But you can breathe. We are not stuck." Malvous narrowed his eyes, homing in on Finch. "I believe you can do something about this."

"They've un-created a house!" Finch tugged at his hair. "They're not supposed to do that if someone is still inside." He flicked a glance at Siggy. "Particularly humans."

Siggy started. "Why particularly not humans?"

"Because you aren't equipped for it," he said. "Immortals can accept the infinite. Mortals require clocks. Boundaries. Windows. Doors."

"Doors?" Malvous stood straighter. "Did you say… doors?"

"Doors," said Siggy.

"Doors," repeated Finch. "What about them?"

"Brownies make doors all the time," Malvous mused. "That's how—"

"How you get around in walls!" Finch cried. He grabbed Malvous' arms. "That is a perfect idea!"

The brownie's brows knitted. "I'm not certain, though. We aren't exactly in a house. Or… a building." He turned to Siggy. "Bros live in the walls of buildings. That's our world. I can create a doorway in the homes where I live."

Siggy cupped his hand around both of her own. "Will you try? Please? We can't be here forever. Or until Laurel and Hardy decide we can come out. Miz Winnie needs us! Mayor Neal needs us! And I"—her eyes swiveled this way and that—"can't keep ignoring the *nowhere* in here forever. I feel like it's swallowing me."

A hand cupped her chin and squeezed her cheeks. Finch drew her face closer to his own. The gold flecks in his eyes danced around in their hazel ocean. "The young mortal is correct." He released her. "Pieces of her are joining the nowhere. We will lose her if we don't act fast."

Now Siggy felt like running this way and that, screaming and flailing her arms. She settled for going from trembling to shivering. The sensation of losing bits of herself hadn't been literal when she'd said it, but now Finch had confirmed that yes, she was actually disappearing. More than at any time since Seaview Haven had begun transforming into Nowheresville, she wanted her mother. As bad as she'd thought things were before—Mama and Papa gone, Miz Winnie disappeared—this was so much worse. She wanted someone else to be in charge, to tell her what to do. Mama had always been the right person for that. Miz Winnie had been an acceptable substitute. Looking for help from Finch and Malvous was like trying to communicate with aliens. They *cared*, but they didn't fully *understand*.

"All right." Malvous threaded his fingers together, stretching his arms wide and inverting his palms. His knuckles cracked. "One Bro door, coming right up!"

Kneeling on the no-ground, Malvous flattened his hands out against a surface that didn't exist. He closed his eyes and concentrated. Slowly, a hairline shape began to emerge from the emptiness. An arc described itself in the beige-gray, shooting skyward until it bent down into an inverted 'U' shape. Malvous sat back, beads of sweat on his brow. "Ta-da!" he announced, gesturing with the flat of a hand. "I give you a doorway." He squinted. "Sort of."

"There's no knob," noted Finch.

Siggy found it hard to stare at the door for very long, but in the few seconds she was observing it, the inverted 'U' began to fade. "It's going!"

Malvous reached to the split in the nothing—and then it was, in fact, gone.

"I will try again," he insisted.

Three more attempts later, and Malvous was dripping in sweat. He lay flat on the nothing, conceding defeat, while his final door disappeared. The second had been more 'O' shaped; this last one 'A' shaped, but they all behaved the same. Here, then gone, in a matter of seconds.

"I am a failure," he nearly wept. "Door-making is the most basic of Bro skills, right after learning how to ask if someone needs that cleaned up."

Siggy was feeling different, too. Less... substantial. Her poorly woven braids (Miz Winnie never had gotten the hang of her style of hair) were coming undone, and each actually felt shorter. At some point, her shoes had vanished. "Finch!" she insisted. "Can you try? I believe in you!"

The fae sat up, as if goosed. He cocked his head. "Say that again."

"What? 'Can you try?'"

"No, the other part. It felt kind of... good."

"I believe in you?"

He paused. "Maybe with a little more... assurance."

"I believe in you!" She clapped her hands together for emphasis.

"You really do?"

Malvous was watching closely, his breathing slowing down.

"I saw you do all those things in Seaview Haven. I *know* you can make things. You can talk to the dirt! You just have to let other people stop deciding who you are. Be your best, um, *Finch*."

The hazel shades of Finch's eyes equalized. They blazed. He squared his shoulders and appeared to sprout a couple of inches.

Malvous reached a hand in the air and closed it around Siggy's. She crouched down to him as Finch began pacing. "Well said, young mortal," he whispered. "I believe you've energized him. Belief is a uniquely important motivator for fae."

Siggy pinched her lips tight, as if trying to swallow the bit of magic she'd just learned she owned. Turning, she watched as Finch held his own palms flat against the nothing. She joined Malvous on the ground and squeezed his hand back.

Something appeared in the nothing. Accoutrements for a door: iron fastenings, hinges, an elaborate curving handle, a knocker in the shape of a gargoyle head, a peephole. But… no *door*. These items hovered in space and suggested the presence of a door, but there was no break in the nothing. Not like what Malvous had achieved. Finch kept his hands aloft, holding everything together, and then the objects began to flicker. They winked, fizzled, and flashed out of existence, leaving behind the scent of ozone.

"Nymph knees!" he cursed.

"Again," said Siggy, feeling powerful. Here she was, ordering around a mythic being.

Finch went at it a second time. A third. A fourth. Each collection of door-related objects was different, but each vanished within seconds under different circumstances. One group went up in a mighty blaze. One imploded. The other turned to sand, which turned to smaller grains of sand, and smaller until nothing remained.

Finch looked heartbroken. He sagged to the floor next to Malvous and lay flat. No one had to say it: being his best Finch was still a failure.

Surrounded by two depressed, dispirited fantastical creatures, Siggy was now also disillusioned. In all the stories, all you had to do was try hard and things happened. You had to want it. You had to be creative. They'd done all the things in the stories yet were still stuck in the nothing. If only she had been able to contribute to the project.

Martin jumped to mind. To the day when he had her hold his motorized chair in place while he crawled on the ground to make adjustments. On Miz Winnie, who wrote all the stories but needed Mayor Neal there to type and edit them. Siggy's 'sciencing' projects needed Martin to help. She couldn't do them alone. And this wasn't a one-person project. This wasn't even a two-mythics project. They needed something extra.

Siggy squinted into the space where Malvous' inverted 'U' door had been. He and Finch had created the exit—a bit. They'd each made it work part of the way.

You can go through this life alone, Mama had once told Siggy, then looked over at Miz Winnie. They'd raised glasses of lemonade at each other. *But having someone along for the ride makes everything much more… possible.*

"Yes!" she shouted so loudly that Malvous and Finch sat up as if shot.

"Please avoid shrieking in the middle of our existential annihilation," Finch pleaded.

"I was transitioning from self-pity to self-abnegation," clucked Malvous. "Now I'll have to start all over again."

"Don't!" Siggy felt Miz Winnie and Mama together, pushing at her. She took one of Malvous' hands, then one of Finch's, into her own and merged them together. "Do it now. Do it together."

Finch made a face, as if he'd tasted something sour. He jerked his hand back. "Please, mortal, that is not how things are done."

"Bros don't do magic with fae." Malvous extricated his own fingers from Siggy's. "It's not the same language."

Siggy glared. "You're gonna make me say it, aren't you?"

Malvous raised an eyebrow.

"You had to tell her, didn't you?" Finch gave the brownie a little kick.

"He did," said Siggy, eyes gleaming. "Brace yourself. This is a big one. *I believe you can.*"

Finch looked both disgusted and entirely inspired at the same time. "Ugh!"

"What's more important, though, is that you believe you can." Siggy coughed. Her hair completely loosed from its twists, the bands holding them gone. A hole had erupted in the knee of her jeans. She tried to keep her voice steady. "You do—don't you?"

"Hmph," said Finch. "Maybe." He scuffed his bare toe on the no-floor.

"I mean, you're not going to let me disappear, are you?" she prodded further. "Or let Laurel and Hardy *win*?"

That last part did it. Finch stood. "Absolutely not." He stared at the nothing. "But I also can't say where this door—this theoretical door we might not even be able to create—"

"Stay positive," Malvous muttered.

"Will take us."

Siggy hadn't thought of that. All she knew was she wanted to be outside of here. With Mama. Or, barring that, with Martin, wherever he was. "Anywhere but here," she said, her voice now sounding like tiny insects skittering across a rock. "And maybe hurry, please."

Malvous got to his feet. He stood behind Finch and held on to the Unseelie-Seelie's shoulders. They faced the same direction. "Now," he whispered. "Focus."

Brownie and fae closed their eyes. Finch stretched out

his arms. "This is different," he allowed. "Haven't read about this in the Guide."

"Silence is golden," Malvous said.

Finch started to retort, then bit down on it. Siggy watched as they both concentrated, as if they could meld together. There were moments when a shimmer slid back and forth between them, blurring both creatures like a smeared pastel drawing. Then something emerged in the no-space. A broad expanse of scrub. Green patches alternating with delicate purple flowers. Stone formations. A small stream unfurled like a carpet, winding through the not-quite-nothing. A gentle rain began to fall on the newly created geography, and in the distance came the baying of dogs.

"Uh, guys?" said Siggy.

Finch peeked first, then Malvous. The Unseelie-Seelie waved his hands. Malvous released him and they stared at the new creation.

"We need a *door*, not a *moor*." Finch rolled his eyes.

"Well, that's not *my* fault—" Malvous caught Siggy's gaze. "Fine. My apologies. I will concentrate better. One giant door, coming up."

The landscape vanished, replaced by beige-gray.

The second time brought a sort of success; the towering door was built for someone approximately fifty feet tall. Reaching the handle would take two ogres and a dragon all standing on one another's shoulders—and probably twice that would be needed to unlatch it.

"Proportion," said Finch.

"Again," Malvous sighed.

In short succession, they brought into the nowhere: a beach ("Not a *shore*, you imbecile," Finch barked); a Viking complete with shield and furs ("That's a *Norseman*, you're getting colder," Finch said); and finally a large, hairy pig with tusks that charged directly across the nothing and, like Finch, circled around again twice before disappearing.

"We're getting nowhere," Finch sighed. "That's a *boar.*"

"If I wasn't disappearing slowly, I'd say all of this is a bore," Siggy quipped nervously. The hole in her jeans gaped now, and her earrings (presents from her mother for being brave enough to get piercings when she was eleven) were gone. The holes weren't even there anymore. She no longer remembered her middle name. Or if she had a middle name. She began to worry that something truly irreplaceable would go next.

"One more time." She gritted her teeth, and this time when Malvous took hold of Finch, Siggy took hold of Malvous. She put all of her concentration into it. She thought of a door, one that might lead to a castle. An old-fashioned, solid thing you'd need a battering ram for. But one with an accessible, easy-to-turn knob. She held on… and believed.

And created.

She felt it happening. Like a piece of yarn joining the three of them together, the—whatever it was, magic, hallucination, belief, promises—jerked forward, and became the outline of a door. She opened one eye to watch that inverted 'U' appear again. After a brief shudder, it held fast. Grew darker, deeper, like an etching. A moment later, the inner section of the 'U' filled with pine planks, held together with iron strap hinges, a matching pounded metal handle and a small stained glass window at the top. It was a door. And it stayed. Didn't flicker. No ozone. A real, gosh-honest door.

Siggy released Malvous and jumped into the air. Her watch fell into the nowhere and vanished. "We did it!"

Finch opened his eyes, face red, hazel eyes glinting gold. Malvous released him, sweating again. They leaped into each other's arms and bounced up and down. "We did it!" cried the brownie.

"I did it!" cried Finch.

Siggy rolled her eyes.

Abruptly, they realized what they were doing and jumped apart, brushing off their shirts. "Ech," said Finch. "I hugged a brownie."

"Pah," said Malvous. "Now I'm going to have to take a very hot shower."

"Guys," said Siggy. "Look."

They turned to admire the gateway. "I knew I could do it!" Finch ran his hand over the pine planks. "One perfect door. Hot and fresh! A door of quality and"—he gestured at the stained glass—"style!" He bent toward Siggy. "You may now pat me on the head."

She obliged. In return, he patted hers and whispered something soft. Her hair twisted up again and held fast. It was like being tickled. Siggy laughed, then coughed.

"We've got to move," said Malvous. "Who knows how long this thing will last?"

"Indeed." Finch picked up Siggy's hand. It was like being held by a loaf of fresh bread, soft and warm.

Malvous picked up Siggy's other hand.

Finch unlatched the door.

"Where are we going?" Siggy asked as they stepped through.

But there was no answer.

The door closed behind them.

Chapter 34

War of Words

Winnie was the writer.

Eve had a life.

Both loved to read. They tore through books at a rate that made the local librarians suspicious.

But if you asked Winnie what else she was good at—aside from reading and writing—she'd have to take a beat. What were her career plans? 'Writer' was number one on a shortlist of, well, one.

Eve, meanwhile, had no particular direction but was good at whatever she set her mind to. That last part was a huge qualification. At one point she was probably the number one expert in everything concerning the band Living Colour; later, she learned how to disassemble and reassemble a carburetor in the dark. She taught herself computer coding, then taught herself Latin. What with her lack of family life at home, Eve had a lot of free time.

Winnie was more of a broad thinker. Once she started writing it was hard to stop, like her brain went into a new gear she hadn't even realized was in her system. She wrote all the time—in class, after class, on weekends, at night. Creating characters was her substitute for having a social life. Eve was the first person she shared her stories with, reading them over the phone to her, then sometimes in person. Her friend soaked everything in and could call back plot points and lines of dialogue later.

One of Eve's greatest attributes was being able to listen, not just hear.

Then in their senior year of high school, college loomed ahead like a dragon that needed to be defeated. Neither of them were trust fund babies, which meant they had to flex muscles of guile and craft they'd never had to think about before. Praying became a part of Winnie's nightly routine.

One afternoon, Eve dropped by after school and handed Winnie a thin sheaf of stapled, typed papers. The title page read: 'DIDN'T COME FOR THE MONEY,' and under that, 'By Evelyn Sommersday.'

To Winnie, the pages might have been beamed from outer space. "You wrote… a story?"

"That's what the name says." Eve looked away, surprisingly shy. "Tell me what you think?"

Winnie stared at the pages. They were a thing that shouldn't exist, same as if Eve had walked up to her and said, "Wanna hold my Heffalump?" And they were clearly coated with some kind of magic dust, because just holding them made Winnie feel a little sick. And a little angry. *This is my ballgame*, she thought. *You can't just stride in here and think you can…*

But Eve could, and she had.

Nausea and rage receded, followed by fear. Winnie's stomach clenched. What if it was any good? And of course it was going to be good. *Because Eve Sommersday is good at everything she does.*

Fear waved hello to guilt. What kind of friend was jealous of her bestie's accomplishment?

All of that created a gumbo in Winnie's gut that took five seconds to prepare. At last, she smiled without her teeth. "Wow, Eve. Congrats."

"I thought about everything you always said about writing and it kind of... poured out of me."

Winnie felt gut punched. At that time in her life, she was far too self-conscious, far too fragile to live in a world where the person she loved and trusted most in the world (who she wasn't related to) could just dilettante her way into the one thing Winnie wanted to be good at.

"Cool, cool." Winnie set aside the daydream of shoving the document into her mom's office shredder. "But how come now?"

"You mentioned the Pepperbush Prize," she shrugged. "I kept seeing all those posters in the library, and, well, community college is nice and all, but I don't really want to go there."

The Pepperbush Prize. Write a short story, win $50,000. Only one kid in the state of Maryland would earn that. It could go a long way to paying for a year, maybe two of college. Some months ago, Winnie had submitted her story ('SPRING TAILS, by Winnifred Arrowmaker').

"Oh." Winnie could only form monosyllables, it seemed.

Eve was already scanning the room, eyes falling on the TV, then to the book Winnie had been reading when the doorbell rang. "Who knows if we'll get financial aid?" she said airily. "So it's either a scholarship or the Army for yours truly."

"The *Army*? You hate going to ROTC!" That had been a strange moment, Eve briefly taking reserve officers' training corps classes. But the Sommersdays were military folks—her uncles, grandfathers and even father had all served.

"It's what we do in my family." She shrugged. "Anyhow, Dad's downsizing in September and I'm gonna have to have a new place to go one way or the other."

Eve's mom had died when she was a toddler. Living with her father had been like living in a minefield; he was either absent, working, or home and drinking. Eve had been spending three nights or so each week sleeping at Winnie's since middle school.

Winnie didn't know it at the time, but she only had about a year left to keep her own bedroom; her parents would turn it into a Beanie Baby display shrine/museum for a couple of years before it became a holding facility for their eBay business. But she didn't plan to stay. Winnie wanted nothing more than to be an adult in control of her own world, not subject to the draconian laws of the out of touch adults who ruled her. She was seventeen, after all. "You could always stay here," she offered.

"That's sweet, but I think we both know that isn't going to happen. Guess I should've paid attention to grades like you always told me to. Like you did."

"Grades are bullshit. You're the smartest person in school."

Eve tapped the story. "We'll see." Her naturally stern expression broke into a smile. "Funniest thing. I sat down to write this story with this idea that it'd be like solving a math equation. Like, okay, how can I science my way into getting this scholarship? I'll write a story that makes everybody cry. How hard could it be?"

None of this helped Winnie's attitude. Eve, acting like writing was a plug-and-play piece of code.

"But then it was like something… happened. I turned off my brain and it—"

"Poured out of you," said Winnie, the words like lemons on her tongue. "I got it."

"So you'll read it?"

Winnie nodded. She was going to have to sack up. Defend her territory. Only one person would win the Pepperbush, and that person had to be her. Because if she couldn't even do that, what kind of writer was she? "I'll read it now."

Eve lit up. "Okay... Okay. But really—be honest. Right?"

Winnie promised. She went out to the porch and sat down with a glass of soda. She took a deep breath and began to peel the pages back of Eve's story.

In fairly short order, Winnie was crying.

Eve had been right.

WINNIE HAD THE Muses—all nine of them—on the edges of their sofa cushions. This was a story unlike any of her others. She'd never committed it to paper until just a few moments ago. She'd never spoken about it with Neal. It had always been too raw; she'd imagined the ink would set any pages on fire. It was the smallest Great Story Winnie could think to tell, but it was also one she never thought she'd share aloud. It was too hard to look at.

The Muses (someone had put out a call, and all nine were in the living room when she emerged from working with Neal) leaned forward, expectant. Some were chewing (more shortbread had been called for). Their faces were eager, expectant, like people who'd seen this movie before but had forgotten the details. Calliope's expression reminded Winnie of Eve's resting face: stony, stoic, giving away nothing. Winnie knew she was on the right track and hated that this was the track she had to be on at the same time.

She gave each of the Muses a brief look, and in that moment saw them not as goddesses. Or even eager listeners. They were vampires. They were feeding. As was the godspell.

"And then?" Eutie asked.

* * *

Winnie wasn't surprised when her friend's story was good. It was precisely the sort of story Eve could—and should—write: funny in places, heartfelt in others. Since Winnie knew Eve, she saw her friend's moves. Eve's reference to a 'forest-bound shack, abandoned and full of secrets' was a place Winnie recognized. Then Eve used the phrase 'gotcha hotcha' twice, which was something Winnie's own grandmother used to say—and in the story, as in real life, nobody knew what it meant. Eve instinctively knew how to craft words, just like she knew how to craft everything else.

It wasn't perfect. Clumsy, really. In places the structure dragged, and the characters were two-dimensional. She also took way too long to get the real story going—something Janus would appreciate. Lots of throat-clearing. And at one point, Eve wrote 'grizzly' when she meant 'grisly.' With every amateur stumble, Winnie felt satisfaction. Eve was not perfect. Eve was not technically adept at writing.

The question became: what to say?

She bought time by starting the story over again but mostly scanning it to gather her thoughts. She caught Eve peeping around a corner at one point, then ducking away. Early on, Winnie had been totally resistant to getting legitimate feedback on her work. Rewriting could be harder than writing. Faced with bigger issues than the occasional spelling error in a story, Winnie crumpled. Start over? Fix things? Winnie had set every story of hers that got walloped into the bottom of her desk drawer. They were her shame. Somewhere in a box in storage on the other side of the Veil sat a thick stack of abandoned stories Winnie had never had the courage to look at again.

A real friend wanted her friends to be successful. A real friend would want to support her friend, no matter what she did. But Winnie wasn't quite herself yet. Not at seventeen. So she called Eve out onto the porch and held out the story. For once, Eve didn't present her usual flat stoicism; there was a hesitation in her eyes, a nervousness in her hands. "So? Piece of junk, right?"

That was the moment Winnie could have done a lot of things.

She might have said, "It's perfect." Or, "It's terrible." Or, "Might want to give it another try." Then they could have gone off to listen to music or ridden their bikes to the mall (neither had a car) or done the things they'd always done. But Winnie had a different idea. She was going to be, as Eve had requested, honest.

Over the next hour, Winnie went over Eve's story in excruciating detail, pointing out every big and small thing that might be an issue to someone, somewhere in the known universe. She chuckled along with Eve when pointing out 'grizzly,' and explained the problems with long, drawn out introductions. Slowly, the chuckling faded. At last, Eve held up her hands and declared 'uncle.'

"So, yeah," said Winnie. "It's good but—"

"Yeah, that's about what I figured." Eve's voice was a cool, distant breeze. "Piece of junk. Whatever. Hey, I oughta go."

"Aren't you staying for dinner?"

Eve had shrugged. "Stuff to do around the house."

And she was gone.

Winnie felt some guilt but considered it a mercy killing. 'DIDN'T COME FOR THE MONEY' had to die the death of a thousand cuts so their friendship could live.

AUDIBLE GROANS FILLED the room as several Muses collapsed against sofa cushions. Thalia was audibly weeping. Winnie paused and met Calliope's eyes. The Muse was flushed and her eyes sparkled. She looked ready to take a chomp out of Winnie's flesh.

For what could offend a Muse more than the thwarting of inspiration? Of talent?

Winnie had exposed one of her ugliest truths, and they heard it loud and clear.

It was a horror story.

Eve never spoke of her story. Or about writing. They went along, more or less the same as ever. Applied for college. Winnie's entry in the Pepperbush Prize contest received third place in the state, and she earned $500 for college textbooks. But the winning stories were all published alongside one another in a storied writing magazine, and being published shifted something in Winnie. She found the courage to keep pushing. To keep writing. To find her feet and get an agent and get a publisher and, in the coming years, start what became her long career of cozy murder mysteries. They never earned enough to buy her Stephen King status, or a huge mansion, but she could contribute to a two-income household with her words. It was something of a miracle.

One day, she swore she'd write something big and important. Something great. In time, something big and important and great found her, and she ended up in Seaview Haven.

Post-high school, Eve and Winnie drifted. Eve set aside college and went into the Army. Recruiters promised her an easy job writing code for them, maybe piloting some drones, but then somebody somewhere in the world pissed off the president and she ended up as boots on the ground. An IUD explosion cost her some of her hearing, and shrapnel left her with dotted scars on her neck and arm. The Army money sent her to the community college, where she got an associate's degree, planning to attend the police academy, but the police turned her down. Her hearing wasn't good enough.

Winnie heard about Eve through mutual friends but didn't really see her again until their ten-year high school reunion. At first, they had an instant reconnection: hugs, tears, comments on how much *older* they'd both gotten. Eve gushed about Winnie's mysteries; at that point, they'd done enough to pay off her student loans. Winnie had the first of her two children by then, having gotten married while Eve was still overseas. Eve was single after ending a long relationship, and working as a security guard at the bank. It was as close as she could get to police work, which seemed to satisfy her soul in a way Winnie hadn't anticipated.

The bar was open at the reunion, and they settled into a corner to catch up as the fruity, frothy drinks flowed. The reunion happened around them.

Then, as midnight approached and the bartender shouted "Last call," Eve fixed Winnie with a glint in her eye. "Good thing you won that prize," she said, toying with the straw in her latest drink. They were each on about four or five by that point. "*Third* prize in the state. Got your motor running."

"Prize?" Then Winnie understood. "Oh, that Pepperdine thing?"

"Pepperbush." Eve flapped a hand at her. "Don't act like you don't remember what it was called, girl. It was *super* important to you."

"Oh, I don't know—" But Winnie blushed.

"Don't act like that. Important enough for you to take a giant dump on my story," Eve continued. "You crumpled up that pretty little face of yours and squeezed hard and—" She cut herself off. "Whatever."

Winnie stared at her hands. Every second felt like agreement. "Look, it needed work. You just had a hard time believing you hadn't been perfect at something from the start."

Eve's face hardened. "Never said I was perfect at anything." She gulped her drink. "Maybe I could've been a writer. If I tried. I just didn't feel like trying. Not after…" She let that go like a balloon.

"Funny, that's what everyone thinks," said Winnie, starting to get angry. "You never hear anybody say, 'Oh, you're a doctor? I always thought I could be one.' But for some reason, everybody thinks they've got a book in them. I don't call myself a wannabe welder just 'cause I think about welding."

"You think about welding?"

"Shut up. What I mean is, if you don't actually make the moves to write, you're not a writer."

"Except, I did." Eve sat up straight. "I wrote something. And it was *good.* Maybe not perfect. But good. Maybe *great.*"

"Not great." Winnie's mouth was sour now. She'd had too much to drink and was going to have to call her husband to pick her up. Probably wake him up, too. But she didn't care about that right now. She was losing an anchor in her life, her friend, by inches. Had been probably since that day on the porch. Maybe it was time to cut the rope and let the whole thing sink to the bottom of the ocean.

"Better than yours." Eve slid from the table and gathered up her purse. Hefting it over her shoulder, she lifted her chin. "I sent that stupid story in, you know. Submitted it and all. Didn't change anything." She snorted softly. "Okay, maybe changed 'grizzly' to 'grisly.'"

Winnie gaped.

"And I won." Eve let that hang there, resting one hand on the chair to steady herself. "Won the whole damn Bushy Pepper Prize."

"Of course you didn't, because—"

"Won it and turned it *down*," said Eve, full of haughty disdain. She seemed bigger than before. "Because I knew you'd never recover. You'd hate it so much that you'd hate *me*, and that wasn't worth it. You go ahead; you call them. Check their records. They'll tell you Eve Sommersday's story won first prize that year, but she turned it down. Fool girl went into the Army instead. All because she didn't want to lose a friend."

Winnie couldn't make her mouth work.

"But it looks like I did in the end anyway." Eve slapped some money down to tip the bartender, eyes bright. Then she turned and flounced out of the restaurant.

Winnie carried that home with her like a sixteen-ton weight out of a cartoon. Let it sit on her shoulders while she brushed her teeth and got into bed next to her husband. (She'd called a taxi, in the end.) And around three in the morning, after falling into a fitful sleep, she sat up in bed and placed a call.

A sleepy Eve mumbled into the phone after picking up.

"Bullshit," said Winnie.

A pause. Then Eve started to laugh.

Winnie hung up.

When Winnie paused this time, the goddesses were giggling. Most of them, anyway. The giggle of a goddess was a spectacular thing, as she learned; the walls vibrated with color and the floor shimmered like it was made of water. Just small vibrations of the universe that reminded her of the one time she'd had a magic mushroom.

But their tittering made her furious. This wasn't funny. For the next twelve years, she and Eve stayed out of each other's way, until the memory of that reunion and late-night phone call felt like a half-remembered dream to Winnie. She was reasonably certain the conversation in the bar had gone sour the way she recalled, but that late-night phone call? How had she known Eve's phone number? And why would Eve have *laughed*?

Again, Winnie met Calliope's eyes. Was she done yet? Were they still hungry?

The giggles trailed off, and the room stopped vibrating. The Muses all looked expectantly at her again.

Calliope made a small sweeping gesture with her hand.

TWELVE YEARS PASSED. Twelve years in which suddenly everyone was connected on social media, including Winnie. It was the best way for her to keep in touch with her children, who'd moved to Colorado and California and who she only saw a few times a year. Every day or so she'd go onto their pages and 'like' or 'love' every single photo, sometimes leaving a comment or two. They spoke irregularly, and when she pushed for them to call *her* every once in a while, her daughter said once, "Fire, flood or blood, right?"

That stung a bit. Winnie had insisted on being left alone while writing her books—which, of course, she was doing all the time—and had a sign made for her office door that read 'fire, flood or blood.' As in: don't bother me unless one of those things is happening. She couldn't deny it—disappearing into her made-up worlds was more exciting than the mundane, everyday existence of laundry or driving the kids to karate class or making dinner. But once the kids and her husband were gone, she didn't need the sign anymore, and the days seemed quite large and empty indeed.

Social media helped. She could be in touch with people on her own schedule. She started digging around for old names, sometimes only curious as to how they turned out, sometimes because she wanted to reconnect. Eve's name came up early on, but it took her a long time to search for her, afraid of what she might—or might not—find. And then she found her: Evelyn Sommersday. Photo and everything. Over the past twelve years Eve had gone to Temple University and graduated with a degree in criminal justice. She'd been married, was now divorced. There was no mention of children. As Winnie would learn eventually, this last part was Eve's greatest sorrow. She'd wanted the family she hadn't been able to grow up with and didn't want to compromise. But then she was forty. And beyond.

But Winnie didn't know any of that as she lurked in Eve's profile. And then, she slipped. She 'liked' something Eve had posted. Maybe it was accidental, maybe inevitable. But it was instantly too late to take it back.

A notification appeared in her mailbox seconds later.

» **I see you there, Winnie Arrowmaker.**

She almost responded immediately, then walked away from the computer. She didn't know what she was supposed to feel. There hadn't been a sweeping, cinematic reason why they'd lost touch. Nobody had slept with the other's boyfriend or husband. Nobody had stolen from or attacked the other.

Winnie didn't know how this story was supposed to end.

Two days after that private message, she had a glass of wine. Then another. Then she wrote back:

» **It's me. I'm sorry.**

Moments later:

» **For what?**

» **For being such a little asshole when I read your story.**

That was where it had all started, at least for Winnie. She paused for a long moment.

» **Did you really turn down that prize for me?**

» **No.**

A pause.

» **I never won it in the first place.**

Winnie stood up, spilling the rest of her wine on her jeans.

» **They gave me honorable mention. I think about a hundred other people got that, too. We got a gift certificate to a bookstore. Twenty-five bucks.**

Winnie did a little dance around the room, happy no one could see her in her wine-stained pants. Her fists drove into the air and down again.

» **Bet you're doing a little victory cha-cha right now.**

Winnie stopped moving and typed:

» **Kind of. But not why you might think.**

» **OK, then why?**

She thought of Eve sitting wherever Eve might be right then. Her face as lined as Winnie's, the lives they'd lived like seesaws between them. One up, one down, one up, one down. But nothing had ever been quite as good as when they'd both been on the same side. Both reading together. Both listening to music on Winnie's dad's ancient stereo system in a mostly empty living room. Both being themselves. And then, as if they'd been whispered in her ear, the words came to Winnie.

Because I think this means we're finally old enough to be friends again.

Another full minute, in which Winnie danced around the room some more. She wasn't nervous. She was as right as the time she'd declared 'bullshit' twelve years earlier. But until Eve responded, she couldn't be sure.

Finally, a picture came through. Eve, raising her own glass of wine to the camera.

» **To us,**

she'd declared.

» **L'chaim,**

Winnie typed back.

After that, the messages—and occasional phone calls—ramped up. Winnie shared her heartbreak over her husband, who'd turned into a giant cliché when they both turned thirty, and he started dating his secretary. Winnie referred to her as 'The Strumpet.' Then he'd become another ultimate cliché by having a heart attack in the middle of one of their sexual escapades. In a drive-through. At McDonald's. It was both heartbreaking and hilarious.

» **They had to call the paramedics to peel him off her,**

Winnie told Eve on a call.

» **She'd been driving.**

» **Think they got fries with that?**

Winnie had fallen on the floor in laughter. By then, it still hurt, but only Eve could make her laugh like that.

For her part, Eve revealed she'd been teaching as an adjunct professor. Pretty good for a former security guard, but she could never seem to make the jump into full professorhood. She was sure it had to do with being Black and was trying not to let it turn her bitter, but it wasn't easy. She never found the right partner; all the men she dated seemed do a quick fade when she revealed her job.

» **Is this as good as it gets?**

Eve once messaged.

» **How do you mean? It's not all that bad over here.**

Still, Winnie had wondered that herself.

» **I'm almost too old to be a mom now,**

she'd written back. This was a common theme with Eve.

» **There's always adoption. IVF. You know that.**

» **I always pictured a baby made of half me and half some guy I was crazy for. Who looked maybe a little like Blair Underwood. Maybe I should've been more methodical, like you.**

» **Trust me, my life isn't necessarily better because I followed the rules. Never forget The Strumpet.**

» **Well, we're gonna be fifty soon enough,**

Eve had written back.

» **There's a door that feels like it's closing faster than I can prop it open. I'd do pretty much anything to have a kid at this point.**

Then Eve had gone silent.

And some months after that, another message:

» **Found a door. Need your help. Meet me.**

And everybody lived happily ever after. Until, of course, they didn't.

Until the goddesses had other ideas.

Chapter 35

Where You Most Want to Be

DOORS. PORTALS. WINDOWS. Holes in the ground. The variety of methods to travel from place to place in the lands beyond the Veil were the very definition of inconstant.

But they were magic. And magic was creation made of equal parts phantasm and emotion.

Magic spent its time hovering, an invisible something just out of reach of those who might attempt to grab it. It couldn't be heard, seen, or smelled, but magic liked to be felt. Magic also thrilled to the new, the unique, the untried. After all, magic was older than any being who attempted to make use of it, including those who thought they were born with it. Magic has been there, done that, and gotten both the T-shirt and the oven mitt.

Except.

Until just this moment, magic had never been summoned by a union involving a Seelie-Unseelie, a brownie, and a young scientifically minded human, in which they combined their efforts to create—of all things—a door. That was unique. And in the beyond-immortal lifespan of magic, anything original was positively not to be missed. So magic showed up for this one.

Curious, though, that the fae, brownie, and human were throwing so much effort into creating a portal *out*, but not *out to* any specific place. All they knew was they couldn't stay in the empty blankness they'd been banished to. They had to be… Elsewhere.

So magic gave them what they desired.

Which was precisely what they needed.

It just wasn't what they *expected*.

MALVOUS BLINKED. TOOK a sniff. Blinked again. Cocked his head toward the sound of music.

No denying it—from the stench of spilled ale to the blare of the jukebox (segueing from The Beatles' 'Help!' into Bruno Mars' 'Count on Me') and the familiar burbling buzz of tipsy Bro conversation, Malvous knew where he was: The Clocked Out. The Bro Bar he visited regularly. The one that usually contained the one fellow Bro he cared to see: Foxtacular.

Malvous blinked once more and looked at his empty hands. No Siggy behind him, no Finch before him. But someone was waving from across the room—waving at him. That same someone patted a stool, one they'd rested a leg across to claim. A someone with a rose-gold pompadour that stood so high it seemed it must fall over at any minute but never did.

The small hairs on the back of Malvous' neck stood on end. Seconds ago, he'd made a door. He'd stepped through it. And he'd ended up… here.

I must return to Seaview Haven, he thought. *Finch needs me. Siggy needs me. It's also my job.*

But the thought drifted from him like smoke from a pipe, which was precisely what the brownie across the room (who was still waving, though it was more like a beckoning now) was puffing on.

Well, maybe just one drink, he thought. *I haven't had a break in a long time. The union would insist.*

Gulping, Malvous took a step forward, boot sticking briefly on the never-properly-cleaned floor. (This was part of the appeal of The Clocked Out; Brownies who spent all day neatening the mess of others could revel in the decadence of a not-very-tidy pub.) As he neared the brownie waiting for him, he let the Bro's smile warm his soul. That pompadour, so soft and swoopy and vertical. That vaguely purplish skin, like a grape waiting to be nibbled on. Those perfectly round eyes. This Bro didn't seem to care that Malvous' were oddly squarish.

Foxtacular Featherweight swapped his pipe for a glass of glowing concoction, taking a sip. Malvous slid into the open seat. "Malvy," said the object of Malvous' hopes and dreams. "About time you got here! Where have you been hiding?"

"Nowheresville," said Malvous, taking Foxtacular's hand.

It was as soft as he'd dreamed.

Maybe even softer.

SIGGY WAS ASTRIDE her bicycle, hurtling down a paved road when she came to her senses. It was afternoon and she rode beneath a sunny, cloudless sky. The woods were full of woodsy noises, rustling and bugs chirping and birds singing. But she was alone. There was nothing on the road except her, and her bicycle.

I went through our door and—

The bike coasted to a halt. She set her feet on the road and took a long, deep breath. Glanced over her shoulder. A faraway light in the distance signaled the end of the woods, and a breath gave her the whiff of salt air, suggesting that maybe she'd left both the nothingness, and Nowheresville, behind.

I scienced it out, she thought, remembering the day

Finch had arrived as she pedaled against the invisible barrier of town fruitlessly. When she'd insisted to Martin that she would figure a way out of town, one way or the other.

But no, science had nothing to do with this. She, Malvous and Finch had made a door and walked through it. This was magic. Good magic, bad magic, she didn't know, but she was aware that she'd never gotten this far down the road out of Seaview Haven before. Especially once the invisible barrier went up.

Where were the others, though?

Why hadn't they come through with her?

Despite the warmth and brightness of the day, Siggy shivered. Goosebumps raised her arm hairs. She couldn't remember the last time she'd been quite this alone in the world. Even at night while she slept, Miz Winnie or Malvous had been downstairs, looking after her. She gripped the handlebars of her bicycle more tightly, expecting fear to take over. But it didn't. Instead, a strange wave of energy flooded through her. She was alone. She could go anywhere right now. No one could tell her to be home for dinner. No one was going to insist she shouldn't be biking on the road out of town by herself. If she wanted, she could run into the woods and never come back. (Not that she wanted to.) She could also turn around and return to Seaview Haven. (She didn't want to do that, either.) The only thing she wished could be a little different was to have Martin with her. He'd have ideas.

Instead, the only person who could make decisions now was Siggy.

She felt grown-up.

Miz Winnie had once shown Siggy a 'laundry list' of statements by a thinker called Sheldon Kopp. Siggy had read it over so many times she practically had it memorized. One line, about how all-important decisions had to be made without having all the data.

Siggy made an important decision and started pedaling. Forward.

About ten minutes later, new sounds drifted out to her: A murmuring of voices. A guitar playing. Someone laughing. All coming from the side of the road, within the woods itself. She coasted to a stop in front of a cleared out area, lined with the stumps of recently felled trees, and discovered an encampment. A few yards into the trees, a scattering of people swirled around parked cars, sat at handmade tables and benches, darted into and out of oversized tents and makeshift buildings. It was a pop-up town in the middle of the woods.

Siggy wheeled her bicycle down a cleared path toward an enormous fire pit—unlit at the moment but still glowing with embers—and stared at the faces of those she passed. They were all familiar, but she didn't recognize anyone. Some stared at her, some barely registered she was there at all. Most let her pass without notice. They went about their business, carrying totes, backpacks, wooden planks, or handmade fishing rods. A few were hauling recently killed animal carcasses.

A flash of movement and someone was standing before her. A tall woman in a tattered polka-dot skirt and smeared white T-shirt knotted at her waist. Her thick hair was held back in a bandana. "Do my eyes deceive me? Is this Sigfrieda Sommersday? Miss Siggy! My dear, where did you come from?"

Siggy blinked at her. The voice hit first, that soft rich tone of authority. Her second grade teacher, Miz Chasnoff, who said 'dear' and 'here' like 'deah' and 'heah,' which Mama said meant she'd originally come from a town called Boston. A place which, she gathered from overheard conversations, was 'wicked good.' Two years ago, Miz Chasnoff had gone camping with her husband and never returned to Seaview Haven.

"I went… through a door," Siggy told Miz Chasnoff now. She understood why the other people she'd passed were familiar but strange: they were all her former neighbors, who'd disappeared. But they were two years older. She was two years older. Something began bubbling in her chest and tickled her heart. "Then I was on my bicycle."

Miz Chasnoff clapped her hands over her mouth. "Anthony!" she cried, and a gangly young man with a buzz-cut hairstyle raced over. "Take care of Siggy's bicycle right now. I have to show her something."

Anthony barked a laugh. "Sigmund the Sea Monster! 'Bout time you joined us!"

Sigmund the Sea Monster. Siggy hadn't heard that one in years. Time was, she'd have hauled off and punched Anthony in the shoulder for making the crack. But he'd been so much smaller the last time he'd teased her at the beach. "Tony Spumoni!" she shot back, almost without thought. "Man, you got tall." She turned to Miz Chasnoff as he wheeled away her bicycle. "Where's he going with my bike?"

"Just putting it in the shed." Miz Chasnoff scooped up Siggy's hand. "Now. Come." Her former teacher walked so quickly that Siggy had to jog, with no time to concentrate on that tickle surrounding her heart. "You see," her former teacher said, her words rushing as fast as her strides, "all of us we ended up here. Like you. The roads won't let us back into Seaview Haven. We've been so *scared*. Some of us went to another T-Town but the rest… we couldn't bear to be so far from home. In case things changed. So we took the supplies we had when we were stranded and set up here—Camp Elsewhere."

Like calling Seaview Haven Nowheresville, Siggy thought.

Miz Chasnoff halted in front of a giant tent whose flaps hung closed. It was actually several tents sewn together into a patchwork to make a larger enclosure. One bright orange swathe across the roof seemed familiar.

Then she knew.

It was *her* tent. From when they'd gone camping.

From when she'd had a mother and a father.

Miz Chasnoff pulled back one of the flaps and began, "Evelyn, I have a surprise—"

But Siggy had already bolted ahead. "Mama!" she cried, heart fairly bursting, tears blurring her vision as she hurtled to the person whose face she would never forget, not in a hundred years without her. Eve Sommersday rose from a folding chair, mouth dropped open, eyes enormous. She dropped the knitting she'd been holding. But Siggy didn't stop until she had her arms around her and they were mushed together as tight as could be.

"Oh, Mama!" she sobbed. "I found you!"

Chapter 36

Butter Be Good

"This is quite a throng," Hardy observed.

"Developing into a bit of a *ruckus*," Laurel offered.

The Unseelie dismantler pair had arrived on the lawn of the mayor's home in Seaview Haven a few minutes ago to find a growing crowd of seething humans gathered there. Quickly determining that this was not festival related (a distinct lack of bunting, and the presence of signs with exclamation marks on them were deciding factors), the fae had slipped between the agitating humans and now stood on the front porch.

The goal, of course, was to finally converse with the erstwhile Mayor Neal Bartleby. But Laurel and Hardy were creatures of chaos. A roiling crowd was actually more interesting in this moment than anything else in the world. It felt like wrapping themselves in a cozy blanket. Transfixed by the collection of milling, muttering, sign-waving townsfolk they tried to puzzle out what was going on.

Laurel counted twenty humans. Hardy counted twenty-eight. An exact number was impossible to determine, since the grouping grew by the moment. They weren't concerned by that fact; humans had no magic, after all. But it was worthy of note.

"Is this what I've heard called a 'pack-nack'?" Hardy wondered.

"I believe the word is 'pick-nick.'" Laurel scanned the crowd. "During such an event, a checkered flag is spread across the ground and someone named Nicholas is placed in the center, then surrounded by food. This does not seem to be that."

"They appear to be airing grievances," Hardy reported after a moment's more attention. "I've tried reading their signs, but their handwriting and spelling is dreadful."

Laurel nodded enthusiastically. "It is! Most beautiful, if incomprehensible." Both were energized by the collection of humanity before them, though just as pleased to be separated from it by the front porch railing. Prior to today, Laurel's personal experience with humans had been cursory and largely relegated to their early changeling-swap days some six centuries earlier. Escaping that had involved being dumped into a river by a raging mob of superstitious villagers, and since then they'd studiously avoided both water immersion and large crowds.

When they'd vied for the Seaview Haven assignment, though, they'd failed to predict that there would be actual human interaction. *Live eternally and learn*, they thought now.

Still, the rising clamor wasn't aimed at Laurel or Hardy precisely. The villagers, none of whom seemed willing or able to get closer to the house than a few feet away, kept shouting the same requests. They all wanted to know what was going on.

"Send us home if you can't fix this damned T-Town!" a gray-haired man wearing spectacles cried.

"Your magic sucks!" said a whippet-thin young man. "I can do better tricks than this!"

"Curious," noted Hardy. "I have always understood that while every grown human *knows* they are in a TROPE Town, they aren't able to express that fact. That is not the case here."

"Seaview Haven is truly broken." Laurel nodded. It was a sensation to savor. Witnessing firsthand the disintegration of a creation as complex as a T-Town was like inhaling savory scents before a feast. "Most agreeable."

Hardy's eyes lit up. "Y'know, we could help things along a bit."

"You mean—"

Hardy nodded enthusiastically.

Laurel squeezed their associate's hand. "I positively love how your mind works." The mission objective of speaking to the Mayor had receded in their mind. The Seelie SMD could wait a bit longer. "Finch may be a hopeless case, but I am beginning to appreciate his dallying in this burg. So much going so wrong. It's hard to want to do the right thing."

"Shall we?" Hardy gestured at the crowd.

"Let's." Laurel bounced on their toes.

Hardy leaped onto the railing that outlined the porch and took hold of one of the roof's supporting posts, waving a hand. "Humans! That is—ladies and gentlemen of Seaview Haven!"

The shouting and muttering diminished. Laurel beamed at their partner, then out at the crowd. A small knot of people at the back had detached and were surrounding something. Laurel ignored them, continuing to bounce.

"Since we can all speak plainly and without wards here, allow me to introduce myself and my partner," Hardy continued. "We are from the Seelie Court Network's Dismantlement of Special Projects Division." They paused, letting that sink in. "We are Unseelie dismantlers, here to consult with Mayor Neal Bartleby and arrive at a mutual decision about the future of Seaview Haven."

Hardy was getting ahead of themselves; they were still only here to report back, but no one said they had to tell the *truth* to these riled-up humans.

Townsfolk murmured among one another as the words sank in. Laurel felt the mood shift and coalesce, a piquant bouquet of unease, fear, and anger. They drank it in like fine wine, feeling more powerful by the second.

"Dismantlement?" A woman's high-pitched voice rose above the murmurs.

"Indeed!" Hardy chirped, their authoritative voice carrying across the yard. "As even the briefest of observations will reveal, this town has had it. We've been sent ahead in anticipation of ending this little experiment forthwith."

Laurel caught some movement around the side of the house. A young human sitting in a wheeled conveyance rolled into view, followed by—was that Felicitous?

Hardy continued fomenting. "Seaview Haven has had a good run, but wiping the slate clean is likely the best—"

Something thudded against Hardy's shoulder, then landed on the porch. A second, similar projectile crashed into his forehead and tumbled at Laurel's feet. A ball? Someone—no, two someones—had lobbed large, yellow balls of some substance at them.

"Ouch." Hardy was more surprised than hurt. "Was that necessary?"

"You want to kill the town!" a woman in a sundress gasped. "That's not right! Just fix it!"

"Save Seaview Haven!" came a second voice. Signs bobbed up and down.

"Dismantle the Unseelie!" cried a third.

Cheeky, thought Laurel.

"Get rid of *them*!" shouted another.

Hardy shook his head. "Madam, that is not our role here. Once our report is submitted, full erasure and dismantlement are likely the best road forward—"

The crowd surged. As a unit, they managed to close the distance between themselves and the house and were now three feet away. Only the last tatters of the wards were keeping them back. A third yellow ball, then a fourth, shot at Hardy. The last one hit them full in the face, and the Unseelie tumbled backward from their perch. Laurel barely caught them, going down on one knee before lowering their partner to the porch. Things had gone bad (and not in a good way) so quickly. Knots and bruises rose on Hardy's face that did not immediately vanish. A trickle of blood ran down their nose and sparkled.

"This is quite unpleasant," Hardy said in a sickly voice. "I mean that sincerely. Ouch. Owie. Drat."

Laurel poked at one of the yellow balls, which was decidedly hard and cold, yet slick and melting against their hand. They gave their fingers a lick.

Butter?

The projectiles kept coming, taking on greater variety while Laurel crouched over their partner. A tomato splattered red next to the dismantlers, followed by a blackened potato, which squished against their boots. Laurel's mind whirled. They wanted to soothe their partner, who looked glassy and pale.

"Perhaps you were a bit *too* effective," they said finally.

The barrage began in earnest; rocks, rotten food, more fist-sized yellow balls, even clumps of mud sailed over the porch railing as the crowd grew more boisterous. Words Laurel hadn't heard in centuries filled the air. They froze in place, still holding Hardy. They had not realized how profoundly terrifying their dip in that tumultuous river had been six centuries ago and were starting to have flashbacks.

Hardy gasped, "This might be too much carnage." Then their eyes fluttered shut.

"You always were incredibly talented," Laurel agreed. Another yellow butter ball rebounded off the house and slammed into the back of their head. They crumpled over their partner.

Both Unseelie dismantlers were down for the count.

"OH, MY," SAID Felicitous as the projectiles began to fly, starting with the yellow balls. He rubbed his shoulder. "Such a waste of good butter."

Martin squinted. "Kind of ingenious, actually."

The brownie sighed. "Your townsfolk have a decidedly *odd* relationship with food."

If only Finch's 'fixes' from the day before had worked better. Martin had learned that yesterday's jaunt around Seaview Haven to familiarize Finch with the place (and hopefully convince him that it was worth saving) had had mixed results. On the one hand, he'd fixed many things. On the other hand, he hadn't fixed them *right*. The gnarly dinosaur-shaped scar on Mr Zhao's son's knee had begun roaring in the night, and now needed to be fed. The grocery bags at Grossinger's had indeed filled up, but with nothing but balls of frozen butter. Customers had been disappointed, but that hadn't prevented them from making off with dozens of the orbs. As for Finch's miracle of the fishes—well, the ocean beyond Seaview Haven's ports had opened up considerably but was now teeming with puffer fish and moray eels. It wasn't even swimmable. Finch had only managed to inflame the town further while simultaneously alerting Havenites that their censorship wards were disappearing.

That had apparently been the cue for locals to start talking and start demanding answers.

Martin thought about seeing Winnie in the garden. How she'd acknowledged him but hadn't moved. How he'd done his best with Siggy's hand signals. But he despaired. What could Winnie do now that wouldn't be too late? Seaview Haven felt like it was collapsing from within.

More projectiles flew. "This is nuts," said Martin. "Felicitous, get behind me."

"I do not require protection," the brownie insisted.

"That's what they thought." Martin pointed at the porch, where the Unseelie rabble-rousers had disappeared. Where they'd gone he couldn't be sure, but that wasn't his problem right now. He didn't know what to make of the scene at the mayor's house. These were his neighbors. It was like watching Jekyll become Hyde. Or was that the other way around? "Now might be the time to roll—and run—away."

"I certainly will not," said the brownie. "You should take cover, though."

"They might hurt you." Martin reached out a hand.

"Why would they do that?"

Martin didn't have the right words. He felt like he should have paid more attention in class and less time writing notes to Siggy. "Because they're-they're not Seaview Havenites anymore. They're like a big beast. Besides, what are you going to tell them? They just think Finch and those weird other fae made things worse, not better."

For all of Finch's half successes and half failures, Martin knew the Unseelie dismantler had meant well. That he was not the same Unseelie who'd dropped into town almost two weeks ago. But the rest of the town was acting like a huge prank had been pulled on them. That they'd been conned while they were already down. No wonder they'd flipped so fast.

"I did need butter." Felicitous held up a sack of approximately five pounds of the stuff. "It will melt if I fail to get it into the refrigerator." He turned to the house. "Trust me, I will be fine."

But as he took a step, a Molotov cocktail hurled toward the house. It crashed against an upper story and spread homemade moonshine across the entire porch roof. Everything burst into flame. A second bottle followed, crashing through a window.

The mayor's house was on fire.

Chapter 37

Throwing Muses (Out)

WINNIE FINISHED TALKING about Eve. She was finished talking, period. She wasn't even sure she would ever write another word; she was so drained. Drained and thirsty. A beer would go down well right now. Turning to the French doors that led out into the lawn, she blinked at the afternoon sun. On the far edge of Neal's backyard sat the bench where she and Calliope had spoken. The bench where she'd seen Martin make a Winnie-bird to remind her of what was important. The bench where she'd decided to tell *this* story.

She'd spoken for more than an hour. Her hands trembled, her legs felt weak, but her voice had been steady. She'd cried during some of the twists in her tale, despite knowing they were coming. Her words had been full of thorns, pricking her afresh each time she reached another break with Eve. The story had wrung her dry.

About halfway through it all, she'd realized it was no ordinary retelling. It was a plea. No, a request. No—a declaration of independence.

But that wasn't right either.

It was, actually, a prayer.

A squirrel scampered across the yard, dug around, then scampered away. Winnie took a deep breath and smelled smoke. Someone must be prepping for a barbecue. But who lived close enough to Neal? That wasn't right.

Behind her, the room was silent. When she'd finished talking and turned away, the Muses leaned into one another, murmuring. No one asked what came next. No one applauded. No one wondered where the ending was. No one sighed and demanded more. Winnie hadn't thought she needed to explain why Eve had brought her to Seaview Haven; they already knew that much. And if they didn't, she was tapped out. It was time to face the music and find out what came next. Winnie turned from the doors.

The room had emptied. There was a mess, to be sure; tea mugs and shortbread crumbs, blankets in disarray. And on a far chair, nine sets of multicolored velour tracksuits sat piled like a collapsed rainbow.

The Pandora's Box™ stood open.

There was no glow in it.

Winnie stood perfectly still, afraid to hope.

"Oh, good!" A familiar musical voice drifted from a reclining chair. Eutie wore a billowing silken robe that flowed over her like water, just as her tracksuit had. Bubbly and pink-cheeked as ever, she'd always been the kindest to Winnie throughout the entire ordeal. "You're with Us again."

"Us?" Winnie's heart sank. Maybe everyone else had run to the kitchen.

"Me," the Muse corrected. "The others departed. I said I would remain for a bit."

"Gone?" Winnie jolted. "As in—"

"The gal-cation has concluded." Eutie spread her arms as if revealing something very dramatic. "I believe My sweet sisters will return to SCN, as I plan to. We have a reputation to protect, and the output from Our offices since Our departure has been either abysmal or nonexistent. There will be a few changes. No one wants to get burned up—"

"Burned out." Winnie couldn't help herself.

Eutie gave her an indulgent glance. "Correcting Muses. Only you, Winnifred. In any case, if you're uncertain that We are truly exiting this TROPE Town, do check the Pandora's Box™."

Winnie took small steps at first, then ran to the side table. It was just a box, now. She'd had no idea what to expect from a dispelling godspell, but she'd thought there'd be more of a bang than a whimper. "Where did the godspell go?"

Eutie smiled. "The spell untangles, then returns from where it had been summoned. Component parts return to their origins, if possible."

"So the story... worked?"

"Beautifully. I wished to remain for a few moments to offer My personal appreciation for your story. For giving Us something not just good, or great, but *grand*. Your mysteries are fine. Entertaining. Not every story has to be enormous and life-changing. Your romance with the Seelie is strange, but We felt the truth of it. With this last tale, you shared a piece of your soul. That only came when you spoke of Eve. Remarkable. Unexpected."

Winnie couldn't resist the compliment of a Muse. Her face heated up.

"The best compositions of any form are more than the sum of their parts," said Eutie. "They are more like—" She smiled. "A song. Something elevated. Epic."

"Hard to believe my friendship with Eve is epic to anyone but us two."

"That's all that matters. When you draw from your heart, it emerges not so much a tale as a—"

"Prayer."

Eutie's dimples deepened. "Precisely. And prayers are what deities hear most clearly, yes?"

Winnie was overwhelmed. "You didn't mind earlier that I cast you all as the—"

Her chuckle was like bells ringing. "It was a fresh way of portraying Us, that's for sure! We aren't bothered by such things. Muses are cursed as much as We are praised." Eutie rose from her chair. "It has been Elysian to spend time with you, Winnifred. We owe you a debt for helping disentangle Us from a spell of Our Own weaving. You will continue hearing from Us, though at a distance. We shall not be strangers."

Impulsively, Winnie hugged her. The Muse embraced the writer in return. Then Winnie was hugging air. Eutie simply disappeared. The space between her arms felt like a cool spring breeze and smelled like pine. Then even her essence was gone, replaced by a strange smoky scent.

Winnie's eyes burned. *I did it. No*—we *did it. Me. Eve. Neal.*

She raced out of the living room.

NEAL'S OFFICE WAS quiet. The whole house, in fact, was quiet; Felicitous seemed to be out. Winnie thudded down the hallway to Neal's office door and flung herself against it, tumbling inside when there was no resistance.

The cyclone was gone. There was no wind. No papers circling the ceiling to the floor. The word tree in the corner had lost its foliage.

Neal was gone, too.

Yelping, Winnie pushed through mounds of paper to the typewriter, nearly tumbling down the sunken room's steps. She'd left him there, typing away. He couldn't have gotten far. He wouldn't have *left* her here—

Well, he left you hanging all that time when you thought he was in a coma—

Winnie couldn't think about that now. They would have to have a conversation—many conversations—about that particular breach of trust. He had paid dearly for his stubbornness and momentary cruelty. She reached the spot where he had been sitting in front of the typewriter and spied a small patch of curly dark hair. Shoving aside reams of paper, she unburied him from his work. Neal was curled up in a fetal position, less gray than he'd been the night before, but far from restored to health. His hands were bent as if he might begin typing again, and his fingers were callused and red. But the moment she touched him, his eyes opened and met hers—not full of the mischievous spark she'd noticed on the first day, but not glassy or distant. He was here.

"I fell over," he whispered.

Winnie helped him sit. "Then I'll pick you up. Can you stand?"

"Not sure."

But he could, if he leaned on her shoulder. "This… might… take… some time." He gestured at his legs. "I haven't used those in ages."

She kissed him, but it was like kissing air. He had no strength to press back. She tried to keep all her concentration on Neal, but in the distance, outside, she heard a buzzing conversation, growing louder. And that smoky scent was getting stronger by the minute. For a moment, she wondered: Were the Muses back? Were they barbecuing?

Neal wobbled so much he nearly knocked them both down. They sat amid the paper. "Felicitous will help when he gets back from the store," Winnie promised. "Then we'll get you into a bed or bathtub or whatever you need."

"Maybe both at the same time." Neal's voice was scratchy and low. He took Winnie's hands and rested his forehead against hers. "So, did we tell a good story?"

"We told a very good story." She hesitated, surprised he didn't recall that she'd returned for a second round. Was it worth him knowing that their romance hadn't been what freed him? *Yes,* she thought. *We're going to start over by being honest.* "But they wanted more."

"*More?*"

"I told them"—she paused, chuckling to herself—"all about Eve. That seemed to make them happiest, because it was hardest."

"But our story was pretty good all by itself, wasn't it?" He wasn't asking about Muses. *We're okay, aren't we?* he was asking. *You forgive me?*

"Our story," she said, "continues to be written."

It was as good as she could give him right now, but it was enough.

Chapter 38

Flame Wars

FINCH WALKED THROUGH a door.

And walked into a kitchen.

Well, this is familiar.

The recently swept, dark wood floors, the stark white walls, the sense of abandonment and hidden decay—yeah, he knew this place. It was the same Cape Cod-style house he'd been inside precisely one time before: Mayor Neal Bartleby's home. He'd gone from a beige-gray nothingness to a house interior built for humans, and stood for a moment, startled. A chilly line traced down his back.

Beneath that flickered a bit of concern—the others weren't with him. He hadn't even seen them go; they just weren't here. *Did they get left behind? Did the door only permit Seelie?*

For a moment, Finch was genuinely worried. What if Siggy and Malvous were still trapped in the gray nothing? Dissolving into bits thanks to Laurel and Hardy's holding spell? He'd never forgive *anyone* if they—

Finch caught himself. Paused. Looked for the irritation, looked for the anger and frustration he should be feeling. Just a few days ago he'd probably have been saying to himself: *So they went off without me. Don't need their help, anyway*. But that wasn't happening right now.

He felt squishy inside. Off-balance. Worry banged around in his head—worry not for himself, but for other people. Maybe for the first time. For no particular reason, he thought of Agatha.

A noise broke him out of his head. A grumble came next. A something caught his attention.

"Felicitous?" he called out. "Bartleby? Winnifred?"

No answers. The house was so still he wondered if he'd walked into another T-Town, or if this was an extension of the Unseelies' spell. Then he heard the sound again—outside. A crowd, as if someone was throwing a party. At first, he assumed it was the Muses. The good-for-nothing goddesses. But Finch listened harder and *felt* harder. He couldn't sense their interfering presence. When he'd last stood in this house, their powers had been so pervasive they'd choked his mind. Made him feel small and useless.

Not this time.

Finch trotted down the hallway and slid open the living room doors. It was a delightful mess in there—crumbs and tracksuits everywhere—but no Muses. They were gone.

A slow grin spread across his face. Winnie had done it. He marveled that she'd found a way and couldn't wait to hear the story that had broken the godspell. *There's something to be learned here*, he thought. *Who knew you could learn anything of use from humans?* But he sensed he was about to start learning a lot over the coming years. He felt like he had to catch up in some way.

So where was the author? The Seelie Showrunner?

More *noise*.

Finch eased over to one of the house's front windows and tugged aside a curtain. The front yard was full of humans, an actual mob of them. They were making quite a fuss, waving signs, and throwing various objects. What would make Seaview Haven's citizens so exercised?

Then he got it. They were throwing a party! Was it a holiday? Someone's birthday? Or could they be so excited from all the spells Finch had flung around town that they were celebrating? Could they have brought this party to the mayor's house to express their gratitude? They wouldn't know where Finch was living, but this house would be a good first guess. No wonder the door had brought him here. This was clearly where he was supposed to be.

Aww, wasn't much, he imagined saying to them. *Just a couple of loose spells I had hanging around. No need to thank me.*

Except he didn't want thanks. He wanted to thank *them*. Siggy and Martin. The Zhaos. Mrs Grossinger. Captain Roberts. Everyone else who had *let* him help them. It had felt wonderful to be useful. To build something. It was like exercising new muscles.

"Felicitous!" he called again.

The brownie failed to appear. Weren't brownies supposed to always be on hand for assistance? He paced the room, trying to decide what to say to the grateful Havenites out there. Maybe he could make a list of what else they needed and see how best he could get that to them. Sure, that was a mayor's job, but Neal wouldn't mind for a moment, he was sure. He could spend an extra day or two here—

Then it all came back to him.

He wasn't here to make lists to help the Havenites. He was here to file a report. One he'd barely started. And that one job that he'd clawed for himself had been usurped by two actually, truly destructive Unseelie who were somewhere in town right now. He'd worked so hard to get here, and now that he *was* here, on the eve of helping tear down Seaview Haven, it was the last thing he wanted to do.

Neal Bartleby went native. Looks like I did, too. Galloping ghosts, what is it about this place?

While trying to figure out what to do, Finch peered outside and observed a strange sight: Laurel and Hardy were crumpled on the porch, splayed across one another. They were covered in grease and food stains. As he wondered, a yellow ball arced out of nowhere and crashed through a windowpane inches from his face. The ball landed at his feet, and he picked it up. Oily and half melted, it was clearly a ball of butter.

Above him on an upper floor, another window broke. A third shattering seemed to come from behind the house.

Finch raised an eyebrow.

Approximately 1/58th of him thought he should run outside and help the fallen dismantlers. A 1/132nd part of him thought, *This is a rather unusual way to throw a celebration.* It was actually more along the lines of one of his Smashes. His mind was racing so much that a bare 1/298th of it recognized that he was not enjoying this chaos at all. Instead, his scalp itched.

Nevertheless, the vast majority of Finch remained steadfast. If Felicitous wasn't here to open the door for him, he could do it himself. He would greet the overexcited citizenry and calm them down. They were obviously not paying attention to Laurel or Hardy. He was the fae who would surprise them with his genuine gratitude.

Time to give them what they wanted.

Squaring his shoulders and tugging his trousers up, he cinched the belt even tighter than before and returned to the hallway. From the kitchen to the foyer of the house his strides were confident, his mood intent. He paused once, thinking he heard something land on the roof overhang of the porch. From the direction of Neal's office, the one with the word tree and the thick piles of discarded paper, came a penetrating odor of creosote.

But Finch was on a mission. He tossed his red-streaked gray hair and shrugged the matter off. All would be made clear in moments. He yanked the front door open, holding his arms wide.

The projectiles ceased to fly. The crowd noises faded, then died.

"Greetings, Seaview Haven!" Finch gestured broadly from the doorway. "'Tis I, Finch! Let's turn down all this fuss and glory in the fact that—"

"It's him!" a cracking feminine voice screamed, and for the barest of seconds another 1/19th of Finch thought, *They're positively hysterical for me*— but then he absorbed the tone. Not love. Not adoration.

Rage.

"You turned my son's knee into a dinosaur!" Mr Zhou waved a fist.

"You gave us *butter*!" Mrs Grossinger dumped a burlap sack filled with more of the yellow balls. "One ton of frozen butter! *Salted!*"

Finch cocked his head, failing to see the issue in either instance.

"And that's it!" the grocery store owner finished.

Several moray eels and puffer fish (dead ones, fortunately) sailed out of the crowd and smacked onto the ground by Finch's feet. "Are you kidding with this? Do you want to poison us?" Captain Roberts shook a fist in Finch's direction.

Finch held up his hands. They'd wanted fish. He got them fish. Eels were fish, weren't they? Why couldn't they be thankful? He was suddenly a lot less thankful for *them*. Didn't they realize he was new at this creation and fixing thing? Next time he would be more specific with his spellcasting. "Oi!" He shook a fist at them. "I did my best!"

"Your best sucks!" cried a young man.

To Finch's surprise, that last curse landed like a rock—or a frozen ball of butter—on his heart. He'd spent his whole life trying to master the Unseelie way, until Seaview Haven, where he'd finally given Seelie creation methods a go. And apparently, he'd failed just as hard at that. They weren't here to celebrate him. They were here to... Finch raised an eyebrow. To do what?

"*GET HIM!*" shouted an old man standing in the front row.

The crowd surged.

Instinctively, Finch held out his hands and *willed* them back. He squinched his eyes and turned his hands, feeling for the ward Neal had established, plumbing its weaker points. But he had no idea what he was doing; maybe he was making things worse. As apparently he'd done yesterday.

The barrier held, barely. The people strained against the magic, faces multiple shades of rose. It was the opposite of comforting. The ward would not hold forever. Finch was backing into the house and preparing to shut the door when a new something flew out of the back of the crowd—a bottle filled with clear liquid, topped off with a flaming rag. It landed just inside the doorway and broke open, scattering alcohol and flame into the house and out onto the porch. The door latched shut and Finch danced backward from the spreading fire.

Behind him, the door to Neal's office flung open and a massive wave of heat pushed out with it. Finch darted to the office and grabbed the handle to yank the door closed, then hesitated, transfixed. The room was on fire. The word tree's spreading branches were crisped and dripping with fiery embers. The back half of the floor was a sea of curling flame, Neal's discarded paper congealing and blackening, the magic in each page turning the flames green, then purple, then aquamarine, then blood red.

He spotted something other than paper, or tree, or fire. Winnie, gasping in the smoke, was trying to pull Neal Bartleby up from the choking sea of paper, hoisting him on one shoulder. The Seelie looked gray and wizened and wrung out.

But at least he wasn't typing.

"The office is on fire!" Winnie gasped.

"The *house* is on fire!" Finch cried.

Neal started to speak, but his eyes fluttered, and he sagged against Winnie. The pair dropped to their knees.

"Finch, *do* something." Winnie reached for him. Her face was soot-smeared, and part of her clothes had been burned off, revealing an angry seared patch on one arm. She coughed. "I can't move him on my own."

Finch barely heard her. She was a gnat in a storm. He stared into the office, taking steps inside he didn't even realize he was making. Two years of story attempts, poems, screenplays and maybe sonnets to rival the works of Shakespeare (though to be honest, probably not) were disappearing into smoke and ash.

It was real chaos.

It was real destruction.

And Finch couldn't take his eyes from it.

"THAT IS *QUITE* the adventure." Foxtacular's eyes were wide, his pipe entirely smoked down by the time Malvous finished detailing where he'd disappeared to nearly two weeks ago. "I suspected something was awry when your hallway wasn't being tended to—no, don't fret, I've fed and watered the Will o' the Wisps and picked up some dust here and there, but no one knew where you'd gone, though I asked and asked." He craned toward Malvous. "And this explains so *much* about where my Muses have been all this time. I'd been relieved not to have to install new windows every few days but…" He leaned even closer. "You were so brave to stand up to that awful dismantler. That was not your job. We should speak with our union rep. Or maybe Janus would give us an audience—"

"Hush," said Malvous.

Astonished, Foxtacular hushed, though he'd leaned in so far Malvous could smell the sage embers from his doused pipe. Malvous cleared his throat and hated what he was about to say. "I have to leave."

"What?" Foxtacular looked as if he'd been slapped. "You can't be serious."

"I must go back." Malvous' hands curled into fists, and he pounded on his thighs. During his recounting of the last few weeks, he'd quaffed mug after mug of the bar's strongest chocolate stout, but it had failed to quash his sense of… well, duty, but not just that: unfinished business. Retelling everything up to and including the appearance of the horrible Unseelie dismantlers Laurel and Hardy left him understanding that Seaview Haven, Siggy, and even Finch were in danger. Siggy could lose her home. Seaview Haven might cease to exist. Winnie's present and future were in question. And Finch, annoying and full of himself as he was, desperately needed help if he was ever going to do something good in this world. They all needed a brownie.

Malvous couldn't abandon them now. Not even if Foxtacular's hand was as soft as a freshly woven silken trash bag.

"You just got here!" the other brownie wailed. "I was hoping we might…" He trailed off, then darted in. His lips met Malvous' and they were—if this was even possible—even softer than his hand. Their kiss was electric, rich, and sagey. Malvous moaned and kissed him back. He'd just gotten everything he ever wanted, or at least the start of everything.

After both a very long and very short time, they parted. Malvous' heart was so heavy he thought it might drop out of his chest. "I have to finish things. Seaview Haven is"—he slid from his seat—"my job."

Foxtacular stared at the floor. Every brownie in the pub would know what the invocation of 'my job' meant.

The song on the jukebox changed from Rascal Flatts' 'I Won't Let Go' to Rihanna's 'Umbrella' and Malvous let Foxtacular's hand slide from his own. He would find a door. He would make his way back to Felicitous' interior exit door. With luck, the other brownie would be home. He wanted to say something romantic like "Wait for me" or "I'll be back for you" but the words wouldn't leave his mouth. This was probably their one shot, and he was blowing it. But Malvous didn't see that he had a choice. Not if he wanted to look at himself in the mirror in the morning.

Swiping at his eyes, Malvous turned to head out of the bar. The door that would be its exit could take him to anywhere any other brownie door existed; he just had to conjure the destination in his mind and start walking. He reached for the back of the bar and heard a loud, raised voice.

"Malvous! You! Uh-uh!"

A pompadour bobbed above the heads of every other brownie in the room, and it was heading toward him. Foxtacular broke through the crowds and halted, wagging a finger. "You do *not* get to walk out on me so fast."

"But I can't stay—"

"Then we will walk out *together*."

Malvous shook his head, heart thumping. "I couldn't ask you to—" But he bit the rest of that off. For once, Foxtacular was chasing him. Foxtacular had kept tabs on his absence. Foxtacular had known that Malvous' floor needed maintenance and had done extra work to keep it shipshape. It was extraordinary.

"You're not asking." Foxtacular pocketed his pipe and tugged his vest down. "And I'm not asking, either." He slipped his oh-so-welcome hand into Malvous' and gave it a squeeze. "I'm telling. I'm coming with you."

Malvous' temperature shot up several degrees. He sensed his usual greenish color had developed an undertone of pink. "Are you… certain?"

"Of course not. I don't know anything. But I'm not going to let you go alone," said the dear, wonderful Foxtacular. "Besides, you sound like you could use a Bro of your own over there."

SIGGY WAS EXHAUSTED. It had been a big day. She'd gone from vanishing in a beige-gray nothingness to helping a brownie and an Unseelie Seelie make a door, to bicycling out of Seaview Haven to finding her *mother*. (Her father was another story, one Mama promised to share later. Yes, he was fine, but no, he wasn't in the pop-up town. Siggy put that aside for now.)

But she couldn't stop pacing. She couldn't stop talking. She went up and down the inside of the tent, spilling everything she could remember since the time her parents had vanished, every tiny detail, occasionally stopping to set her hands on her mother's cheeks, just to make sure she was real. So many things, concluding with the horrible beige-gray room of nothing and nowhere and the door that she, Malvous and Finch had created that sent her to this very place. She went on and on, restless and excited and oh so tired but unable to stop.

Then, she stopped. She ran out of things to say. Also, she needed some water. Her mother handed her a bottle, and she gulped and gulped, suddenly hearing the silence in the tent. Turning from her mother's shining, joyful face, she spotted Miz Chasnoff. And then another person. And a few others. Then she was all turned around and realized the entire giant tent was positively *packed* with people, all of whom were watching her.

Siggy stopped drinking.

When had all those people come in? Why were they staring?

"That's all," she said in a small voice. "Show's over."

Of course, it wasn't. She'd been kicked out of Seaview Haven just as things were getting ramped up. She'd left behind Laurel and Hardy and their meddling, Winnie was still in the mayor's house, and the Muses were totally in charge. Plus, if Martin had been right, the rest of the town was getting pretty riled up after Finch's day out. And Finch! And Malvous! Where were they all this time? Why hadn't they ended up on the road with her?

For some reason, though, she kept thinking about Martin. About what he was doing, right now. Was he safe? Was he arguing with Finch?

In the quiet, the pop-up villagers began leaning to one another and murmuring. Siggy heard suggestions: *If the wards are weak, we should try getting back in again… We'll show those Muses a thing or two… No way am I going back there, you couldn't pay me enough….*

Siggy and Eve looked at one another. And for just a split second, Siggy saw her mother in a different light. She was a mom, not just Siggy's mom. She was a wife. But she was also a person. Siggy hadn't really thought about it like that before. A person, plus all those other things. "Mama," she began. "I wanted to—"

A zipping sound came from one side of the tent, a deep rumbling purr. The tent hushed again, and everyone turned to the flaps, which were a) tied open and b) did not feature a zip but were c) the only entrance and exit from the stitched-together contraption. What could be making that noise?

Then Siggy saw it. An inverted 'U' shape unzipped itself in the middle of reality, sending people scattering away from the noise and the creation of a… well, a door. Someone on the other side knocked.

No one in the tent moved.

But Siggy knew what they were looking at. This was the same door she'd helped create in the nothing. But whoever'd created it this time couldn't just walk through. Someone had to open it. So she stepped forward and pulled on the handle.

Out stepped Malvous. But not alone. Malvous was with someone else who looked a lot like Malvous, except for a really huge hairdo that flipped back as he passed through the door. They were holding hands.

"Well," said the brownie with the hair.

"Well," said Malvous. "This was not where I expected to go." He turned to his friend. "I told you we should take the *other* door. This is the one I used to get here from the empty—" His gaze landed on Siggy. "Oh. My goodness. Sigfrieda!"

Siggy waved and pointed at her mother. "Look, Malvous!" she cried. "Mama is here!" She waved around the room. "And so are a lot of others from my neighborhood!"

Malvous and his friend stared in awe at the humanity around them. "Fascinating," said Malvous. "It appears that this door has many exits. It brought me to"—he turned an adoring eye to his friend—"Foxtacular."

"And it brought me *here!*" cried Siggy.

Eve rose from her chair and set her hands on her daughter's shoulders. "Neither of you are Felicitous. But you do appear to be brownies."

"At your service, lovely lady." Foxtacular bowed deeply, his pompadour bobbing with the movement.

"And you appear to have a door that goes where people *need* to be."

Malvous turned to the door, turned to Foxtacular, then to Eve. "That is an astute observation, indeed. I hadn't considered that."

"All it takes is a bit of sciencing it out," said Eve. She hugged Siggy from behind. "And a daughter who has a very good sense of recall."

Siggy started to wriggle out of her mother's grasp, then sank into it.

People began standing in the tent. "I have a place I need to be," said one man in a turned-around baseball cap. Siggy thought she knew him from down by the piers.

"Me, too," said Miz Chasnoff, turning to Anthony. "Go fetch your father. Now."

Anthony fled the tent.

"What are they doing, Mama?" Siggy turned to Eve.

"Just watch," said her mother, pointing.

Malvous and Foxtacular barred the door with their bodies. "Now, wait, good people. We can't be *certain* how this door will behave. It would be a violation of Bro code to simply let humans wander through a magic door without knowing for certain where it leads."

"It leads Somewhere!" cried Siggy. "It might even lead to Nowheresville!"

"And that's still better than here," said Eve. "I wish to go home with my daughter. We volunteer to be first."

"We do?" Siggy gulped.

Eve fixed her with the gaze of one adult to another. She did not bend down; she did not make her voice lighter for Siggy's sake. "I am the Sheriff of Seaview Haven. I have a best friend who's in danger. I have a whole town that's about to be torn down. You bet your bicycle I'm going first, and there's no way you're not coming with me." She addressed everyone else in the tent. "You all should make your own decisions. Think carefully." Turning to Malvous and Foxtacular, she gave them a nod. "Stand aside. You've done your duty. Now, I need to do mine."

Malvous touched foreheads with Foxtacular, who nodded. They clasped hands briefly.

"Then I will come with you," said Malvous. "Foxtacular will remain here to ensure the portal remains open until everyone who would like to use it has passed through."

He held open the door.

Siggy took his hand and then took her mother's.

They stepped through.

Chapter 39

Smoke and Mirrors

SWEAT ROLLED DOWN Finch's face and neck; the backs of his hands were beaded with salt water. He was transfixed, held in place by the raging flames consuming Neal's office, while fully aware that the conflagration was eating up the front foyer. Soon this whole place would be soot and ash and—well, what did happen to an immortal creature engulfed in flames?

Probably nothing good. Finch might be able to swim underwater to help a Kraken plug up the ocean, but he couldn't stay submerged forever. He could fall from the sky and (usually) not end up damaging himself, but he couldn't fly. And within a mighty blaze, he could likely stay alive far longer than many creatures, but that didn't mean he wouldn't experience agony once the flames reached his skin. He was immortal, but that was only if some grave accident didn't befall him. Everything had limits.

The fire was truly beautiful. Yet it didn't move him. He didn't feel like cheering it on.

Certainly, the fire spoke to whatever part of him remained Unseelie. That was the part that had left the dot on his toe for hundreds of years, the part that wanted to lash back at his idiot human brother for making his early years so awful, the part that created the Smashes that demolished his beautiful garden every year—all to prove he was properly Unseelie. That part wanted to touch every flame, to roll around in the fire and really, really get to know it. Because he'd always aspired to be like flame. Like fire. To consume and leave nothing behind.

And the longer he stared at the flickering orange-yellow-red-blue-magenta-teal-violet flames, the less they urged on that part of Finch. Instead, they called up flashes of the last few weeks: the joyful ride on a young human's motorized wheeled contraption, the wind in his face. Hours spent reading books in Winnie's library. Freshly squeezed lemonade with honey. Summoning plants in Winnie's garden to bring on a second harvest. Learning to tolerate Malvous and his grumbling and needling. Being vulnerable with a foot that wouldn't heal for the longest time. Choosing (even though goaded into doing so) to assist an injured child, a failing grocer, and an ocean.

He'd bungled quite a lot of those things, it seemed. He wasn't any more inspired as a creator than as an un-creator. At least destroying was easy. It was so simple to tear things down that took time to create. Building was much harder, and perhaps he didn't have that in him, either.

Might as well throw myself into the flames and let them do whatever they do to our kind. At least then I'd be useful at something. I could be part of the entropy.

Something bit his leg.

MARTIN AND FELICITOUS had been quite busy since the Butter Ball Assault began. Once the warfare moved from (reasonably) harmless dairy products to taking out the Unseelie on the porch, they did their best to keep in the background and not get caught up in the fracas. Then the crowd had started hurling moonshine Molotov cocktails, and Felicitous made a decision.

"We can't let them singe," said the brownie, pointing to the porch, where the Unseelie rabble-rousers had fallen. "If the house truly is ablaze, we must save them first."

"We gotta save *Miz Winnie* first!" Martin shouted. "She's inside!"

"Where we do not have access at this time," said Felicitous. "This is known as Tree-Aging, if I understand the human phrase. You must decide what you *can* do before attempting to move to a more difficult aspect."

"That's triaging," said Martin. "And I'm going to go inside—you can't stop me!"

Felicitous shook his head. "You can do many things in your wonderful, wheeled contraption, but I cannot suggest that being an effective fireman is one of them," he said, and passed easily through the ward. Martin tried to follow but was blocked. *You have so many things to do at home. Where is dad? What about your homework?* flooded his brain, and he rolled away from the porch. Immediately his brain felt less addled.

Meanwhile, Felicitous had lifted Laurel under one arm, Hardy beneath the other, and clambered down the steps. He gave the seething crowd his most severe, Bro-est look of all, daring them to interfere. This seemed to work until Martin sensed—

A flash. A flutter. Just in the corner of his vision.

Siggy appeared out of nowhere, alone. Walked out of thin air—well, thin air shaped like an inverted 'U,' which promptly vanished behind her. Martin goggled. So much for sciencing; magic truly did exist.

"Siggy!" he cried.

"Martin!" she shouted.

They met one another in an embrace neither had ever realized how much they needed.

Behind them, cocktails and butter continued to fly.

* * *

Astonished, Finch turned to find a furious Winnie staring up at him from the floor. She coughed. Neal lay in a heap by her side. "Stop"—cough—"fire-dreaming and *do* something!" she cried.

"You bit me!"

"We're *dying*."

Before he could respond, two pairs of hands simultaneously shoved Finch aside. One pair latched onto Winnie's outstretched arms, while the other dragged Neal's slack form. Whirling, Finch was astonished to find Malvous and a tall human with a cloud of downy, dark hair held down with a bandana. She reminded him of Siggy.

"Eve!" Winnie gasped, eyes welling.

"Eve?" Finch wondered.

"Eve." Eve Sommersday coughed into her fist, bent over by Winnie's weight.

"Eve!" Winnie cried again.

The woman shook her head, barely comprehending what she'd just walked into. "There was this brownie door and—" Eve whipped around in one direction, then the other. Finch followed her frantic movements and watched as she spotted Siggy on the other side of a window, standing outside with her friend Martin. She gave a quick nod, then refocused.

Meanwhile, Malvous had set Neal aside and bounded into the kitchen, returning with several soaked towels. The trio of helpers wrapped the cloths around Winnie and Neal's heads, and Eve covered her mouth with the final one. "Where did the door go?" Malvous scanned the room. "That's our way out!"

"The door's on fire." Finch pointed at the front of the house.

Malvous groaned and rolled his eyes. "I mean the one we created! It's gone!" He whirled on Finch, who had never seen the brownie so angry. Actually, he'd never seen him angry at all, so perhaps he was misreading the narrowed eyes and gritted jaw. But probably not. Eve, after all, was giving him the same look.

Oh, right, thought Finch. *I was about to actually* do *something useful*. "I'm on it!" he shouted. "Watch this!"

"Better hurry," Malvous rasped. "We're all going to be crispier than a peach cobbler if you don't get us out of here right now."

"That way!" Finch ran down the hallway and hefted the living room doors open. The Muses were gone, and the fire hadn't yet reached this room. The French doors hung slightly ajar, leading to the green garden. "This way!"

Eve and Winnie staggered toward the living room and Finch waved them through. Malvous appeared next, with Neal hefted over one shoulder. He was nearly at the back doors when he turned to see Finch still standing in the house. "Come on!"

Finch heard him but didn't respond. The flames were still calling to him. He flapped his hands at Malvous, tuning him out. "I can't. Not yet. I've unfinished business—"

Malvous strode back over and cracked him across the face with the flat of his free hand. "Snap out of it!" growled the brownie. "Here's my final piece of advice. Create. Don't create. Doesn't matter. You're here to *transform*. And not just yourself. This whole town needs transformation. So you can let it all burn down, or you can take charge and *make* something out of this!" He turned and ran to the doors, shouting, "One more thing! I quit! Again!"

Then he was gone, through the living room, and out those sliding glass doors, seconds before the ceiling crashed down and blocked the final egress from the house.

Finch was alone, surrounded by flames.

Transform.

The word echoed like a penny dropped down a well. Take something, turn it into something else. Something better. He'd been doing some transforming of his own these past weeks. Investigate, discover, understand, transform. Those were things he could do here, too.

"Thank you, Malvous!" he shouted to the conflagration. "Thank you, Winnifred! Thank you, Siggy! I get it now! At least, I think I do!"

Finch's hands began to glow. A tingling spark flickered in his chest. The beads of sweat on the back of his hands evaporated. His fingers vibrated. He felt like a light switch that had just been turned on. He ran back into the hallway and faced Neal's conflagration-filled office.

Striding inside, Finch stretched his arms out into a cupping, hugging motion. A wild energy swirled in his body, building and building. He pulled the flames from the draperies, the floors, the walls onto himself. As he drew the fire inward, it disappeared from the room, the colorful flames ebbing lower and disappearing, leaving behind charred curtains, singed walls, pieces of partially incinerated paper. He pulled and pulled and pulled, drinking not the flames themselves but their pure energy. It felt familiar, like the moment the Muses had nearly overwhelmed him with their ideas, their music, their inspiration. But this time, Finch was the one drawing down. Taking in. Absorbing.

Transforming.

Now he felt like he'd just *eaten* a Muse. Or nine. His hair stood up like luminous red sparklers. The gray was gone. He was full of fire and purpose. Fire that could destroy, but fire that could also create.

Finch caught a glimpse out the office windows of the garden as Winnie and Eve hugged tightly. Malvous stood to one side, supporting Neal. From inside the office, Finch twirled his fingers at the yew hedge, and a small hole opened up, enough for Siggy to squirm through. The girl raced over and attached herself to the women like a second skin. Brownie and Seelie watched the three humans with exhausted and smudged looks on their faces, but both were smiling with delight.

Yeah, I got this, thought Finch, returning to the remaining flames. *I can do this. I just needed a kick in the behind. And a knock on the head. And a couple smacks in the face. And a Siggy and a Martin to show me the way.*

Finch made a choice.

And began to create.

Chapter 40

Leave of His Senses

FINCH BENT OVER a stack of papers, twisting his mouth. As an immortal creature he had all the time in the world, but somehow getting Seaview Haven back up and functioning again was taking *forever*.

"Can't we just"—he leaned forward over his mahogany desk—"clear the decks in one fell swoop? Start over? I've got just the spell—"

"Don't even think about it." Neal glanced up from his knitting. Once Winnie had taught him how to use the needles during his extended convalescence, he'd started making a scarf and never stopped. After a month of needle clacking, it was 71.3 feet in length and could wrap around the necks of dragons. Multiple dragons. "This is a slow, methodical process. You're *my* intern for the time being, Finch, so you'll learn how to do it *my* way."

The former UDIP intern investigator Finch, now of pending designation but technically assisting the Mayor of Seaview Haven, let out a frustrated breath. This was his fourth sigh of the morning.

At least the new mayor's office was pleasant. Oval-shaped, painted a soothing, light blue and decorated in curved bookshelves and a twenty-five-foot glass-domed roof that let sunlight onto the word tree sapling planted at its center. Creating the office had been one of Finch's first decisions, as he learned to harness the fire he'd absorbed. Winnie said that where she came from, the oval was a shape of power. So he'd made the kitchen and the resting room that shape, too. That was as far as he'd gotten because the needs of the T-Town constantly took precedence.

The resting room was for Neal. The official Seelie SMD had recovered nearly all of his capabilities since the Day of Mayhem a little over a month ago, but he wasn't very agile. He'd taken to co-opting Finch's old cane and moved with a halting step.

"There's just so much *paperwork*," Finch sighed.

"Well, all the records were burned in the fire," said Neal, fixing a stitch. "You just have to sort through every one of the newly submitted histories of town residents to determine who gets to stay, and who'll be leaving us. It's only a couple hundred."

"Try two thousand!" Finch reached for a tube of ointment. "Besides, paperwork is giving me hives."

"Spend less time moaning about the paperwork and arrange more interviews with Havenites." Neal lifted his chin. "You'll have to meet every single one of them."

Finch growled and squinted at the folders. When the Day of Mayhem faded, much had changed. Neal was in no shape to run a T-Town, but neither did it warrant being canceled and torn down anymore. Finch had a long conversation with the recovering Seelie and made a heartfelt plea to remain in town to fix whatever needed fixing or create whatever needed creating. There was no need to rush back home now that he'd been tossed out of the UDIP internship program, and he was left with a lot of fire inside that needed redirecting.

With SCN's tentative approval, Neal gave him a provisional position. *We can revisit this matter once I am more fully myself.*

There was much cleanup around town to accomplish, and Finch had been busy for nearly twenty hours each day. With the Muse-installed barrier gone, he'd repaired the road leading to and from town. That led to missing Havenites returning, each with a complaint or twenty to file. Neal guided the criminal complaints to the Sheriff, Eve, while Finch worked with more domestic issues. No matter how many hours he put in, though, the new Seelie's to-do list was now nearly as long as Neal's scarf.

Finch had also fixed his initial 'helpful' spell errors. Yulong's dinosaur scar was now non-sentient. The grocery store went back to receiving supplies (though there was an ongoing issue with spices). Finch blurped with Terri the Kraken and together they ensured the ocean was now rich with edible, non-poisonous fish species. Fine-tuning a T-Town, he was discovering, was a continuing education.

All of this fixing and transforming and creation had changed Finch. These days his mane was lustrous, bold, and bright red, reflecting his inspiration. He planned to keep it that way. As much as it grated on his soul to take orders, he promised himself to listen to Neal's guidance. But there were some areas that confused him—like how to sort the returning Havenites' paperwork.

"Why is there a category called 'Leave to Remain'?" Finch asked. "You can't both leave and remain at the same time. Then you have 'Leave to Leave' on the other stack and that's just repetitive."

Neal shrugged. "It's a human affectation. I saw the phrasing in an office in Birmingham once. If you hate it, create something better."

"My brain hurts from all this creation." Finch gave a sigh, his fifth of the morning.

Ice pellets began falling on the domed glass ceiling. "Uh, Finch, any chance you forgot to calibrate the weather for today?"

"Maybe?" Finch squinted.

"It was bright and sunny a minute ago, and now we're getting hail. Hail will get in the way of the rest of the day's plans."

Slumping, Finch clasped his hands together and made a small gesture with his fingers. The rat-a-tat ended. "I had no idea there were so many fiddly bits in this whole town maintenance thing. How am I supposed to even know what month it is? I never used a calendar with squares before." He despaired that he'd ever get a handle on everything. Most things in a T-Town didn't come with handles. "Can't you deal with some of the fiddliness?"

"I could," said Neal, his needles clicking back and forth, "but I am still weak and unuseful. Besides, I was of the impression you wanted to know how the whole SMD situation worked."

"Of course, it's just… a lot." Finch wasn't sure why it mattered; he'd only be an assistant here until Neal got his act together and started running the place again. But he didn't want to say that.

"Besides," Neal continued, "you'll want the weather to be on its best behavior for our guests."

Finch leaped to his feet. His scalp tingled. "Wait. That's today?"

The oval office door (also oval-shaped) flew open, revealing Felicitous. The brownie wore a pair of squared spectacles and had taken to donning vests and utili-kilts. "Your Eminent Mayorship—Ms Winnie, Sheriff Eve and Siggy are outside. You must depart now if you are to greet the portal arrivals on time."

"Excellent," said Neal. "I'm looking forward to seeing ɮ— again. It has been quite a while."

Panic jolted Finch from his chair. He raced around the office in a spiral. "Saddle up my bicycle! Inflate the tires! Where's my hat?" Reaching the tree at the office's center, he rested his hands on the bark. "Where's the lemonade? How much shortbread do we have?"

"Done, done, on the coatrack by the front door, out by the bandstand, two hundred pans' worth." Felicitous was eternally cool under pressure.

The Mayor caught Finch by the arms and held him still. "You'll do fine. Well, you'll do adequately. Take a breath and compose yourself. We'll see you at the Common."

"Where are you going?"

"There is a beautiful writer waiting for me out front," said Neal. "And I will not keep her waiting. Not again."

After Neal left, Finch collapsed into his seat. He'd pushed today out of his mind for so long because today was when he learned what the next part of his immortal life would look like. Exile? Firing from SCN? Or... maybe even the chance to continue interning in Seaview Haven? All options were on the table. His chest contracted.

Just then, a puff of purple smoke appeared in one of the oval room's curves. There were no corners, after all. The smoke smelled like toasted marshmallows and disappeared as it rose to the glass-domed ceiling.

Agatha, Witch of Backyard Sheds and Third Tuesdays, materialized in the room.

"Hello, Finch," she said.

He clutched the armrests of his chair, back sweating. "Afternoon," he gargled. "You lost?"

"Well," said the witch who had formerly been one of his closest friends. "I wanted to inform you that your gift has arrived."

Finch stared at the floor. A few days after he'd absorbed the fire, he'd taken a good, hard look at what he wanted to do with himself. He was alone for the first time in ages; Winnie and Neal were recovering, Malvous had left town to be with Foxtacular, Siggy and Martin were racing off to the water tower together. His thoughts had turned to

Winnie's garden, then to Agatha's destroyed patch. As wrecked as their friendship.

It didn't have to stay that way. Finch might not be able to fix things between them, but he could perhaps make them a shade better.

"Glad it arrived safely," he said. "How does your garden grow?"

Agatha waited for him to meet her gaze. "At least I now know it did come from you. What's a witch to think when she goes to bed one night with a scraped-over mess of a backyard and wakes up with a blooming, bursting garden with way too many plums?"

Finch smiled faintly. "I do plums pretty well, it seems." He'd looked at Winnie's garden one night, admiring the hard work he'd put into it, along with the correctly-ordered spells, and had a bright idea. Could one *copy* a whole garden and *paste* it somewhere else?

Turned out, the answer was *yes*. It took him most of the day and night to work out the combination of spells, but eventually, Finch had pulled it off.

"Not enough rue, though," she said. "I'll have to fix that."

"Mistakes were made. In the past. And they're ongoing." He sighed. "I am sorry, Agatha."

She raised an eyebrow. "So it's true, then. You must be Seelie. Because Unseelie never apologize."

Finch squirmed. "Still getting used to that. But… you knew it all along."

"I had suspicions." She gazed around the room. "Now it sounds like you're on the brink of a really coming up in the world."

Finch shook his head. He really didn't know. All his work repairing, tweaking, and adjusting Seaview Haven over the past weeks might not be enough. The executives at SCN might decide he was a complete failure even in his newly-accepted Seelieness. They could decide to file charges of tomfoolery, shenanigans, and overall failure to declare himself as not fully Unseelie with the Seelie Court. So much was in their hands.

They'd never let him *run* this place, that much he was sure of. Neal had announced he'd like to hold a more emeritus position in the town; his time under the godspell had been hard on his body and soul, but nothing said that Finch should be the one next in line.

"Oh, they won't want me running a whole T-Town," he said. "I don't know anything."

At last, Agatha smiled. "That is a good place to start, though. It means you know you need help. Need to ask questions. Running a TROPE Town properly can't possibly be a single-fae operation."

Finch stared at her. She could have written a thank you note, sending it by passenger pigeon. Or by T-Town mail. Or by spell. She could have completely ignored his apology gift. But Agatha had come in person, to see him once more. "Neal did a good job for a while," he said. "But me—I'll take help from wherever it comes." He stood. "Especially if it comes from the Witch of Backyard Sheds and Third Tuesdays."

Agatha's smile was even more genuine now. "I'll think about it."

"Truly?"

"Of course. But first, I want to have a long catch-up binge on the last several weeks of *La Ciudad Grande* episodes. Have you heard about Marsha and Ted? I think they're making a huge mistake!"

Finch strode over to her and kissed the back of her hand. "Not a word. I've been, you know, a little preoccupied. How about we meet up next week?"

"What, on a third Tuesday?"

Finch grinned. "Well, it is the best day of the month."

Chapter 41

Fair to Middling

SEAVIEW HAVEN'S VILLAGE common wasn't very large, but it sufficed. Sufficed as an assembly point when things were falling apart. Sufficed for the Counting. Sufficed for holding a Market. If the mayor's house had been the brains of the town, the Common was its heart.

Today, that heart was being taken over by a fair. Jaunty red-and-white striped tents sprouted from the ground, linked to trees and each other with bunting and flapping flags. Residents swarmed the midway, ducking in and out of the tents, testing their various offerings—live music, games of chance, homemade treats made with ingredients most locals hadn't tasted in two years, craft items, and handmade wares for sale. Camera-laden drone bees had been unleashed to capture Bee Roll, which could be used in movies. The trees were again sprouting with cameradryads, emerging from a long hibernation, and re-learning their focuses and apertures.

Two amateur fortune tellers, who in a gaffe of coordination had been set up side by side, were giving each other the evil eye.

"Someone should have seen that coming." Winnie nudged Neal as she polished off her second ice-cream cone. She gently hooked her arm through his, sighing at the sheer pleasure of having him all to herself.

Neal took a beat, then laughed. She loved that he didn't always get her jokes instantly. The blank look on his lovely, if careworn, face made *her* crack up.

"Perhaps they are… *fair* weather friends," he noted.

Winnie blinked.

"Who had the bad *fortune* to be paired together?"

"Oh, my." She pulled him closer. His punnage was turning her on. "That was awful. And I loved it."

Grinning, Neal took in the grassy expanse before them. "This looks marvelous. The fact that this fair has come off without more issues is entirely due to the fact that Finch had virtually nothing to do with it. We'd have ended up with a triangle-shaped Ferris wheel and hot dog flavored cotton candy and toffee-covered rocks."

"Hot dog cotton candy sounds kind of interesting." Winnie coughed, partly from amusement and partly due to the ongoing tickle in her throat. Inhaling smoke had done some damage, and she planned to see a specialist on her next trip across the Veil to see her children. This time, she might convince Neal to come with her. "He's trying, so give him some credit."

Neal made a seesawing motion with his hand. "He's overwhelmed, but it's good training for making movies later on."

"Gardening to an SMD is kind of a huge leap. You might blow his circuits."

"Oh, that won't happen for *ages*, assuming it happens at all. And he's not in charge yet. But I've never seen a fae who wanted something this much. They *assigned* me to this place. I learned to love it. But it's like he feels he was reborn here."

"He was." She pinched Neal's sleeve. "Promise me again: if they release you, you're not leaving, right?"

Neal stopped walking and hooked his cane over one arm. He held Winnie's cheeks in his hands. "I'm not going anywhere unless you are. I'm happy for all the time we get as your in-house editor."

Winnie closed her eyes as he kissed her forehead. She knew this. She had to stop asking. But it was hard to fathom, really, that at some point Neal would cease being Seaview Haven's Mayor. Not that she'd stop writing, no matter who was in charge. Eutie had told the truth: the Muses might not be physically present, but they spoke to her daily now.

"I might even turn on that crystal computer SCN sent down," he whispered. "Can't be afraid of all keyboards for the rest of eternity."

"But no more typewriters." Winnie nuzzled his neck. "Understood."

Across the midway, Siggy waved, then raced over to Winnie with a small plush lion in hand. "I got the ring over the milk bottle!" She high-fived Winnie, then Neal.

Eve came up behind her, finishing a curl of sugar-coated fried dough. "Next time I need to corral some renegade glass, I know who to call."

Winnie gave her a side hug, not wanting to let go. Since her return, the women had stayed up many nights into the wee hours, drinking on Winnie's porch or a swing in Eve's backyard, catching up in great detail. Winnie wanted to hear all of Eve's adventures over, and over. Eventually, Winnie told Eve exactly how she'd gotten the Muses to leave. Eve held her hand toward the end.

I'd forgotten how jealous I was. You wrote a good story, and you hit it out of the park on your first try at bat, Winnie had admitted. She wondered if there would be a time when they didn't feel a need to mutually soothe one another on this.

Eve had smiled, her expression somewhere between abashed and amused. *That wasn't true, actually. I wrote a lot. I just never showed it to anybody before you.*

If you write something new and don't show it to me, I will shake you until your teeth rattle, Winnie had said.

Eve had linked their pinkies and made her promise to be honest. *But not mean.*

I'm better at that now, Winnie had admitted.

Mostly, though, they talked about Siggy. Eve had missed many months of her daughter's life and wanted to know every tiny thing. Being away from Siggy had been agonizing. Wrenching.

Much harder than losing Hal, Eve had admitted.

Siggy's father had never been a fan of TROPE Town living. He'd been on the verge of leaving when he'd fallen for Eve and stayed for her. But he'd always been distracted, Eve told Winnie. Once Siggy was born, he took to wandering for hours, sometimes staying out overnight. When the pair of them had driven away on that fateful afternoon, he'd abandoned Eve the moment she was settled with the refugee campers.

Not a word since, she'd told Winnie one night, well into their second bottle of Moscato. *I'm pretty sure he had a family back on the other side of the Veil. I think he went back to 'em. We were always a stopgap. I'm okay now, I guess. But it's harder on Sig.*

Indeed, for several weeks Siggy had been much quieter and sadder than Winnie had ever seen her. But one evening Winnie passed by the Sommersday house and spotted Siggy and Martin on the porch, talking. Winnie sat down with Eve in the backyard for a glass of wine and to watch fireflies, and on the way out Siggy was waiting on the front steps. The girl had been practically luminescent.

He's a good kisser, Siggy had giggled at Winnie, then run into the house.

And so a new adventure begins, Winnie had thought.

Now flanked by her friend on one side and her love on

the other, Winnie squeezed both of their hands. No one had to say a word; they were all thinking the same thing.

Thank everything that I have you.

As in most TROPE Towns, the Common was situated smack in the geographical center of the village, with a bandstand smack in the middle of the green space.

Seelie constructors liked things to be as neat and orderly as possible.

Finch stared at the bandstand, considering moving it a few feet to the left. Just a bit off true. But not today. He was fretting about the imminent arrival of the Seelie Court Network programming executive who would decide his fate. All possibilities were on the table.

Why did I write that report? Did I have to be so... inventive?

But he had been. Finch's personally penned report had spun a harrowing tale of how the Muses had marauded through the T-Town streets, stealing every scrap of food and clothing—and even toys—from the locals, who were left huddled in hovels and bewildered in backyards, unable to accomplish the complex tasks involved with mystery re-enactment for the benefit of the cameradryads. It was full of detail and drama, some of which approximated the truth. He'd glossed over the godspelling with Neal's permission, merely noting that it had sent the SMD into a writing tailspin following a knock on the head. Instead, Finch underscored the malcontented mob that pelted the mayor's home with precious butter reserves, then set the place ablaze in their desperation to be heard. During all that, Finch (with some help from Felicitous) had whisked the agitating Unseelie dismantlers Laurel and Hardy to safety and convinced the Muses to take refuge by returning to their regularly scheduled desks at SCN.

Nice piece of fiction for an Unseelie-Seelie, Neal had noted. *How'd you do it?*

Finch didn't know. *Mixed truth and wishing?*

Neal had nodded. *Now, that's some insight I could have used two years ago.*

Finch had looked away. *Anyway, the SCN execs will never know the difference.*

Laurel and Hardy might, Neal had noted. *So might the Muses.*

Finch wasn't worried. *I'll take my chances. My guess is the Muses have already forgotten about this place. As for Laurel and Hardy—well, I hear they've been relocated. They'll never be reliable witnesses.*

Felicitous had been the one to report that bit of welcome news a few days ago. Apparently the Unseelie were being punished for inciting the human riot by being demoted in the rankings and sent to assist in some of the most tedious deconstruction Finch had ever heard of, starting with the Mongolian Sandworm Sandcastle Expo. Each meticulously created sand sculpture had to be demolished grain by grain, with each grain labeled for future reassembly. The job would keep them busy for a century or so.

Finch's report should have been the end of it. After all, at SCN the motto was: *Observe humans. Enjoy humans. Avoid humans.* Executives rarely visited T-Towns personally. But Finch's letter had been so compelling and convincing that it had two unintended consequences: one, it prompted an investigation into the role gods and goddesses had in SCN affairs—an investigation whose findings were now sealed in a vault in the deepest sub-sub-sub-basement of HQ, after several high-level deities threatened dire retribution if their roles were questioned further; two, it convinced the EVVVVVPCTTAP known as ɮ— that she ought to visit a T-Town, rather than observing it from the lofty heights of a dynamic map on a table in a conference room. She'd sent a message: Expect her on the thirteenth at noon precisely on the bandstand in the Common. Sharp.

That had sent Finch into a whole other kind of panic. The room had spun around him. He'd summoned Felicitous for a cool compress and took a long nap in the oval resting room. Then he'd sprung up three hours later with a solution to everything.

A fair.

After all, bunting hides a multitude of sins.

FINCH ALLOWED WINNIE and the other villagers to take the lead on coordinating the fair but asked local vendors to prepare a tasting menu of wares for their incoming guests. He'd ordered the musicians to vacate the bandstand and set up to one side, playing an upbeat tune as the fae executives arrived. He'd told all the vendors to shut their tent flaps at 11:55am so that the entire village could be available to greet their lofty guests.

He was sure he'd forgotten something.

At 11:57am, Finch stood next to Neal in the bandstand, with VIP others—Winnie, Siggy, Eve, Felicitous—standing behind a velvet rope on the ground. Most, if not all, of the T-Town residents had gathered, and stood around sipping drinks, eating fried items, and clutching soft toys.

Finch started to hyperventilate.

Neal set a hand on his shoulder. "Breathe."

"I am"—he puffed—"breathing."

"That's a little too much breathing," said the Mayor. "Question: when do you plan to adjust the weather?"

Finch's mind blanked. "Butterballs!" Closing his eyes, he raised one hand and twiddled his pinkie, then placed his palm to the ground. The temperature plummeted from ninety-one to eighty-six degrees in five seconds.

Down on the ground, the overeager band saw the gesture as their cue and launched into the raucous opening of AC/DC's 'Back in Black.'

The crowd craned toward the bandstand with interest.

"No, no, no!" Finch flailed his hands at the band, who took that to mean that they needed to turn up the volume and obliged. Turning pink, Finch drew a hand across his throat to get them to stop, but they were too lost in the beat. The sky darkened. The temperature continued to plummet. Citizens lifted their collars and curled against one another as a chill wind began to blow.

On the bandstand, the portal crackled.

Then the sky crackled.

Finch made a noise he'd never uttered before. It was not a crackle.

Neal grabbed Finch's flailing hands and clapped them together. The temperature halted at fifty-four degrees. Finch came to attention.

"Calm down," Neal shouted over the growing wind and the band, which insisted on crashing through the song as if they were the orchestra on the *Titanic*. Behind them, bunting loosed from the tents and many Havenites hurried away. "I can't fix this. I'm not strong enough yet. But you can! Turn off that storm!"

A pack of tarot cards fluttered in the wind, while boxes of freshly picked blueberries danced in the air. A handmade birdhouse crashed to the ground. More locals jogged away to find shelter. Siggy, Eve and Winnie huddled together. The portal continued to crackle.

Finch couldn't catch his breath. His hands wouldn't move.

A cold deluge of rain fell, instantly soaking anyone not under the bandstand. The band—finally—abandoned the song and escaped with their instruments. Everyone stared out over the ruins of the fair as tents ripped from their moorings, tables overturned and a herd of prize cows stampeded down the fairway, booting a crystal ball ahead of them. One of the amateur mediums ran after the cows.

That's what I call bovine intervention, Finch thought wildly.

The bandstand crackled once more, and the portal opened.

A chorus of harps and strings erupted from the portal, crescendoing as ꜩ— emerged, flanked by her Left and Right Side Assistants. The portal clapped shut, cutting off the fanfare. All four newcomers were dressed exquisitely in white—ꜩ— in trousers, the others in skirts—and wore matching gloves covered in intricate, tiny, sculpted grass patterns. ꜩ—'s coiffed hair held fast in the breeze, though. ꜩ— quickly assessed the situation, and without a word raised one eyebrow at the rainstorm, then twisted her left wrist. An invisible wall sprouted to enclose the bandstand, creating a quivering, iridescent bubble of protection around everyone inside.

The silence was instant, and terrifying. Finch forced a grin. "Greetings, Superior One." He bowed deeply. "Seaview Haven"—he winced as a giant stuffed teddy bear tied to a line of bunting smashed up against the bubble and lay pasted there, like a bug on a windshield—"welcomes you?"

Behind him, Neal, Winnie, and Siggy began murmuring to one another. Eve made no sound, transfixed by the newcomers. But Finch couldn't concentrate on the mortals and the Seelie. The unreadable look on the EVVVVVPCTTAP's face was his only focus. It was the one thing he had no idea how to change. "Everyone." He gestured around him. "Please allow me to introduce the

Executive-Vice-Vice-Vice-Vice-Vice President in Care of TROPE Town Allocation and Programming, ɮ—."

ɮ— observed the ongoing storm from inside the bandstand, then nodded at her assistants one by one. Each scribbled notes in the air with unseen styluses.

The storm, the storm, I have to fix the storm, Finch thought. *I have to fix something.* But he felt only coldness where his creation fire usually lived. He knew about breathing. He knew he had to calm down and collect himself. But nothing was coming. He was blocked.

Closing his eyes, Finch thought about his last encounter with ɮ—. He'd leaped on that T-Town map and pointed out Seaview Haven, declaring it was his. He'd been bold. Fearless. Partially tethered to a bag full of brownie. (He missed Malvous in this moment, not for the first time, but the Bro had gone on a long vacation to Atlantis with his boyfriend and had no plans to return to Seaview Haven once they were finished.) But that table-dancing Finch had felt he had nothing to lose. This was different.

He could lose something he very much wanted. Not just something he *pretended* to want.

Opening his eyes, he tried a smile. "We'd hoped for better weather today, your Worship, but there's been a slight hitch. I'm afraid that I—"

Neal stepped forward. "Pardon me, but I'm the one who erred. It's been so long since I had my hands on the weather that I overrode Mr Finch and… I seem to have gotten a bit carried away. But Mr Finch"—he gave Finch a severe look—"you were about to re-adjust the weather, weren't you?"

Still, ɮ— said nothing.

Finch swallowed. His brain calmed a few degrees. He could almost think again. He just needed a few more seconds.

"Wow, you're *gorgeous*," Siggy piped up from the back

of the bandstand. Neal shoved Finch to the side as the young woman blinked up at the newcomer and gave a small curtsey. "How do you apply your makeup like that, ma'am?"

ɮ— raised an eyebrow. And part of her mouth. Not quite a smile, but at least in the neighborhood. She rested a finger beneath Siggy's chin and turned her face this way and that. Then she leaned in and whispered into Siggy's ear.

While they were occupied, Neal closed his grip on Finch's arm and hissed, "You're out of time! Start doing the hand-wavy thing!"

"But Siggy—"

"Shhh," he continued. "Ignore her. Just do it."

Closing his eyes once more, Finch pinched his fingers together. Warmth ignited in his gut. The wind died away. Clouds un-clouded. The rain ceased. And in a matter of seconds, both the sun emerged and the temperature climbed. He blinked his eyes open again and swore he heard the twitter of a distant bird.

Neal ruffled Finch's rocket-red hair, which now featured a lone gray streak.

"Ta-dah!" Finch started to declare, then noticed the wreck of the fair beyond their bandstand bubble. "Oh dear. Again."

Winnie sidled up to him. "It's not so bad. Know how many stories of mine I got right on the first draft?"

Finch didn't understand. "All of them?"

Winnie laughed and coughed. "None at all. Know what you do when your first draft crashes and burns?"

"You give up?" Finch was trying to follow along.

"No!" she cried. "You start over again. Better. Then you do it again, until it's *right*. And again, and again and again. Until—" She glanced at Neal, then Eve. "Until you convince the Muses that it's a Great Story after all."

Finch tilted his head. The human might be on to something.

ꜩ— had finished speaking with Siggy. The teenager held her hands over her mouth, as if she'd been handed a tremendous secret and didn't want to let it out. ꜩ— made a reverse twirling motion with her wrist, and the invisible wall around the bandstand vanished. A warm breeze swept into the small, no-longer-enclosed space. The stuffed teddy bear slid to the ground with a soft thump.

Finally, the Seelie executive spoke. "Mr Finch," she declared. "I am officially bringing you on board as Seaview Haven's Showrunner-in-Training, for a probationary period of either four seasons or two completed made-for-streaming movies, whichever comes first. The Mayorship and Director aspects of this position will be considered after you surmount this first hurdle. My assistants have prepared the paperwork."

Finch's gut rumbled, the fire within sparking. His chest swelled and he couldn't stop grinning. "You like me? You really like me?" He bounced on the balls of his feet. "I knew if you gave me a chance I could just—"

ꜩ— laughed, the sound like spring birdsong. Rosebuds sprouted from the ceiling and bloomed. "Dial it back, show-off. You're getting ahead of yourself. Two minutes ago, I was prepared to turn around and return to my office, where I won't get wet or assailed by flying blueberries. Obviously, Seaview Haven is not supposed to behave like this. And whatever celebration you had planned has been turned upside down. If that is your idea of a welcoming party to show off your prowess as a creator, Mr Finch, let me know right now and I will re-do the paperwork."

Finch shook his head so fast his brain rattled. "No. You're right. I screwed up. You saw it. But there's so much to *think about*. There are a million little corners to reality!"

"Well put."

"And besides—" He heard what she said. "You agree?"

"I do. And there is but one reason I've re-reversed my thinking on having you as Showrunner of this town." She clasped her hands behind her back. "You have a team, Mr Finch. In a matter of seconds, the Mayor tried to convince me the storm was his doing; a young girl who will clearly never need to wear makeup for one day in her life asked me for tips; and our esteemed author-in-residence has given you sound advice on craft. Whatever shortcomings you may have, Mr Finch—well, not *may* have but do have—you have a valuable set of experts by your side to ensure you learn the ropes. Your retaining of the position of Showrunner-in-Training rests on your ability to maintain the team. After all, we don't want you to be a Sh-IT forever."

Finch blinked.

Behind him, Siggy giggled.

Eve and Winnie collapsed against each other.

"Hm." ɮ— gestured at her assistants. "Perhaps we should re-think that nomenclature." She cleared her throat. "In any case, you may be our *Creator*-in-Training until you get the hang of things." She eyed the bandstand. "May I assume that all of you are part of this project, then?"

One Seelie and three human heads nodded.

"Good. Mr Finch is a bit of a mixed-up bumbler, but he's a good gardener." ɮ— nodded at her assistants, who conjured visible pages in the air. "Your signature, Mr Finch."

With a shaking hand, Finch made his mark on the pages, which immediately disappeared.

"Excellent. That is part one. For the second part, this whole identity crisis of yours must be resolved in a proper Seelie Court session, Mr Finch, so you will join us in one week to submit your evidence of Seeliehood. After that, we will see what we can conjure up." ɮ— nodded severely at Siggy. "You, young woman, should visit us one of these days. I believe we may have some interesting outlets for your particular expertise."

Eve slipped an arm around her daughter. "Not any time soon. I just got her back."

"So you did," said ɮ—. "There is no hurry. Now, if that is all—"

Finch held up a slightly dampened tote bag and offered it to the executive. "I'd hoped to have a whole feast for you," he said. "But this will have to do. Felicitous makes an excellent shortbread."

For the first time, ɮ— smiled with her eyes and her mouth. "*That* is how you seal a deal, Mr Finch."

WITH THE PORTAL sizzled and vanished, and ɮ— and her assistants headed back to SCN, the happy quartet descended the bandstand steps into the warm sun and onto the soggy grass. Martin emerged from one of the few still-upright tents and gave Siggy a wave.

Siggy couldn't think of a moment when she'd been happier. Well, except maybe the other night, when she and Martin had kissed for the first time. "What'll you do first?" she asked Finch. "Can we get a horse stable? What about a zip line? How about—"

"Now, hold on a minute, missy," Eve told her.

"I'd like a horse," Winnie admitted.

"Er—" said Finch.

"Hey, who's that?" Siggy pointed in the distance. Two locals were bounding across the muddy fairway, crying, "Mayor! Mayor!"

Together, Neal and Finch stepped forward. "Yes?" they chorused.

Neal gestured at Finch and Eve. “Speak to all of us.”

The huffing and puffing humans were Mrs Grossinger and her son. Both had on aprons. She bent over to catch her breath, and he gasped, “The store! It’s been *robbed*!”

“The money’s gone?” Eve hustled over.

Mrs Grossinger righted herself and shook her head. “No! The spices finally came in—oregano, cardamom, marjoram, cinnamon—and someone ran off with the sack! All gone! Just as we were starting to get back to normal!”

Eve and Winnie leaned forward, and Siggy noticed they had the same spark in their eye. “Fascinating,” said Winnie. “This happened during the fair?”

Grossinger’s son shook his head. “The storm! Something about the storm. I don’t know. We let people wait out the storm in the store and when we checked, the spices had vanished!”

“So there are a lot of people to speak with,” Winnie said consideringly. She turned to Eve. “Sounds like something the Sheriff ought to get in on.”

“Naturally,” said Eve.

Finch held out his hands. “Oh, I can conjure up some new spices—”

“Uh-uh,” Neal warned.

Winnie wrapped a hand around the Maybe-Seelie’s shoulders. “Don’t you dare. This, my dear Finch, is what we call the start of a story. Something unexplained has happened. These things occur all the time when Seaview Haven is running properly. And as the new Sh-IT—”

“Creator-in-Training!” Finch corrected her.

Winnie chuckled. “Fine, but the other way’s more fun. Anyway, it’s time we walk you through an investigation. There’s an excellent chance you’ll end up making a movie about this.”

“Soon, in fact,” added Neal.

Winnie guided Finch to the bicycles. "So much to learn, CIT Finch. Evidence. Fingerprints. Motive. Means. Opportunity." She let out a long, happy breath. "Boy, I've missed this!"

Finch sent a pleading glance over his shoulder at Neal.

"Don't look at me," said the almost-ex-mayor. "I'm just a consultant. This is all yours now, Finch. The whole wide world of Seaview Haven is yours."

Finch clenched his teeth. "But how does it *work*?"

"What, the whole wide world?" Winnie raised an eyebrow.

"Yes!" cried the CIT, or Sh-IT, depending on how you looked at him.

Siggy mounted her bicycle as if it were a mighty steed and briefly touched her chest, right where her heart was thudding. "Nobody knows," she said, and pressed on the pedals. As she set off from the Common, she called out, "That's the best part! It's a total mystery!"

End Credits

Unlatches smallest violin case ever invented.

Between April 2025 and March 2026, I had three books published. What you hold in your hand right now, *We Interrupt This Program*, is the third of those three.

And you know what, folks? Be careful what you wish for.

On the one hand, I couldn't be more fortunate. Not only as Solaris Nova allowed me to continue writing and publishing this fun, funny, sometimes maybe possibly insightful *Tune*-iverse (yes, that's what we're calling it and if you have a better idea, where were you a year ago). I love the fact that Trope Towns are a thing. I love that brownies are still openhearted helpers and Seelie are still up their own nose about how wonderful they are and that Unseelie now are getting a moment in the sun.

On the other hand, this past year has been… a lot. Aside from everything else in life and freelancing, trying to edit, revise, develop cover concepts and tag lines, solicit blurbs, write back cover copy and publicize three books in less than a year has rather eaten my life. On top of that, I've been writing the *third* book in the *Tune*-iverse and with luck that'll be out in the near future – right now we're calling it *Don't Touch That Dial* – and so, yes, time for a nap.

There it is, the opening notes, played on that smallest violin ever.

What some aspiring writers may not realize is this: Beware of saturating your own market. If you're someone who dreams of putting out more than one book a year, be prepared for the fact that some of your readers may not *need* or want to *buy* more than one of your books in a year. Be aware that not all press will be open to you. It sounds delicious, it sounds like you're Someone Important, but what it really means is you're Someone Exhausted and you could be giving some of your books shorter shrift than they deserve.

Not mine, of course. All of mine are my children and they are equally as pretty. I just have to find more folks who want to see their slide shows.

The fun thing about *We Interrupt* is this: I'd written it even before I was sure Solaris Nova would want more *Tune*-iverse. But thanks to their new imprint Solaris Nova moving some of the goalposts, thanks to the enthusiasm of my wonderful editor Amanda Raybould, and thanks to *all of you who bought the last book*, they wanted *two more*!

Surprisingly, another publisher also wanted two of my older books that had never found homes, and that's how we ended up with nearly simultaneous signings for two more *Tune*-iverses; and two totally different dark fantasies *Leave no Trace* and *The Only Song Worth Singing*. If you've got them all, I salute you! You are among my favorite people. If you've helped me promote them, you're *also* among my favorite people.

And these people include but are not limited to: Carol Gyzander. Nicholas Kaufmann. Alex Shvartsman. Ian Randal Strock. Amy Grech. Amanda Cherry. David R. Stokes. Rebecca Hoffman. Alexis Gerard. Lynda Del Genis. Julia Reddy. Ellen Kushner. Delia Sherman. Zin E. Rocklyn. The list could, and probably should, go on. Apologies to everyone I forgot.

It is one hundred percent accurate that I am now playing the world's smallest stringed instrument like a rock guitar. But every time I think about this past year in terms of the volume of work and effort and time and money and *everything* it has taken to get here, I have to laugh. The synchronicity of multiple deals for multiple books all at once has been a kind of miracle.

Writers live in a world of famine, and then an entire supermarket drops on your head.

If you're lucky.

We Interrupt this Program has been a happy place to return to – and I've been so delighted to insert some of my own experiences, hopes, and fears as a writer into it. Too many ideas? Check. Not enough time? Check again. Not enough energy? As an over-fifty-year-old woman, absolutely. Plus, I have gleefully been inspired by some particular, wonderful friends I've met along that writing journey to flavor many of my characters.

Let's all put more trips to the *Tune*-iverse on our calendar for the future.

Meanwhile, many thanks are always warranted – to my families of all kinds, near and far. To my wonderful husband, who *finally* got his own dedication. To Amanda and to all at Solaris Nova who believed in the unreality of the *Tune*-iverse and have allowed me to continue the silly, punny, insidery stories within. To my Amazing Agent, Bridget Smith and all at JABberwocky Literary Agency, for having my back and making sure those contracts read like they're supposed to.

Big hugs to my inspirational, celebrational and Muppetational dear friend, potter, gardener, philosopher, author, and massive Doctor Who fan L. J. Cohen. She is a whirlwind, a creative mastermind and all around incredible listener. If she happens to bear some vague resemblance to Winnifred Arrowmaker, well…

I met L. J. a million years ago through the terrific organization Broad Universe (BroadUniverse.org), and would not be here if I hadn't signed up for the latter and befriended the former. You never think your life will change in your forties, but I'm proof that it can happen.

Many thanks to everyone who has supported, continues to support, and will in the future support all my writing efforts. I am forever surprised that no one has yet told me to shut up about my books, that people buy them from me, and even write reviews that make me tear up. It is always a journey, and you never know where that road will take you next.

We Interrupt This Program is all about the story. Who tells it, who gets to tell it, who approves of it and who says, *This is not good enough, you can do better*. It's about how story builds our lives and perceptions and our worlds. (Sometimes more literally than others, especially when the Seelie Court Network gets involved.)

For now, here's where the story pauses.

But not for long.

As Christine Mason Miller reportedly said, at any given time you have the power to say, *This is not how the story is going to end*.

Stay tuned. Much more story to come.

About the Author

Randee Dawn is a Brooklyn-based author and journalist focusing on speculative fiction across the categories (science fiction, fantasy and horror) at night, while writing entertainment and lifestyle stories during the day for publications including Today.com, Gold Derby.com, Variety, The Los Angeles Times and Emmy Magazine.

Her first novel, *Tune In Tomorrow*, was published by Solaris in 2022 and re-issued with additional bonus content in 2024 via Solaris Nova. Her other novels are *The Only Song Worth Singing* and *Leave No Trace*.

She resides with the love of her life, with a lot of books and never enough mangoes.

Find Randee Dawn at RandeeDawn.com and join her newsletter for updates!

If you're in the New York City area, Randee hosts Brooklyn Books & Booze every third Tuesday at Barrow's Intense Ginger Tasting Room. Come out for a sip and a story (BrooklynBooksBooze.com)

FIND US ONLINE!

www.rebellionpublishing.com

/solarisbooks

/solarisbks

/solarisbooks

/solarisbooks.
bsky.social

SIGN UP TO OUR NEWSLETTER!

rebellionpublishing.com/newsletter

YOUR REVIEWS MATTER!

Enjoy this book? Got something to say?

Leave a review on Amazon, GoodReads or with your favourite bookseller and let the world know!

www.ingramcontent.com/pod-product-compliance
Lightning Source LLC
LaVergne TN
LVHW041057080826
845145LV00007B/1601

9781837867752